WHERE THE WIND BLEW

a novel

What they're saying about *Where the Wind Blew* ...

"*Where the Wind Blew* is a story of the past and an allegory of the present. It reaches inside to your most primal secrets and shows the ravages of remorse. Bob Sommer hears the music and voices of the past and gives you what America has become today. Do Americans like what America is today? *Where the Wind Blew* has the scope of an epic, the darkness of *Crime and Punishment*, and the pace of a suspense novel. This is some reading matter that you'll wanna read!"

—Mason Williams

"I found *Where the Wind Blew* engrossing and heartfelt. Bob Sommer tells a story about the unintended consequences of our actions, even when they may be justified. It is a very human tale about convictions, love in its multitude of forms, the insensitivity of the system, and the unforgiving nature of time. Emotionally taut and historically intriguing, this novel explores the psyche of a man whose past finally catches him. Although set in the past, its themes transcend time."

—Ron Jacobs, author of
The Way the Wind Blew: A History of the Weather Underground

"I had a hard time putting *Where the Wind Blew* down.... As a veteran of the sixties I appreciate that it takes us back to the days of the movement to show the anger, frustration and helplessness we felt as the war in Vietnam continued to escalate in spite of everything we did to oppose it.... There are many veterans of the domestic war who would be sympathetic to Peter Howell's plight."

—Robert Pardun, author of *Prairie Radical: A Journey through the Sixties*

WHERE THE WIND BLEW
A NOVEL

BOB SOMMER

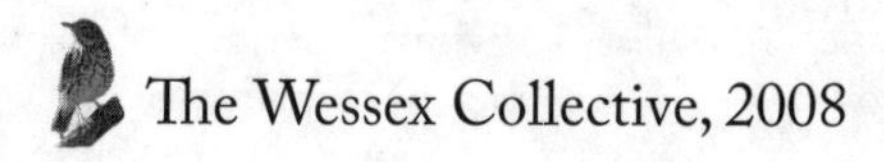
The Wessex Collective, 2008

First Edition

ISBN 13: 978-0-9797516-1-5
ISBN 10: 0-9797516-1-6

Published by The Wessex Collective
P.O. Box 1088
Nederland, CO 80466-1088

Web: http://www.wessexcollective.com
contact: sss@wessexcollective.com

Acknowledgements
Sandra Shwayder Sanchez and R. Peter Burnham of The Wessex Collective have been nothing less than enthusiastic about this book since I first brought it to them. The exhaustive effort they made in transforming the manuscript into a book exceeds my ability to thank them.

Cover design by Christine Potter; cover photo by Bill Irwin

BISAC code: FIC019000 (literary fiction)

For my wife Heather

and my children, Alex, Francis, and Erin.

You encourage and inspire me,

and I am blessed by your love.

...and every wind
In the world is howling around me.

Odyssey, V, 306–7

Chapter 1

Thursday, April 22, 1999

"*Fffkkgghh!*"

Not even a word.

A guttural noise…as if the car itself swore, as if he and the car had already fused into something more than mechanical but less than human.

He'd glanced up as a red-tailed hawk skimmed the tree tops, crossing the narrow band of sky above him, and then the Jeep banged into a gouge in the road with such force that it shivered the car frame and sent a volcanic jolt through his spine and into his chest, where it erupted in a raspy grunt.

The bird fanned its tail feathers, yawing, almost hovering, and then it was gone as the front end seemed to drop into nothingness.

Groggy from driving for almost twenty hours and barely sleeping in days, he slowed the car as underbrush lashed the doors and fenders and clawed at the metal. The road was little more than a pair of ruts in the slushy ground.

He must be close to the lake. He bounced through pits and over rocks hidden in the patchy snow, climbing all the while, with the altitude pressing on him, as it had hours ago, when he drove through Berthoud Pass, where the road took him over two miles high. The nausea later subsided, at lower altitudes in Tabernash and Hot Sulphur Springs, but he never stopped feeling queasy, and now it was rising, as he went higher once more, and the crowding forest and looming darkness only made it worse. The day was overcast and drizzly. Clouds gathered. He lost track of the sun and no longer knew which way he was headed.

His throat was raw, dry. He brought a water bottle to his mouth, but just then—bang!—the car hit another bump. Water splashed on his lap, soaking his thigh, and he swore again, shouting into the windshield. Short of breath from the altitude, from fatigue, from wondering where he was going and what he was doing here, he lowered his window and the engine's roar flooded the car.

He thought this was a fire access road, unmarked on most maps, and if he took it he could avoid registering for a campsite. Once he tucked himself away somewhere, no one would bother him. He never saw a ranger when he camped here with Todd last year, and even then it occurred to him that the national forest, with its network of unpaved roads and remote campsites, would be a place you could lose yourself for a while, if you had to. But now he was uncertain if he'd taken the right road. Perhaps this was private property. The crumpled map on the passenger seat was useless and turning back would be difficult. He had either made the right turn or he hadn't. The green digital figures on the dashboard read *6:12*. The days were longer now, but with the overcast sky, darkness would fall soon.

It was stupid to bolt like this, to take off for nowhere once his mask had been ripped away, but the instinct to run had overwhelmed him like the reflexes of a drowning man fighting his way to the surface. He'd seen it coming for days, maybe a week, watched his whole life crumble, even resigned himself to it. But as the end came, as the final moment approached and he could still do something before the choice slipped away forever, the impulse to leave overwhelmed him. Still uncertain of what he'd do next, he withdrew money at an ATM, collected items from his file cabinets, and told Cherry he might be in Topeka for a couple of days on school board business. But he still hadn't decided, still hadn't resolved himself until there was only a day left, and then he panicked and began wildly gathering things and throwing them into the Jeep. In the storeroom downstairs, he trudged past the unfinished model on Todd's workbench with armloads of camping gear. He rifled through his bedroom closet as the familiar musky floral scent of Cherylee's body lotion filled his lungs. He stumbled through the upstairs hallway and past the open door of Emma's room, where mounds of rumpled clothes lay scattered around her unmade bed. And he thought he should stop where he was, just stop right there and sit on the stairs and not do another thing until Cherry came home and he could tell her everything. But the momentum carried him forward, and he loaded the Jeep, stopped at another ATM, and then he was gone, just like that. No plan, no destination, no idea of what he'd do next. Without a note or a call, without even a word to his wife and children. It wasn't just that he'd let the chance to try and explain slip away, to tell them he was not who they thought he was, but he didn't know if he could face them. Things had happened fast, and he wasn't ready. He always knew that the veneer might one day crack and his life would shatter, but even so, he'd allowed himself to get comfortable with who he'd become and the life he was living, and he wasn't ready when it all came apart. And now...

He'd have to go back. He knew that. This impulsive dash to nowhere was foolish and would only make things worse. He'd have to go back for his family's sake. He couldn't just leave them like that. But maybe...maybe he could at least gather himself here before he surrendered. A few more days would make no difference after all these years. He could steel himself to face what lay ahead, to face his family. He didn't know what would be worse, spending the rest of his life in prison or an hour with them.

The car rumbled through the brush for a few hundred yards more, and then the ground leveled off and daylight glowed through the pines and cedars. The lake was close. He rolled forward, peering in every direction, straining to see through the trees and thickets for signs of human life, colors that were not part of the forest, movements, other vehicles. He stopped well short of the break in the trees at lakeside, shut off the engine, and climbed out of the car, unfolding himself from the stiffness, drawing moist air deep into his chest. The forest floor was wet and the air damp and thick. At the edge of the lake, he hunched up his shoulders with a chill. The lake was as large as a dozen football fields and enclosed on all sides by trees and foliage. A cliff rose beyond the woods at the far end and several waterfalls careened through the rocks with run-off from the snowmelt above the timberline. The stillness of dusk pervaded the lake and the woods. It was early in the season for vacationers. School would not be out for weeks. With darkness approaching he had to find a place to park and camp. The car erupted into the quiet when he restarted it.

The road forked, encircling the lake from each direction, and he turned right, away from the tourist road on the other side. He drove at a crawl, with the window open, and spotted an orange tent cover near the edge of the water on the far side—possibly where he and Todd had camped—but there were no people and no sign of movement, only a corner of the tent poking through the foliage.

He neared the rushing waterfalls and knew that if he stayed too close the noise would camouflage other sounds, and he shuddered, realizing that old instincts, dormant and stiff, like muscles he hadn't used for years, were reawakening. People had said he was clever and resourceful, but perhaps more than anything else, he was cautious—and determined. He survived even as others were caught or simply grew weary of the life and turned themselves in. His group's plans to go underground had collapsed before they ever had a chance to gather themselves, collapsed in the dust and debris of an explosion, and he had been left alone, with a few names and phone numbers, and his instincts. Maybe being alone was the key to surviving. Maybe others relied too much on their networks and on each other. The so-called safe houses never felt safe to him. There was always some guy who wouldn't cut his hair or some honey who wanted to argue when neighbors complained about overflowing garbage pails and loud music. His visits to these places were always brief, and he trusted no one, long hair or short, even when they shared their dope and their tales of lawlessness. He thought being around such people just increased the odds of getting caught. Who would the shoes be watching? Not the people who complained about the music and kept their own trash pails covered and tidy. He would move on quickly, after a few nights, long enough to eat, clean himself up, and on one or two happy occasions—and no more than that over a year or two—even get laid.

With the car backed into a clearing and the engine finally shut down, he was too exhausted to bother with the tent. He took a leak in the brush and looked across the lake once more, but he saw no other camps besides the orange tent. He felt like puking, but nothing came up. Inside the car he drank more water and put the driver's seat back, bunching up a sweatshirt for a pillow. The overcast sky felt close. The wind pushed through the trees, ebbing and flowing like the ocean tide.

He twisted and shifted in the seat. Sleep was impossible. He got out of the car to heave again, steadying himself against the hood, but again nothing came. The whirling of the altitude sickness left him miserable whatever he did. If he stood, he needed to sit. If he sat, he needed to walk. He fumbled through his bags looking for aspirin, but found none. He hadn't eaten more than a few bites since leaving home, but just the sight of the thin plastic grocery bags bulging with cans and packages of food made him gag. The groceries looked so random now, so absurd. He had stopped at a convenience store in northwestern Kansas and rushed through, grabbing things from the shelves and tossing them into a basket. But now he couldn't imagine eating any of it—beef jerky, pepperoni sticks, cans of tuna and beans and fruit, boxes of cookies and snacks. He'd thrown in anything that would keep without refrigeration. Instant coffee, peanut butter, crackers, bread. He made extra trips to his car with jugs of water. The kid at the counter snorted a laugh and asked if he was stocking up for Y-2-K, and he grunted, "Yeah," without smiling. The kid rolled his eyes at another clerk, he thought without being noticed.

He remembered buying ibuprofen, but he couldn't find it. Then he couldn't recall whether he'd actually bought it or just thought of buying it. He couldn't seem to focus on one thing and tried to think about what to do next. What was the point of running? If he didn't turn himself in, they would find him. His family didn't know where he was or why he was gone. He didn't have the strength for this any longer. He should have just waited—for his family to come home, for the FBI to arrive, but now here he was, in this dense forest, with the wind blowing and misty rain falling, wrestling with his heaving stomach, tormented by guilt and worry and fear, and thinking he should just drive down to the main road in the morning and surrender. He might be in prison for the rest of his life—fifteen or twenty years at his age amounted to the same thing. He'd read of others like him who had resurfaced after two decades or more and gotten some tough sentences. But even if he accepted whatever was coming, his family would still be dragged into a nightmare that would last for months, for years; that would scar them forever. And his betrayal would be the worst scar of all. He would infect them no matter what he did.

Yet even as the layers of his identity came off and this mudslide into chaos began, he had felt moments—not even moments, just isolated stabs—of relief that now he could finally shed the invisible leaden overcoat he'd worn for so long. Over the years, he sometimes considered turning himself in, but how could he bring his family's world to a crashing end just to assuage his own conscience? Instead, he carried on, even convincing himself at times that the terrible burden of this secret guilt was how he would pay for his crimes, and that it was a worse fate than sitting in prison. What a fool he'd been! And what a coward, to be here, so far from whatever had by now descended on Cherylee and the kids!

This deep, searing betrayal was like nothing else, not even close to having an affair or gambling away savings and home. The man Cherylee had married and raised two children with did not exist, and the person who was now gone was someone she had never known, a complete stranger. He had concealed everything from her, and despite a couple of close calls, she never suspected that he was anything other than what he seemed. And while he always knew this could happen, was perhaps inevitable, she had no chance to prepare herself, as he did. Maybe he should have confided in her. He had considered it over the years, but wouldn't that just give her an unwanted burden? Wouldn't that make her complicit, too? She deserved so much better than this. He had left her with money, put things in her name—the house, the cars, even the business. She owned everything, and he owned almost nothing. But what was that compared to what must be happening to her right now?

He was out of the car again, now in complete darkness. Fog had settled over the lake, and the thick moisture gave him some relief from the nausea, but it was cold. He wanted to run the engine to warm up the car, but the noise would echo across the water like a bulldozer. He noticed how full of sounds the forest was—rustlings in the underbrush, melting ice and snow dripping from the trees, the persistent rush of the waterfalls, the eerie nasal mooing of elk. He heard a firm swishing and stepping, twigs cracking, followed by snorting. Elk? No, it was alone—probably bear. He sealed himself back inside and listened and watched in the cottony thickness, for how long he couldn't say, but he did not hear the sound again.

He clicked the ignition key backward to check the clock: *9:28*. But he was on Mountain Time now, 8:28 p.m. The whole night lay ahead. He tried to settle himself again, refolding the sweatshirt with Emma's high school logo emblazoned on it—a grinning Indian chief dancing with a tomahawk. Over a year ago, he had decided that the logo was offensive and he made a public stink about it, and Cherry and Emma weren't too happy with him either. Cherry didn't like controversy, and Emma didn't like attention. His letters in the Hawkings and Kansas City newspapers and his complaints to the school board embarrassed them. But lately he'd found it almost as hard to ignore such things as it was to keep the secret he guarded. It was his own fault that he was here now. He didn't blame that kid from Emma's school newspaper. She just kept digging and digging. He could see it. He knew she'd find something sooner or later. He'd beaten the FBI for almost three decades, but a high school kid unraveled everything.

He pulled a wrinkled manila envelope out of his bag and slid the contents onto his lap and studied them in a narrow flashlight beam. He'd practiced signing the name Peter St. John many times before he wrote it on his first fake driver's license, but the pen had slipped when he made the actual signature and he retraced the upper curve in the *S* while a clerk at the DMV watched. Still, the smudged-up card had never been questioned when he showed it for job and apartment applications, though he always worried it would be, and since then it had spawned many renewals. He sniffed, not quite ginning. Did it mean something that he used a saint's name? Metaphysical coincidences played no part in his world view. The name was just random. St. John was the first good match he'd found that day in the cemetery with Robin. The old license was useless.

He unfolded a fragile, gray clipping he'd quietly torn from a newspaper in a North Carolina library decades ago.

> *Groenkill, New York, September 17, 1971.* Almost a year after a bomb tore through Merval Corporation headquarters, killing four people, the trial of two members of the terrorist group responsible for the attack has ended.
>
> Terry Finnegan and Lawrence Keubler were each sentenced to twenty-seven years in a federal prison.
>
> The victims included Richard Kleeman, a Merval vice president, and three of the terrorists, Robin Conforti, Benjamin McManus, and Corinne O'Reilly.
>
> Another Merval employee, maintenance worker David Reed, lost his arm in the explosion, which ripped through the corporate offices on a busy weekday afternoon.
>
> Merval manufactures radar systems for the military.
>
> Still at large and wanted for the bombing are Simon Phelan and Peter Howell. Both are believed to have been in the building at the time of the explosion.

He had tried to put the past away, just as he'd stashed these artifacts in an envelope in the back of a locked file drawer, but the people, the memories now poured out and surrounded him. Not memories, but a reality he was still living. As he read their names, he realized that for him, they were still young, always young, but now the logic, the linkage of events and ideas that led them to put a bomb in that building, was so distant, so frayed that it would be easier to reassemble a cobweb from the clumpy strands on the whisks of a broom than to reason his way back to that rash act. Yet the insistent thought that no one was supposed to get hurt had always stayed with him. The newspaper writing was clinical, cold. It conveyed none of the feelings that led them to that point, none of the fear that shrouded them, the endlessness of the war, the government's entrenchment, how it turned its guns, its agents, its force on the people it was supposed to protect. There was nothing political in this account; it was just a crime report, with more than a hint of smugness in its tone.

At the end of the article, Peter and Simon were conjoined in a dark immortality. It sounded as if they had escaped together. But in all these years, Peter never learned what became of him, whether he was dead or alive, free or in prison. Peter had looked, too. He followed the infrequent news articles that appeared for a couple of years after the bombing. There weren't many. The group was so much smaller than they all had imagined. They believed they would shake the very core of the system, but they faded into oblivion instead. Peter wondered if Simon was even alive, or Terry or Keub.

In a pocket notebook that still had a price sticker of ten cents and the name of a drug store in Groenkill, Peter turned pages filled with lists of items: vinegar, alumina, alum, chalk, lime, seltzer, cleaning fluid, muriatic acid, peroxide, sand, battery acid, and on it went—the raw stuff of a bomb. If they couldn't steal dynamite, they would make it themselves. Magnus could make anything. More lists appeared on the pages that followed: grocery items for the safe house; addresses, phone numbers, schedules; log notes from watching people come and go at different office buildings, including when the guards on the dog-watch took lunch. How methodical they'd been! How much care and effort they invested! Now, the lists and log notes were even more nauseating than the altitude. He had to destroy this stuff. It could still be used as evidence.

There was also a concert program. *The Senior Recitals for Music Majors, Saint Celixine College, April 1970.* The cover was sky blue, with the college emblem depicting a missionary priest holding a cross and a book, and blessing an Indian who knelt submissively. In ornate gothic script, the words *Educans et Suffens in Nomine Christi* encircled the image. The program was smirched with the imprint of a boot that had stepped on it thirty years ago. Peter found it among some papers when the students occupied Celixine Hall, and it was still creased from when he stuffed it in his back pocket that day. Listed for Friday evening, April 30th, was Susan Mallory, playing the Bach Cello Suites.

He had been able to go for long periods as his children grew and his business consumed him without wondering about her, but he had kept the program, the same as he might have kept a photo of someone he'd killed in an automobile accident. All of his guilt and regrets, it seemed, could be funneled into this one piece of paper. Now, and many times over the years when he was alone with his darkest secrets, he could look back on missing that recital as the moment in which a fragile object of great value was still in his grasp, just before it slipped from his fingers and shattered on the floor. This was all that remained of the moment before everything changed. He had no photo, no yearbook, no other artifact of her at that age. Maybe …an insane notion flashed before him…to find her again before he turned himself in, just to see what had become of her, to look from a distance.

He sputtered and sucked air. It was the altitude.

Fucking crazy…wasn't all this bad enough already?

He'd find a police station in the morning. Coming here had already made things worse.

He clicked off the light and hunched in the corner of the driver's seat, watching the fog roll through the woods and across the lake. He considered trying the radio to see if there was anything on the news about him, but he was too tired to care. He dozed in fits, startled by rustlings outside, often thinking sounds were other than they were—the quiet had a voice of its own, many voices, and he thought they were all talking about him.

Chapter 2

Sudsy pink foam spilled from the roof and fenders and dripped onto the concrete in globs as the Expedition rolled through a storm of sprays and mists in the cavernous chute. The car lurched forward on the track, and Cherylee St. John walked along beside it, watching through the lobby windows with her cell phone to her ear.

"I don't know…about fifty dollars," she said, shrugging, and catching the movement of her shoulders in the shadowy reflection in the window. She was irritated: How did Jean always get around to the cost of things?

Sixty was closer, not including the car wash, which would have been *a lot* more if she'd let that smarmy kid talk her into the full hand waxing. But a glint in his eye, just the slightest hint of a grin as he described in an eager, nasal voice how important it was to protect the car from corrosion, made her wonder if the car needed waxing as much as he needed whatever little bonus he got for talking her into it. Besides, hadn't she just recently had this conversation with a greasy man in a stained tie when she bought the car and then added the undercoating at a price that seemed ridiculous as she watched them put the car up on a rack and spray black tar under the fenders? Ten minutes—all it took, and for that price! Peter had been right; her experience buying the car was already paying off. She saw through the kid—and being assaulted like this spoiled her fun. She had looked forward to getting out early this morning—it was such a bright and pleasant spring day—to have the car washed and vacuumed, and then to watch its creamy luster renewed from beneath the dust and splatter as a pair of boys wiped it down and cleaned the windows in the sunshine that poured into the bay outside the carwash. Well, she'd gotten past the smarmy kid and would tip the boys outside, unless he showed up there, and now here was Jean pestering her yet again about what she paid to fill the SUV's tank. Jean hadn't let up since she bought the car—about the size of it, the cost of it, the sales tax, the insurance, and of course the gas. But none of that compared to what she said when she found out that Cherylee had bought the car on her own, without Peter, and had paid *cash* for it—which was nothing. The forty grand was worth it just to see the look on her face. *Cash!* Yes, indeed, and she'd done the whole deal, from start to finish, without Peter so much as setting foot in the dealership.

But Jean didn't get it. This purchase wasn't about money. It was an accomplishment, an achievement. Cherylee had done it by herself! When Peter first suggested buying a new car without him a few months ago, she wanted nothing to do with it, but he seemed so pleased with himself once he latched on to the idea that it became as much his project to encourage her as it was hers to buy the car. She knew that she was too dependent on him for financial decisions—in fact, for all of the big decisions about the house and the business—and she always meant to learn more. He had encouraged her, too, she had to admit, and now he sensed an opening, an opportunity. "What's the worst that could happen?" he laughed, while she imagined a lemon sitting in the driveway, leaking oil and rusting away before her eyes. Between the business and now the school board election, he just didn't have time, he'd said when she first mentioned (with some hesitation) that maybe it was time to consider buying a new car, but then this notion came to him and he wouldn't let it go. She was right! he agreed. The Jeep was getting old, and it was too small for all of them—especially when Jean was along for the ride. (They both nodded and smiled, thinking of Jean cramped in the back seat between the kids with her knees pulled up to her chest and her purse jammed on her lap.) He would sell the Honda and take over the Jeep, and she would drive the new car, which she would buy! And after pacing dozens of showroom floors, enduring endless "follow-up" calls—*Hey, Mrs. St. John! Brad down at Hawkings Ford, and we're ready to deal today!*—and then negotiating with creepy salesmen and managers and that slimy guy in the stained tie and even the service manager, who talked her into buying a set of rugs that she thought should have come with the car, she felt like she had done something, proven herself—to herself, even more than to Peter, or Jean—and she was proud of the car, and the decision, and all that went into it.

And now she enjoyed the car all the more—seeing it stand out across a parking lot at the grocery store or mall, settling herself into the soft leather driver's seat high above the road, with the sleek dashboard and digital speedometer in front of her. How could she explain the feeling she had about this car? Her children would be safe in it. The whole family would be safe! They would take trips together, go on vacations. Emma could plug her earphones into the armrest while Todd watched a video on the drop-down screen. Peter would enjoy it too. It was so...*outdoorsy*, so like him.

She tipped the boy waving a towel beside the open door and climbed in. The car smelled like new shoes.

"Oh, I'll be home soon. I just wanted to get the car washed. Has Peter called?" she asked.

Why did she let Jean rattle her? She was more worried about Peter right now than what the gas cost.

"No," said Jean. "Where is he?"

That tone! It couldn't be just a simple question, ever. She had always disliked him. But Cherry didn't know where he was. He hadn't come home last night, and he hadn't called. Above all, she didn't want Jean to know *that*. "In Topeka," she answered. "Some school board business. I'm not sure exactly." And she wasn't sure. He often went to Topeka these days. It was just that she hadn't heard from him. She should have been more assertive.

"Well, if you ask me, he'll do some good if he gets elected and finally stops them showing movies all week in school. Did Emma tell you what they saw this week?"

"Yes, yes, I heard all about it."

"M*A*S*H! That's what!" Hearing all about it wouldn't stop Jean. "Is that a history class? M*A*S*H?! The teacher thinks that watching Alan Alda brew martinis will teach them about the Korean war! I asked her who was president during the Korean war and do you know what she said?"

Cherylee did know and was now trying to merge her three-ton vehicle into traffic while she looked for an opening in Jean's rant to tell her—again!—that she'd be home soon.

"Lincoln!! That's who she said was president...Lincoln!!"

"Okay, Jean..."

"Oh," Jean added, "there was one call, from Regina Claymore. She wants you to call."

"Okay, bye." Cherry snapped the phone shut, not waiting for another syllable from her sister. Jean had known about that message all along and just mentioned it now, when Cherry could have returned the call while she was in the carwash lobby. In addition to wondering where Peter was, she now worried about why the high school principal would be calling her in the middle of the morning. She decided to wait until she got home. If Emma had gotten in trouble again, she didn't want to be driving while she tried to sort it out, and she might have to write something down.

She thought it would be such a pleasant morning, too, first getting the car washed and then stopping for coffee on Freestate Boulevard. She'd have to skip the coffee now. She always liked coming down this way. The road was smooth with fresh new pavement. The center island of the four-lane parkway through East Hawkings bloomed with lovely plants, with native tall grass, with carpets of green grass freshly watered by in-ground sprinklers. On each side of the road shopping centers brimmed with restaurants, movie theaters, and all of the stores that had once only been names on catalogues in the mailbox—Williams Sonoma, Coldwater Creek, Pottery Barn, even Saks!—all part of the growing patchwork quilt of suburban townships just over the state line from nearby Kansas City.

As a native of Hawkings, Cherylee appreciated all of these improvements far more than newcomers could. She remembered when the town was little more than an exit on the interstate highway where the pavement gave way to a dirt lane and a dusty, run-down truck stop. Everyone knew that back in the fifties the interstate highway finalized the division between East and West Hawkings that began almost a century earlier when the railroad tracks that still ran alongside the highway first came through. For generations, the people of Hawkings were particular about mentioning from which side they came, East or West, and some still were. Even newcomers seemed to pick up on this before long, perhaps goaded by real estate agents trying to sell the "charm" of West Hawkings or the affluence of East Hawkings.

The west side was the old, old section of town, the site of cattle drives, of granaries, of a vast railroad yard and a belt and buckle company started by one of the town's first settlers. West Hawkings had the pride of long history. It was where "the good people" lived, that is, where the granary and railroad workers lived in clusters of boxy houses that sprawled outward in dense neighborhoods on each side of The Shawnee Trail, the busy main street at the center of town.

East of the railroad tracks and the old downtown, the cattlemen and business owners bought swaths of green, rolling land and removed themselves from the smell and commotion of the railroad yards, the factories, and the general filth of poverty. Trees, hills, and distance insulated their large, serene homes. But although they had the money and the land, they could never call themselves "the good people," which over a hundred years later was a distinction many in West Hawkings still felt.

To Cherylee, it was fresh paint on rotting wood.

Cherylee and Jean Horstman grew up in a two-bedroom ramshackle house near the center of West Hawkings, aware every day of their lives of the social and financial distance between themselves and the people in the plush neighborhoods to the east. Jean, the older of the two, always knew how narrow the margin was that separated their family from impoverishment. Her father labored in the railroad yards and loved to tell people that he had lived the American dream. Over the course of thirty years he worked his way up to foreman and paid off their small home and gathered a pension and insurance benefits from the railroad. Her mother cleaned houses in East Hawkings until Jean was in high school, so Jean was old enough to preserve a clear memory of June Horstman arriving home well past six in the evening, after she had cleaned the bathrooms and kitchens of strangers, and then making dinner for her own family. Jean knew that a long sickness for either parent, or even a contrary unwillingness to go on, a personal revolt against the oppressive sameness of each day and the utter boredom of the work, would mean the loss of their home.

But Cherylee was five years younger than Jean, and by the time she was an adolescent, June had cut back on working. Family life seemed stable, settled. How things were paid for didn't concern Cherylee. She felt the same way about it as she did the ingredients of hot dogs—the less she knew the better. Her mother's meager attempts at home decorating seemed to Cherylee just bad taste, though June always thought long and hard before choosing a vase or lamp on sale at the five-and-dime on The Shawnee Trail, or later at Wal-Mart, after the plaza opened in West Hawkings. Cherylee would endure her mother's wrath if she bought a fashion magazine. More painful was the click of her father's tongue and slight shake of his head when he saw the new records she brought home. Everything, it seemed to Cherylee, was valued by its cost and never by the pleasure it gave. She saturated herself in the Supremes and the Beatles and—best of all!—Elvis. She imagined herself among the wealthy and famous, among people who never judged anything by asking, "Whadja pay for that?"

And here she was today, driving her new luxury vehicle along fashionable Freestate Boulevard to her lovely home in East Hawkings. What difference did it make if the gas cost fifty dollars, or even sixty? She could afford it. Peter's business had taken off, and he said their stocks had done well over the past couple of years. Everything in Cherylee's life and community conspired to success and growth, and she relished it all—the new subdivisions and schools, the clean and smooth pavement, and of course, the shopping. The stores in the East Hawkings Pointe Shopping Center still weren't open, but they were all there, waiting for her. Maybe she would return later and look for some pasta bowls at Williams-Sonoma.

Things hadn't come easily for her and Peter. They had struggled for years, but now, with his catalogue business flourishing, he was even running for office. Yet she was worried about him, if maybe the election was too much, if maybe all the politics—the meetings and phone calls and campaigning—were just more than he should have taken on. He seemed so stressed lately, especially the past week or so, as if the effort to run the business and keep up the campaign had just imploded on him and he was no longer in control and things were coming at him too fast. He hadn't slept much, even less than usual, and he'd become cheerless, absorbed, and she'd begun to think—though she never said it—that maybe losing the election would be for the best, though he seemed to be doing well and should have been happy about it.

She knew to the day when it all started—his interest in politics. A Saturday, several years ago. It was that book about lesbian girls that set him off, when the school board wanted to take the book off the library shelf. "They can't do that!" Peter exclaimed, rattling the newspaper in his fists. "What?" Cherylee asked. She had the exhaust fan on over the stove, while bacon sizzled and splattered in front of her, and she missed it the first time he said, "Ban books!" She was glad that Emma was still in bed and Todd downstairs watching TV when he told her what book the school board wanted to ban, which sounded reasonable to Cherylee, who was certain she didn't want her kids reading a book about two teenage girls falling in love with each other. But the next evening, after dinner, there was Peter, sitting in the living room absorbed in a new copy of that same book, even reading passages aloud to her, and she had to hush him so Todd wouldn't hear. "Whacko fundamentalists!" he muttered. "They're in the schools!" He stayed up late to finish the book and the next day wrote a letter to the *Kansas City Star*, which prompted a flurry of letters in response and began an angry debate in the newspapers and radio talk shows that went on for a year.

Up until then, he had sometimes made sarcastic comments about conservative politicians or made fun of TV preachers, which made her uncomfortable (she didn't care for them herself, but she didn't like Peter's irreverent jokes about them), but he was so busy at the warehouse that his interest never amounted to more than idle jokes or offhanded remarks. The schools, though, the idea that the children were being influenced by these people, that riled him in ways that surprised her. Now he began monitoring what the kids were studying, even quizzing them at dinner—sometimes too aggressively, she felt—about things the teachers said. He called the high school principal because he thought there were too many religious songs in one of Emma's choral programs, and he exploded when Todd came home and said his teacher told them that the Book of Genesis was right and Darwin was wrong. And then there was that business about the high school logo. Cherylee just didn't like all these...controversies, but he wouldn't let things go, and she found it difficult to argue with him. He would start talking about the Constitution and quoting this author and that politician, and she wondered where all this was coming from, as though it had just all backed up inside him and now it was spilling out. As far as the book about lesbian girls went, it wouldn't have bothered her a bit if the school board banned it from the library, and she made sure that Peter's copy was tucked away in their bedroom closet. Lesbians, indeed!

As the mall entrance approached, Cherylee's phone chirped. It was Jean again. "Where are you?" Her tone different. There'd been a car accident. Someone was hurt, dead. Todd and Emma were at school.

But where was Peter?!

"What, what is it?"

"Just come straight home! There are men here, from the FBI...and a police car. They want to talk to Peter. They won't tell me why. Come straight home, Cherry!"

✢

Cherylee watched his lips move, his tongue undulating behind uneven, recessed teeth, and she fixed her gaze on a tuft of whiskers he'd missed shaving in the curve of his chin. If he let the beard come in, it would be thick and dark, and grow rapidly. His head was shaved to a glistening sheen, and his eyes never wandered from her, though they must have when he wrote, for the notebook on the kitchen table somehow filled itself with scribbling as she sat there, across from him, avoiding his eyes and trying to find in his words, no, not even in his words, but in the very movement of his lips and tongue and teeth, and the tuft of unshaven hair, some meaning, some idea that had anything to do with her—with her children, with her husband. And there was none. He might as easily be a creature from another world who not only didn't speak the same language, but lived in a dimension that had none of the same parameters as hers, as though gravity, or time, or light were incomprehensible, as incomprehensible as his words were to her, as the questions he kept asking.

"I don't know!" she gurgled through her sobs. Her voice was hoarse, cracked, desperate. She'd already said it so many times. Her cheeks were soaked, but he seemed indifferent, even accusatory, as though she were part of this fantastical story, this lunatic invention that he was spinning around her, web-like, enclosing her house and her kitchen, and *her*, until she was nearly immobile, with darkness engulfing her and the small gaps of daylight still left in this nightmare that spun wildly all around her closing up, sealing her in. "Why do you keep asking me about this...Peter Howell, or whoever? I don't know anyone by that name. There must be some mistake. My husband's name is Peter St. John. This is all a mistake!"

Jean sat beside her, a hand on her arm, though she didn't feel it. She felt nothing physical, yet feeling nothing consumed her as if she were paralyzed. Others were here, in the room with her, with him, but they were mere shadows in her peripheral vision, entities but not people, shades. A man in a dark suit glanced at papers on the kitchen desk, where everything from bills to school papers accumulated. Two Hawkings police officers in clunky shoes stood by the hearth and watched, their shoulder radios sometimes burping as the FBI agent questioned Cherylee. His voice had the throaty roughness of a smoker. "Mrs. St. John, we need to talk to your husband. Do you know where he stayed last night?"

"In Topeka. I told you that already," she pleaded.

"Where in Topeka? What hotel?"

"I don't know."

"Your husband went out of town overnight without telling you that he was going to be away or where he'd be?"

He made it sound criminal, awful. No, they hadn't talked since yesterday morning, and it did bother her that he hadn't called. She'd tried him last night, and again this morning, after Jean's frantic call, and both times it went straight to voice mail. But there was a reason, she was sure—an all-night meeting, a caucus. He probably thought it was too late, or too early, to call by the time he had a chance. How could a slight misunderstanding like this sound so...conspiratorial?

"I told you that already. It's not the first time. Sometimes his meetings are late. He doesn't want to wake me up."

"Mrs. St. John, did you ever wonder if he was having an affair?"

"Oh!" Jean bristled, clutching Cherylee's arm too tightly, sending a jolt that brought Cherylee back from the coma into which she was slipping. "What does the FBI care if someone has an affair?!"

"We don't, ma'am, but I don't understand why Mrs. St John doesn't know where her husband would stay."

Ma'am!?

Both sisters heard it, the comedy of this man in a plaid suit, with a careless shave, bringing these surreal accusations and bizarre stories before them, and now sounding like Joe Friday.

"You're the FBI," Jean said, gaining courage from the absurd moment, "why don't you just check all the hotels?"

"We are, ma'am." His sharp tone shredded the farce even as he called her *ma'am* once more. He turned back to Cherylee. "Mrs. St. John, what do you know about a terrorist group called The Circle?"

"I…I've never heard of it."

The phone rang. It was in the clutter on the kitchen desk. The dark suit stepped aside as Jean picked it up, and she let it ring again as she took it into the laundry room and shut the door. The muffled sound of her conversation filled the silence in the kitchen as Cherylee sat alone with the four men. Friday scribbled in his notebook, and one of the uniforms answered a call on his radio that now took him out the front door. Cherylee saw him pass outside the window.

Jean emerged from the laundry room. "Cherry, we have to go over to the school. Emma is in the principal's office. We have to pick her up."

"What?" asked Cherylee. "What happened?"

"I don't know," Jean said, though Cherry heard the lie and turned abruptly to the agent, saying, "We have to leave now."

"We have some more questions."

"No," said Jean, "you have the same questions, over and over, and I want to know if you have a right to stay here if we don't want you here. Do you have some sort of warrant or orders? Don't we have a right to consult a lawyer?"

"Your cooperation is entirely voluntary right now. We do not have a warrant."

"Then we want you to leave and we have to go to the school."

"I understand," he said. "We appreciate your assistance. We'll be calling again."

The remaining uniform was already halfway to the front door, and the two suits followed him, though they were still sitting in their cars in front of the house when Jean and Cherylee backed down the driveway. There were other vehicles outside, too, and as the two women pulled out of the driveway, a flurry of cars doors opened and people ran toward them with microphones and tape recorders. There was a van with the logo of a Kansas City television station. Jean feared that Cherylee might hit someone as she backed out. A man knocked on Cherylee's window, and she jerked the car to a stop and lowered her window.

"Mrs. St. John, can you confirm that your husband is a fugitive from a terrorist organization?" Like tentacles, hands with recording devices crawled over the reporter's shoulders and head. Before she could answer, another voice asked, "Mrs. St. John, where is your husband right now?" A man with a video camera now positioned himself in front of the car. Cherylee babbled, "I don't know…go away! I have no idea what you're talking about!"

People were on Jean's side of the car, too. "Go away!" she scolded over the clatter, as if shooing pigeons from a picnic. "We don't know anything! Go away!" She looked behind them and in a low voice ordered Cherry, "It's clear. Let's get out of here!"

Cherylee never even looked at the rearview when she released her foot from the brake. As they drove past the FBI agents in their car, Jean saw from her elevated seat in the SUV that the dark suit was on a cell phone and the plaid suit was writing in his pad.

"What is it?" pleaded Cherylee. "What is going on? What happened at school?"

"She's all right, and she's not in trouble. But the principal said that something about Peter had appeared in the school newspaper this morning, the same business those agents and reporters were asking about…as if he wasn't who he said he was."

"Not who he said he was?!"

"Cherry, please slow down."

They took the right turn at a red light without so much as hesitating at the corner. The Expedition swerved into the far lane and then crossed back to the right side of the road.

"I won't slow down. I have no idea what's going on! Oh my God, there were FBI agents in my house! I'm going to try Peter again." She fumbled in her purse for the cell phone.

"I'll do it," Jean said. "Just drive." She had volunteered for a task she wasn't sure she could do. She did not own a cell phone herself and was not certain how to dial Cherylee's once it was opened and lit, brightly awaiting whatever it was supposed to do next. "What's his number?" she asked.

"It's on the speed dial… just…oh, for God's sake, Jean! Give it to me." She snatched the phone from Jean's hands, and Jean watched helplessly as Cherry steered the monster with her left hand and worked the cell phone with her right. In a moment, Cherylee had the phone up to her ear, waiting for an answer. Jean heard Peter's voice on the recording, and Cherry left yet another message, the third since Jean had called her about the agents showing up, this time her shortest. "Peter, call me!" She snapped the phone shut and dropped it in the console tray between the seats.

‡

Scrunched over, eyes down, arms folded, a tightly-wrapped package, Emma St. John sat in the farthest corner of the waiting area across from the receptionist. A gaggle of students had watched Cherylee and Jean enter the building and cross the hallway to the office as classes changed in a hasty turmoil.

With her eyebrows raised and a scowl on her mouth, the receptionist nodded toward Emma as soon as she recognized Cherylee. Jean frowned, wondering if there wasn't also a glimmer of satisfaction in the woman's eyes. This wasn't Emma's first visit to the office.

Emma ignored Cherylee as she sat beside her and put an arm around her shoulders. The girl often wore her long dark hair pulled around behind her head and flowing into a pony tail halfway down her back, but now it was loose, wrinkled from the scrunchies that cinched it, and it surrounded her face—her last bluff of camouflage. "Are you all right, honey?" Emma said nothing. Her lips were pursed, her eyes focused on the floor. Cherylee said, "We're going home and you can tell me what happened later."

Emma glanced at her mother and hissed, "That bitch! I'm going to kill her."

"Who? I don't even know what's happened."

Emma sneered, "You never know what's going on!"

"Okay, honey. We'll talk about it at home."

"Bitch!" This time it was more than a hiss, and the receptionist tilted her head toward them with the quickness of a predatory bird.

Jean came over and said, "Cherry, the principal wants to talk to you. I'll stay here with Emma."

Cherylee gave Emma another squeeze. "I'll be right back, honey, and then we'll go home and sort this out."

As she stood, the principal greeted her. "Mrs. St. John, I'm Regina Claymore." Cherylee had met the woman on more than one occasion, so the introduction made her seem aloof, as if they'd never met. She was angular and stiff, with bony hands, and she spoke with a mild drawl, which Cherylee knew was from Texas. The principal had just started at East Hawkings High School last September after moving here from Lufkin. Her predecessor had been the target of Peter's occasional complaints, though Cherylee was certain she knew of them. "I'm sorry you had to wait. I was on the telephone when you arrived. Please come inside."

The reception area was large and busy, with several assistants working at desks, and teachers and counselors coming and going to check mailboxes and use the copiers. No one failed to turn at the sight of Cherylee and her sister and daughter in the waiting area, and now all watched as she followed Regina Claymore through the maze of desks and down the hallway to the office. Cherylee felt every soul there focused on her, and she avoided looking back, matching the rapid stride of the small woman in front of her, following her as if they marched single-file through a narrow tunnel.

Before the door was shut, Cherylee exclaimed, "What in God's name is going on!? Policemen at my house, and reporters, and FBI agents! And now I'm here because my daughter…well…what? What am I here for? What has happened to my daughter?"

"Please sit down, Mrs. St. John." The principal gestured to a chair and she sat behind her desk, leaning forward with her hands folded on top of a newspaper. Behind her several large windows offered a view of the parking lot and driveway in front of the school. Cherylee recognized Brenda Rojas pulling up and leaving her car in the fire lane as she rushed toward the door and out of sight. "I am terribly sorry, Mrs. St. John. This article appeared in today's edition of *The Raven*, our weekly school paper. We've done everything we can to keep copies from circulating, but it's put out in the hallways and common areas, and the students take their copies for free. I want to assure you that this was not approved or condoned by the school."

"What? What does it say?"

Regina turned the paper toward Cherylee, who read the headline on the front page in horror.

SCHOOL BOARD CANDIDATE MAY HAVE TIES TO SIXTIES TERROR GROUP!
by
Marcia Rojas

Cherylee read the column to the bottom of the page.

> Local businessman Peter St. John, who is seeking election to the Hawkings School Board, has gaps in his resume. While he claims to be a graduate of Saint Celixine College, a private Catholic school in upstate New York, there is no record that he was ever a student there.
>
> In a telephone interview with the alumni director at the college, this reporter confirmed that no one by the name of Peter St. John ever attended the institution. However, a striking resemblance exists between Peter St. John and one Peter Howell, a student there from 1968 until he dropped out in 1970 to become part of a terrorist organization called The Circle. That group was responsible for bombing Merval Corporation's headquarters in October 1970. Three members of the terrorist group and one executive at the company were killed. Peter Howell has not been seen since then.

There was more. The spread inside the paper included flyers from the radical group, headlines from newspapers in a place called Groenkill, New York, describing the bombing, and several mug shots of sour and unkempt young people, as well as a yearbook photograph of a shaggy young man in a crew neck sweater who bore a stunning resemblance to Peter, at least what he might have looked like at eighteen or nineteen. Cherylee had never seen a picture of him at that age, but the resemblance, his deep liquid eyes, his head tilted to one side as he smiled for the camera, was unbearably familiar. The sensation she felt sitting across from the FBI agent now returned with dizzying power, as a wave of heat swirled through her chest and arms and surrounded her head.

The principal rushed from behind her desk as Cherylee swayed in her seat, leaning over beside her. "Are you all right? Can I get you some water?"

"Oh!" she sobbed. "Oh! I don't understand any of this!"

The principal sat in the chair beside her. "We don't either, Mrs. St. John. This article was not approved, and no administrator or faculty member saw it before the newspaper staff went to the printer last night."

The intercom buzzed, and Regina reached over and hit the button to put it on speaker. "Yes?"

"Mrs. Rojas is here to…"

She grabbed the handset, awkwardly trailing the cord as she walked around behind the desk again and put the phone to her ear. "Please bring her into the conference room," she responded, "and call the student out from class and bring her directly there also."

When the principal hung up, Cherylee said, "That's about Marcia Rojas, isn't it? She wrote this thing. That's who Emma was calling a bitch outside. You bring her in here, and her mother too. I saw Brenda walking into the building. I want to know what's going on!"

"I can't do that right now, Mrs. St. John."

"Why not?!"

"Mrs. St. John,"—the principal's tone became stiff, defensive, Friday-like—"we have to find out what happened here. I should tell you that copies of the paper were given to the *Hawkings Record* and the *Kansas City Star* this morning. Apparently when the students retrieved the papers from the printer, they brought copies to the local papers also. All of this was done without the sanction of the school."

"Sanction?! You're more worried about being blamed for this than the damage you've done to my daughter and my family!"

"Right now, I am worried about your daughter and another student, and about keeping order in the school. I think it will be a good idea for you to take Emma out of school for several days, at least until we have time to find out what has happened here. I'll make arrangements to have her schoolwork delivered to your home."

Unfamiliar with the offices outside, Cherylee looked around on her way out but could not find the conference room where Marcia and her mother were waiting for the principal. As Cherylee strode past the receptionist, she said to Jean and Emma, "Let's go home."

Classes were now in session, and the halls and front walk were deserted and quiet, though Cherylee, humiliated, angry, and confused, might not have noticed if all of the students and faculty had lined up to watch them leave. She walked ahead of Jean and Emma, and opened her cell phone to see if any messages had been left, but there were none.

Chapter 3

"We are people of this generation, bred in at least modest comfort, housed now in universities, looking uncomfortably to the world we inherit."
—from The Port Huron Statement

October 1969

A repetitive clanking stirs Peter from sleep. A clanking, followed by a grinding, then the flick of a match, and more clanking—the cast iron lids on the gas stove that heats his tiny apartment.

"Shit!"

A whisper, a breath.

Susan rarely swears. He grins and stretches in the single bed. He has it all to himself. It's cold outside the covers. She must have just gotten up and now she's trying to get some heat. The knob is tricky. You have to press it and quickly turn to the right while you bring the match up to the burner inside the stove. If you're not quick enough—"Shit!"—a safety valve shuts it off.

He groans from the achy stiffness at the back of his head. "C'mon back to bed. I'll start it in a little while."

The cycle of noise repeats itself, concluding with the epithet.

He calls, "I'll do it soon."

"Just tell me how."

The outside temp must be near freezing, and the apartment is almost as cold. "It's easier for me to do it than to tell you how."

More clanking and match-lighting and swearing, this time a religious oath. She never does those.

The cold floor stings his feet, and the ache surges through his neck and head. She has on his sandals. With the blanket wrapped around him, he takes the matches and lights the stove on the first try. Flames whoosh through the burner, and he heads back to bed as she runs water into a saucepan. "You want tea?"

"No, nothing."

"Peter, it's almost eight-thirty. Don't you have a class?"

"Not going."

"Why not?"

"What's the difference if I sleep here or there?"

Sloshing of water, clanking of saucepan, striking of match, whooshing of flame. She sends the noises to him—a dissonant song of annoyance. "You might wake up in Saigon, if you're not careful."

She flips through his albums and puts on The Moody Blues. A symphony orchestra swells up around a deep voice reciting a poem filled with mystical images of moonlight, shifting colors, illusions, and reality. The voice recedes into symphonic music, gentle and humorous. It lulls Peter.

But his head still throbs.

Finally, he pulls the blanket around him and trudges to a chair at the kitchen table. The room is warmer. "How come you're in such a rush?"

"I have a rehearsal at ten and I have to go back to my room first. My cello is there."

"Why didn't you just bring it here?"

"Because I didn't know I was coming here. Besides, I can't. This apartment is an ice box at night. The heat's either on or off. What's wrong with that thing?"

"I don't know. Something with the pilot light."

"Peter, it's a gas stove! We could die in our sleep!"

"I'll call the landlady. I keep forgetting."

She opens a box of teabags, and he says, "Coffee for me. There's some instant in back of the shelf."

"So you're going to class after all?"

"I'll have coffee and then decide. My head hurts." He adds the last remark as a joke but it comes out whiny.

She shivers in the bedroom as she pulls his sweatshirt off and finds her clothes in the pile on the steamer trunk, shifting her feet like a child on hot sand.

He leans over for a glimpse of her in between clothing but only gets elbows and knees. She is a thin young woman, with sapphire blue eyes and straight red hair clipped at her neck and freckled skin with light orange down on her arms. She often regards her broad face as too broad and too flat. She wears glasses to read, and to perform; she's always peering through them in photos of her playing the cello. Clothing frustrates her—trying to find things that fit. Everything seems to hang from her like shapeless robes on a thin nun. Not a chance she'll ever go braless in public. To her, the braless women always seem to have heavy sagging tits and large round nipples outlined in their sleeveless tee-shirts, and she wonders at times if the whole burn-your-bra movement is really about freedom or just about showing off. She's two years older than Peter and two years ahead in college. She's a senior, a music major. When he found out she was a musician, he thought the flute or violin might better suit her wraith-like frame, but then he attended a recital last year and saw her wrap herself around the cello, engulfing it, swaying as if she were part of the instrument, and he imagined that he was the cello.

The water boils up and Peter abandons the blanket to turn down the burner. He rinses a pair of mugs from the mess in the sink and gazes through the window at the Hudson River.

"What a view!" she exclaimed on her first visit to his apartment.

"I guess," he shrugged. "But the place is so small, and it tilts. You notice that?"

She looked around as if the speckled linoleum would reveal the tilt. Indeed, the floor was uneven. A marble would roll straight from the stove to the door. Outside, they noticed that the whole building leaned to one side. "But it's still a great view," she said.

Whitecaps jitter on the brownish gray water, enlivened by cross currents of wind. Across the river to the west, hills rise up from the railroad track at the water's edge. The tapestry of orange and yellow in the trees is dusky. Snow might fall.

"Is there milk?" Susan examines her mug and wipes it out again before pouring water into it. She's tired, the apartment smells, and she wants a hot shower, which looks like it will have to wait until much later in the day. Peter's bathtub has no showerhead, and she would go a month without bathing before she would sit in it. She has rehearsal, followed by an officers' meeting for the orchestra, of which she is secretary, and then classes.

Peter is an unattractive sight right now, with his hair matted and skewed, and a thin, patchy beard spreading from his cheeks along his neck and throat. She wishes he hadn't grown it. His face was so flush and handsome, with thick waves of dark brown hair falling over his brow. His pockmarked cheeks give him character when he has shaven and brushed his hair, and he has a way of leaning his head to one side when he listens, when something has grabbed his interest, that triggers his smile, not a smile of humor but of recognition, of acknowledgement that whatever he's hearing is especially worth hearing. It's that look, that smile that drew her to him and made her feel that she somehow completed him, and he completed her. He's tall, over six feet. He'd been a point guard in high school, and his skill and quickness were obvious in the college's intramural league last year. She stopped by the gym a few times when she knew he'd be playing, even before they got to know each other very well. He was vibrant and confident when she first met him, so much so that she didn't realize he was a freshman. She found herself at a table full of people in the cafeteria one afternoon over a year ago, and he was there, and she couldn't stop laughing as he did impressions of some teachers.

But he moved off campus this year, to save money on room and board, and now he was partying more and not eating very well, and he was out of touch with campus life, not even playing intramurals. He lingered in cafes and bars around town, and she thought it was just easier for him to blow off school work. He told her that if it weren't for the draft he probably wouldn't even stay in school. And his major in English seemed little more than a random card pulled from a deck. He liked to read, had always done well in English classes, and had some natural writing ability that pushed his papers to the top of the grade curve, when he got them done and turned them in on time. But the draft had trapped him, not only to stay in school, but to keep up with his class. If he weren't a "true sophomore" and passed all his courses with at least a C, the draft notice would arrive in the mail before next semester's tuition bill, and now the pressure of working to stay out of the army, and out of Vietnam, seemed to have the very opposite effect it should, deflating his interest in school, draining any other purpose from the work. She wished he had stayed on campus instead of moving into this frigid little box underneath the looming, black railroad trestle that crossed the Hudson.

Oh, but she's also angry at herself for getting sucked into last night. They were just going out for pizza, but then he convinced her to go to a party he'd been invited to, and then convinced her to come back here, which she thought was what he really wanted all along, and even seemed to her like a good idea after two glasses of wine. She began sleeping with him last May. She remembers every detail of their first time (it was the first time for both of them), in her dorm room, after exams were over and her roommate had cleared out for the year, and they held their breaths and swallowed their snickering as one of the nuns clacked past her door in the quiet hallway—but she had no plan to disrupt the week like this.

"If there is, I'd be wary of it," he says.

She settles at the table while the tea steeps and The Moody Blues bounce through another song: *Tewwwsss-day aaaf—ter-nooo—ooon!*

He spoons coffee from a crusty jar and pours water. "Where you gonna be later?"

She's not certain that she wants to be found. How many hours until she can go back to sleep in her own bed—alone? "Not sure. I have to practice and then write a history paper. Maybe the library."

She squeezes the teabag between the thick fingertips of her left hand. She showed him one time how her fingertips bulge from the calluses.

"Maybe?"

"I'm just tired, Peter."

He reaches for her arm and strokes it, but she stirs the tea without looking up, without responding.

"Those people…whose house was that? Who invited you?"

"Keubler." Peter uses his last name, like the others last night. "He's in one of my classes," he adds.

"Mmm."

"What, you don't like him?"

She shudders, as much disdain as cold. "He's like a used car salesman in hippie clothes."

"He's okay."

Her left nostril curls up.

"Hey, I just remembered…that guy, Simon, I was talking to, he wants me to write something for his newsletter."

"You? What about?"

"About the war."

She frowns skeptically and looks down, into the mug, as she raises it to her lips.

The idea seemed not only clearer to him last night, but vital, even urgent, and the conversation comes back to him now—how they sat for a long time on rug beside the coffee table, passing joints and downing beers, while Simon picked the tobacco of unfiltered cigarettes from his teeth and described his tours in Vietnam—to Peter, to a couple of others nearby, but mostly to Peter—described the sharp, booming explosions of the five-inch guns on the *Maddox* in the Gulf of Tonkin in '64, firing hundreds of rounds into the darkness, hitting what Simon never knew, he said, ammo bunkers, VC, children, water buffalo, maybe Americans. *What the fuck were we even shooting at?* he asked Peter, leaning close, lowering his voice into a sharp whisper, as if Peter might explain it to him, might finally clear this up, and he waited until Peter shrugged helplessly and then continued, *There's no sense to any of it, man. No sense!* He described his second tour, also, this time on a swift boat in the Mekong, where he saw a stack of rotting bodies on a buffalo path alongside the river, and what it was like to unleash the fifty-cal into a free-fire zone without a clue if they were hitting the enemy or just terrified villagers who had the bad luck to live where the VC wanted to hide. *But Peter, these people—the North Vietnamese, the Vietcong—they just want their country back. They want everyone out—the French, the Americans, even the Communists. They're nationalists, Peter. Their country's been overrun by foreigners for decades, for centuries.* He squinted, knowing what Peter would say next before he said it, and asked, *Did you know that Ho Chi Minh wanted Truman's help against the French before he went to the Communists?* No, Peter said, as expected, trying to follow him, trying to piece together the fragments of unfamiliar history in his narrative, trying to listen as people came and went, as laughter and talk surrounded them, as someone strummed a guitar along with a Beethoven symphony booming through the stereo speakers; as he tried to fit classical music into the kaleidoscope that whirled around him, and to connect the water buffalo and the North Vietnamese and Truman, searching for a pattern, an image, a story woven into the fabric of Simon's talk. At times Susan would glance expectantly at him from where she sat talking with Corinne. ("Betty Rubble meets earth mother!" she later called her, laughing when they got back to Peter's apartment.) Peter couldn't follow it all, but he was fascinated, enraptured by Simon, by his war stories, by how intently he spoke, how intimately. They became confidantes, friends, in the space of hours. Peter couldn't leave, wanted only to stay and listen; he'd never had a conversation like this before, never been this close to death and violence, to war, never heard anyone describe it this way. Simon flooded back over him now.

"Oh Peter, have you ever read it?"

"Yeah, some."

Not exactly true, he knows, and she does too, though she gives him a pass. He's seen it on campus, in the lounges and cafeteria, a chaotic and dense weekly of political diatribes, poems, cartoons, ads for head shops and music stores, and classifieds full of ride information, concert tickets, used furniture, stereos, and pirated eight-tracks. Maybe true in the sense that he's seen it and knows what it is, but he's never read one of the editorials past the first graph or held the paper in his hands longer than it took to visit a bathroom stall.

"It's already winding down, Peter. That's why Nixon got elected. It'll be over soon."

"Maybe I'll write about the draft," he offers, but he feels himself probing, uncertain. She's right. The war, the protests, politics—they've all been noise until now. They've never had a face until he met Simon.

"Drink your coffee and go to class." She kisses his cheek, and adds, "I'll see you later."

In the stairwell, she wonders if she was too sarcastic. She's just tired, she decides. She'll see him later.

⁜

He's late…and he's fucked.

More than half of the students at Saint Celixine College commute to school, and the parking lot is full when Peter arrives. He snakes his way through the rows of the lot, a vast unmarked field of gravel and tar, punctuated by a few light poles, until he spots a girl with a rucksack skipping down the steps from the quadrangle, leaving puffs of steamy breath behind. She's blonde and wears a colorful sweater. Peter cruises behind her until she climbs into a white Volvo. If he wasn't in such a rush he might talk to her, but instead he waits for her to vacate the spot, which she seems in no hurry to do. He tries beeping lightly, but the horn of his old Plymouth sticks when he taps the chrome bar on the wheel and an obnoxious honk bellows at the Volvo. The blonde hair swishes around, and the girl scowls. Then the car jerks out of the space as she struggles with the clutch. So much for his prospects with her.

It's almost twenty after the hour by the time he trots across the quad to Driscoll Hall.

The classroom door has an unfortunate location across from the frail wooden lectern that now bears almost the entire weight of Brother Joseph Stedman, who has draped himself over it as he listens to one of the students. His dark brown robe flows to his shoe tops; the hem is soiled and frayed, and his shoes have thick support soles. He was teaching this same course in English Renaissance literature when Peter was in kindergarten. His gaze seems fixed in a permanent state of incredulity, which he accents by raising his bushy eyebrows and looking over his reading glasses. As Peter enters the room, Brother Stedman glares at a student lounging in the back with his head against the wall, his legs stretched out in front of him, and a Bic pen flickering in his fingers. The thirty-odd students in the class have all turned, watching the student in back as if he were a condemned man approaching the block.

Peter tries to seat himself quietly, but the professor interrupts the student-who-will-soon-be-headless. "Mr. Keubler, would you be so kind as to repeat your question for the benefit of Mr. Howell, who has just joined us and will be at a distinct disadvantage when I respond?"

Mr. Keubler smiles expansively. He has large white teeth. He enjoys entertaining the bloodthirsty mob, and the executioner. "It wasn't really so much a question as…"

"Wasn't there going to be a question somewhere in your rambling discourse on the *relevance* of Milton?" Brother Stedman's lips curl around the word *relevance* as if he just discovered gristle in a chicken salad sandwich.

Keubler opens his hands and arms. The final swing of the ax is imminent. He will die well. "No, I was just commenting on how Milton's…"

And then it falls.

"You see, Mr. Keubler, there's our problem. You have put it squarely before us! Your classmates' parents have not paid for *your* comments but for *mine*, whether they happen to be *relevant* or not, at least in whatever manner you define *relevance*. I suppose we could look at the rhetorical uses of the word, as for example, to presuppose that there is an object of relevance, as in relevance *to* some *thing* or some *idea*. We might consider Milton's *relevance* to the state of our political structures in the latter half of the twentieth century, but then we'll learn nothing of Milton and his *relevance* to *his* world. We'll merely treat history as a mirror for ourselves. You see—and with apologies to the rest of you, including even Mr. Howell, who thought well enough of our enterprise to join us for at least a small part of it (my digression is nearly at an end)—this is our problem. Let me put it for you bluntly, Mr. Keubler. Your comments exemplify what is wrong with most American students today, a cancer, even, that has grown within academia, and what is that cancer?"—he pauses and looks over the entire class, though no one risks an answer—"I will put it plainly for you! It is that you *worship…your…navels*!" Another pause, this time to ensure that his students appreciate his unique blend of profundity and earthiness. Brother Stedman grins at the class and continues, "The stripes and stars of the American flag should be replaced with the image of a human navel, for we believe ourselves to be the center of all, and as we sit on the quad, cross-legged, strumming our guitars, admiring bra-less coeds, and smoking things that were not produced by the tobacco industry, we turn our attention inward and stare at our navels. We examine them with great care and particularity. We compare them with one another's"—an undercurrent of skittish snickering spreads across the room and feeds the professor's diatribe—"we watch them for changes in size and shape. We admire them, and we interpret the world through them. The navel is the doorway to the universe, and our biggest problem is figuring out how to fold ourselves back up inside our own navels."

And with that Brother Stedman looks up from Keubler and offers a wide, tight-lipped grin to the rest of the room, finally landing on Peter, where it lingers. Then he takes up the book on the lectern and says, "Let us now continue our examination of Milton's use of mythological allusion in the *Areopagitica*."

⁂

Peter and Keubler bob and weave on the busy quadrangle walkways after class. Peter had slogged through the rest of the hour with his head aching, but Keubler now seems to have an astounding level of energy and good cheer for someone who was not only at the same party and smoked the same dope and drank the same booze as Peter last night, but was beheaded less than thirty minutes ago. Even now, he laughs and re-enacts Brother Stedman's performance. Peter misses some of his jokes as they navigate the walkway, but he enjoys his humor nonetheless. Keubler is easy to find in a crowded room. He laughs a little louder, cracks wittier jokes, and always seems to have some special accessory that distinguishes him, like an expensive camera, or a girlfriend with an exotic dog, or even now, a wide-brimmed fedora hat and a bandana fluttering from his belt loop like a sash. He carries only a spiral notebook covered with doodlings and a Bic pen, which protrudes from his mouth at no small risk to passers-by, as he chews it like a cigar and retells the tale of his own execution. He is a theater major, and Peter saw him play the fiery Mercutio in a production of *Romeo and Juliet* last year. Peter feels plain beside Keubler, still wearing his old crew neck sweaters and penny loafers. His hair is shapeless and shaggy, while Keubler's long hair is neatly parted at the middle and flows to his shoulders. His beard is trimmed like Richard Harris's for the role of King Arthur. In fact, with his hat off, Keubler somewhat resembles Jesus.

Sunshine has broken through the cloudy morning, and the day warms enough for students to settle among the fallen leaves on the grass in between classes. Passing one group in a grove of trees, Keubler abruptly stops and twitches his nose like a squirrel. He grins at Peter. "A little maryjane in the air."

"You know any of them?" Peter asks.

"The short girl, with the bazooms...she's in the company."

From past Keubler dialogue Peter has gleaned that *the company* means the theater department, and from his smile, that Keubler knows the short girl with the bazooms well.

"But I got better stuff than anything going around here. Wanna get a toke?"

Peter has heard that Keubler deals drugs, but that just adds to his mystique. What's the big deal about getting a few nickels for your friends? The stuff has to come from somewhere. Better him than some sleazebag.

Peter's biology lab is next hour and he has notes to complete. He figured he'd get some Twinkies and finish his assignment. His mouth is dry and his head hurts.

Keubler's eyebrows flicker. "C'mon, man. Let's get a toke."

It isn't a decision for Peter as much as an impulse, a sudden folding into Keubler's world.

Keubler grins, and they veer off from the walkway and across the grass to a service road between the administration and fine arts buildings. The place is isolated. Peter glances up at the windows overlooking the alley.

"Don't worry," Keubler says. "I've been back here before. Over this way."

Peter follows him to a cove behind a dumpster, and Keubler pulls a tightly wrapped joint from his shirt pocket. "Ta-da, man!"

The cove is quiet, and after he kicks aside some broken glass and paper trash, Peter decides that it's not unpleasant. He settles on the ground with his back against the wall and the rusted green dumpster filled with the accumulated garbage of two buildings looming before him and sheltering him from the wind. The smoke eases into his throat and lungs with a surprising smoothness. He looks inquisitively at Keubler as he passes back the joint.

Keubler grins. "Good shit, ain't it!"

"Is this what we were smoking last night?"

"Nah, that was just some party-grade Mexican. This is way too good to pass around among so many people." He snorts a laugh, holding up the joint like a connoisseur and imitating a crusty English accent, "It's very fine, indeed! Direct from the forests of Colombia!" He sucks another toke and holds it in his chest, and his words leak out, "I can get more if you wanna buy some."

"Maybe." Peter tries to calculate whether he'd need to cut into his rent money, but the dope slowly overtakes him, like sleep, he thinks, only you're awake to enjoy it and watch yourself fall asleep.

They sit and enjoy the sensation, and as Peter stares at the dents and rust on the dumpster, he notices a pattern, a web-like map, which he follows from a crease just below the splotchy sticker with the refuse company's phone number, through a network of cracks in the faded paint, to a valley of dents near the lower corner just above the rear wheel. He retraces the lines, pacing himself through the journey from the sticker in the upper corner again, but now finding his way to a patch of rust at the edge of the dumpster's back panel. "It's like Middle Earth," he observes.

Keubler had been staring at the dumpster also. "Middle Earth?"

"Yeah, can you see it?"

"Where's Middle Earth?"

"It's...have you read *The Hobbit*?"

Keubler shakes his head. "I heard about it, though."

"You should read it, man. The dumpster... it's like the map, from Bilbo's house to the dragon's lair."

Keubler laughs, "I told you this was good shit, man!"

Recognition envelopes Peter like a draft of warm air, and he laughs too. Then they settle into another meditative quiet, glowing in the warmth of the isolated cove.

Suddenly, the growling of a truck's diesel engine in the alley startles them, and the dumpster jolts toward them as the steel prongs of the truck's lift jam through the slots on each side of the container. With a howling roar, the dumpster rises over their heads in a series of jerky movements, higher and higher, until it turns upside down, delivering its contents into the back of the garbage truck with the fury and violence of an erupting volcano. Without waiting for the dumpster to fall back to the ground, maybe on top of them, they dart out of the cove and down the alley to the parking lot at the rear of the building. Terror gives way to laughter, as they roll on the ground, swatting each other, howling and retelling the tale of their escape in unfinished sentences completed by yet more laughter.

The truck passes them, with the driver scowling, a thick and grizzly man in his forties, disgusted at the spoiled rich kids who have nothing better to do than roll around on the grass in the middle of a weekday.

Breathless and high, brushing each other off, they gather themselves and start back towards the quad. The bell from the tower on top of Celixine

Hall rings once, a resonant and deep note for the bottom of the hour.

"So you still goin' to that class, man?" Keubler asks.

Peter snorts, "Not much point. Might as well try to explain the absence and the late notes all at once."

"Let's get some food."

"Food!" Peter grunts and follows Keubler...

‡

Professor Anne Ritchdorf might have once been a nun. That, at least, is the general speculation among her students. Short and trim, with closely cropped salt-and-pepper hair that might have been permanently matted down by confinement in the white cardboard and brown woolen cowl of the Celixine nuns, she appears now in the attire favored by nuns who have recently crossed back into secular life—a navy blue skirt covering her knees and a crisp white cotton blouse with long sleeves and a modest piece of jewelry, a pin that glints over her heart, a single eighth note in plated silver.

She suspends her baton over the music stand as the roar of a garbage truck in the alley below engulfs the room. She grins through pursed lips, while her eyes convey the resolve of suffering one of the many challenges of teaching and conducting in the midst of chaos. The class snickers. It's the same every Thursday during this hour—the truck arrives at the same time. Often the orchestra is already playing, sometimes softly. The truck never seems to appear when the cymbals are crashing or the tympani thundering. The professor and her students all know this; it is their shared joke.

Susan holds her bow over the strings of the cello, where she will keep it as long as Professor Ritchdorf has the baton up. The truck's engine grinds and echoes in the hollow of the alley, piercing the large, thin panes of glass, rattling the blinds, vibrating in the strings of the double-basses. The pattern is always the same. The professor lowers the baton, and Susan and the other string players rest their arms. The truck has made its entry into the alley and now must raise the dumpster. Professor Ritchdorf bobs her head sideways, a small mime of the pattern. Susan smiles and straightens the music on the stand. The truck's engine roars as the dumpster is lifted; then follows the crash of its contents into the truck's open yaw. One of the horn players leans over to the student next to him and whispers something that results in laugh. The professor fears losing control of the class if the interruption lasts too long, but she makes no attempt to speak over it. It becomes a study in sound, a foil for the music that will soon fill the room. The professor steps off the conductor's stand and leans toward the window as the dumpster is lowered back to the ground. Two students have bolted out from the cove behind the dumpster. She assumes they went there to smoke a joint. She's noticed it before. She should say something to the dean about it, but in the past she's forgotten as soon as she became reabsorbed in the music. She'll have to say something this time. She turns back to the class as the truck growls through its gears and fades into quiet. She waits until the room can absorb the silence, the absence of noise, of sound; it is a music of its own. True musicians, she has told her students, appreciate the pauses as much as the notes. "Ready now!" she says, drawing a breath into her chest and stiffening herself to attention as an example for her students. She raises the baton again and the bows resume their ready position.

⁜

From thin monotone speakers in the low ceiling of the Cavern, the jingly-jangly echoes of Roger McGuin's twelve-string "Mr. Tambourine Man" drift into a fog of cigarette smoke and mingle in the babel of conversation and clatter of dishes below. Commuter students eat and kill time between classes here, lingering over soda cans rank with butts. The theater people always camp at the same table, and at another, the editors of the literary magazine abuse the latest submissions and read their own poems aloud. A rock band and its hangers-on sprawl at a cluster of tables against the wall while one of its members picks at an unplugged electric guitar. And the black students occupy a table that none of the white students use even when it is empty. Some on the faculty consider this place an infected abscess that should be lanced and drained. It is not a stretch to imagine that Brother Stedman would be one of these. But others, like Father Alfonse LeClerq, the college's president, and Brother Luke Finnegan, Peter's freshman composition teacher of last year, find that life flourishes here, as it might in the hidden coves beneath an Antarctic ice shelf or on the mucky bottom of a swamp.

Simon waves to Peter and Keubler, who peer through the dim light, still glowing themselves with the buzz of Keubler's Colombian. The bright Indian summer day outside barely pierces the narrow windows shaded by the concrete dock of the cafeteria upstairs. Simon has short, unbrushed sandy hair and a goatee that fades into his unshaven cheeks, and he wears a paint-stained oxford shirt and khaki pants, also covered with a splotchy rainbow of paint. He gives them each a soul shake and laughs as he holds on to Peter's hand. "Late night, huh?" he says. "Your old lady okay?"

"Yeah, she's good." Peter nods, grateful that Susan isn't there to hear that she's his old lady.

A pastiche of faces from last night surround the table, and as Peter tries to fix them in place again, Simon nudges him. "Hey, listen to this," he says, and turns, "Keep reading, man!"

A student in a denim shirt with a wooden cross that hangs from coarse twine around his collar reads from a sheaf of onion-skin pages: "And behold, Spiro went among the Republicans who had paid one hundred dollars to take bread with him, and he saith unto them, 'A spirit of national masochism prevails, encouraged by an effete corps of impudent snobs who characterize themselves as intellectuals.' And as the Republicans ate and drank, he saith that students of today 'now goeth to college to proclaim rather than to learn.' He warneth the Republicans against Communists and radicals and drugs, and then he broke bread also."

Everyone at the table laughs and claps.

"That's great, man!" Simon exclaims. He turns to Peter, "Wasn't that great?"

Through the undulating tunnel that surrounds him, Peter refocuses on Simon. "Yeah, what is it?"

"That's Terry's column this week. You know Terry?"

"No."

Terry reaches across the table grasps Peter in a soul shake, and another voice adds, "He's my young cousin!"

Peter now recognizes Brother Luke at the end of the table, a stout, bearded man in brown robes and wearing horn-rimmed glasses.

"Brother Luke, I didn't see you there!"

"I try to blend in," he laughs, "but the robes are a dead giveaway."

Others laugh too, Corinne sitting beside Simon, and Magnus, smoking and grinning at Peter through a thick mustache that droops over his lip. (*He knows,* Peter thinks, *knows I'm high.*) Magnus flickers his eyebrows and unfolds his grin into a broad, hairy smile. Peter smiles back—now they both know. He's still sharing telepathy with Magnus when Keubler brings a chair up to the edge of the group, and then Peter grabs a chair also. Copies of *The Word* litter the table among the dirty plates and overflowing ashtrays, and Peter realizes he should take one, should read it. He stares at the papers, trying to decipher an upside down headline.

American troops are dying for Wall Street!!

He's worked halfway through the line, maneuvering letters and syllables around like Scrabble chips in the fog, when Simon jars his focus by ruffling the paper to pull a plain white book with black lettering on the cover out from beneath it. "Hey, Peter!" he exclaims, "you're an English major. You ever read any poetry like this in class?" And he reads aloud with an exaggerated Southern drawl:

How to be a Toad Sucker?
No way to duck it.
Gittchyseff a toad,
Rare back and suck it!

He looks up and explodes into laughter, which spreads through the group.

Keubler nudges Peter, "What do you think Stedman would say about that?"

Now they've all turned, waiting for him to respond. Beside him, Simon still chuckles from the reading. Peter snickers along with Simon and then frowns and lowers his head, as if looking over a pair of reading glasses. He purses his lips and says gruffly, "Mister Keubler, I find no classical overtones, no brilliant metaphor, nothing for posterity in these driveling lines. I find only toad sucking, sucking of toads, and then more *toad-sucking!* Let us hope to hear no more of this sucking from the barren yaws of this illiterate toad-sucker!" Peter pushes his eyebrows upward, and mimicking Stedman's tight-lipped smile, sweeps his gaze around the table, surprised once again at the sight of Brother Luke, who laughs and applauds with the others.

"That's him! You got him, Peter!" Simon exclaims, and shakes his hand again.

"Well, I have a class," Brother Luke says, rising, and he adds, "You should come out for the play, Peter."

"You should, man!" Keubler pats him on the shoulder.

Brother Luke waves a hand over the table. "But Simon, these newspapers are a problem."

"I know, Brother," Simon shrugs, feigning shame, "but the word has to get out!"

Brother Luke grins at the pun, a grin of familiarity, warmth. He's known Simon for years, though he never had him as a student, but Simon has been a fixture around the campus even after quitting school to work full-time at the newspaper. Brother Luke likes the paper, its wit, its irony, and he agrees with its anti-war stance, though he wishes it was expressed less stridently at times. Still, seeing his cousin Terry and other students exercise their writing skills with such energy and passion he thinks can only be a good thing, though he's in the minority among his faculty colleagues in thinking so.

He takes Simon by the elbow and says, "You've won the good fight, Simon. The administrators gave you space in the newspaper racks on campus. We're not talking about the First Amendment. Just litter. No one picks up the unread papers. See over by the doorway." He points to a tumbling stack of papers sliding off the rack. "Your last three issues are still there."

"I'll get them," Terry says, and he nudges Magnus. "Give me a hand, Mag."

As their chairs scrape backwards, Simon throws up his hands. "See that, Brother! No sooner said than done."

"I'm on your side, Simon. But they're just looking for an excuse to keep the paper off campus."

Brother Luke nods to the rest of the group, and as he leaves, Peter worries that his impression of Brother Stedman may have prompted Brother Luke's abrupt departure—and he wonders, too, if it will find its way back to the source of his inspiration.

‡

By mid-afternoon, Susan is running on Coca-Cola and a Three Musketeers. She's desperate to go back to her room and shower, and she may need a tampon, also. The cramps are familiar and unwelcome. Poor Peter, she thinks. He really didn't know all that was hitting him. She may have another day before her period descends. She can get a napkin in the ladies room in the library, if she needs one—and at least she doesn't have to worry about being pregnant this month. That was a big chance a couple of weeks ago, right in the middle of the month.

After gobbling and gulping her way across campus to the library, she has settled at a table beside a window overlooking the quad, where she tries to plow through a dense chapter on the collapse of feudalism in the late middle ages. But in the quiet and heat, she soon finds herself drifting off, staring into the seam between Celixine Hall and Kieran Union, which offers a glimpse of the Hudson's gray water. And she soon finds herself bothered by how parsimonious that glimpse is, with the buildings disrupting it, and now she focuses on them, noticing, perhaps for the first time since she came here, how different they are from one another: Celixine, with its dark maroon bricks and gothic arches carved in mortar over its windows and doors; and Kieran, shaped like an oversized concrete bunker, but with rows of pillars, all painted in primary colors, enclosing the bunker in a colorful and bizarre cage.

Father Alfonse often touts the contrasts of traditional and modern, Celixine and Kieran, side by side, when he promotes the college to the Groenkill Chamber of Commerce or to prospective donors and trustees. And Susan heard a similar speech at her freshman orientation, but now the buildings seem strikingly ugly to her next to each other, as if the college can't make up its mind what it wants to be and the skyline pays the price. If they weren't there at all, she thinks, she could watch the river flow past from where she now sits. But then, where would everyone eat and sleep, and gather for plays and concerts? It's all too confusing...isn't that Peter in the Kieran parking lot—with someone? She recognizes the fedora hat. She told him she'd be here, but now he's leaving campus, heading for the parking lot. He has a class...shouldn't he be in lab right now?

That she's fallen in love with him is not something she wants to admit to herself. She decided before college that an attachment might deter her from becoming a professional musician. But now, watching him disappear down the steps on the far side of the quad, she knows only the sorrow of absence, of neglect, and a vague sense of waste because she had played badly today and now can barely focus on studying. The whole day was lost to...well, what was it? She wanted to be with him last night, against her own instincts, but she just wanted to be with him, and now he seems to be pulling her into places that she doesn't want to go, but where she goes anyway.

He is changing before her eyes, but she doesn't blame him, or herself. Everything is changing so rapidly, it seems. She'll go to class and then crash. That's all that matters right now.

Chapter 4

Marcia was vibrating when she got home from the warehouse. She had to turn on the computer and start writing while it was all still fresh. That's what she'd do. Write. It would keep her from thinking about what was next, what would happen after the article appeared…if it appeared, if she didn't kill it herself, or if someone else found out. For now she wouldn't think about that either. Just write. Don't think. Write.

She was home alone. Her father worked until after eleven at a Kansas City television station, where he was a news producer, and her mother was working a twelve at the hospital.

Once the computer was up she dialed into the internet. There was e-mail from Jaycee:

To: marcyr@unilink.com
From: perrywhite@raven.net
Date: April 20,1999

yo Marcy! u all right? had a parent thing tonite—gramma's birthday. still on for deadline? let me know how many words. i was worried!

How many words, she mused. They should run a special edition. This wasn't who wore what to the prom. She had scooped every paper, every news service, every everything in the country, even her own father! She wondered if a high school kid get a Pulitzer.

No, she wouldn't kill the story. Not herself. It was hers.

She didn't even want to reply right now, but she had to let him know she got back safely, as if anything could have happened, but still...he said he was worried. They'd lost the signal when she called from the car.

> Gotta write—send you an e-m later—don't know how long, maybe 1,000—maybe more—we need a photo spread inside, and the cover too—don't call—gotta get busy.

She had to start writing. Her head was spinning.

She wasn't out to get him. It wasn't like that at all. It was just a simple assignment—interview him because he was running for the school board, and then do the usual background stuff, talk to one or two people who knew him, check out his *curriculum vita*. You could do most of that on the Web.

He had been so nice the first time she talked to him at his business a couple of weeks ago, which surprised her, since Emma turned out so weird, with her black clothes and now hanging out with all those goths and skaters.

She'd known Peter St. John since she was a child but had never spoken to him alone until that day. He waved to her from a work table as she wandered through the open garage door of the warehouse. There was no reception area. The wide doorway opened on to the production floor, where row upon row of tall gray steel shelves towered like canyon walls in the vast warehouse. But still, it seemed like a fun place to work. Birds fluttered among the rafters. A forklift beeped, spiriting about with flashing lights. Workers on roller blades whizzed among the aisles filling baskets that were then delivered to the production floor. A dozen or so people gossiped and laughed as they packed goods at the long tables.

Mr. St. John—she still thought of him as mister—wore a khaki safari jacket and slacks. His hair rounded the sides and back of his head. What was left of it was bushy and thick, falling over his ears and collar. He was packing items alongside his employees. He saw Marcia and smiled. One of the workers dropped a package at that moment, and shredded newspaper blew out of the box in every direction. Marcia tossed her backpack aside and helped gather the paper as the wind swept it across the floor. The woman who dropped the package laughed and said, "I'll get it." Marcia noticed how relaxed and happy she seemed, even though she had just possibly damaged some goods right in front of her boss. "Just leave it," she added. "I'll get a broom."

Unsure of what to do with the newspaper shreddings, Marcia turned to Peter, who was holding her backpack and pointing at a waste bin. "Stuff happens," he said, smiling. "Let's go into the office." She followed him into a glass paneled room off the production floor where photos of his wife and children lined a shelf behind his desk. She knew that he made a lot of money in this business. Her mother sometimes grumbled about what snobs the St. Johns were, but now it all seemed so unpretentious. The photos were in cheap drug store frames. The office itself was no better than a shift manager at any warehouse might timeshare with the other managers. Her own father had a nicer office. But the understatement of Peter's clothes and office, and of his manner, conveyed the ease and confidence of having money.

She expected him to offer some platitude. *So when did you become a young woman?* But instead he asked if she wanted coffee and whether she had any trouble finding the warehouse.

"No," she said. "But I didn't realize there were so many buildings out this way."

"There weren't always. When I first leased this place the last mile or so was a gravel road. Now it's a whole industrial park."

She thought he sounded regretful, even guilty, as though he had opened the door to the progress that now spoiled the pristine farmland and prairie.

"Oh, well. Now, you're here about the school paper?"

"Right. It's just an interview, sort of a profile of the candidates."

"Yes, yes," he said. "Great project, good idea! Are you interviewing the other candidates too?"

"Maybe. Not yet…I'm not…I mean, the editor may send some other people out to do that."

"Well, I'm glad you drew my name. What can I tell you?"

And so it went. Nothing of particular interest. At least, nothing beyond what she already knew from her research. He opposed the evangelicals on the school board. He wanted more funding for the music and theater programs. He thought teachers should be paid more. As he spoke, Marcia was trying to find the hook for her article—maybe on the book-banning thing. She liked that issue. She wanted the piece to have an edge.

His *CV* said that he had gone to school in New York, a small private college—Saint Celixine College—and then he lived in North Carolina and Florida, but there wasn't much detail about what he did after college, so she decided to probe that. "It must have been something to be in college when you were. Didn't Kent State happen then?" She already knew the answer from browsing the internet and checking dates on his *CV.*

He was glancing at a copy of it. "Yes." He thought for a moment and added, "It was in the spring of 1970."

"Tell me about that." (She was proud of herself for asking a good open-ended question.)

Peter pushed his hand over the wisp of hair on top of his head. "Wow, it was so long ago. Yes, Kent State. What a tragedy."

"But what was it like for you? What were you doing when you heard about it?"

"Hmm. I was…you know, I'm not sure where I was. I just recall hearing about it…you know, later. People were upset, angry. There was a rally on our campus, a lot of speeches." He seemed thoughtful, as if he was playing a movie in his head but she was behind the screen and couldn't see it.

She tried another tack. "After all that happened then, with Vietnam and the draft, the rallies, all of it, what was it like when you first got out of school and got your first job?"

"My first job?"

"Yeah."

"No one ever asked me that before. Having your own business isn't something you interview for, so I guess I'm out of practice at being interviewed. I'll have to think for a minute."

She avoided doodling or writing, trying to keep eye contact with him, but she found herself studying his pitted cheeks. He must have had terrible acne as a kid, she thought, wondering what he looked like when he was young, with a full head of hair and a sprinkling of zits across his face. His nose was knobby, flattened at the tip; maybe it had been broken. She wanted to ask about it but was afraid of offending him, like asking a woman if she's pregnant only to find out that she's overweight. She watched his eyes drift away from her, looking at something that wasn't in the room, and now she thought it odd that an answer didn't pop right out. Wasn't this one of those questions that always made people grin with fond recollections of how far they had come? Wasn't this a story that was told and retold? His enthusiasm for the interview seemed to be fading, and she feared losing it altogether if a phone call or knock at the door gave him an easy out.

"Oh," he finally said, "I worked at various jobs after college."

"Like what?"

"Oh, different things. The stuff a young guy does when he hasn't figured out what he's going to do." The first hint of the usual patronizing she got from adults.

She decided to press. "Well, gimme a for-instance." She smiled.

"Hmm. I was a roofer for a while." He said it almost as if thinking something up to satisfy the question. "I waited tables," he added, and then he thought for a moment and said, "A bunch of different things. I met Emma's mother in Florida, in 1982, and then we came back here and I started this business in the garage at our first house. I was amazed that people kept calling and buying things. I had no idea we'd grow like this. There are fifty people working in this building now! We've shipped something to every state in the union and over a dozen foreign countries. I still show up here each day in a state of amazement. And this internet thing—it's going to turn into something, too. It'll save us a lot of money, and the customers too."

He was coasting into the success story of his business while she still had questions about his background, but he gained momentum and now it was too late, and she sat through anecdotes about his employees, about weird requests from customers, about arranging deliveries to obscure places, and even about brushes with fame—the movie star who would only place her orders directly with him, the hockey player who cursed him out for delivering his girlfriend's gift to his wife. Marcia was afraid there were more stories to follow, and the thread into his past now seemed hopelessly broken. She wondered later if he'd been more skillful than she gave him credit for in steering things that way, turning from the sincere friend-to-all-things-living and into just another Rotary Club member who wanted to tell his success story. What a ploy to make sure your audience isn't really listening! She realized later that he had many years of practice at exactly this kind of confrontation, and undoubtedly with much more skillful and aggressive questioners than herself.

But she had liked Peter. He was an unusual sort of businessman, from his casual manner of dress to how friendly he seemed with his employees. And she thought he was courageous, too, saying some of the things he did in this conservative, Bible-belt town. She even worried that her profile would show a bias in his favor.

The night after the interview she found his school's Web page. There were photos of an attractive campus with old brick buildings and stained glass windows overlooking the Hudson River. The images were serene and rural, lush and green in the summer and snowy and pristine in winter. It was much different than she had imagined New York state, which she only knew from images of congested Manhattan streets that she had seen on television. The more she looked at the college's website, the more appealing the college seemed, with football games in the autumn colors and crew races on the white-capped river. She wondered if they had a journalism program.

Alumni weren't listed on the website. But Marcia persisted. She wasn't looking for trouble, but the way he steered around some of her questions nagged at her. Maybe he had tax troubles. She wasn't given much to speculating. She just liked to have all the pieces in place. She clicked open a link to the most recent alumni report, thinking he was so successful that he'd probably be listed as a donor. But when she scanned the donor lists (a surgeon from Peter's year had given $10,000!), there was nothing. It was late and she was certain that she missed his name, so she saved the file to review again later when she wasn't so tired and e-mailed a copy to the computer at the school newspaper office to print it out there.

Jaycee saw her looking over the file after school and asked about it.

"It's weird," she said. "You'd think a guy with that much money would be a big deal for his college."

"What about the other stuff?"

"Well, it's all stuff that we already know about. He doesn't give any names of places he worked in Florida or North Carolina, just says he worked in construction and waiting tables. I thought if I could find someone who knew him from college, like a professor or whatever, it might add a little spice, you know, a surprise angle, on the piece."

"But you're saying that he might not have actually graduated from the college he put down on his resume?"

"No, all I'm saying is I didn't find his name in the alumni report, which is probably true for a thousand other people who didn't donate money, and ..."

"And what?"

"Well, it was just...there was just something about the way he kind of spaced out when I was asking him about that whole time period. You know, nothing he said. I thought people liked to talk about stuff like that. Maybe he's afraid we'll find out that he smoked marijuana."

"That he inhaled!" Jaycee laughed.

She smiled, and he left her to the computer, where she stayed until a custodian appeared and told her that he had to lock up.

The next day, she called the alumni office at Peter's college on her cell phone. A dry female voice advised her that they did not give out personal information about alumni. When she identified herself with the press, the dry voice asked what paper, and she avoided mentioned her high school as she said, "*The Raven*."

"Never heard of it. Hold on," the voice said wearily.

An assertive male voice now came on and said, "This is Dr. Williams. What can I do for you?"

Marcia stuttered, intimidated by the change in tone. "I'm trying to verify some information about one of your graduates for a story."

"What paper are you with?"

"*The Raven*."

"Never heard of it."

"We're just outside of Kansas City. It's a small town, Hawkings, Kansas?" Her voice lilted upward—a teenager turning a declarative sentence into a question. She felt her thin veil slipping off. His tone changed.

"Never heard of that either. Is this a school paper?"

"Yes."

"Young lady, we don't give out that information…"

There it was—*young lady!*

She jumped in, talking fast now. "Excuse me, sir. Our school newspaper is running profiles of the candidates for the school board election. One candidate, Peter St. John, lists himself as a 1970 graduate of Saint Celixine College. We're simply trying to verify this information for our story." Encouraged by her own brazenness, she continued, "Also, we'd like to find someone who might recall him as a student there for an interview."

"Well, I don't think…"

"I can have my principal call you. Or, I know! You can call us back, so you know this is legitimate. Here, I'll give you the Hawkings High School website, and you can see for yourself. It's w-w-w-dot- …"

He surprised her by taking the address and looking up the school as she waited. She guided him through the website to the school paper and even to a group photograph of the newspaper staff that included her. Then he said, "There's very little I can share with you about any of our graduates. Hold on for a moment. What year did you say?"

"1970."

Music came on the line, a thin segment of Vivaldi's *The Four Seasons*, punctuated by a congenial female voice offering free information for prospective students. Marcia considered calling back for a packet. Then Dr. Williams' voice returned. "We find no listing of a Peter St. John."

"Are you sure? Is there a question about spelling the last name? Saint is usually abbrev…"

"We're quite sure how to spell *Saint*. No one named Peter St. John graduated from the College." He said *college* as if there could be no other.

"The profile lists 1970, but that could be a misprint. Maybe it was 69 or 71."

"It's not."

"How can you be sure?"

"Because we checked the entire database. As I said, no one by that name *ever* graduated from the College."

She was befuddled. Surely it was a mistake. Or maybe there was something amiss in the profile. But why would he mention that college if he didn't graduate? That was it! Maybe he didn't graduate!

Jaycee pitched in some of his own money, along with forty dollars from Marcia, and a few dollars from the school newspaper budget they needed to make up the price so they'd have enough to purchase a copy of the 1969 yearbook for Saint Celixine College. They had found a website that sold yearbooks, and this was the only one available for that period. "Slightly marked up," the description said. The book listed for almost a hundred dollars, plus taxes and shipping costs. But they decided to buy it. Marcia wasn't satisfied and she didn't want to embarrass herself or hurt Mr. St. John without verifying her facts. They paid for overnight delivery, and Jaycee had the unopened package at the newspaper office.

"I waited for you to open it," he said. She sometimes wondered if he liked her.

She tore open the envelope, and gritty liner stuffing scattered on the desk and floor. In the junior section, under the S's, the photos went from Sabin to Suzinski. There were pages of students listed under S, but no one with a St. or Saint, nor was there anyone listed with the surname John. They checked the other classes too, looking through the same alphabetical sections of tiny one-inch-square black-and-white photos of boys with bushy hair and girls wearing caftan tops. They leafed through the activity photos, snickering at the clothing and hairstyles, until Marcia noticed a student in a gleeful group at an outdoor activity, perhaps a picnic or tailgate party. Everyone was laughing and splaying their arms and legs in every direction. One student bore a startling resemblance to Peter St. John.

"There!" she said.

Before she could point to him, Jaycee exclaimed, "Yeah, I see it!"

"Go back! We have to find that student."

And they did go back, now paging through all of the underclass photos until they found a student listed in the class of 1972, with a wave of dark hair over his brow and more hair covering his ears and collar, wearing a crew-neck sweater and button-down shirt, with his head tilted slightly to one side, and the name Peter Howell below the picture.

"Do you think it's him?" Marcia asked.

Jaycee snorted. "Do you think it's not?!"

"Holy shit! What is going on?"

The door of the newspaper office was open. Metallic cleats echoed in the hallway as baseball players came in from practice and headed into the locker room down the hall. Jaycee looked in both directions before shutting the door. "I don't know."

"If it's him, why does he have a different name?"

"Maybe it's nothing big. Like, maybe he was in show business and changed his name. Was he a musician, or maybe an actor?"

"Why wouldn't he want people to know if he was an actor?"

"I don't know. I mean it's not like he had some long Polish name or whatever. You wouldn't have to change a name like Howell."

"What now?"

"I don't know, Marcy. But we better keep this between us. Let's see what we can find out about Peter Howell. I wonder if *he* graduated."

"You think he didn't?!"

"Hey, we don't know anything right now. Maybe you should call the college again."

"I guess…but I don't know if he'll give me any more information."

"Yeah, it might send up a flag too. We have to keep this on the D-L while we check it out."

She shivered, and she knew that Jaycee had the same jitters. She felt as if they were far out on an ice-covered lake and had just heard the first ominous crunch beneath them. She wanted to stand very still and take the next step slowly—and she didn't want Jaycee to make a sudden leap that might send them both crashing through the ice and into the cold deep water.

"Here's what we'll do," she said. "I'll do some searches on the Web and if I can't find anything, I'll call the school again. At least they already know me. I can play stupid if I have to, like, 'Sorreeee, I must have got the wrong name from the editor,' like this is just something I do when I'm not in fashion club and cheerleading."

"That's good!" Jaycee laughed. "Chomp on some gum when you call."

"I'll twirl my hair, too, even though they won't see it!"

They laughed, but the shoreline was far away, and the crunch of the ice had been resonant and deep—and they had both heard it.

‡

"Holy Jesus!" Jaycee muttered as he sat beside her and leafed through the articles and photos she found on the Web and at the public library that described the activities of a radical student group from the 1960s. She had microfiche printouts about a campus riot instigated by a group that called itself The Circle in the wake of the Kent State shootings. Jaycee turned the pages slowly—she already knew what was coming—and now he lingered over an article about a bombing in upstate New York. And then he turned to the next item, about the trial and conviction of the terrorists who had planted the bomb, and then the next, about the manhunt for two terrorists who had escaped.

Peter Howell was one of them.

Jaycee held up a small copy of his mug shot, taken after an arrest for vandalizing the administration building at the college. His lips were parted, though it seemed as if he wasn't even breathing.

She knew the sensation; she had felt it herself hours earlier, sitting at the microfiche reader.

His voice quivered. "You gonna go see him?"

She felt light, both warm and chilly. "I don't know."

"You have to, Marcy," he whispered. His eyes were glazed. Then he added, "We have to run something. What are you gonna write if you don't find out what this means?"

"I don't know," she said. "Besides, we still don't know for sure that this is him, do we?"

"No, but I wish I wasn't sure it is. We have to find out. Does anyone else know about this?"

"No."

"We'll never get this past Holbrook."

"I know."

"We'll worry about that later. Here's what you do, call and tell him you're coming to see him, that you just want to confirm a couple of quotes—and your facts, but—that's it!—just kind of add that, like it's an afterthought—and that you only need a few minutes of his time. Ask him if you can stop by his office after school."

"Okay."

"Wait ..."

She watched his eyes dart around, not fixing on anything, and then he took her hand—he'd never touched her before, not like this, never more than a pat on the shoulder—and said, "No, you shouldn't go. Forget what I said. You shouldn't go."

"Why?"

"It might not be safe. Maybe we should just call the *Star* or tell your father or something. Maybe we should tell Holbrook."

Her hand had been limp, but she gripped his fingers now and said, "Not a chance—especially not Holbrook. This is ours. Our story. We're gonna run it."

"But look what he's done!"

"We don't know that, and anyway, I've known him my whole life." She shook her head and curled her lips up, not quite a smile. "He drove me and Emma to soccer practice."

Now she squeezed his hand. She was tempted to kiss him, but it was too much right now, too much.

When she made the call, Peter seemed almost saddened to hear from her, as if she was a customer who had just cancelled a big order—and not at all surprised, either. She considered not telling Jaycee, afraid he'd insist that she not go. Instead, now he wanted to go with her, but she said no, she had to go alone. And she rallied, adding, "Besides, maybe he had a lousy day, and I'm just one more headache."

"Call me, Marcy, as soon as you're done. Call me."

"Okay."

⁜

Her second visit to Peter's office was altogether different from the first, right down to the blustery and cold weather that seemed like it blew in just to make her feel worse. Her car was buffeted on the way to the warehouse, and she had to steer with both hands. She had not figured how to begin the interview, even as she struggled across the parking lot, grasping her jacket and clutching her backpack. This time the warehouse seemed damp and vast and shadowy. Yes, it all seemed worse this time. She passed several workers on her way to the office, and she felt conspicuous.

Peter was at his desk, with his back to the door, facing his computer, and he quickly closed the screen as she said, "Mr. St. John?"

"Hello, Marcia," he said. "Have a seat." He sounded like a teacher who thought she'd been cheating. This time would be different.

She held her bag and kept her coat on. He didn't offer any soft drinks, but got up from behind his desk and closed the door.

She could see it now, his face, his eyes, the tilt of his head, even the pattern of waves in what remained of his once thick hair. It was him! She was sitting before the young man in all those photos. He had vandalized the school, taken over a building, set off a bomb, killed people! She had no doubt who he was, and now he was right in front of her!

She had requested the meeting, and it was up to her to start, but now she just sat in front of him, clutching her bag and waiting for him to say something. His face was ashen, gray, and his eyes shadowed and puffy. He looked like he hadn't slept. He finally said, "It feels strange to see you again like this, just you and I. I've known you since you were little but never really talked with you so much. You and Emma were in so many things together, scouts and soccer and all of that. We've known your parents for years. They're good people, and your mother always stayed involved in your activities. But you and Emma aren't that close anymore, are you?"

Marcia shook her head. She had no idea where this was going.

"No," he continued, leaning his head to one side, a slight grin crawling up from the corner of his mouth, "I didn't think so. You always sold the most cookies in the troop. Emma could never beat you at that. You've always been very ambitious. I'll bet you get good grades, don't you?"

Marcia just said, "Pretty good," though she had straight A's.

"Mmm," Peter mused. "You'll be very successful. Well, about this story. I'm guessing that by now you've run across some of the different roads I took in my life, and that's why you want to ask me some more questions."

Marcia had not even taken out a notepad, but she was too stunned to write. "It's just that…well, I…we came across some inconsistencies."

He smiled and used her phrase. "Gimme a for-instance."

Now she fumbled in her bag for the notebook. "The college on your resume…"

"Saint Celixine."

"It says that you graduated from there?" She winced at the upward lilt in her own voice.

"I guess that's a bit of an overstatement."

"We found…we got…" She couldn't find the entry point. She took a breath and fumbled in her bag again, this time pulling out the yearbook. She saw a palpable change in his demeanor. He stroked his beard with the back of his fingers as she opened it to one of the bookmarked pages. "There's a picture in here. We didn't know what to think. Maybe it's just a coincidence." She held out the yearbook with the page open to his class photograph.

He stared at the picture but said nothing.

She pulled out a folder stuffed with the Web printouts and copies of newspaper articles she'd found. "This is probably all a mistake," she said. "We just didn't know…what all this was."

He leafed through the articles. It was all there, even more than he imagined. He shook his head. "I figured that when you called to ask more questions, you had probably either reached a dead end or found the entrance ramp to a superhighway. I guess it was the superhighway. You know, it's been over twenty-five years since I talked straight with anyone about that time in my life. Like I said, when you own your own business, no one interviews you for the job, and when you go to the chamber of commerce meetings, everyone just accepts what you say about yourself as long as you stay on top of the heap. We all wear masks, even people who don't seem to have anything to hide, or at least anything that might send them to jail."

"Mr. St. John…"

"Marcia, you already know that's not my name."

‡

Jaycee's e-mail was cryptic—and alarming.

To: marcyr@unilink.com
From: perrywhite@raven.net
Date: April 21, 1999

Gotta talk—come to the office 1st hour—bring your notes—Holbrook!!

She had been up most of the night and could not recall when she trudged over to her bed and flopped on it, still fully clothed. The soft chime from the computer announcing the e-mail's arrival blended into the warble of a bird outside her window, but then it roused her. "Omigod!" she exclaimed, when she realized that the computer was still on line and the phone had been tied up all night.

Before the meeting, she made a diskette copy and printed two paper copies of her article, one of which she slid under the floor mat in her car.

Her mother's car was in the driveway and her bedroom door was shut. She must have come in from the hospital and gone straight to bed.

The secretary in the principal's office sent her to the conference room, where Jaycee sat alone on one side of the table, with Mr. Holbrook across from him and Mrs. Claymore at the end. Marcia slid in beside Jaycee, the first time she'd seen him since the interview. They'd spoken only briefly after it, long enough for her to tell him she was okay and that she'd work on the piece that night, and then her cell phone had cut out. She couldn't reach him later because he'd gone out with his parents. As soon as she was seated, Mr. Holbrook said, "Good! Now that Marcia's here, maybe we can get an explanation of what's going on. Could either of you explain this?" He opened a folder and took out the invoice for the yearbook that Jaycee and Marcia had ordered.

"What is that?" the principal asked.

"These students purchased a yearbook from a college in upstate New York for the class of 1969, and I think they should explain why they used newspaper funds for this and why computer resources are being used to print lengthy reports from this same college. Is one of you planning to apply for the class of 1969?"

His sarcasm even fell flat for Mrs. Claymore, who turned to the students and asked, "Do you have this yearbook?"

"I have it," Marcy said, and she opened her backpack and put the book on the table, now stripped of all the sticky notes and bookmarks that had filled it.

Mr. Holbrook pulled it toward himself and began to leaf through it.

"Well," said the principal, "I'm confused too. Let's start by you telling us what you're working on right now for the paper."

Jaycee said, "Profiling school board candidates. We ordered this yearbook for background research on one of them."

"With money from the newspaper fund," Holbrook mumbled as he turned the pages.

"But mostly our own money," Jaycee shot back.

"Which candidate?" the principal asked.

Jaycee and Marcia glanced at one another, but neither responded.

"Which candidate is it?" she asked again.

Holbrook now shut the book and rested his hands on top of it.

"It's…too soon to say," Jaycee said.

Mrs. Claymore seemed to find the situation almost humorous. "You mean you don't know which candidate you're researching, but you ordered an expensive book to do the background research?"

"They know, Mrs. Claymore." Mr. Holbrook now pulled more papers from his file folder, and Marcia recognized the media profiles done by all of the candidates. "There's only one candidate who lists any connection to this college, Peter St. John, who is a graduate."

"But he's not in there!" Marcia spoke for the first time since she sat down.

"Well, so what?" Mr. Holbrook responded. "It says here that he graduated in 1970, and this is a 1969 yearbook. Maybe he transferred into the school. Just what is it you're doing?" But before either student could answer, he turned to the principal. "I don't like this, Mrs. Claymore. Mr. St. John's daughter is a student here, and I think we're getting into risky business if we start printing allegations that a school board candidate didn't graduate from the school on his CV based on flimsy evidence like this."

"How much did this book cost?" Mrs. Claymore asked.

Jaycee answered before Mr. Holbrook could speak. "It was a hundred dollars, but we only used twenty dollars from the paper's funds. The rest was our own."

"But they never cleared that with me," Mr. Holbrook added.

"I see," Mrs. Claymore said. "So you two put up eighty dollars of your own money just to buy a yearbook from the wrong year. You're both honor roll students, so I don't think you're stupid enough to buy the wrong yearbook. Why did you want this one?"

"It was the only one we could get," Jaycee said. "There wasn't one from 1970."

"Okay," she asked. "Perhaps you can explain why you needed a yearbook at all, then."

"Exactly my question," trumped Holbrook.

Marcia was bleary with fatigue, but throughout the exchange, she was trying to figure out how much she could share without spoiling her story. Jaycee still didn't know the full extent of it, and she was also worried about having parts of the story leaked if they gave away anything right now. The principal might call Peter. Word would get around that something wasn't right with his background. Holbrook would for sure shoot his mouth off. She knew the story would explode, and she could not compete with professional journalists if any of them got a whiff. Even as she had sat reading microfiche days ago, she considered not submitting copy to the faculty advisor before it appeared. And now, the story was bigger and the chances for leaks would increase exponentially. She had to go mum, and she had to get Jaycee to go along with her.

"It was a dead end," she blurted out. "I just wanted to get the facts straight and maybe interview some people that might have known Mr. St. John. So I talked Jaycee into getting the yearbook with me, and I printed out the alumni report without telling him, because I knew he'd be worried about using up all the ink and paper. But then I couldn't figure out how to reach some of the people from the school. The professors are retired or dead, and the alumni report wasn't much help after all because you can't figure out who he might have known."

"Well, why didn't you just ask Mr. St. John?" Holbrook said, now relishing Marcia's obvious naivete.

She nodded, as though she regretted not asking his advice sooner. "I know, I know. That's what I should have done. That's what I'll do." She turned to Jaycee, whose face might have shattered into pieces if it were stroked with a feather. "That's what we'll do. Mr. St. John can give us some ideas about who to ask. Is it too late? When does the article have to be submitted?"

"Uh, no," he said, confused. "We have a few days. Let's...uh...do that. We'll get a couple of interviews for your piece and then we can put together all of the profiles."

"Well," said Mrs. Claymore, "it sounds like a plan to me, and now we'll all have just enough time to make second hour."

Mr. Holbrook began to put the yearbook back into his briefcase, and Marcia nudged Jaycee, who said, "Mr. Holbrook, we can we have our book?"

"Your book?"

"We still might need it. We can pay back the newspaper, if that's what you want."

"I'm sure that won't be necessary," Mrs. Claymore added. "Mr. Holbrook, why don't we let the students have their book?"

"I suppose." He left it on the table and headed out the door to his class, but before Jaycee and Marcia could leave, Mrs. Claymore stopped them and said, "I'd like to read your profile of Mr. St. John before it goes to the printer, Marcia. When would that be?"

Marcia looked at Jaycee, who said, "Tomorrow night."

"Good! Well, you bring me a copy before it goes out. Now, don't be late for your next class. You can get a hall pass at the desk."

Outside, Jaycee said, "What was that all about?"

"I can't tell you right now. I gotta go."

He was still standing in the empty hallway when she reached the stairwell at the end of the hall and looked back before bounding up the stairs to her history class.

Chapter 5

Concealing yourself, Peter had learned many years ago, is something you do in public. You blend into the crowd or landscape. You don't attract attention. You observe the speed limit and make full stops.

You don't steal—unless you have to.

You get straight.

In the hour after the blast, he drove on back roads all over Groenkill County, shivering with fear, sobbing, trying to figure out what to do next. Every driver he passed seemed to be peering through his windshield at him. There was no one left to call. He was alone.

He stayed with a friend of Keubler on a farm outside New Paltz for a few days. This was supposed to be a safe house, but it turned out to be where his drug connection lived. Keubler never showed up. There was dope and partying—and too many people coming and going, too many ways he could get snatched. Strange cars coming up the long dirt driveway to the house or faces he didn't recognize passing joints in the living room brought an overwhelming fear that this car might be the heat or this strange face belonged to an undercover pig. It wouldn't be long before his fears were confirmed, before paranoia turned into reality. He left without telling Keubler's friend. Just got in the car and never went back.

He drove straight to a barber shop in New Paltz, the old-fashioned, Floyd-the-barber kind of place that the university students avoided. Floyd-the-barber thought Peter was on something when he asked for a buzz cut on the sides and a little long on top, but he dove into his work, while a couple of legionnaires watched from waiting chairs with unconcealed glee, as if Floyd had just caught one of the vermin loose on the streets and could now buzz and clip him back into the human race. Peter paid the man, brushed himself off outside, and climbed into his car to begin his journey into a parallel universe, living a life not his own, recreating himself to fit his I.D. cards. He dressed like a clerk in a hardware store, wearing clothes he bought at thrift shops and a baseball cap and sunglasses if there was even a glimpse of blue sky. He made sure the tail lights and headlights were working. He stayed in cities when he could, traveling south through Philadelphia and Raleigh and Atlanta. He felt safer in rush hour traffic on interstate highways than alone on back roads in the middle of the night.

When he settled anywhere, working in a restaurant kitchen or at a construction site, he kept regular hours; he kept his place neat and spare; he was cordial to any neighbors he met, even friendly, but he avoided chatter that might lead to questions. He stopped using drugs. It was too risky to buy a nickel from a stranger, and there was the aroma, the risk of getting caught holding. He even stopped drinking rather than put his fake license at risk every time a store clerk carded him.

He passed briefly through a couple of safe houses for which he had contacts, but he never felt safe there, and after a while he gave up trying to become part of anything like the Circle again. Besides, the movement seemed to dissipate as public support for the war eroded, as the country figured out that Nixon was indeed a crook, and as the troops came home. The movement's success brought about its own demise, and Peter ended up becoming what he thought he had revolted against, not by choice but by osmosis, by years of concealing himself in public.

Now, in a national forest in Colorado almost thirty years later, his instincts were stiff, fossilized. A ranger stopped at his campsite to remind him about the ban on fires. Peter said, "No problem," and after the ranger disappeared into the brush, heading back to the path around the lake, Peter sat on the ground, shaking and gagging. He couldn't stay here long. When he was breathing steadily again, he locked the car and walked the perimeter of the lake to see who else was nearby. There were only a few other campers. The orange tent turned out to be a couple of young women from Boulder with climbing equipment who said they planned to scale the cliff on the western end of the lake. Peter wondered if they were lesbians. He didn't talk to anyone else. Near a campsite with a pickup truck, a man waded into the water with a fly-fishing rod.

The other empty campsites offered nothing better than where he was, so he set up his tent and sorted through his groceries and clothing and equipment. He had a little over $1,000 with him. He broke it up, keeping a few hundred in his pockets and folding some bills into a plastic baggie in his fishing vest. He also taped a tightly-folded $20 bill into his left shoe, wondering how bad things would be if he ever needed that bill, and why he even bothered stashing it there. He was going back…but not yet—in a day or two. He wasn't ready yet.

Once he set up camp, he had nothing to do and no way of communicating with anyone. He still had his cell phone, but there was no signal here, and knowing little of how they worked, he decided not to try it, fearing the call could be traced to his location. He scanned the few stations he could get on his car radio, but there was no mention of him on the news, and he couldn't risk running the battery down, so he shut the radio off after fifteen minutes. He tried napping during the afternoon but couldn't even doze.

He was only a couple of days removed from the life he had created over nearly twenty years with Cherylee, and while guilt and worry for his family tore away at him, the remoteness also gave him moments of detachment. He was isolated, alone, just as he'd been for many years after the bombing. Yet now he felt nothing like he did after driving away from the safe house in New Paltz. Now, he carried the experiences of watching his own children blow out birthday candles, of hearing a cough from down the hall in the nighttime, of staying up on Christmas Eve to put out gifts for the children and then surprising Cherry with a present. He had left much behind the first time he fled, including his mother, but there was so much more now.

Days passed, and he experienced moments of serenity, of relief that the burden of fear he had carried for so many years about, not whether, but when he would be uncovered and his life unraveled was finally gone. But these waves of calm were followed by storms of despair, the numbing, short-of-breath kind, when something as simple as spooning powdered coffee into a mug ends in sobbing, which spent, then gives way to overpowering fatigue. Once he was accustomed to the altitude, he slept in epic doses, awakening to piss, and to eat, though he didn't have much appetite, only occasional cravings, for oatmeal at night or beef-sticks at dawn. The tapestry of his imaginings took him back through the choices that brought him to this moment. He would turn himself in soon. He wouldn't survive long if he didn't, not as he had back then. He had no papers, little money, and no identity—none; it was all gone. And the world was such a small place now. An FBI computer in Alaska was as close to information about him as one back in Kansas City. He didn't have the strength to go on, but he wasn't yet ready to return.

His reluctance lasted for weeks. Campers came and went, and Peter moved from one place to another, finding recesses in the woods, mostly staying out of sight and away from others. He remained in the same vicinity, seldom venturing far from his campsite. It rained frequently, and he sat in the car, dozing, brooding, fretting, sobbing. The car turned funky. He thought often about simply starting up and going to the local police station. Just a flick of the wrist to start the engine and drive away, but he could never bring himself to do it.

When the skies cleared, he watched other campers cast fly rods or scramble on the rocks at the base of the mountain. Rain and high winds blew into the valley and out again with surprising abruptness, and intervals of sunshine sometimes brought torpid heat that lingered over the lake and then gave way to near-freezing temperatures at night.

By the end of May, while Emma prepared to graduate from high school despite her father's disappearance and all the chaos that descended on her because of it, the melting glaciers fueled the waterfalls to almost deafening pitches. On the very day of commencement at East Hawkings High School, Peter wandered into the meadow at the far end of the lake, where he'd seen elk grazing. The field was now thick with the reds of paintbrush and the yellows of golden banner. He had never gone beyond the field until this afternoon, but he followed a path to the bottom of a rock scree that might have been delivered here by a glacier tens of thousands of years ago. From his campsite, the scree looked like a field of gravel just above the tree-line, but now he found that it was a vast field of boulders spread out over a space as large as his subdivision in Hawkings. He began hopping and stepping from one boulder to another, and soon he was halfway up the field, sweating, but invigorated, and now determined to get to the top, to a ledge he'd seen from below.

The outing was spontaneous, so he had brought nothing with him, no water or food or even a jacket. He was not used to exercise and had gained weight over the years, but after many weeks of lethargy he now pitched himself forward, scrambling across the rocks, and soon his brow and his shirt were soaked in sweat. The area had an unseen life of its own. Chipmunks and marmots skittered among the rocks. Patches of moss and wildflowers grew in places that appeared barren from below. Once or twice, he stepped past large holes dug under boulders and looked fearfully around for mountain lions, though he saw none.

The ledge was wider than it appeared, like a platform overlooking the scree, with the lake and valley spread out before him. On a distant hill, beyond the treetops within the national forest, earth-moving machinery carved its way through the woods for a new road, and the engines churned through the constant rush of wind on the mountainside. Below, he found his campsite, a few scraps of tarp and the aging Jeep, now his whole life, all that he had left. Exhausted and thirsty, he regretted leaving the camp without water.

The boulder field had taken an hour or more to cross and the walk back looked even more imposing than the climb up. He found himself in the dilemma of a child who has climbed a tree and now discovers that the footholds and handgrips that got him to the top are out of reach. In the confusing jumble, Peter had already lost track of rocks he'd climbed over just minutes earlier. His mouth and throat were so dry that his voice would have rasped if he spoke. He worked his way along the edge of a nearby stream, to where the water plashed over the rocks, and soaked his face and neck. Cupping his hands, he slurped down water so cold that his teeth and throat hurt, and then he rested on the ledge, his face drying as the wind picked up from the west and whisked across the scree in noisy gusts. Tired, and not eager to tackle the hike back through the maze of rocks, he sheltered himself from the wind behind a boulder and settled on a tuft of grass where he could shut his eyes for a few minutes. He would rest and then head back.

As Emma crossed the stage in her gown, taking her diploma without a smile or eye contact, seeking again her anonymous place in the rows and rows of graduates, camouflaging herself in the sea of maroon gowns, Peter found his few moments of rest on the side of this mountain busy and frenetic. It made no difference if he was out in the sunshine and fresh air or brooding in the funk of his car. Sickening tremors of nausea and fear were constantly with him. He had lost track of the days and didn't know this was graduation day. But he thought about his children, and his guilt pounded away at him in the grinding rhythms of the distant machinery. As the familiar cycle of his few options once more spun through his head—go back, keep going, call Cherry, who did he know, where could he find anyone—he recognized that beneath all of it, he was terrified of going to prison, and he knew it would be for a very long time, possibly for the rest of his life. This wasn't like the few nights he spent in jail when he was young. Even with the beatings that he and Simon and the others got, they knew they'd be back on the street in a couple of days, and they had the camaraderie of their group, of everyone who was there for the cause and who made noise and harassed the pigs and cheered each other up. This was different. It wasn't jail, it was prison. And he was older now. He would not adapt well, if at all. It wasn't just the confinement that frightened him, perhaps that least of all. No, it was the harsh routines; the endless pressure of fearing all those around him, whether inmates or guards; the constant, infinite presence of people everywhere; the open toilets; the noise and light. And knowing that there would be no end of it. He had imagined this, too, many times over the years.

He had known this fear when he was younger, before he met Cherylee, a deep, primal fear hidden beneath layers of rhetoric. As he eluded capture, going from one place to another, he convinced himself for a while that he would continue the cause, the revolution, that he would eventually find others from the movement whom he could trust. For a time, he believed he was searching for such a group as he wandered the eastern seaboard in the early seventies, from New York to Florida, until he realized that there was no more movement. The momentum had withered like a wildflower that resists even brief survival in a vase of water. Without its roots firmly planted in the wild, it had no life, and so the movement had died off, many of its participants now drawn into the needs of their young families, their individual lives, their jobs and businesses and homes.

But that same primal shudder quaked within him again, like silt churning up at the bottom of a clear stream. He felt it now even more powerfully than when he was young. It was a fear he could no longer suppress, as he had for so many years by caring for his family and building his business, all the while convincing himself that if he did these things, they would insulate him. He buried his fears under the layers of the life he invented. But here they were again, stirring him to shift against the rock on which he now leaned.

His life in one sense had stopped when he was barely twenty years old. Peter Howell, he sometimes imagined, had been abandoned like the offspring of some cold-blooded creature, and the shadow within him had simply inhabited another being, which it slowly absorbed and overcame until it re-emerged like a visitor from another world, with no history, no identity, no personhood within the species in which it now found itself. At least, that was the fiction he continually tried to create for himself, but in fact his history and his regrets were always with him, one of those being that he had left his mother without saying goodbye, had, in fact, left her with the debt from his jail bond, for he was already in trouble when the bomb went off and he went underground. He called her once, months after that, when he thought the shoes might not be tapping her phone any longer. He was in a booth in Durham, North Carolina, and knew he couldn't stay on for more than a few minutes and that he'd be out of state by morning anyway. She gulped sobs and said no more than a few words, so overcome was she at the sound of his voice. She never mentioned the money from the bond. There wasn't time for him to explain anything, and besides, he didn't think he could, not in any way that would have meaning for her. He told her he was all right, that he was sorry and missed her, that he loved her, and that she might not hear from him for a very long time. He stayed on the phone longer than he should have. The air in the tobacco town smelled like the inside of a cigarette package, and he listened as she cried, and then he hung up and drove through the night. Over the years he sent cash to her, wrapped inside sheets of paper and in envelopes with no return address, sometimes he wrote letters, but there was little he could tell her about where he was or what he was doing. A couple of times he tried to explain why his cause was important enough to bomb a company that manufactured weapons, but as he imagined her reading what he wrote, it sounded empty, thin, and he tore up the letters and wrote vaguely and predictably about his health and how much he missed her. Finally, he learned on an attempted phone call that she'd been ill for months and had just recently passed away. The voice on the phone was familiar, a neighborhood friend of his mother. He hung up just as he thought she recognized him, and felt, not grief, but just an overwhelming emptiness, as if remembering grief, as if confronting once more—and with finality this time—that he was tied to nothing, belonged nowhere, in effect, didn't exist. No one was left to care what happened to him, and he had no one left to care for.

But still, there was Susan. He often wondered over the years what became of her, and then, just a few years ago, he had an encounter of sorts, at a concert in Kansas City. Cherylee had surprised him for their anniversary by getting a subscription to the symphony, and as they browsed through their programs one evening before the concert, she pointed out the ad for the orchestra's fundraiser and said maybe they should go. They chatted and he flipped the pages of his own program, and then he suddenly recognized Susan's name on the page that flew by. He turned back and there it was, Susan Mallory. She had composed the final piece to be played that evening, a choral work called "Beckonings." Throughout the concert, until it was played, Peter could think about nothing else. He looked all over the audience, fearful, anxious, wondering if she might even be here for the performance. He read and reread the short biography in the program. Her music degree from Saint Celixine College had earned only a sentence in the list of conservatories at which she studied and taught. She had trained with a famous composer in Europe and received numerous awards and made many recordings. But there was no personal information about her, whether she was married, had children, or where she lived. Her music, it seemed, was all the public needed to know about her.

He was captivated by her piece, recognizing a melody she had practiced long ago on the cello, and now he fantasized that she'd written it for him, perhaps thinking that someday he would hear it, a message of regret, and maybe also of forgiveness. The audience was completely taken with it, and when it ended, Peter calculated how to wipe his eyes without Cherry noticing.

Afterwards, driving home from the concert and still vibrating from the shock, he was afraid that if he even mentioned the music to Cherylee he would give himself away. She talked about someone she had seen in the lobby and about attending the fundraiser, and Peter clung to his solitary thoughts as he negotiated the traffic. But then she turned to the music and said she liked most of it, until they got to that weird thing. Those were her words, *that weird thing*, by which Peter knew, or was supposed to know, that she was referring to Susan's piece. Cherylee added, "Why do people write things like that? So depressing. I go out to enjoy myself, to forget about things. I like music to be pleasant."

He had no idea what to say. The music had penetrated his cover with greater force than if someone stepped out of the crowd in the lobby and said, "I know who you are!"

He pulled up short behind a car that abruptly stopped for a caution light.

Susan's voice had been so clear in the music that he thought he would have recognized it even if he hadn't seen her name in the program.

"I don't know," he said. "I liked it. It was…different, unusual." He struggled for the words. He couldn't bring himself to just shrug it off and agree with her. It seemed like such a betrayal. What came out instead was mush, while turmoil raged inside him. But what did it matter? What was left of himself after so many years of lies, half truths, equivocations? The lies were not just to protect himself any longer, but to protect her and the children.

"Maybe," she said, "but it seems like all the modern music is so gloomy, and weird. It hardly even sounds like music."

By now they were on the interstate, whizzing south to Hawkings, and the speed and the monotony of the highway numbed the chaos within, and as they neared their exit, he asked, "What do we have to eat at home?"

He later found some of Susan's CDs at Borders, and he bought one of everything with her name on it. All of her compositions had the same flavor as the piece he heard at the concert. Peter played her CDs in his office and kept them out of sight in a drawer, but he was disappointed to find that the biographical information in all of the albums was the same as on the concert program, word for word, with no hint of where she might be living and whether she had a family. The CDs were now in one of his bags in the trunk of the car. He'd packed them to avoid leaving behind any connection to her. He knew they'd be found. He had no way to listen to them now and thought he should get rid of them, but he didn't want to leave them behind.

⁜

He probably dozed for no more than twenty or thirty minutes, while the commencement address went on for much longer and Cherylee and Jean sat awkwardly on the gymnasium bleachers with Todd squirming between them. Cherylee snapped a photo of Emma in the sea of maroon, but she would be indistinguishable when the photo was developed. Peter had never lost awareness of the wind shifting and coursing along the slope of the mountain. The sound of hooves roused him once, and he peered over the top of the boulder to discover a herd of eight or ten mountain goats grazing on the slope. He watched them grunting and snuffing, together yet indifferent to one another, lingering and then easing past him. When they were gone, he resumed his doze, while the graduates and their families milled about in the high school commons, posing for pictures and hugging one another, and Emma took the long way around, outside the building, to return her gown to the band room and wait by the car until her family discovered her there, by herself, and they all rode home in silence.

When he was fully awake, Peter again drank from the stream and threw water on his face. The goats were gone, perhaps to the cliffs above the scree, where the young would be less vulnerable to mountain cats. The lake glistened in the orange glow of the sun just above the horizon to the west, and he saw the red and blue and green tarps of the campsites below, and here and there the glint of a vehicle among the trees. On the shoreline across from his own campsite two fishermen in waders, perhaps separated by thirty yards or more, were casting into the lake. Now he realized that a vehicle was at his own campsite, a tan pickup truck, and then he saw people checking out his site. The vehicle was marked with the emblem of the park service. He began to scramble down through the rocks, but the way was confusing and difficult, and he became disoriented among large boulders that blocked his view of the descent. It was getting cold, and he scraped his legs along the way and stumbled in his haste.

It was dusk when he arrived back at his campsite. The rangers were gone, but a cardboard ticket dangled from a string on the driver's door handle. He'd been cited for camping without a permit and instructed to go to the ranger's office to pay the permit fee and a fine. The ticket was written in blue carbon ink; the ranger had the original—and Peter's license plate appeared in a box at the top. Nothing inside the tent appeared to be disturbed.

He had stayed one day too many. The park service computers might not trace his tag right away, but an FBI computer search would find out that he had been here soon enough. Still sweating and out of breath from the hike, he took down his tent, gathered his belongings, threw everything into the back of the Jeep, and headed for the narrow trail that had brought him here. Once he was clear of the lake and on the trail, he became more aggressive as he drove, bouncing wildly along the path that he had so cautiously negotiated weeks earlier. Where he would go next didn't matter as long as he was clear of the national forest. With his tag number now in the computer database, or likely to be there very soon, he would not be able to use similar campsites elsewhere. Although he knew this should have been the signal to turn himself in, he found himself running, as if from habit.

The highway that accessed the unpaved road was itself remote and isolated, just two lanes and no shoulders, with some stretches barely wide enough for two cars to pass. He saw few vehicles until he reached a crossroads that turned onto a busy four-lane state highway, and he turned west with no idea where he was going or where he would stop next. The back of the car was a jumbled and smelly mess, with the damp and dirty tent thrown on top of everything else. It was dark as he drove through small towns with unfamiliar names and then over long stretches of lonesome highway in the mountains.

For some time, his stomach had been cramping up, which he thought at first was just from nerves, but now it was tightening and he was so overwhelmed by the urge to shit that he didn't think he could drive another mile, much less wait to find a gas station. Traffic was thin and the road unlit. The urge became so powerful and the pain so intense that he feared he would soil his pants, so he pulled to the side of the road, and after stumbling through the brush, relieved himself in a diarrheic fit, with his intestines cramped and rumbling. His insides felt as if they were being twisted and rung out like a wet towel. It was the stream water, he realized. He'd caught something from drinking it. He had to go again, once he thought he was done, and again one more time. By now he was sweating and panting. He could not tell if he was overheated from the effort or if a fever was coming on. Unable to clean himself well, he was miserable in his soiled underwear, now feverish, tired, and with nowhere to stop.

A few hours later, the car needed gas and Peter needed sleep. In the indigo night sky on the horizon, he couldn't distinguish the rolling mountain tops from clouds. He had no idea where he was, only that he needed to stop and that parking on the roadside would invite a passing cop to check him out. Somewhere on the western side of the mountain range, he spotted a dim electric glow in the distance, which turned out to be a gas station at the crossroads of two county highways, the only building at the junction. An old mechanical pump sputtered and chimed, and Peter tried to adjust his pants while he waited for the tank to fill. He rummaged in the back of the car and found a pair of briefs from a few days ago. Inside, the clerk pointed past a rack of potato chips to a door that opened into a dirty, cramped, and smelly men's room. Peter stuffed the old drawers into the waste bin, pushing them under the crumpled paper towels that overflowed the rim, and after washing one more time, he went out to the tiny convenience store and read the headlines on the papers.

"Them's all yesterday's," the clerk said. He had a gray beard like a brillo pad and a baseball cap glittering with pins. "New ones'll be here in a couple of hours."

Peter nodded and paid the man for the gas. "Any motels around here?" He looked out into the vacuum of darkness beyond the rim of neon light around the gas pumps.

"No motels."

Peter sighed. "How about campgrounds? I just need to get some sleep." He suddenly felt chilled and his gut began to rumble and cramp again. He needed to go back to the wash room.

The clerk postured his chin forward as though to think about it and then shook his head no.

Peter went back to the men's room and unleashed another torrent of diarrhea into the muddy mess already in the toilet. He buried his nose in the crook of his shoulder while he sat there and then washed hastily and tried to flush again, but it just stirred and settled without draining. He shivered now, and passed through the shop without a word to the clerk. He decided to drive on and pull off the road whenever he found a shoulder wide enough. If he was picked up, so be it. He would surrender soon anyway.

Within minutes after he left the station, he was feverish and shivering, and the cramping in his gut returned. He would need to stop and shit again soon, very soon. When he saw a road sign with a picnic table on it, he didn't even hesitate but pulled off the road, into the darkest section of the picnic grove past a couple of weathered tables, and squatted in the weeds a dozen feet from the car. He took his pants off beside the car and cleaned himself and then climbed back into the driver's seat, folding the sweatshirt behind his head and wrapping himself inside his coat. He shivered and dozed, startled by infrequent vehicles on the road, and had to step outside several more times, now puking and gagging.

As he dozed, he fully expected to be awakened by a flashlight beam in his face and a squad car with whirling lights in his rearview mirror. Images of his family—of helping Todd build a model or watching Emma sing in the school chorus—were so painful that he was reduced to sobbing as they came to him. He thought of Cherylee, who probably hadn't slept since he left, pacing the house, sitting at the kitchen table, no doubt herself often in tears. He pulled out his cell phone, but there was no signal. Then he took out his wallet and turned on the dome light so he could gaze at the photo he carried of the four of them. It had been taken a year ago. Emma and Cherylee had argued about what she would wear, and there was a hint of Emma's crossness in the picture, not quite a frown, but not a smile either. She had always been willful. He could see Cherylee in her—the hazel eyes and rounded chin. People said Todd looked like Peter, and now he saw that with his wavy dark hair, Todd resembled him as a boy. He would look like Peter one day. They both had the same round, liquid brown eyes. They both looked vulnerable. Peter snapped off the dome light and clutched the photo as he pulled the coat tightly around himself.

The sound of tires crunching slowly behind the Jeep woke him. This is it, he thought, as the car door slammed shut. But he opened his eyes to see a man dashing from his car and into the brush in the gray dawn.

Peter was cold, but the fever had broken. The urge to piss felt like a normal morning urge. He waited until the car was gone and then got out himself. Traffic passed, sweeping by at terrific speeds and throwing gusts into the weeds on the roadside. He had no idea where he was. He opened a jug of water and threw some on his face and rinsed out his mouth before drinking. He was weak, shaky, even woozy, but he thought the worst might be over. He hadn't slept in a bed since he left and decided that's what he wanted. He would check into the first motel he could find and sleep in a bed until there was knock at the door. He drank more water and climbed back in the car, panicking for a moment when he couldn't find the photograph in the rumpled mess in the front seat. He propped the picture on the console and pulled into the traffic, once again heading west.

Chapter 6

Magnus's lime-green Ford Econovan glows in the darkened driveway of Corinne O'Reilly's house on Brook Street. Ancient oaks give the neighborhood an aura of quiet and stately conservatism. Most of the houses were built some fifty or sixty years ago; ponderous and gabled, with thick columns and wraparound porches—and now heavy with a sense of decaying affluence. Some have been subdivided into apartments. Ramshackle additions and unmatched siding pockmark the neighborhood. Cars crowd the driveways and street. You climb a few steps up from the sidewalk to gain Corinne's lawn, and in the dark, you watch your step on the rippled slate walkway that takes you up to the shadowy porch.

Corinne grew up in this house and inherited it when her father passed away a decade ago. She was a psyc major at St. Selly's, but her degree has been less helpful in dealing with the bi-polar dentist in whose office she is a receptionist than her natural warmth and generous spirit. She smiles easily and prefers listening to talking. Her wiry brown hair is always frizzy because she does nothing more than run a pick comb through it after a shower, and she's as apt to laugh as to cover herself with a towel if one of the many people who come and go in her house passes her with nothing on in the hallway. The house is filled with exotic souvenirs from her year in Africa with the Peace Corps—masks, blankets, pottery, and photos of herself surrounded by smiling Ugandan children.

The college remains part of her life. Students who want to join the Peace Corps come to her for guidance. And when Simon returned from Vietnam, he enrolled there to study art. She cleared out her enclosed back porch, with its bright southern exposure, so he could paint, and he filled canvases and paper with images that continually floated up from his memory like hot, glowing embers from a stirred fire. But he soon became disillusioned with his art professors, who wanted him to bend and distort the harsh and violent realism of his work into stylized images. *Decorations!* he bitterly called the lifeless geometric canvases they produced with masking tape and spray paint. *Colorforms!* he sneered. He abandoned school after two unhappy semesters.

The Word began in Corinne's dining room with a mimeograph machine and a pair of Royal portable typewriters, to circulate anti-war flyers and mostly to publish the dozens of feverish letters and editorials that Simon wrote and the newspapers refused to print. The pages multiplied as other voices joined Simon's. With students and volunteers crowding into Corinne's house, it soon became unworkable, so she and Simon found a cheap office near the wharfs and began selling ads to cover the lease and printing costs, and now *The Word* is a thick and widely-read tabloid. When Abbie Hoffman quoted one of Simon's articles in a speech, Simon re-dubbed the house cat Yippie, and it was Yippie's sinister and smiling face at the center of a barbed wire circle with a stick of dynamite about to blow—a design of Simon's making—that Peter and the others later had tattooed on their shoulders.

The urgency of the moment, of the daily atrocities that appear in headlines, of the misleading speeches by those who run the war and the apathy of those silent millions who could stop it if rallied to the cause, now drive Simon to run the paper at the same frenzied pitch he brought to his art. His canvases and drawings fill the newspaper office walls. He paints less now, but he can't dabble at it. He binges, sometimes disappearing into his studio for days, then sleeping for twelve or fourteen hours, and then throwing himself back into the paper for weeks until the need to paint once more consumes him.

After picking his way along Brook Street for several blocks, Peter spots the bright green van and recognizes the house from last night's party. He flips on his dome light for a glance in the mirror. He had parted his hair in the middle, but the part won't hold and an absurd wave crests on top of his head. He presses it down and climbs out, stumbling on the walkway with his quick step. Simon told him to stop by tonight. He said they'd talk about the paper. He wanted to show Peter his paintings.

No one answers the door, but it's unlocked. Classical music blares into the hallway from behind the French doors on his right, not exactly classical though, chaotic, confused, and oddly mixed with the pungent scent of cannabis. Peter follows the noise and smell and finds Simon lounging on the sofa with a book and Magnus hunched over the coffee table, sitting crossed-legged on the floor, while he plugs a stopper into a chemical flask.

Simon looks up from his book. "Hey, Peter!" But just then, as Peter starts through the doorway, he raises a hand. "Listen! This is the best part!"

The music is dissonant and unfamiliar, but the whining strings and bellowing horns now coalesce in a celebratory chorus, a joyous finale. And then, *KKRRCCH!!!* An electric belch crackles through the speakers and the needle jumps back a groove and repeats the fractured chord.

"Awww, shit!!" Simon leaps up.

"Bummer!" Magnus says.

In the abrupt quiet, as Simon lifts the turntable arm, Corinne's voice surprises Peter. "Put it back on." She stretches her legs out from a club chair behind the door, her eyes closed. Without opening them, she adds, "Hi, Peter."

"Hi!" he says, smiling. And she smiles back, her eyes still shut.

"It's gone now! The moment is gone! Holy shit, you wait all the way through to get there, too! We have to replace that one."

"What was it?" Peter asks, still puzzled at this odd music.

"The Firebird!" Simon exclaims. He squats before a row of albums, fingering his way through them. "You never heard it?"

"No."

Simon's eyes widen as if Peter just said he never heard of Santa Claus.

"Stravinsky! I love that piece! Everything comes together at the end, when the phoenix is reborn from the ashes." He brings his hands together and then raises and separates them, wiggling his fingers as the newborn bird flutters away. "You have to hear it! A song of hope! Hope in the midst of chaos. Little enough of that nowadays, ain't that true? We'll get another copy and listen to it. Hey, Cor, what about having a Firebird new-album party?"

She grins. "I'll make hash brownies."

Magnus smiles. His teeth glow in the dim light.

Simon puts on another album, and Dylan's wiry voice groans over the steady strumming of his guitar. "Come on in, man." He takes Peter by the shoulder, and they sit on the sofa. "You got that thing ready to stoke up?"

Magnus nods and lights the bong, and water bubbles up as he sucks on the rubber tube, moiling the smoke into a thick cloud inside the flask. He hands the pipe to Peter, who pulls on it, surprised at how smooth and cool the smoke is, filtered through the bubbling water.

"Hey, Peter, do you know Robin?" Simon asks.

Peter holds the smoke in his chest and shakes his head, whispering "No" into the cloud as he lets it go.

Simon takes the pipe and draws the smoke in, and they listen to Dylan, with the rhythm coursing through them and the urgent lyrics pressing on them. He brings the pipe over to Corinne and holds it as she lifts her head for a pull, and then the smoke eases from her lips and into Simon's face as he leans over her, his lips parted in front of hers, and they smile, staring at one another, until their smiles collapse into giggles.

Simon hands the pipe to Magnus and stands beside the turntable, lip-syncing along with the last song on the side:

"Oh, help me in my weakness,"
I heard the drifter say,
As they carried him from the courtroom
And were taking him away.

He sings aloud now and sways through the end of the song, and then flips the record and tosses himself back onto the sofa. "She went into the city for the moratorium," he says.

Peter hands him the pipe. "Who?"

"Robin."

Nodding, absorbing the name, Peter asks, "Who's Robin?"

Magnus lights a cigarette, bouncing his head with Dylan, watching Simon, waiting as he draws on the pipe, waiting for him to respond.

Words seep through Simon's lips, through the smoke, "She's...wait... why did you ask that...about...Robin?"

"Cause you asked if I knew her."

"Do you?"

"No."

"You should, man."

Corinne's laughter erupts over the music—rich, throaty laughter, infecting Magnus, who gets it, the same joke. "It's like you're in a movie," she says, coughing out the words.

Peter and Simon now laugh, too, until it subsides and they settle back, inside the music now, absorbing the lyrics, following the chord changes, finding wonder in them, a pathway through them, patterns they've never heard until this moment.

When the album ends, Corinne puts on The Band, and Simon leans his shoulder into Peter's. "I'm thirsty, man. You want some juice?"

"I always want juice when you're thirsty," Peter laughs, and Simon laughs too and leads him into the kitchen, another world, bright with fluorescent light. The music fades; it's distant, not part of this world. They drink orange juice in silence, like children gulping cold drinks by the refrigerator on a hot day. The light feels harsh, clinical.

Peter asks, "Where are your paintings?"

"Yeah," Simon nods, as if remembering there are paintings in the house, and that they're his. Then, as the recollection surfaces, he grins, frowning as he does so, almost sinister, and Peter wonders if he offended him. But that was why he came, wasn't it...why Simon invited him...to see the paintings?

Simon drains his glass and crosses the kitchen, opening a curtained door into darkness and then pulling the string from an overhead light. The porch is cold and the windows black with nighttime. Their reflections surround them on three sides. Simon turns on more lights, utility lamps, the kind auto mechanics hang under an open hood while they poke at a butterfly valve and tell you how much it'll cost to fix.

The room is a collage of images and color, with canvases stacked against the walls and drawings taped on the windows and spilling from the table. Simon kicks aside a drop cloth and places one of the canvases on the easel, and Peter looks at it for several moments before realizing that it's a close-up of a leg, torn at the knee, now in two pieces, or almost two, for all that holds it together is a blackened strand of skin. The image is uncomfortably close, and Peter has the urge to step away, but he can only back up half a step in the cluttered room and now realizes that it's the close-up view rather than his distance from the canvas that renders the effect.

Simon replaces it with another, now of a soldier, greasy with sweat and filth, his face indistinguishable in the shadow of his helmet, his shirt sleeves torn off at the shoulders, dragging another soldier through the mud, obviously dead, and leaving a trough behind. Simon watches Peter absorb the scene, offering no hint as to what he should think of the sullen image, and indeed, Peter is unsure of how to respond. He's never seen art like this—and with the artist hovering nearby as he studied it—nor has he ever seen war portrayed in such stark and somber imagery.

Viewing a painting without some clue about what he's supposed to think is a new, and discomfiting, experience. Here he is, in this frigid room, with the painting before him, not even hanging on a wall, still on its easel, with no museum or gallery surrounding it to let him know that its very presence here means it has already been judged worthy, and with no caption to describe why it represents this movement or that historical moment. Just him and the painting. These raw and painful images. Simon watches him absorb them. The thick, glistening mud; the lifeless, sagging body, heavy and resistant; the soldier dragging it himself lifeless, shorn of hope, an upright version of the body in the mud—they could each be the other.

The picture offers neither comfort nor hope, nor anything to help him decide how to respond, but he now recognizes a kind of power in it that derives from that very effect, that the artist can stand by confidently and pass judgment on *him*, on his ability to judge, without waiting to hear what he says, without shuffling expectantly, hoping for praise, fearing criticism, which is how Peter has felt on those few occasions when he's shared a poem or story he wrote with others and then waited to be validated by them. He senses that Simon would change nothing if someone else thought he could improve the work in some way; that for him, this is a naked revelation of what he's seen and how he's seen it, and that anything else would be a lie.

Simon has already pulled a sketchbook from a shelf and opened it on a drafting table, and as Peter looks on he turns page after page of drawings, rattling the paper sharply, offering the images almost as if he resented sharing them because doing so meant acknowledging that he'd produced them, as if they were demons and these were his failed efforts to exorcize them. The pencil strokes are pressed harshly into the paper, definitive, sharp strokes. Charcoal shadows ripple in dark waves. Soldiers look out from the pages, staring back at the viewer as they lounge on ammo boxes or peer out from behind trees and foliage; their faces wear the horrors they've seen and inflicted; their eyes seem to ask why they're here. Dead bodies—soldiers, both American and Vietnamese, civilians, children, the elderly, women—lie in contorted positions, rumpled on bunkers, in roads and fields, some dismembered, some of them also looking up from the page through lifeless eyes.

Peter feels as if he's being guided through a nightmare. Sensing the impact of his work, Simon offers a sardonic grin and quips, "Heavy shit, ain't it?" And as Peter nods, he adds, "Here, you gotta see these before we go back inside." He shuts the sketchbook abruptly, though they're only halfway through it, and now props a portfolio case on the table and flips through a series of watercolors, benign scenes of villages, of peasants turning irrigation valves, of others leading water buffalo. The scenes are pastoral, relaxing, with gentle pastels and easy brush strokes that sometimes give way to stray drips or dried clumps of color at the edge of a cloud or the corner of a wagon. The mis-strokes add a measure of ease to the scenes, as if the artist had no care for his carelessness and the subjects had no care for anything but doing their tasks.

"These are so different from the others," Peter says.

"This was before and that was after," Simon responds, and after a pause he exclaims, "Cartoons! That's what Gould called them. Cartoons!" Then he hisses, "Prick."

Peter never liked Professor Gould either, and more sure of himself now, he says, "But they're amazing!"

Simon offers a tight smile and nods, less appreciation than an acknowldgement that Peter said something. Voices and laughter arise from inside, more voices than they had left behind, and now the voices pour into the kitchen. Terry is here, and Keubler, with the girl who played Juliet last year, and others. Simon folds the portfolio and turns off the lights, as if to avoid drawing them onto the porch, as if he had shared something with Peter and doesn't want it diluted by having others seep into the studio. They rejoin the party, and soon more dope goes around, and more music is played, and more wine drunk, and later cookies and peanut butter sandwiches are wolfed.

Much later, when Peter has settled into the sofa cushions and it no longer makes sense to go home—or even move—he loses the rest of time until a low, gruff voice near his head barks, "Hey, hey! Wake up!" He opens his eyes to the face of a gaunt woman in wire-rimmed glasses. She grabs his arm and shakes him. "You okay!" Less a question than a declaration. She snaps the blinds up, and sunlight assaults him. Then she struts down the hallway and into the kitchen, and Peter watches her black military boots recede. Voices in the kitchen, banging of doors. The woman reappears, now wearing a black beret and an army fatigue jacket. She extends a hand, which he thinks he's supposed to shake, but she pulls him up from the sofa with surprising strength for her lanky frame.

"I'm Robin," she says, once he's standing.

"Hey, I'm Peter," he rasps.

"Yeah, I know. You all right, Peter?"

His mouth is so crusty he can barely move his lips.

"I'm okay," he musters.

She laughs, "You're in bad shape. C'mon, let's get some breakfast. I hate driving. You can take me to the office."

His head seems encased in crust, and a familiar pain shoots up through his neck as he remembers swigging deeply and often from the wine bottles that went around. His foot slips on the clutch, stalling the car, and Robin chuckles in sharp snorts and asks, "You sure you're okay?"

"Yeah," he says, restarting the car, over-revving the engine, pushing the heater lever on and blasting frigid air into their faces.

She watches, bemused, and waits without shivering until he lowers the fan.

Driving with her silently beside him reminds him of learning to drive, how his mother sat in the passenger seat while they wandered neighborhood roads and later highways around Nassau County and she said nothing while the car was in motion and little at stop lights, stoically enduring the jolts as he shifted gears, stopped abruptly, stalled the car, and coasted perilously into crossroads. Robin now sits beside him with a similar stoicism, masking whatever fear she has, if any at all.

Her conversation amounts to one-syllable directions. "Turn there." "Left here."

Still dazed to find himself driving when he'd been sleeping coma-like only fifteen minutes earlier, he feels as if she's more behind the wheel than he is, guiding him through an unfamiliar section of town, among the canyon-like warehouses near the Groenkill wharfs, well north of his neighborhood. She tells him to park in front of a building that looks abandoned, and he wonders if this is the newspaper office, but she leads him up the block at a brisk pace to a coffee shop he wouldn't have spotted if they passed it, so recessed is the doorway. Everyone inside is black, customers, waitresses, and the two cooks at the steaming, sizzling grill, one of whom barks orders to the other employees. When he sees Robin passing along the aisle behind the counter stools, he calls to her, "Are we free yet?"

She snorts a laugh, "I'm workin' on it."

They squeeze into a table on the aisle, and Robin orders eggs and sausages and hash browns and toast. Peter asks for coffee and a roll, not even wanting the roll, just for the sake of ordering food.

"Never been here, have you?" she asks. Her lips curl around a sarcastic grin. She already knows the answer. Her cheeks are shadowed, sunken below her high cheekbones, and her skin has the pallor of sunlessness and smoke. She might be pretty, Peter decides, if her frown weren't fixed into her eyebrows, as if the muscles had been trained to stay in place, and if she allowed some sunlight onto her face. She smokes while they wait for the food, and Peter notices that her cigarettes are unfiltered, like Simon's, but the brand is different. Something he's never seen, a French name.

He shakes his head, looking around.

"Being white feels different all of a sudden," she says.

"I guess."

The food arrives and Robin jokes easily with the waitress before she leaves.

With her cigarette still burning in the ash tray, she slices a wedge from her eggs with a fork and says, "Don't worry, you're safe here."

He shrugs, "I never thought I wasn't. I've just never been here before, that's all."

"Yeah, right."

Her edginess puzzles him. He doesn't remember her from last night, or from the college, and he's too groggy to parry her sarcasm, or to figure out how not to offend her, which he seems to do just by sitting here.

She eats without speaking, and he asks, "Are you a student at the college?"

"Sometimes. Not much these days."

Unsure of what that means or how to respond, or if he should at all, he hesitates, fearing that more questions will only lead to more sarcasm. She's been friendlier to the people who work here than she's been to him since he awoke.

"You were at a rally yesterday, in the city?"

Her mouth is full and she nods, swallowing impatiently, but she's less edgy when she responds, perhaps relaxed by the food, by the warmth of the place and by the jocular chatter all around them. "One of them. There were rallies all over the city. A few of us went down to Bryant Park. McCarthy was there, but you couldn't see him through the mobs. Not that I cared much. I doubt if he'd have been any different if he won."

"Why not?"

"None of them are any different. Nixon said he'd end the war, but he was full of shit."

Her comment reminds him of Susan's only the morning before, or was it the day before that? Now he can't recall what day it is. He missed almost a whole day of classes, and now...is this Friday? Maybe it's Saturday. He looks around at the customers perched on stools and hovering at the front counter, trying to decide if they're on their way to work. Their clothes could be anything, a weekend or weekday. Not a suit in the place. He sneaks a glance at his watch. It's after nine, late for the breakfast rush on a weekday—and really late for him if it is a weekday. His first class on Friday starts at nine.

"You got a class or something?" Robin asks.

"Maybe."

"Maybe?!"

He notices that her laughter is always punctuated by a sardonic and vapid snort. Stupidity and incompetence seem bountiful sources of humor to her, doubtless confirming what she already thinks—about him, about Nixon, about the world as he knows it. His trouble driving had especially frustrated him because he thinks of himself as a good driver, at home with the gears, with speed—and now he doesn't even know what day it is. He can't decide if he's here because she needed a ride or because she wanted him out of the house, or maybe both, but oddly enough, he doesn't dislike her. He rather finds himself bothered by the mysterious tension that surrounds her, and that he seems to feed by saying or doing exactly the wrong thing, no matter what he says or does.

The coffee has brought him around, though his head still hurts, but he's already here, already so late he probably won't even make his next class, if there is one. He gives up. Right now he's just as dumb as she thinks he is. "So what day is it?"

"Guess." It's the first time she's smiled at him.

"Saturday."

She shakes her head and taps another cigarette from the pack.

"I was just hoping," he said.

"Hope is a thing with wings." She offers him the pack, but he declines. The last time he smoked was years ago, and from within his hangover he feels tinges of the nausea from way back then, just before he threw up in the bathroom after smoking with his friends, hoping his mother wouldn't hear him while she sewed in her bedroom across the hall.

"So what did I miss last night? When did you arrive?"

"Probably nothing. You were out on the couch when I came in around two and went to bed. We took a train up from the city."

"You live there, in that house?"

"It's Corinne's place. Yeah, I do. Magnus does. Terry might as well live there. Simon lives there with her. What about you, Peter?"

"I'm a student."

"Keeping that deferment, huh?"

He shrugs.

"So, what do you think about the war? Simon said you could help with the paper. He said you can write. We need writers."

"I don't know what I can write." He hesitates. "Simon thought I should write something about the draft. I don't know a lot about the war. Seems like we can't just let the Communists take over."

Her congenial humor evaporates with a shake of her head. "They are so good at selling that shit," she declares. "They keep repeating the same bullshit day after day, the same lies, the same sugarcoating, like we're winning, and the commies are on the run, and if they say it enough, if they just keep repeating it, it becomes true, because people believe them and never look at the facts or think for themselves or read anything but the headlines and sports pages in the *Daily News*. America's been brainwashed, Peter, by Nixon, by the government, by the corporate media. You think a peasant in Vietnam cares about communism? He's just trying to survive, trying to figure out who has the power. What're we doing there?"

He has no answer but she doesn't wait for one.

"Feeding the starving, gluttonous military-industrial beast we've created, that's what! This isn't about fighting communism, Peter. It's about feeding capitalism. And the way it's going, a nuclear bomb will fall on millions of innocent peasants who won't even have time to wonder what happened before they're vaporized." She flicks ashes and pulls on the cigarette, leaning over the table. "Have you got any idea what napalm does to people, Peter?" she whispers, squinting.

He shakes his head again, trying to avoid admitting that he doesn't know what it is, now finding that he's been knocked down to his earlier status.

"That's the trouble," she laughs. "It's not that people support the war. It's that they're so ignorant about it they don't even know what's really going on. You see truck drivers with little American flags in their windows, putting their mindless nationalism on display like a chip on their shoulders, daring someone to knock it off. But if foreigners occupied this soil and set up their own power structure, and stole our resources to profit billions of dollars while the people of this country remained impoverished and powerless, what would they think then?"

"I see your point," he says.

"Maybe you do, maybe you don't. You're worried about keeping your student deferment, about staying out of the draft, but what about those who don't have that choice? What about them? As long as the war doesn't affect you, you don't worry about why we're fighting. Have I got that about right, Peter? Is that a fair statement?"

"I suppose so."

"You run across Immanuel Kant yet, while you're staying in school and out of the draft, the categorical imperative? What if everyone made the same choices as you? In fact, what choices have you really had to make? Does it take more courage to stay in school or to burn you draft card? To go to Vietnam or to Canada?"

She stubs out her cigarette and puts some money on the table. "Well, go home and get some sleep or go to class, or whatever. Why don't you come by later? I'm not sure what you can write, but I need someone to help me edit Simon's stuff. He can't tell a semi-colon from a quotation mark."

"Yeah, okay." He considers adding *Nice meeting you*, though it seems like an odd thing to say right then, but before he makes up his mind, she catches the waitress's eye and shares another joke, and then heads down the aisle without another word to him.

He watches her cross the street with a long masculine stride. He likes her black boots and wonders where he can get a pair.

Chapter 7

Jean wanted to bang the phone down, just slam it into the cradle—bam!—the way you could with that hefty old black Ma Bell rotary phone, the one from her parents' house, the one she still had in a box in her basement. You could slam that old phone down, set the little bell inside to chiming, send a message for sure. But all she could do now was press the OFF button with the tip of her forefinger, press it with all of her might, her arm stiff, her elbow extended, press as hard as she could, holding the phone with one hand and pressing with the other.

The phone beeped. A tiny, sharp note. Cheery, insipid.

"Darn thing! What is that? Touch a button! What's the satisfaction in that?! Well, we just won't answer it again today. That's enough. Let it ring!"

Emma squirmed at the kitchen table, her knees pulled up on the seat and her bare feet dangling over the side, more limbs than she knew what to do with. She got her height from Peter, but Jean saw in her face a pastiche of dead relatives, dead before the girl was born, Nanna Horstman's pointed nose, a birthmark near her ear from a great aunt. Peter was more obvious in Todd—those large brown eyes, the hunch of his shoulders. But who were Peter's relatives? Now Jean wondered.

"The ringing wakes Mom," Emma said.

"I know, honey. I'm just tired of talking to these people."

"You can change the number of rings so it will go right to the answering machine."

"Oh," Jean said. She went back to the sink, where she was rinsing lettuce. She allowed the running water to muffle her voice as she added, "Well, maybe someone could have said so a week ago."

When the water stopped, Emma asked, "It's all true, isn't it? What Marcy wrote, what they're saying?"

"I don't know, dear. You should eat something. At least some toast. Can I put some toast in for you?"

Emma shook her head, a slight movement, barely enough to jitter her hair. She studied the ingredients on a Dr. Pepper can. "But if it's true, then our last name isn't even real. We don't have a last name!"

Jean had thought about that, too. They all had. One of the many horrors that had descended on Cherylee and the children since Peter left was that of all the things that turned out not to be true, or at least appeared so, even their very name might be a lie, not just a fake name, as if they had another real name, but nonexistent. *They had no last name!* Jean had already held her sister in her arms as she sobbed almost the very words that Emma had just spoken. Still, both Jean and Cherry outwardly maintained the position that nothing had been proven, nothing confirmed—and they had yet to hear from Peter, who might be injured or dead, perhaps the victim of a crime or a car wreck or a pernicious smear attack for reasons they couldn't imagine—but this idea curled through the wreckage that surrounded them like the first scent of fire before the smoke even appears. Cherry never conceded the truth of anything that had come out, whether talking to the children or trying to parry questions from the police and the press, but in recent days she'd become so debilitated by all that happened that she hardly left her bedroom.

Emma now seemed more thoughtful about the idea, even intrigued, in a bizarre and pained way, as if it perhaps confirmed all that she already suspected was false about life itself, as if she had long known that people wore masks and could be counted on to lie, and now here was the proof. But…if even the lie was gone, then what was left?

Jean sat beside her, putting her hands over the hands that held the soda can, and said, "I'm sure there's more to it than what that girl said. What could she know?"

"Bitch!"

"Oh, Emma."

"Well, she is! And don't think she's not enjoying every second of this. Can't we sue her?"

"Emma, this doesn't help. There's so much we don't know."

"And that too! If even half of what she said is true then my dad's been lying to us for my whole life."

Indeed, Jean had already reached this conclusion on her own. She had never trusted Peter, not that she'd ever imagined something as large and tragic as this. But she always felt there was a kind of arrogance about him, not from having success and money, because she'd felt this way long before those things came to him and Cherylee. Rather, he had a manner—which, she had to admit, he directed more toward her than others, at least as much as she ever saw him among others—that conveyed that he was smarter, more experienced, more worldly than she was, though she seemed to be the only one who wondered how he gained that worldliness. Maybe he just felt threatened by her, by her doubts about him, by the fact that she was more educated than Cherry, and just naturally more inquisitive. She had earned a master's degree in archeology, had traveled on expeditions and digs to remote places in the Middle East and South America. She wasn't stupid, or unworldly, far from it, though all that was many years ago, before the fatigue of travel and competing for fellowships began to drain her ambition, and at about the same time as her father's emphysema from a lifetime in the railroad yards made it clear that she needed to be here, close to her parents. She gave up her academic ambitions and took a job at the DMV—temporary at first, she thought—and now she has issued new license plates for almost two decades.

However their mutual distrust had begun, and then played out over the life of Cherylee's marriage to him, she knew, as she sat beside Emma, grasping the hands that held the soda can, that it didn't take a master's degree to see how much pain this betrayal had brought to this child, and to the rest of this family. All of Emma's teenage rebellion—her strange outfits, streaky hair-dyes, and the rows of piercings that lined her ears—now appeared to Jean as meaningless as a crumpled costume on the floor of a child's bedroom in the morning daylight that follows Halloween. Emma was doing what she needed to do to manage her pain. Peter had swirled her in circles to the music of Judy Collins when she was a child; he had danced the Twist with her at her girl scout troop's Father & Daughter dance (a photo of them stood across the room on the hearth); and he had cheered at her basketball games in middle school, before her interest in sports and most other activities faded. And now he had abandoned her, with these startling, unbearable truths emerging like the details of an unfamiliar landscape as the fog lifts. Yes, Jean would admit that Emma's recent antics sometimes put her off, that she'd had little tolerance for the girl's fashions, and music, and attitude, but here she was, a child after all, a child experiencing pain of a confusing, unnameable nature, and Jean had no answers for her because she had none for herself, though she'd always had her suspicions.

She sat with Emma until the girl finally raised her head and offered a tiny scowl from the corner of her mouth, and then Jean squeezed her shoulders and returned to the sink, hiding her own tears and shaking the salad bin so hard that water splattered her blouse and face, which seemed a small blessing, as she now had an excuse to wipe her eyes. She grabbed a paper towel, but it ripped off only partially and two feet of paper towels unraveled from the dispenser.

"Darn!"

Emma smirked.

Maybe the blessings had multiplied. Even the smallest mattered now.

"You never swear, Aunt Jean! Why don't you just let one rip? Wouldn't it feel good just to let out a good *Fuck*?"

"Emma!" A grin muscled its way into Jean's eyes and mouth. She feared a new rupture of tears.

"Go ahead, Aunt Jean! Let 'er rip!"

"Oh, indeed, that's not...well, you swear enough for all of us."

The phone rang.

"Let it ring," Jean said.

The moment of relief faded before it ever fully took shape.

Emma went to the desk and beeped the phone on, hesitating and listening before saying "Hello," almost inaudibly. Whoever it was did all the talking.

Emma turned her back to Jean, but from across the kitchen Jean heard that the caller was still talking as Emma took the phone from her ear and beeped it off. The voice sounded female.

"Who was that?" Jean asked.

"Nobody, just another reporter."

"She had a lot to say."

"Yeah. Hey, how did you know it was...?"

"I could hear some of it. What did she want?"

"Same as all the others. I'm going upstairs." Emma slouched across the room and up the stairs without looking back. The moment had indeed faded.

Jean's hands were still damp when the phone rang again. She wondered how to change the rings as she picked it up: a woman's voice again, but not a reporter; this time Rita Maupin, Peter's assistant at the warehouse.

Jean had seldom spoken with her, never more than a greeting or comment about the weather when she visited the warehouse with Cherylee, who had nothing good to say about her after such visits. She complained that Rita made her feel uncomfortable, that she was even rude to Cherylee, not overtly, but in subtle ways, like never speaking to her in more than monosyllables, or making her feel that if she didn't phrase whatever she said precisely when she called or stopped by, that Rita would have no idea what Cherylee was talking about. In short, doing her best to make Cherylee feel small, and even stupid. Meanwhile, she seemed to have an abundant reserve of warmth and cheerfulness on tap for Peter. By proxy, Jean didn't like her, never had. Even her appearance. She had the squat shape of a shoe box. And how she walked, with a short, deliberate step that made her appear to glide officiously from one place to another. But this call, or one like it, was inevitable. Jean knew little of Peter's business, but she knew that no business could run for long without someone in charge.

Rita said she'd put off calling as long as she could, but she'd been swamped with calls from reporters asking if Peter had returned and wanting to interview employees. (Jean now wondered if she would read a quote from Rita in tomorrow's paper.) Rita also said that someone claimed on the radio that the business was just a cover-up, maybe for drug trafficking or an underground terrorist network.

"Who would say such a thing?!"

"Oh," Rita said, almost dismissively, "it was M-P-G."

"Who?"

"Melvin P. Gash. You never heard his show?"

Her tone...was she enjoying this?

"No, I've never heard it." Jean said.

"It's on the radio every afternoon."

"I don't have time to listen to the radio during the day." Jean felt herself tightening, as if her throat were being squeezed. She couldn't decide who made her more angry—Rita or this...Gash person, whoever he was.

"Well, anyway. The payroll is due. A deposit needs to be made, and the checks signed. I can do that in Peter's absence, of course."

"I'll talk to Mrs. St. John."

Jean thought she was done, but Rita added, "The deposit has to go in by two or the funds won't clear."

"I see. We'll be there shortly."

Jean felt like a brushfire had just been fanned into a blaze. Did Rita have to wait until now to call, with only a couple of hours remaining? Still, she winced at saying *Mrs. St. John*, which must have come off as haughty. Peter always insisted people call him by his first name, even children. Well, Jean didn't agree with children calling adults by their first names, but things were off to a bad start with Rita. And what about Cherylee? Jean wasn't sure she could deliver her, and even if she did, neither of them knew anything about the business.

Cherylee had been quiet for so long that Jean expected to find her asleep. Maybe she had taken a pill. But there she was, in the easy chair in the corner of the bedroom, her hands on her lap, staring in front of her, wide awake. She had not answered when Jean tapped at the door, and now she looked at Jean with a mild inquisitiveness, her eyebrows raised. Not, who called? Or what happened now? But what was Jean doing here? There was a numbness in it. She had the jaundiced pallor of a severe case of flu. She seemed drained of energy or interest in anything, simply numb.

"It was the warehouse, Cherry. We have to go down there."

"Why?"

"They don't know what to do. And reporters have been bothering the employees."

"But I don't know anything about the business."

"I'll go with you. We'll see if we can help. It's not fair for Rita..."

"Rita?"

"Oh, Cherry, Peter doesn't pay her enough to deal with this mess." Jean didn't know where her sympathy for Rita suddenly came from, perhaps just seepage from seeing Cherylee in this state, or salesmanship to move her along. Jean offered a hand to her sister. "C'mon, I'll help." But Cherylee ignored her.

Jean couldn't recall ever seeing her this vulnerable, this weakened, certainly not since before there was Peter. If you could be awake and still be comatose, that was how she appeared to Jean. She had been unpredictable since soon after Peter disappeared. Her moods swung in loops, like a tether ball being pushed back and forth around a pole, high and low, in long arches and short circles, and Jean didn't know what she would get at different times. Cherry would snap into the phone at reporters. She brazenly spoke back to the police and FBI agents who interviewed them again, so much so that Jean was afraid they would think she was involved in whatever Peter did.

Jean admired how she tried to shield the children from the chaos that surrounded them, but over the past few days, her energy and will seemed to flag. She was confused, exhausted, spent. There seemed nothing she could latch on to in this whirlwind, so she had given up and simply withdrawn, eating almost nothing, sometimes dozing, seldom leaving her bedroom. Jean requested time off from work just to stay here and make sure she didn't do something rash, maybe harm herself, and to take care of the children and fend off the calls.

It was simply unthinkable what had happened to Cherylee. You couldn't make this up, Jean thought. The very idea that her sister had lived with—been married to!—a man for seventeen years, that they were raising children, living in this big house, all of it, and she didn't even know the man's real name! Emma was right. That was one of the most unimaginable parts of it.

Cherry now appeared so fragile. Her marriage and children had given her a self-confidence and sense of purpose that Jean had not thought possible when they were young. Jean had once thought of her sister as... well, shallow...yes, and self-absorbed, too. Movie stars, pop singers, and gossip took up most of her energy when she was in high school. Jean used to make sarcastic remarks about her not being able to find Canada on a map or that she couldn't name a single Supreme Court justice. But maybe Jean was no better for knowing those things if it just meant you could use them to humiliate your sister. And now, she saw not only how much Cherry had been hurt, but how deeply she felt the pain and confusion of her children. And there was so much they all still didn't know. Maybe Peter would call soon—or be found—and then they could move on to whatever was next. It was clear to Jean that she would be spending a lot of time here.

"The thing is," Cherylee said, "I don't even know what was real."

Jean settled on the ottoman.

"I keep thinking back through different parts of our life, different times, and I wonder if I could have known any of this, if there'd ever been a hint of it, and I can't. There was nothing! We've been married all these years. How could I not know anything about him?"

Whatever Jean's own thoughts were, she knew what she had to say. "Cherry, it's too soon to assume anything. All we know is what that girl wrote. The rest of it is just...speculation. Those reporters have to print something. They probably make up most of it. You don't even know where they get their information."

"They were talking about us on TV last night. On TV!"

"Who was?"

"Oh, I don't know. I was just flipping the channels. I couldn't sleep. Three or four heads in little boxes like Hollywood Squares were all talking at the same time. One of them said Peter would go to jail for twenty years or more. They were talking about us—our family!—in front of millions of people! Oh God, Jean, they said twenty years!"

Jean leaned over and wrapped Cherry in her arms. "Those shows don't mean anything. By tomorrow no one will remember what they said. Besides, they probably have Peter mixed up with someone else."

"Where is he? Why doesn't he at least call?"

"I don't know, Cherry."

"What is it they want at the warehouse?"

"Rita said they needed to write payroll checks and there wasn't enough money."

"How could there not be enough money?"

"I don't know. We should go there. I'll take you."

Cherylee dried her eyes and nodded, refusing Jean's hand as she pushed herself out of the chair.

⁜

The warehouse always seemed barren and depressing to Cherylee. The parking lot was unpaved, just a weedy open space of limestone gravel and dust, while other nearby businesses had blacktopped parking lots surrounded by festive arrangements of prairie grass and azaleas and yews. She had encouraged Peter to fix the place up, give it some street appeal, but he always said that it was a waste of money, that his customers never saw the place or came here, that money spent on things like that would come out of their profits, which would effectively be spending money of their own on something of no value, so what was the point? He didn't even have a sign for his own parking space, but that seemed less about the sign's cost than his instinctively democratic manner of running the business. His car was always just another car in the dusty lot. If it was closest to the side door, that was only because he arrived before anyone else, turning on the lights at six or sixty-thirty and brewing the first of dozens of pots of coffee that would brew throughout the day, and he seldom left before seven p.m. He ate lunch along with his employees in the break room or at the picnic tables behind the building. He had lunch brought in at least once a month and threw a frisbee with the employees on the grass. He sometimes went to the chamber of commerce breakfasts or out to lunch with vendors, but this was where he always preferred to be.

Cherylee hadn't been involved in the business since she helped him pack and ship boxes from their garage in a rented duplex over a dozen years ago. And he never seemed to expect that she should work there. In fact, just the opposite. Emma had already come along when he got started, and when Todd came later, Peter was thrilled that the business now gave them the freedom for Cherylee to stay home with the children and run the house. She almost felt left out at first, but he said no, the business was really succeeding because of her, because now he could give it all of his energy.

Maybe she'd been there from the start, maybe she had helped him succeed, but now she felt like a stranger in her own world, as if she were seeing the insides of her own body and had no idea what any of the organs did, or even what they were called. And one of the strangest of all was Rita Maupin. It had always been a wonder to her that Rita had such an important job, that Peter trusted her, even liked her, as much as he did.

Now Cherylee stood before Rita, who sat behind her desk outside Peter's office, surrounded by photos of her teenage children and the tow-truck her husband operated, wearing jeans and a maroon golf shirt with the company's logo on it, and watched her speak to Jean as if she wasn't even there.

"We haven't got funds for the payroll," she said—snidely, Cherylee thought, almost as if she was getting some satisfaction from this, though her own paycheck was among those that wouldn't be paid.

Jean had withheld from Cherylee the unpleasantness of her earlier conversation with Rita, had, indeed, been encouraging, even cheerful as they drove here, sharing the almost laugh she'd had with Emma. But Cherylee drove with the numbness of someone on the way to the doctor and expecting to hear bad news. And if Rita had been sympathetic and helpful and polite, Cherylee might have remained numb, but now she felt something that approached gratitude to Rita for bringing her around again. Rita, in short, had pissed her off.

"Why not?" Cherylee snapped.

Rita cocked her head toward Cherylee, glancing up at her as if to say, *Isn't it obvious why not?* and then looked away again before she responded in a low, dry tone, emphatically the opposite of Cherylee's, "We met the last payroll, but the account has been drawn down and a deposit has to be made."

"And it's due this afternoon?" Jean asked, repeating what she already knew, trying to muffle the tension.

"By two," Rita affirmed. "I usually print the checks the day before. Peter always signed them himself. As I said, I can sign them, and technically, Mrs. St. John can too. The accounts are in her name." Her eyes remained focused on Jean.

Cherylee drew a breath at hearing herself spoken of in the third person, at the insinuation that she didn't even know that the accounts were in her name. Peter had put everything in her name. He always had. She knew that. He said it was for tax purposes, or in case something happened to him, which she always thought had to do with insurance or estate planning, but now she began to wonder what that something was.

"How much is it?" Jean asked.

Rita reached past Jean, bumping her hip as she opened a drawer and took out a calculator. She mumbled as she tapped the keys, "Forty-eight people…two weeks…Lynn took two personal days…Karl was out sick…." She tapped, scribbled on a pad, and tapped some more before announcing, "About $45,000."

"Accounts?" Cherylee asked. Rita looked at her, and she added, "You said accounts. Are there others?"

"Oh…yes, the others."

Cherylee knew she couldn't have been clearer, but she watched Rita hesitate, even appear puzzled before she answered a question about information she dealt with every day.

"There are other accounts?" Cherylee repeated.

"Yes, there are others."

"What others?" Cherylee asked, her voice tightening, rising.

"Peter transferred funds from a money market to meet the payroll and pay vendors. The checking account doesn't earn any interest, so he never kept more than a month's expenses in it. There's a brokerage account, too. He talked with the broker a couple of times a week."

"So you can access these other bank accounts?" Cherylee asked.

"Uh-huh." Rita clicked her mouse and turned the monitor for both sisters to view. She scrolled through the activity summary and then stopped abruptly. "Hunh."

"What? What is it?" Jean asked.

"There…those withdrawals. That was…." The monitor glass chimed as she tapped a fingernail on it.

Cherylee and Jean stared at the figures on the screen, deciphering the confusing ledger entries, until they recognized the dates of Peter's disappearance and the day before it, with two ATM withdrawals of $500 each.

Whatever confidence or strength Cherylee had gained from tussling with Rita now seemed to drain away as her knees and legs became wobbly. Tears welled in her eyes. She gasped and reached for the desk to steady herself, and then turned away and stumbled out the door, where she leaned on the wall and sucked in air that she wouldn't have to share with that dreadful woman.

Jean didn't understand at first, but she followed and took her by the arm, asking if she was all right, telling her to wait, wait for just a moment, just one moment, while she went back inside and told Rita to print and sign the checks, that they'd go to the bank and transfer the money, and as Rita began to explain that vendors still had to be paid and another payroll would be due in two weeks, Jean resorted to her thickest DMV voice—a flat, indifferent, monosyllabic, lifeless grumble—to say, "Write the checks," and then she went back to Cherylee, shutting the door behind her, shutting Rita out of the space she shared with her sister. And now she saw it, too. She understood. There it was! Peter had planned his departure. And that dreadful woman might have even staged that little drama, knowing what they'd find when they came to the ATM withdrawals. How could anyone be so cruel?

Jean put an arm around Cherylee and tried to walk her out of the building, but Cherylee clung to the wall.

"I don't care what he might have done in the past," she whimpered. "None of that means a thing to us. But this…he just walked away from me, from his children!"

They stood in an open area inside one of the loading docks. Across from them, at some distance, a group of people worked at long tables, packing boxes and stuffing them with shredded newspapers and crumpled sheets from rolls of manila paper. The overhead doors were shut, and Jean tried to pry Cherylee away from the wall and toward a nearby access door. As she took hold of Cherylee's arm and began to walk her away, a girl with a long blonde pony tail zoomed by on roller blades pushing a cart. "Comin' through!" she announced, as she whizzed past and disappeared into the stacks of shelves.

Jean had noticed a woman at the work table watching them, and now, without looking down at the box she'd just packed, she zipped a length of tape across it, sent it on its way down the conveyor belt, and approached them.

"Mrs. St. John!"

Cherylee knew few people here besides Rita. Hearing her name startled her. The woman wore a baseball cap and tee-shirt.

"Mrs. St. John," she said, when she was closer, "I don't know if you remember me."

Cherylee squinted. The woman's face was partly veiled in the shadow of her cap. Her skin had the dry pallor of a smoker. Clumps of hair sprouted from under the cap like overgrown vines. "I'm sorry, but I don't ..."

"Luanne. I'm Luanne Higgins now, but you knew me as Dicarlo? I went back to my maiden name. Our boys were in t-ball...oh, that was years ago now. You remember Stevie Dicarlo? He played with Todd?"

Cherylee's lips widened, not quite a smile, just recognition, acknowledgement. "Yes...yes, I do." Still gathering herself, she wiped the dampness from her cheeks with her fingers and asked, "How is Stevie?"

"Fine, he's fine," Luanne responded, almost dismissively. She peeled away some shredded paper that had stuck in the sweat on her arms. "Mrs. St. John, I'm so sorry about all that's happened to you and your family. We all are. I wanted...well, we just wondered if you'd heard from Peter?"

Other workers now gathered.

Cherylee shook her head, which seemed to deflate them. More workers appeared, but no one said anything for an awkward moment. The empty conveyor belt whirred. Roller blades clattered somewhere among the storage shelves. Jean looked at the expectant gathering and wondered how best to get her sister out the door, but just then Cherylee asked Luanne softly, almost as if no one else was there, "You went back to your maiden name?"

Luanne scowled, nodding. "After the divorce...but I have custody," she added triumphantly, and then said, "Stevie's in Todd's class this year."

"Oh, I'm sorry." Cherylee spoke as if she'd been told the boy had cancer. "I should have known that."

Jean leaned over to take her sister's elbow, certain that the group would expect no more from them, but Cherylee lingered, looking around, as if realizing for the first time that Luanne wasn't the only one there.

The girl on roller blades now whirled up to the edge of the cluster, dragging one skate as she slowed herself in a tight pirouette. She appeared more at ease on wheels than the rest were on their feet, and taller too. She didn't wait to hear what was being said but just blurted out, "Are we gonna keep our jobs?"

Jean winced at the girl's bluntness, at the very idea that Cherylee should even consider such a question right now, much less be expected to answer it.

But Cherylee frowned thoughtfully and looked at the girl almost as if she saw something behind her, as if yet another layer of this catastrophe had now been pealed away and what it revealed was that there would be many more layers, many more consequences, and she had thought of none of them until now.

The girl was possibly no older than Emma, but her look of expectancy, and her directness, suggested that she had grown up much faster. She was probably the youngest employee in the group, but she seemed to be speaking for all of them, perhaps even asking the very question that Luanne would have asked if she'd been more brazen. They all waited for Cherylee to respond.

"What's your name?" Cherylee asked.

"Kelli."

"I…I don't know, Kelli. I don't understand all that's happened …" she trailed off, as if mentally spinning through a deck of flashcards for an answer, but they were all blank.

Jean said, "We're just starting to figure …"

But Cherylee interrupted, her voice trembling, absent of pride, careless of what secrets she might reveal—what was left to hide? What could she conceal from these people that they didn't already know? What did any of it matter now? She'd had enough of lies. All that was left to hide now was her fear, which itself was no more hidden than her face was when she played peek-a-boo with her children so long ago.

"I'm not sure," she said. "I can't answer that. I don't know anything about the business." She turned back to Luanne and asked, "How long have you been working here?"

"Almost six years."

Cherylee smiled faintly. "When the boys were still in t-ball," she said, as if finishing the sentence aloud that had already formed in Luanne's head.

Luanne nodded recognition. That had been her very thought. "Just started that spring," she said.

People now clustered at the end of a storage aisle.

Jean noticed Rita watching them from behind the office window.

Cherylee panned across the entire group and glanced around at the building too, as though seeing it for the first time. She felt like the only passenger in a lifeboat who knew for certain that there was no land beyond the horizon, and kidding themselves was pointless.

Her voice cracked as she said, "I don't know what's happened to him."

"Cherry," Jean said, "we should go."

Cherylee nodded. "I'm sorry," she said to Luanne. "I just don't know."

"It'll be all right," Luanne said, patting her arm. "We'll be thinking about you."

Outside, Jean was ready to unleash a tirade about Peter's assistant, but before she could say a word they were approached by a reporter with a microphone. He was older than some of the others they'd seen, with a hairline that ran high up across the top of his head and thin, stringy hair dyed the reddish-brown of a well-oiled baseball glove. He lumbered toward them in an uncomfortable trot. "Mrs. St. John! Pardon me! Mrs. St. John!" Behind him, listing perilously alongside a drainage ditch in front of the building, a tall panel van colorfully announced the presence of KBOM Radio. Script lettering below the logo boldly exclaimed, *"We want to know!"* An antenna arose from the top of the truck like a barren metallic cornstalk, adding to the dangerous tilt of the vehicle.

"Excuse me, Mrs. St. John. Mel Gash, with radio station KBOM." The high-pitched sputter of his voice would have led no one who had just met him to guess that he was a radio announcer.

The women were halfway across the gravel lot to the SUV when he stopped them, blocking their way. Clouds of dust swirled in the warm spring wind. Cherylee's hair blew in front of her face, and Jean clutched her handbag. They couldn't have been more disarmed if he had walked in on them in the bathroom. A young man in jeans and shirttails guided cable from the truck to Gash's microphone. Then another man appeared, this time with a TV camera. A second reporter in a suit rushed up behind Gash, who turned abruptly to him and said, "Me first! But you can keep your camera rolling." Then he turned back to the women, who could not find a path through the apparatus and people now encircling them.

"Mrs. St. John, do you have a few minutes for our listeners?" Gash continued, "They want to know what has happened to Peter St. John." Before she could answer, he perked up at a sound in his earpiece and raised the pitch of his voice as he spoke into the microphone, "We're here live at the warehouse of Peter St. John's successful specialty gift business just outside of Hawkings. I'm with Cherylee St. John and...and you are?" He pointed the mike at Jean and waited.

"Jean Horstman," she said, wishing instantly that she had stopped herself from answering.

He sputtered on, "M-P-G live on the spot from Kaaayy-bomb! with an exclusive for our audience. *We want to know!* Well, folks, today we want to know *what happened to Peter St. John*?! Missing in action since a spunky high school student broke the story that he has been living a lie, living in hiding—indeed living as one of us in this fine community—a fugitive from the sixties—a terrorist, a bomber—maybe even a murderer—*allegedly!*—and now going so far as to run for public office—an office of trust, of responsibility for our children—the school board here in quiet Hawkings—but your own M-P-G is on the scene with an exclusive. You know where on the dial you can go for the most miles per gallon! It's to M-P-G! We want to know!" He turned back to Cherylee, bearing down on her. "Now, Mrs. St. John, are you also a fugitive? Are you part of a network of underground fugitives hiding from your crimes of decades ago? What is your real name?"

Jean was outraged. She had to stop this catastrophe. Her poor sister! So vulnerable now, so fragile! Only moments earlier she'd been hit anew with the devastation that had befallen her family. And now this!—this demanding and dreadful individual, piling one question on another before she could say a word!

Employees gathered on the loading dock to watch the spectacle in the parking lot. The cameraman swirled around behind the women, as dust blew into their faces.

Cherylee tried to speak. "I don't know what ..." She only wanted to get out of the hot wind, away from them, all of them, and seal herself in the quiet of her car.

But the torrent of questions rolled on.

"Are you saying that you were unaware of your husband's involvement with the terrorist underground of the sixties and seventies?"

"She hasn't said anything yet," Jean spoke up.

"Miss Horstman..."—he turned on her like a jackal on a wounded antelope—"...you are...Mrs. St. John's sister?"

"Yes."

"Were you involved with this network of terrorists also?"

"How can you even suggest that?! We don't know...my sister and I don't know anything about this!"

"Mrs. St. John...Cherylee," he continued, "have you heard from your husband? Has he communicated with you since the Hawkings high school newspaper scooped every news organization in the country with this incredible story of a fugitive of thirty years living among us?"

"No!"

"No!" Jean repeated. "And since the questions you ask between your self-promoting speeches are ridiculous, we're leaving now!"

Gash whirled back on her again, pulling the microphone up close to his lips, which flapped as he spoke, as if they too were caught in the wind like the women's skirts. His comb-over came unraveled as he turned, now blowing from one side of his head like a banner. "Are you saying the people have no right to know?!" he demanded. "Don't you think the public should know if terrorists are living among us?"

"No!" Jean exclaimed. "I mean, yes, but you ..."

Cherylee spoke up. "I want to say something."

"Cherry, don't!"

All of the reporters now pushed into Gash's space, holding out microphones and recorders. The cameraman swooped around in front of her, nudging a reporter aside and kneeling on one knee at a lower angle to her. Even Gash suddenly grew quiet.

"I do...I want to say something. You people haven't left my family alone since this whole mess began. I don't know where my husband is, and I don't know anything about whatever you think he's done. When he decided to run for the school board, it was to help the children, not for himself, for the children, and now look at all the good that's done for him. Just please leave us alone!"

She took Jean's arm and forced her way past the cluster of news people, but before they could close the car door, Gash again put himself in the way and said, without a microphone or camera now, "Would you come on the air as my guest to tell us more about the kind of man your husband was, to tell us more about him?"

Jean's instincts raged. "Cherylee, don't! It's a setup!"

But Cherylee said, "I just want all of this to stop!"

The sun glared over his shoulder, and she squinted up at him.

"Maybe if you have a chance tell your story," Gash said, leaning in toward her, "it will bring an end to all of the confusion."

"Oh, Cherylee," Jean moaned, "don't do it."

But she seemed taken, seduced. Maybe this would be the end of it.

"All right," she said.

"I'll call you," Gash responded, and he shut the door as if protecting her from the snarling pack before the reporter behind him could approach.

Chapter 8

"Who was that?" Brenda Rojas asked.

Marcia lay the phone beside her on the bedspread. She hadn't heard her mother in the hallway, but now Brenda pushed the door back, stepping inside, waiting for an answer. She still wore her bathrobe and her hair was tussled, unbrushed. The shadows that ringed her eyes betrayed more than fatigue from her nightshift. No one in the house had slept much, and probably wouldn't have even if a spate of anonymous calls hadn't disrupted their lives. Some of the calls were likely from Emma's friends—nasty and foul, though probably harmless—but others...well, they didn't know. Extremists? Friends of Peter? They didn't know. And of course, there was the endless harrassment by reporters and the surprise visits from the FBI. No, they hadn't slept well in the Rojas house.

She knew.

Marcia could see it in the weary, intense glaze of Brenda's eyes. They were set widely on her face, and the whites stood out from her bronze skin, which now seemed yellowed, drained.

Marcia shrugged, stuffing her hands under her armpits. She couldn't wrap herself up tight enough to hide from the questions, the endless calls, the strangers coming out of nowhere to talk to her.

Brenda pursed her lips and drew a breath through widened nostrils. "Was it about the St. Johns?"

Cunt! That's what someone called her yesterday as she navigated the hallway between classes. Treacherous territory, now full of dangers she never dreamed of, never imagined.

Brenda sat on her bed. "Marcy, those people have had enough. You have to leave them alone."

Yes, that's what she wanted too. But she felt like she'd blown up the world, and she knew that's exactly what she'd done to the St. Johns. She had no idea he would take off for god-knows-where after she interviewed him, probably on the very night that she and Jaycee were working on the layout for the paper. She kept thinking back over the interview, his tone, how he sat there telling her about living with a group of revolutionaries, burning his draft card, using drugs, going to rallies, finally setting off a bomb in a building. Marcia was entranced. She quietly slid her notebook out once he started talking and scribbled as he spoke, afraid to interrupt him, afraid that any distraction would crash the interview, but he kept talking, telling her things she wouldn't have even known to ask about, describing the people he was involved with, what they did, why it mattered to them. She felt as if she'd been plugged into a wall socket, she was so charged, so anxious to go home and start writing, so fearful of losing the narrative, of allowing the ambience to fade before she got the story down. When she finally shared it with Jaycee, it was too good, too rich to allow it to get away—and they knew that the school, that Holbrook and Claymore both, would suppress it, so they did what they had to. It was their story—*her* story—and she wasn't going to read about it a week or a month or maybe a year later when some other reporter finally uncovered all that she'd already discovered. But the fallout didn't belong to her. It belonged to Mr. St. John. She was just the conduit—a by-stander in these events, not a participant. All of this wasn't supposed to happen.

But she couldn't have been more wrong. The FBI questioned her. Then they questioned her again, and probably not for the last time. She was, it turned out, the last person to talk with Peter before he fled. She might have information that could help them find him, or further incriminate him. She could become a witness at the trial, when he was caught. The phone rang endlessly. Cars slowed and people gawked in front of the house. And then there were the calls, awakening them in the middle of the night. Her mother would be so upset that they'd all be up until dawn.

Marcia stayed out of school for several days after the article appeared, and when she returned, she felt like a bundle of raw nerves, with everyone watching and talking about her. Teachers whom she thought liked her suddenly went cold; others that she barely knew now befriended her. Kids from different cliques openly ridiculed her. She was afraid of being alone in the locker room. There was never a moment when her story about Peter was not at the center of her life.

It affected her father's work, too. The news editors at his TV station pressured him for interviews with Marcia, and he got calls and e-mails from reporters and editors at the other networks, and radio stations, and newspapers. But his understated praise for her tenacity and research—offered quietly, and when Brenda wasn't around—was perhaps the only glimmer of satisfaction that Marcia found in the hell that had descended on her, and beneath all of the fear that she now suffered, she knew she would do it again to earn that praise. Within it, too, she heard echoes of his own frustration at the tiresome business in which he found himself—covering the police blotter, local barbecue festivals, and dog stories. He had pointed out to her one time that there's always a dog story on the local news. *Dog saves kid! Dogs suffer in heat wave! Dog befriends lonely senior citizens!* One in every show, he said. Now she couldn't watch the news without trying to guess how a dog would be worked in. If she stuck with journalism, her worst fear was that she would have to cover dog stories.

Maybe if she wrapped herself up tightly enough and waited, her mother would leave soon. Marcia knew the pattern. She just had to wait.

Brenda said, "Just stay out of it now. It's none of our business any more."

Marcia nodded.

Now softening, Brenda added, "I have to go out to the store. How about spaghetti for dinner?"

Marcia shrugged. She hadn't been hungry lately.

"I'll get some spaghetti. It was always your favorite."

"Okay." She thought Brenda would try to unravel her into a hug, but she only kissed her on the forehead and then left. Marcia wouldn't have minded the hug, but she might have cried. She didn't want to cry. She felt sorry for her mother, too. It wasn't fair that this mess came down on her.

Marcia had hoped that Emma wouldn't be the one to answer when she called. It had taken so long to get up the nerve, and then, there was Emma, saying nothing, and in her harsh, deafening silence reminding Marcia that she had done something so terrible, so horrific that it could never be forgiven and never fixed. On her first try, Emma's aunt hung up almost as soon as Marcy asked to speak to Cherylee. It was probably a good thing that *she* didn't recognize Marcia's voice. Then, on the second try, Emma went silent as soon she heard Marcia, and then she hung up on her too.

Marcia wanted to talk to Mrs. St. John. She wanted to apologize. Cherylee and her family were the real victims. Marcia saw that now. She had never considered, never imagined what this would do to them. It simply hadn't occurred to her.

Marcia and Emma had never been close friends, but they were stuck with each other almost from the time they started school. They would never have chosen one another as companions or friends, yet their lives had always been entwined through school and activities. They had gotten along at different times when they were young, going through cycles of friendship and indifference, but by the time they reached high school, they had almost nothing in common. Marcia generally thought of Emma as gossipy and cliquish. Her sudden transformation into a goth seemed forced, unnatural, and the look was so weird, her black clothes, bizarre lipstick colors, and heavy eye makeup, and she hung around with a couple of girls who looked like clones. The few boys at their lunchroom table were skaters who came and went with periodic school suspensions. Marcia knew that Emma was smart, but she was barely doing what she needed to get by in school. It was so odd now to think that they had competed at selling girl scout cookies—and that Emma's mom had been the troop leader.

Marcia heard her mother on the phone downstairs, her voice muffled. It was her father—they were talking about her.

She turned on her computer. When the line was free she would check her e-mail.

The phone call lasted another few minutes, and then Brenda came back upstairs to dress. As she passed Marcia's room, she looked in again. "Spaghetti okay?" Her voice was sprightly now, masking the phone secrets.

Marcia nodded and waited until the garage door rumbled open and Brenda backed out before she got on the internet. There was e-mail waiting from Jaycee, from just a little while ago.

> hey m, u gonna do a followup piece on the stjs? last issue – gotta get everything to the printer tmrw nite.

What was he thinking? He'd been after her to write another piece, even saying it was a way to make up to the St. Johns, a sympathetic piece. They were lucky they were still on the paper. Marcia thought about whether there was a dog story she could write. She'd dismissed the idea of writing anything more about Emma's family from the first time he mentioned it, but he hadn't let up. She replied, no! not another word—said enough already!

Within minutes a message came back:

get off and answer the fone

The phone rang minutes later, and Jaycee asked, "What's goin' on?"

"I never should have done this!"

"Oh, man, Marcy! You so should have. It was all gonna come out anyway. You're not the one who caused it. I mean, think about it. Just forget for a minute that this man was actually wanted by the FBI for terrorism and murder. Just forget about that for a minute and think about him getting married and having kids—and he isn't even who he says he is!?"

"That's all I think about! But that's not what the story was supposed to be!"

"Marcy, you gotta stop doing this to yourself. You get more calls? What's going on?"

She felt herself starting to cry. She hated to do that in front of anyone. She held onto the phone, but she said nothing.

"Still there, Marce?"

Silence.

"I know you're still there, so I'm gonna stay on the phone." He paused. "You know, this whole thing is gonna pass."

"It's not! The police are out there looking for him, and his family's been destroyed. People treat me like I'm a freak!...God!!" Her voice cracked, and she wept silently.

"Marcy, but what you did...it's so totally awesome. I mean, you may have a whole career and never get a scoop this big ever again."

"Great."

"No...but...people...like at school ..."

She heard him trying to find any entry point, something to console her, but there was nothing. There simply wasn't one. Nothing good had come of this, and it couldn't be undone. "They hate me!" she blurted. "They all hate me!"

Now Jaycee was silent, waiting, abiding with her.

When the wave had crashed and ebbed, and she was calmer, she asked, "Do you ever think about what made him do it?"

"What do you mean?"

"I mean back in the day...that someone...that these people thought it would be a good idea to bomb that building?"

"Jesus, Marcy, they were a bunch of anarchists! I know there were protests and all that, but these people were crazies!"

"He didn't seem crazy. He was actually pretty nice. Like an aging hippie, you know...like my father."

"I can't believe that."

"No, I mean, he just doesn't seem like someone who'd want to hurt anyone."

"They were making bombs, Marcy!"

"But when I was talking to him...listening to him...it made sense, you know. He said no one was supposed to get hurt. They wanted to destroy the building but not hurt people. He was so convincing, I believed him. He was talking about the war and all, you know, and he said it just wouldn't end. They kept dropping more and more bombs, and thousands of innocent people were getting killed. The government was lying about all of it. He got me wondering...what if they were right?"

"Right?!"

"Yeah, like, what if that was the only way anyone would listen?"

"You couldn't avoid listening. They were shouting in the streets."

"But it didn't stop the war. That's the one thing that kept coming up in all the stuff I read, and in the interview, that no one would listen to what they were saying. No one would listen to them. The war was wrong. Kids were dying. What does it take to get people to listen?"

"Marcy, you're way too far into this stuff."

"Yeah...and now his family. Oh, what a mess! It'll never end."

"It'll pass, Marcy."

She paused and said, "I wonder where he is."

"Me too."

"You know what he told me?"

"What?"

"He said that he never saw his mother again after the bombing."

"Are you serious?!"

"Yeah. He said he called her a few of times and sent some money, but he never saw her again. She died several years later, and he didn't even find out until afterward."

"God, Marcy!"

"I keep thinking, you know, that he wasn't doing anything wrong now, just running his business and all. He was taking care of his family. Maybe I shoulda just left them alone."

"You're so wrong about that, Marce. It was gonna come out." Jaycee paused and asked, "Did you see Emma at school?"

"No…is she back?"

"I heard she was. You worried about seeing her?"

"Yeaahh."

"It'll be all right."

"I don't think so."

"You gonna write something?"

"No, I can't."

"Well, I gotta fill in something."

"Do a dog story."

"A dog story??"

"Oh, nothin'. It's a joke with my dad. I hafta go. I wanna get on the net for a while before my mom comes home."

"See you tomorrow."

"Okay.

Marcy put the radio on, and Edwin McCain's raspy voice crooned the waltzy lyrics of "I'll Be."

‡

She did not see Emma face-to-face the next day, or the day after that. But she caught glimpses of her at the center of her group, moving from one class to another like a rock star surrounded by hangers-on and body guards.

Marcia's fears proved justified. Emma's posse vilified her with malicious gossip, spiteful remarks, and name-calling. Ugly notes were stuffed into her locker. Nasty, threatening e-mails appeared. Hateful flyers circulated. Though Emma remained in the background, even when she returned to school, a small militia of her friends had taken up her cause, and the program of tormenting Marcia took on a new life now that Emma was back.

With just days left before school ended, she and Jaycee worked late one afternoon to clean up the newspaper office. Jaycee had gone out for food when Emma appeared in the doorway, eyeing the room as if it was a filthy gas station bathroom.

"What were you calling my mother for?"

"Oh!" Marcia jumped. She sat cross-legged in front of a pile of old galleys headed for the trash, but as she looked up and saw Emma, she noticed the box with her research about Peter overflowing on a table near the door.

The hardness in Emma's appearance seemed unnatural and forced to Marcia. She wore a tight, sleeveless black top and had a streak of purple running through her hair. Yet her voice was tightly strung, high in her throat; it quavered. Whatever came out next had been gestating violently. Still, fearful as she was, Marcia now recognized how much pain the gloss of Emma's clothing and make-up covered.

"Emma, I'm sorry. I didn't know."

Emma scoffed, "Didn't know!? That's pathetic. You expect me to believe that? Miss Overachiever? You didn't know!? What did you think you were doing?"

Marcia now wondered if Emma's bravado was for her benefit or for the girls who just then appeared, leaning in the doorway. One had a backpack slung on her shoulder and the other was empty-handed, her arms folded and a cigarette behind her ear. She'd get busted if there were any teachers around, so the hallway must be empty. Marcia felt vulnerable seated on the floor, but standing up might seem confrontational. She wondered when Jaycee would return.

"I called to apologize to her, to your mother," Marcia said. "That's why. Nothing else."

Emma scowled. The girls had slid into the room and were peering around, as if it were a lab full of specimen jars. Then one of them noticed the box with Marcia's research. "Hey, Emma. Check this out!"

All three turned and descended on it, rifling through, pulling out files and papers.

"What is all this?" Emma asked.

Now Marcia was up from the floor, but she couldn't stop them. They elbowed her back, and the girl with the cigarette turned and faced her. "What are you gonna do?"

"You can't have that stuff!" Marcy said. "You don't belong in here." She started for the door, but the girl stepped in front of her. By now Emma and the other girl had emptied it all over the table. There it all was, everything, photocopies, notes, even the yearbook.

"You little cunt!" Emma exclaimed. "Look at all this shit! You were prying into my business for months!"

"It wasn't like that, Emma. It didn't start out that way."

The girl with the knapsack turned pages in the old Saint Celixine yearbook. "God, look at their hair! And these clothes! People really wore shit like this?!"

"What is that?" Emma asked.

Marcia said, "It's a yearbook from your father's college."

"He's in there?"

Marcia nodded. "A couple of photos in the paper came from here." She reached for the book, but Emma pulled it away.

"I'll show you where," Marcia said. She took the book and paged through the freshman class for the photo of Peter Howell and then handed it back to Emma.

The girl with the cigarette glowered at Marcia, while the other girl now leafed through a stapled photocopy of *The Word* that Marcia had found on microfiche. She stared at an article for a moment and then said, "What a pile of shit!"

"What is it?" the other girl asked.

"This thing? Listen to this shit." She lifted her voice as though reading from a textbook in front of the class, stumbling over the unfamiliar words. " 'The masses have cap-i...capi-two-lated to the military...military-industrial complex, which has gained a foothold in every fa-...facket of their lives, from the mindless gibberish on their glowing TV tubes to the pro-... pro-pa-gan-dis-tic di-...a-...di-a-trib-es of the Nixon-Agnew political machine.' "

"That was one of Peter's articles," Marcia said. "He wrote that,"

Emma hadn't looked up from the photo of her father, and now she turned the pages of the yearbook and asked, "Where are the others?"

Marcia noticed that she was calmer, even curious now.

"What, photos?" Marcia said.

"Yeah."

"There's another in back of the book." She turned to the one that showed Peter at the tailgate party. "And there's this too. We didn't use it because the quality was too poor." She reached past the girls, leafing through a file and pulling out a photograph on filmy paper that depicted Peter without his shirt, his head bandaged and his eyes nearly swollen shut, displaying bruises all over his chest and arms. The caption read, "Here's a picture of the First Amendment in practice! Peter Howell was released from the city jail only hour earlier, after participating in an act of civil disobedience that caused bodily harm to no one!" The banner at the top of the photo declared the name of the publication to be *Liberation Now!*

"That's my father?"

Marcia nodded. "The photo was staged to show his injuries. That's why his shirt is off. He and Simon Phelan, the leader of the Circle, were arrested at a campus rally and taken to jail and held for several days. They were beaten up several times. The cops were supposed to hit them in the torso and legs, where the bruises wouldn't show, and the damage would all be to internal organs, but they got carried away. It took months for your father to recover. He told me that this incident put him over the top and turned him against the system and the government. He went to the bathroom a lot, didn't he?"

The knapsack girl exclaimed, "What the fuck kinda question is that?!"

Emma looked at the girl and turned back to Marcia. "Yeah, he did."

"It was because of damage to his kidney that they did back then."

Marcia saw that Emma was taking all of this in for the first time. The vast, dark underworld her father inhabited had opened up before her, and Marcia was standing beside the doorway into it. Emma's father had urinary problems that Marcia knew about, had been arrested and beaten up; he had written things that Marcia had read and about which she knew nothing. Until now, Emma had simply spun in the whirlwind of chaos that began weeks ago. Now she was glimpsing what some of it meant, and it was a more complicated beast than she ever imagined.

At that moment, Jaycee appeared in the doorway with a sack from Dairy Queen and looked around. "What's goin' on?"

Emma clutched the yearbook. "I want this."

Marcia nodded. "You can have it. Go ahead and take it."

The girl with the knapsack sneered at Marcia as she passed by, and the three of them filed past without another word.

"What was that all about?" Jaycee asked.

"Nothin'," Marcia said. She began to gather up the papers and files scattered about by Emma and her friends.

Chapter 9

I have reminded you time and again that the militancy of the New Left is escalating daily. Unless you recognize this and move in a more positive manner to identify subversive elements responsible so that appropriate prosecutive action, whether federally or locally initiated, can be taken, this type of activity can be expected to mount in intensity and to spread to college campuses across the country. This must not be allowed to happen and I am going to hold each Special Agent in Charge personally responsible to insure that the Bureau's responsibilities in this area are completely met and fulfilled.

Very truly yours,
John Edgar Hoover, Director
—memo to FBI Field Offices, July 23, 1968

December 1969

"So how do we get out there, Mag?"

Simon stands before a tall chain link fence that runs across a Thruway overpass and all the way down the embankment to the roadside.

Traffic is sparse. Occasional cars and trucks rush into the cavernous belly of the overpass, leaving a wake of metallic echoes.

"Down this way," Magnus says.

He wades into the brush along the slope. Behind him Corinne clutches Simon's hand. Keubler, Terry, Robin, and Peter follow. A grocery bag full of spray cans rattles in Robin's grasp as they stumble through the shadows.

"Here!" He pulls at a section of the fence, tugging with bare fists at the jagged wire edges and pealing back an opening barely wide enough for a small dog. "I'll hold it while you crawl through."

"We'll never get through that," Keubler mutters.

Magnus lets go.

Corinne winces as the fence snaps back.

"Okay, wait a minute!" He fumbles through his rucksack and brandishes a wire cutter.

"You're a goddamn boy scout!" Simon laughs.

Magnus cuts through a section and yanks it away.

Once on the other side the group finds itself on a narrow ledge above the highway. Stumbling would mean ending up a bloodied sack of broken bones on the roadside. They navigate the ledge, gripping the chain links, until they reach the immense girders that support the overpass, where they huddle in the shadows as a semi-trailer passes on the road above them. The overpass rumbles.

Magnus grins. "Man, this is fucking real!"

Simon tightens his grip on Corinne's arm, and she smiles broadly.

"Tell me again how we do this," he says to Magnus.

"Hey, nobody should go out there who doesn't want to! Anyway, there's not enough room for all of us. Watch!" He edges out on the girder. "Keep your feet on the ridge and hold onto these struts overhead." Now he swings freely, holding on with one hand and supporting himself on one foot as he cavorts thirty feet over the roadway.

Simon blows a breath. "God, Magnus, you're a crazy fucker!" He turns to the rest of the group. "Okay, we're not all doing this."

"Bullshit!" Robin exclaims. "I'm going out there. I want to see my handiwork on those girders in the morning."

"Okay, what about you, Peter?"

"I'm good."

Simon grins. "You don't sound so good, man. It's no big deal. Just hang out here." He turns to Keubler and Terry. "How about you guys? We need lookouts."

Simon's right: Peter is scared shitless, but he rallies himself and now insists, "No, I'm good. I'm going out there."

Simon pauses, nods approval, understanding—he's going out there. "Cool! Okay, man. Terry?"

"I'll keep watch here," Terry says. "Maybe Larry can go upside and whistle if someone comes."

"Man, don't call me that!" Keubler exclaims. "I hate that name!"

Terry smiles at Peter, a smile of patience, of resolve. He'll try to say it right next time.

Peter grins back, sharing the quiet joke, and wishing now that he'd said the same thing as Terry, had thought of it first. Terry didn't even hesitate—this wasn't for him and that was it. He seems braver for staying behind than Peter feels now that he's committed, now that there's no turning back.

Heights never bothered him much. He climbed trees brazenly as a kid and liked going up on the roof with his father when they turned the antenna to get the baseball games on TV. He easily scaled the ropes in gym class all the way to the rafters, but this...these dark, imposing girders, the traffic below, the gray pavement, the height. He's never done anything like this. Still, he said he would. He's going. Whatever happens happens.

Corinne grabs Terry's arm, huddling with him. They're teammates.

"All right," Simon responds. "What about it, Keub? Can you keep watch on the bridge?"

"Yeah."

"Okay, what's next, Mag?"

"I'll go first, all the way across, and do the first word. Then the next person and the next. We spread out and each do a section. Outline the letters with one color and then fill in with another. Big bubble letters!"

"Big bubble letters!" Simon laughs.

Robin opens the grocery bag. "All righty, kids, here's two cans each."

Magnus shakes his cans, rattling the mixing balls, and stuffs them into his waist and then hustles onto the girder with the agility of a monkey, working his way across the northbound lane to the far side, over the southbound lane, almost disappearing in the shadows under the bridge.

Robin undoes a button of her flannel shirt and tucks her cans inside, clanking as she edges out, her lips tightly pursed. In a crease of light, Peter notices how she clenches her jaw muscles, like an ostrich, he thinks, and he wonders how fearless she really is, as she grasps the struts and sidesteps along the girder and out over the roadway. Yet she seems indifferent to the danger—and her own fear—as if it's just something that stands between her and what she needs to do, an obstacle, not a threat. Nothing distracts her at that moment.

"I'm next," Simon declares. He follows her, with two cans jammed in his belt like a cowboy in an old Western.

Peter has the shortest distance to go, just halfway across the near lane, but the height over the road is the same for him as for the others, and as he realizes that he could die here, he gains courage from the thrill of doing something that could kill him. Simon's already out there painting... having fun! It's a roller coaster ride, a daring bicycle jump, the highest tree in the neighborhood! As Peter plants his foot on the girder ledge and grabs a strut, crusty with bird shit and rust, and edges himself out, Simon laughs, bellowing with joyful fear. But now his voice, the rush of cars passing below, the hissing of paint cans—all the noises and activity around Peter seem to fade from his awareness just as the cheering from the bleachers and shouting of his teammates on the bench had on the night he scored fifty points in a game, setting records that still stand at his high school and in the city league. Nothing distracted him that night, nothing bothered him. His energy grew as the game went on; he got quicker and faster. Every move he made was the right move, every decision the right decision, every pass, every shot, the right pass, the right shot. None of the others here knows he set that record, had that game, the greatest game he ever played, but now the sense of purpose, and focus, that swells through him feels the same as it did that night, and he hasn't felt that way for a very long time.

They've all spread out over the highway. A car passes on the bridge overhead, and they brace themselves. The vibration courses through them like turbulence on an airplane.

Below, traffic blows through the tunnel. Magnus said that northbound drivers might notice something going on, but by the time they realize what they saw, they'll have zoomed past. Even if they want to report it, the next rest stop is twenty miles, so the group has plenty of time to do the graffiti and be gone. The real risk is smoky.

Peter now feels as comfortable on the girder as if it was the lowest rung on a ladder. The cold nighttime air and quiet between passing cars are invigorating and pleasant. He had shoved his paint cans into his pant waist like Simon, but as he twists this way and that, paint hisses from a leaky can and soaks his shirt. Every move leads to more hissing and more paint. A soggy red blotch covers his belly.

"Holy shit, man!" Simon calls. "Are you all right!!"

Peter looks down and laughs. "Yeah, I'm okay. It's just paint."

Simon's howl of laughter echoes through the metal and concrete under the bridge. A car approaches, heading north, and slows as it nears the bridge. They watch and listen until it speeds up again once it's through the tunnel.

"What's goin' on?" Magnus hollers, already working his way back.

"Thought we had a casualty," Simon responds. "Peter looks like he's taking fire."

Robin has finished her section and now eases along the girder ahead of Magnus. "C'mon," she says. "That car made us. I'd rather get busted for something better than this."

Peter and Simon haven't finished, so Robin and Magnus wait, clinging to the girder. Magnus holds on by one hand.

Keubler suddenly yells from above, "Something comin'! Hold on!"
"What now?" Robin groans.
Magnus takes hold with both hands.
Simon chuckles, "We gotta finish. What the fuck! Either we're busted or not."
Peter's can is clogged. Paint fizzles and bubbles under his finger. He shakes the can, but it's useless, so he throws it on the roadside below.
"Here!" Simon tosses a can, but Peter's fingers are wet, and it slips away and falls, bouncing off a car roof and then clanking on the pavement. The car slows and stops on the far side of the overpass.
Above them, a pickup truck whisks across the bridge. They hold tight through the rumbling until it's gone.
Keubler leans over the railing and calls, "Coast is clear!"
"Check on the other side and see what that car's doing," Magnus calls back in a loud whisper.
"Okay."
Robin hands a can to Simon, who passes it to Peter. As he grabs it, he notices the same bemused scowl on her face as when she watched him stall the car months ago, but then she wanted him to drive. Now she looks as if she'd just as soon finish the job herself. He sprays wildly as car doors slam and voices reverberate below.
"Let's go!" Simon whispers.
The footsteps below have increased to a trot, and suddenly two men appear on the roadside. The group freezes and watches them inspect the area. They could be construction workers or football players. Both are bulky and thick, wearing jeans and short jackets. Their movements are purposive, aggressive. They look around the roadside and underneath the bridge. One of them kicks the paint can that Peter had tossed away.
Up above, the group remains as silent and still as a cluster of gargoyles.
Just then, Keubler appears at the railing and calls, "Hey, I think they're coming back!"
"Jesus, Keub!" Simon mutters.
The pair on the road now look up and explode into a barrage of oaths, while the four on the girder hustle back to the ledge, where Terry yanks them in, one-by-one. One of the men throws the paint can, which clanks off the metal fence between Peter and Terry. Now the men scramble up the embankment, slipping on the concrete, as the group wiggles along the ledge and runs for the opening in the fence. Simon and Magnus remain

there until everyone gets through.

"We can take these fuckers!" Magnus exclaims.

Simon shakes his head, snickering, "Not tonight, Mag. Let's get outta here. C'mon."

Keubler had sprinted for the van, about fifty yards down the road, and now pulls up alongside. As the group piles in, Magnus shoos him from the driver's seat. "Got it, man," he says.

The men struggle through the opening in the fence and close to within reach of the van as it zooms off, with its passengers laughing and howling insults from the windows.

"We'll find you!" one shouts. "You can't hide that piece of shit!"

Slowing the car, Magnus leans out and gives them the finger, shouting back, "Come and get me, man! I'll be waiting!"

"Let's go," Simon urges.

Jolting everyone inside, Magnus stomps on the gas, slams the Allman Brothers into the eight-track, and lights a joint in one seamless motion, while Simon climbs in back and lights another, leaving Magnus to his own world in the driver's seat, where he tokes and bounces to the music.

His prank.

This was his prank.

An inspiration that came one morning as he sped along the Thruway in the swift current of drones rushing this way and that, bustling to and from the hives of industry and government—Albany just north of here, the capital, with its hordes of state employees and lawyers and politicians; Kingston and Poughkeepsie to the south. Middle managers, accountants, engineers, workers, and more lawyers rushed this way and that. He smoked a joint and thought about the people in the cars, most of them alone, and he thought, too, about the highway, the true religious icon of America—the interstate highway system, created by (and named for) President Dwight D. Eisenhower to move weapons rapidly all over the country. He'd seen too many tanks and trucks stuck in French mud and jammed up at Italian intersections, and he wasn't going to let that happen here. And all the drones now buzzed along on a little artery in this unthinkably massive weapons delivery system. How fitting a place to send a message! Magnus studied the overpasses, calculating how to paint one, examining the girders, the fences, the signs and lights, the exit and entrance ramps. He stopped at exits and scrambled through the brush to study the I-beams. He returned at night and climbed out over the highway alone. A rush! An adventure! Had to be shared! He told the group, and they smoked and imagined the impact of their message—the delayed moment of recognition, the epiphany hitting a driver hours later, though he'd barely noticed the sign as he drove along with radio drivel filling his head...but then, the words would gel, the meaning would take hold, the double entendre would explode, and the idea would awaken him from dronehood. He would become one of them.

They took Magnus's slogan and never considered another.

BRING THE WAR HOME!!

Wired from the outing, from the near-miss at scrabbling with the Neanderthals, and now thoroughly buzzed, spaceship Magnus flies through the winding and narrow canyons of back roads enclosed on each side by towering walls of dark trees, his window open and the speakers blasting Dwayne's tough, lyrical slide riffs into the darkness.

Simon pops into the passenger seat again and thumps him on the shoulder. "It was good, man! It was good!"

Magnus nods. It was good.

‡

Susan eats cherry Jello with bananas floating in it, while Peter watches. The dinner crowd has mostly gone and they're alone at a long table near a window trimmed with cardboard garlands and Christmas lights. Outside, the early darkness of winter has fallen.

"I don't know how you can eat that stuff," Peter says.

She smiles, poking at the quivering mound. "I like it. It reminds me of when I was little." Her silliness amuses him. She's older than him, yet she delights in such childish pleasures. "Have some." She scoops a spoonful of the glistening, ruby gelatin and offers it to him.

"I didn't even like it as a kid," he says, mocking disgust, but he scarfs it down and grins.

"See, it's good for you," she giggles. "It makes you smile."

He reaches across the table for another, this time carving a slice with banana.

"You just don't want to admit you like it," she adds.

He feeds her a spoonful, pulling the spoon slowly through her lips, and then another for himself.

"Hey, are you coming tomorrow?" she asks.

"What's tomorrow?"

"I told you last week..." She hesitates as his face goes blank. "Oh, you forgot already!"

"Wait, wait...I know this!"

Her frown betrays still more delight—he hadn't forgotten, he was ahead of her, of course he'll be there. A wide smile brightens his face. She loves his smile—it infects her with joy. He doesn't smile only because he's happy, but because others are, because she is, because he's made her happy. Yes, he'll be there. No, he hadn't forgotten.

"But...where is it again?" he asks.

"The gallery. It's the opening for Professor Gould's new paintings."

"Ah, more masking tape and spray paint."

He hears the echo of Simon's words in his voice, but she just laughs.

"Something new this time...collages...people floating through the sky. Besides, I didn't ask you to come for the paintings. I thought you'd like to hear us."

"I would. I'd like to hear *you*."

"Will I see you over the break?"

"Maybe...sure. Hey, maybe you could come into the city. I could meet you there and we could do city stuff...Rockefeller Center, Jazz at Jacques... spend a day." She livens at the thought, and he adds, "It's just...I'm staying here practically till Christmas. Only be home for a week."

"Your mother will be disappointed." Which she says more to express her own disappointment than his mother's. She hoped he'd come over to Jersey, even spend a night. Maybe they could drive to New Hope. It's so pretty in wintertime. He's never been to her house or met her parents. But the city would be fun too, though she dislikes driving there, and the train ride is so long.

"I know...it's the paper."

"I've hardly seen you all week...since your article came out."

"Didn't want the mud to splatter on you."

"Was it that bad?"

He shrugs. "My car got egged. Rotsees snarl at me on sight. You must have seen the campus paper."

"I know. I knew there'd be a reaction when I read it."

"Yeah...that's one way to put it. I've had calls in the middle of the night too. But you know...it sort of juiced me up, I mean getting that kind of response. If I pissed them off, I must be doing something right."

"I guess. Do you have to go that far, though?"

"They don't get subtle—they're too thick for it."

"Not them, but other people. You'll never convince them, but shouldn't you try to win over other people too?"

He frowns lightly, hesitating, "You didn't like it…my article."

Now she scrapes the Jello bowl, toying with the spoon, tracing patterns in the globby remnants, avoiding his gaze, as if she'd just been caught in a lie. She feels her face go flush.

"No, it's not that…I did like it. Peter, you have a gift, but I don't even think you know what it is yet. You do have something special…I hear it when you talk about some of these issues now…but your article… you sounded like…I don't know…you're using all these expressions… 'technocrats' and 'subverting the mass consciousness'…. It just didn't sound like you at all. And you sound so angry, too…like you're trying to sound like one of them."

"Them?"

"Oh, those people, those radicals. Some of them aren't even students here."

"It's about the war, not about who's a student and who's not."

"I know. And I'm not saying you shouldn't write about it, but you don't sound like yourself. It's not your voice, your own voice, I mean." But now she sees that her words have stung him. The smile has long melted.

"What should I sound like?"

"Oh, you're hurt."

"No…not hurt. Goons have been screaming obscenities at me all week, and they didn't hurt me."

"But you are…I'm sorry…I just…oh, everything I say makes it worse…"

"What?"

"It just sounded so extreme. It had a high pitch, as if you were yelling. And people listen better to someone who's not yelling, that's all, that's all I meant."

He'd considered driving her up the Thruway to show her the bridge the day after they painted it. He wanted to share the exhilaration he felt when he stepped off the ledge and onto the girder, with the concrete below and only his grip on the rusty metal to keep him from splattering on the highway. He felt liberated that night, and defiant. And later, he felt accomplished. He'd overcome his fears. He'd done this thing. He was emerging, part of a movement, part of something important. And he'd felt the same way when he wrote the article trashing the ROTC. No one at *The Word* offered anything but praise for his writing, and the jeers and threats from rotsees and jocks when he crossed the quad had only reinforced that praise. But he went alone to see the bridge, wanting to see it first for himself, as if suspecting what he eventually saw when he approached it and not wanting to subject himself to two disappointments at once. Indeed, the sign appeared far less dramatic than painting it was. The letters were streaky, sloppy, especially his, because he had rushed, and the luster of the effort didn't shine through in the message on the girders, though they had risked their lives to put it there. He knew then that she wouldn't share what he'd felt that night. And now her criticism is altogether different from the outrage his article provoked, and in some elusive way he knows that he didn't show her the bridge because he feared the same reaction she's had to the article. At once he recognizes a chasm between them in the different ways they see things; that she'll never step over the line to challenge authority; that his—and the others'—willingness to provoke anyone, from the thugs at the bridge to the thugs in Washington, is something she'll never understand. Yet he also recognizes some truth in what she's said; that he appropriated language for the article, tried to fit what he wrote into the style of the paper, if the paper could even be said to have a style; that in the most fundamental of ways, he still hadn't fully liberated himself, perhaps because the looming cost of liberation was still higher than he was ready to pay.

"I'm sorry, Peter. I really don't know much about all that..."

But he knows it's not about *all that*. It's about *him*, not the war, not the movement, but about where he belongs, about hearing his own voice and not someone else's.

"No, you're right."

She sees him smile again, but not like before, not sharing her joy, because that's been drained now...just recovering, steadying himself, but from what, she can't see, something more than a trifling comment about his article. She's suffered harsher criticism from music teachers. That's what makes you better, isn't it?...and stronger, too. She wants to ask him about his classes, his exams, but now she's afraid to ask anything—she's already gone too far. Still, she worries about what he may be involved in that doesn't appear in print, that the rotsees may beat him up (she doesn't like them either, but she's always been too busy to pay much attention to them), that he may get arrested or suspended if he goes too far. And there's also the draft. If he fails any courses, he'll be drafted. Without a doubt, he'll be drafted.

She has to ask.

Make it sound like changing the subject. She's steadying herself too. "So when's your first exam?"

Not even close to subtle, and he sees it, smirks, smiles, sniffs a chuckle, warms again.

"I don't even know. I'm so far behind now that it won't matter. No way Stedman will pass me."

"Oh, Peter," she whispers.

"I can't worry about it."

"Peter, you have to stay in school."

"It doesn't matter if I do. I won't go. I'm not going."

"But it's not just the draft."

"That's all it's been for me, and I can't let it run my life any more."

Her eyes moisten as she gathers the trash on her tray, and he asks, "What time are you playing?"

Which brightens her and now seems to lift her whole body. She pushes loose hair on one side behind her ear.

"At seven."

As she separates her utensils and trash, he imagines her as a child, meticulously following the nuns' instructions to organize her tray before she brought it to the window. He'd learned the same way.

⸸

Simon tromps up the wooden stairway to the back porch and rattles the blinds on the kitchen door as he bursts in. "It's tonight! We're gonna do that place tonight!"

Corinne follows, out of breath, carrying a bag of groceries and trying to manage her purse. The shoulder strap had slipped down to her forearm and the purse dangles at her knees. She pushes through the door as Simon closes it on her, excited about his news, about finding Peter and Robin at the kitchen table, littered with typewritten copy and clippings and photos.

"What place?" Peter asks.

"The ROTC office over at the campus. We're gonna trash it tonight!"

"Who's we?" Robin asks.

"A couple of SDS guys said they can get us inside the courtyard."

She groans, "Chauvinist assholes!"

Simon looks at Peter. "You gotta come, man. It's the rotsee office! They're yours now!"

Peter's lips part and he draws a breath, without responding.

"What is it, Peter?"

"Nothing, I just had something else to do tonight, that's all."

Robin laughs, "Don't want to foul the nest?"

"No, but I don't see the good of it. Why not protest in front of their recruiting tables where everyone can see us?"

"Marketing," Robins sneers, "that's all that is! What good are words and signs without action?" She snatches a couple of pages from the table and holds them up. "These are just the means to action, Peter. It's all about getting people to do something, not just writing for its own sake."

Simon grabs his shoulder and says, "Don't worry about it, man. Do what you can when you're ready. I just thought this was up your alley."

"Yeah…I was supposed to be somewhere else, that's all."

Corinne laughs as she empties the grocery bag, "Peter's gonna get laid, you dopes!"

Simon laughs too, and Robin shakes her head, allowing the clippings to slide from her hand as she mutters, "You can't have it both ways." She lights a cigarette and Peter watches her jaw ripple and her cheeks collapse as she pulls on it. Minutes earlier they'd been working on the paper together, laughing at Simon's bad grammar, sneering at Nixon, and now Peter has ceased to exist, though he's just a foot away from her.

Simon casts a frown at her from behind and says, "It's okay, man. We got enough people anyway."

But Peter has trouble reading Simon, too. His tone has an edge. And trashing the ROTC office did sound like fun—like revenge—but why tonight? He'd hardly seen Susan all week and hadn't spent a night with her in…when was it? Weeks. Many weeks. Simon was right, they didn't need him. He'd done his part. He wrote the article. He went out on the bridge. They would avenge him.

And he might have let them too, might have skipped out if Robin hadn't snorted and chuckled just then, as she gathered the papers on the table, "Well, it won't matter either way, Peter. You'll still get blamed for it."

Later, outside, still glowing from the joint they smoked while they read some of the new copy to Simon, and with his car keys jangling in his fingers, Peter notices two men sitting in a dark blue Buick across the street and a few cars down from his. They don't seem to be doing anything, not talking, not moving. His gaze fixes on them, locked in by his buzz. He squints curiously at the car, and just then, the driver raises a camera and takes his picture. At first, he's puzzled, and then startled, as he realizes what just happened. He fumbles with his keys and hustles into his car, uncertain what to do next. Going back inside would be too obvious. He watches them over his shoulder as he pulls out, and then through his rearview as he shifts into second, and then third, now almost a block away, but the Buick stays put.

‡

The art gallery is a chaotic space, angular and asymmetrical, painfully emphatic about its modernism. The wall paneling clashes in dizzying geometric patterns, and the room is nearly devoid of right angles. Even the stained glass windows depicting scenes in the life of St. Celixine high up on the west wall, where the afternoon sunlight can brighten them, appear strained and distorted by their jagged edges, as if the images had been assembled from broken glass, as if de Kooning had reinvented the college's patron saint.

Susan's group is confined to a corner beside the stone fireplace, a tight space where the ceiling runs at a long, precipitous angle from St. Celixine praying with the Indian children up above, and down to a low wall, just behind her, with barely a foot between her head and the ceiling. She has to crouch to get in or out of her seat, but now she sits and struggles through a Brahms quartet along with her group amid the clatter of dishes and the din of conversation. Work-study students in white shirts and aprons circulate with platters of hors d'oeuvre, and clusters of people talk and laugh, admiring the paintings and decoupages on the walls, sometimes stopping to observe the musicians and then wandering on.

Susan can't see the main door from her seat. The crowd is too thick, but she sometimes glances over her music, wondering if Peter will emerge from the crowd. Brother Stedman drifts past, in his long brown robes and white collar, nodding encouragement to the musicians and approval to Professor Ritchdorf, who returns a stiff smile as she perches on the arm of a nearby chair, quietly stewing about the conditions in which her best musicians now perform. Father LeClerq glances over from a gaggle of trustees, who listen politely as Professor Gould explains the inspiration for his new series of decoupages. The trustees gaze up at a panel depicting a blue sky and white clouds, with bodies floating through the air. Celebrity faces have been pasted on them and varnished over, clipped from magazines and newspapers. Robert Redford as Butch Cassidy, Charlton Heston as Moses, Art Linkletter, Ed Sullivan, Katherine Hepburn, Sidney Poitier, Walter

Cronkite, and a dozen more—all flailing their arms and legs as they fall through the cartoon-like clouds. As Professor Ritchdorf sends a piercing glance to Father LeClerq, Professor Gould tilts his head thoughtfully and smiles at a comment from one of the trustees, who wags her free hand as she talks, holding a plastic cup of rosé wine in the other. He folds his arms and leans forward. He is balding on top, but he retains long flowing waves of graying hair that drift over his ears and collar. He nods vigorously. He agrees with her. Yes, how perceptive. They turn and study the images on the wall again.

Susan now leans into her instrument, delivering a stiff line of pizzicato notes, bowing forcefully, booming through the noise that surrounds her, saturating herself in the music even if no one else hears its nuance, or its power. The violinist across from her glances up, a quick grin, and Susan smiles back. They've launched their protest. Pursing her lips and lifting her chin, Professor Ritchdorf now turns back to her students, releasing Father LeClerq to admire the cartoons on the wall, as she quietly and proudly enjoys the spirited surge from her quartet.

Susan loses touch with her surroundings, hearing only the music, hearing precisely where she'll plunge in with the other players after a rubato. Beneath the din, they hear themselves play the final movement better than they've ever played it. They bow strongly, with stiff forearms and loose wrists, raising the final crescendo above the noise, unaware that the talk has diminished, that the trustees and Father LeClerq, and even Professor Gould, now watch and listen, as do Brother Stedman and a dozen others who surround the fireplace. The musicians pull their bows across their instruments for the final note and discover…silence, a moment, a pause, and then the room bursts into applause. Professor Ritchdorf rises from her seat clapping, holding an arm out to her group, who smile and nod their heads. And when the applause fades and the chatter resumes, Susan looks around, for Peter, hoping to see him smiling at her through the crowd, but he's not there.

‡

The ROTC office is on a narrow corridor downstairs from the gallery in Kieran Union. The crowd has long since dispersed, and the building is dark and quiet, and locked, when Peter and the rest of the group make their way through the courtyard outside the office. Walkway lights from the main quad on the other side of the building cast a dim glow on the narrow path through the garden.

Michael Kennedy, the SDS chapter president, had earlier taped the lock on a doorway that gave them access to the courtyard. As they approach the office window, he says, "I'll get it," and he produces a small crowbar. But before he can step up to jimmy the latch, Simon exclaims, "Fuck that!" and swings his foot in a clumsy karate kick, smashing it. The explosive noise startles them.

"Why'd you do that?" Kennedy says.

Simon shrugs, "What the hell, man!"

Once inside, they tear into the place, sweeping papers, in-boxes, and family photos off the desktops. They pry open filing cabinets and scatter the contents. They push over credenzas and pull down wall decorations, spray painting the walls with, "Che lives!" "Power to the People!" "Fuck the Pigs!" "Out of Nam now!"

Suddenly Robin asks, "Hey, where are all the banners and chin-up bars?"

They all look around and Kennedy mutters, "Oh shit!"

"What?"

"We're in the wrong office."

"Fuck!"

At that moment light floods the hallway and courtyard, and the office door slams open, with a campus security guard carrying a Detex clock in front and two city policemen behind him. The guard stands aside as the cops sweep into the office, and Peter and the others dash for the window, but now a bevy of cops trot through the courtyard flower beds to greet them.

Scrambling into each other, ducking the fists and clubs of the police, the students are pushed and beaten to the floor and then dragged through the hallway and down the stairs in front of the building, where a half dozen police cars have lined up, their lights whirling. Robin takes bare-fisted blows to her ribs and back. "Get your fuckin' hands off my boobs!!" she shrieks, kicking futilely at the cop's groin. He clubs the back of her legs and hobbles her, and then drags her across the quad.

Lights go on everywhere, and students gather to watch the commotion, with more piling out of the dormitories. Spectators fill the windows.

Michael Kennedy lands in the back of a squad car with Peter and Simon, shaking his head, bleeding from above one eye, hair caked to his forehead. "You asshole!" he shouts at Simon. "You brought this down on us! You fuckin' asshole!"

Simon laughs. "You people are so full of shit! You talk about revolution, but as soon as one of the pigs lays a hand on you, you start whining and looking for someone to blame. Man, this is what we're here for! You gotta be ready to lay yourself out. You think this was just some trick-or-treat thing? Just spray a little paint and turn over a few waste cans, and then go home and sleep in your own bed. It's a revolution when people know you're willing to put yourself out there, when they can see what these pigs are really all about, when they ask why we're doing this! Besides, you dumb shit, this crew didn't get put together in the time between us breaking that window and them busting in the door. Look around at all these cop cars. You think that old security guard brought this down? Hell, we were set up, and it wouldn't surprise me if an undercover pig in your little preppie SDS group did it."

Simon jostles in the middle of the seat as he argues with Kennedy, pushing Peter into the corner. His hands are scratched and cut. The cops wrenched his arms behind him and jammed the cuffs on quickly and tightly, and now the pain in his shoulder is so severe that he wonders if it's dislocated.

Hundreds of students have emerged, including a large group led by SDS who chant and swear at the cops. One of the deans is out on the walkway in slacks and a sweat shirt, talking with a police officer, and he is soon joined by another administrator. Peter thinks he may be the one whose office they trashed.

ROTC students shout at the protesters. The crowd is dense, and Peter can't see into the cars behind them.

The dean addresses the students through a bullhorn, but his voice is muffled inside the squad car, with Simon and Kennedy arguing and the radio crackling static and chatter.

The protesters close on the police cars, and now the ROTC students form a line on the grass to stop them, which only agitates the protesters, who greatly outnumber the thin line of military students. Soon the two groups are nose to nose, shouting at each other.

A beer bottle smashes on the fender of the car, and as two cops climb into the front seat, Simon taunts them, "You pigs gonna run squealin' back to the sty now that the people are out?"

The cop on the passenger side sneers through the grating, "You shut the fuck up! You're gonna find out what we do back at the sty."

His partner starts the engine, and Peter now sees that three of the cars are leaving together. He looks back at the line of police cars along the quad, certain that an unmarked blue sedan there is the same one he'd seen earlier in front of the house.

Chapter 10

Fall 1999

Peter dunked a clutch of fries in the eddy of mustard and ketchup on his platter and shoved them lustily into his mouth, stymied at chewing until he could suck a gulp of Coke through his straw. The mound loosened, but before he'd even chewed through it, he tore a bite off his burger. He sat by a window alongside Route 191, outside of Jackson, Wyoming, as a slate gray sky darkened and swirls of light snow turned into a snow storm on a September afternoon. The woodstove at the center of the dining room gave off an agreeable warmth and the inviting scent of burning oak. In a nearby booth, a group of bikers in black leather and bandanas debated whether the snow would stop. Their bikes were covered with blue tarps in the parking lot.

Peter curled the toes in his left shoe and felt the edge of the twenty dollar bill taped there. A few twenties and tens stood between him and that bill—another tank of gas, a bag or two of groceries. He still had valid credit cards with him—or he thought they were valid—but he knew he'd be quickly found if he used one.

He put the burger down and watched the snow churn on the whitened and hilly range across the highway. There were few cars and no bikes on the road. He should nurse the meal. It would end soon enough. The booth was a piece of real estate; this table and seat, the fireplace, the view from the window—those were what he was paying for. How many meals had he eaten in the past and then rushed off without worrying about where he'd go next? If he lingered, how long was it before he turned from a customer into a vagrant?

It would be over soon, he thought. He'd spent months in the car, driving all over Colorado and Utah and Wyoming, staying at campgrounds and roadside rest areas, eating canned food and peanut butter sandwiches. His money was nearly gone, and the instincts and fears that had pushed him to keep running were fading like dying embers. When he passed Grand Teton earlier, he thought maybe he'd just walk into the forest and let the snow fall on him. It couldn't be worse than what he would face if he was caught or surrendered. It was an option he would ponder while he sat here. He often thought such things now. He had decided to eat a hot meal in a warm place while he could still pay for it. Whatever happened next, he'd about run out of chances like this.

He knew that his victims never had such choices. One was killed instantly, never knowing what happened, and the other was maimed and died a few years later. Peter had pushed them out of his thoughts for stretches of time, but even before Marcia appeared with all her questions, those two men had begun to preoccupy him again. He had looked them up on the internet and read about the families. He even considered sending them money anonymously. When he realized that Marcia had raised the lid on his past, he knew he would have to face them. The very day that she came to see him for her second visit, he was looking at an article on the Web about Richard Kleeman's son, who was himself now a Merval executive. The company still held an annual commemoration of the bombing, and Douglas Kleeman declared in the interview that as far as he was concerned, the case was still open and he hoped it would one day be solved. Money would mean nothing to this man, Peter knew. He'd quickly collapsed the Web page as Marcia came into his office.

Going back to Teton was a possibility. He had already decided what he would do. He would follow one of the hiking paths that surround the mountain and just keep walking until the snow was too deep to go farther, and then he would settle there and wait for the end, for darkness, for the pain to stop. But he knew it wouldn't end for his family, and he wanted to see them again. Memories flooded his imagination along with his doubts and fears. In all these months, he had yet to call them.

After he finished eating, he decided to find the town library and see if he could use the internet. Thick wet snow coated the pavement outside the restaurant, and the wiper blades rattled impotently over the ice on the windshield. The wiper fluid valves were encrusted, so he scraped the windows with a plastic tent stake. The storm was getting worse and the temperature dropping. He would go to the public library for a quick look at the internet and then move on before dark. An expensive and touristy place like this had nothing for him. Maybe he could find somewhere out near the mountains to park for the night. He would decide then what was next.

The waitress's directions to the library seemed clear when he stood at the cash register but confusing once he reached town. He missed the turn and lost a half hour trying to find his way back in traffic that moved in fits and starts while the snow continued to fall.

It was already dark by the time a librarian showed him to a computer carrel and turned on the monitor. He thought she might be keeping him at arm's length when she leaned around him to bring the computer screen to life. He must smell even worse than he looked. The librarian's brass name tag said Kristen. Salt and pepper hair fell straight and loose to her shoulders, and reading glasses hung from a chain around her neck. Her features were Indian—high cheek bones, dark eyes, and tawny skin, like a fading leaf. As she helped with the computer, he was distracted by the terracing of colorful necklaces she wore, and by her bracelets and the large topaz stone in her ring. She spoke in a fragile, quavering voice. "You should be all set now. What are you looking for?"

"Nothing special," he said. "Just catching up on the news."

She lingered, perhaps to make sure he didn't look at pornography. He typed the address for *CNN.com* and stared at the screen until she wandered back to her desk.

His chances to use the internet had been rare and short, and frustrating. On most of his attempts at public libraries, he needed a library card, or all the computers were taken, or the system was down. Something always seemed to conspire against him. Still, he'd been able to follow some of his story from the Kansas City and Hawkings newspaper and TV websites. He saw the explosive reaction of the media in the days after he fled, saw the faces of people he hadn't seen or spoken with in decades, saw images of headlines from thirty years ago as reporters dug into the story, following Marcia's lead. But then it died away and fell into brief notices in the back pages. There was nothing new to report. The same stories reappeared the last couple of times he had a chance to look on the internet.

But today he found a link he'd never seen before, to the website of a radio talk-show host in Kansas City named Melvin P. Gash. Peter clicked it open and suddenly midway music exploded from the speakers. Nearby patrons turned abruptly from their books and computer screens, and Kristen at the reference desk frowned, jangling her necklaces as she looked up. As quickly as he could, Peter muted the sound and offered an apologetic shrug. She nodded, peering over her glasses, and turned back to the patron at her desk.

What he found sent a dizzying and sickening rush of heat through his neck and scalp. A carnival of animated pictures, pop-ups, and crawlers danced on the screen, most of them about him. He saw articles about the Circle and the explosion at Merval, about the FBI tracking them and other radical groups, about the riot at St. Celixine after Kent State. And then there was the current stuff: his business, his entry into politics, even some of his letters to the editor. And *his family!* He saw Cherylee and Jean at his warehouse with a pudgy man with a bad comb-over and a microphone. Peter'd never seen this photo. Cherylee looked straight into the camera, so distraught—and so lost!

It got worse.

Gash had interviewed her on his radio show.

Peter was sweating now. He'd kept his coat on in the warm building, ready, as he always was, to get up and walk away at the first hint of trouble. He also wore a dirty and frayed cable knit sweater that Cherylee gave him last Christmas and a yellowed tee-shirt underneath that. The shirt was damp at the small of his back, and his armpits were as wet as if he'd just come in from shoveling snow. His brow and neck were moist. He pulled the coat off and dropped it on the floor beside the chair.

She was so vulnerable. How could he have left her at the mercy of bloodless vultures like this? He wanted to hear the interview, hear her voice. The website offered a link to replay it, but the noise…he couldn't listen here. He settled for reading a transcript of the interview:

> *Melvin P. Gash*: We're here, fellow citizens, as we are everyday, because *we want to know!* And today is special indeed, my friends, because you have heard me chronicle the story of Peter Howell, also known as Peter St. John, who was a citizen of our community for over fifteen years, and all the while he concealed from everyone, from his neighbors and friends and the very constituents he beguiled into putting him up for office, that he was in fact Peter Howell, a terrorist from the age of anarchy in the sixties, a time when the foundations of our society were undermined, and for which we still pay the price in the moral decline of our country. For all these years, Peter Howell lived among us in the open, not hiding in some remote mountain shack or

third-world country, but right here, in our midst, a business man, a member of the chamber of commerce, and most recently, a candidate for office! Well, my friends, today is special indeed because his wife, Cherylee St. John, has agreed—no, offered!—to discuss her life with this terrorist-in-hiding and share what she can about him. Thank you for being here, Mrs. St. John.

Cherylee St. John: You're welcome.

MPG: Now, let's start off with whether indeed I should call you Mrs. St. John, for that, after all, is a fictitious name. What is it like to find out that you're living under a false name?

CStJ: It's nothing of the kind!

MPG: Well, all right then…may I call you Cherylee?

CStJ: Yes, I suppose.

MPG: Cherylee, then. Now, tell us, Cherylee—because only you can answer this—what is it like to live with a terrorist?

(*pause, air silence*)

MPG: Forgive me, Cherylee, as a journalist, I should know better. I meant *alleged* terrorist.

CStJ: But Peter didn't do these things! He loves his children. He runs an honest business. He pays taxes! Don't those things count? They've been printing such awful things, and you keep making these accusations on the radio. You have no proof of what you've said. For all I know my husband was in an accident or murdered or kidnapped. My children and their friends hear what you say! All you've done is bring us more pain. Hasn't my family suffered enough? I thought you were going to give me a chance to clear some of this up, and now…

MPG: And now, I'm afraid we need to go to a break to pay some of our bills. We'll be right back.

Following commercial break.

MPG: Friends, we're back with Cherylee St. John, the wife of *alleged* fugitive and terrorist from the nineteen-sixties, Peter Howell *a-k-a* St. John. Now Cherylee, you're here to set the record straight, and I welcome the chance to hear what you have to say because—say it with me at home, friends—*we want to know*! You claim I have no proof, but I would never make false accusations or betray my listeners' trust. I have here, Cherylee, copies of some of the documents used by that feisty student reporter, Marcia Rojas, to bring the truth about your husband to light. And my own research staff has been looking further into this matter. Here, please, look these over. I'm sure you've seen some of this before. It's irrefutable, Cherylee! Peter Howell has been living in our community under a false name for all these years…

CStJ: It's not true! No one has proved this! You're just showing me thirty-year-old pictures of someone who might have looked like him! It's a big leap to conclude that that's him. Now you want to dump all of this on my husband!

MPG: Well, let's back up for a second, Cherylee. I can see that you're upset. Can you tell us whether you have heard from your husband and where you think he might be right now?

(pause, air silence)

CStJ: I haven't heard from him…it's been months since I've seen him, since he left. He went to Topeka for a political meeting. It seemed like he was going to a lot of meetings in the past few years, one thing after another, and sometimes he stayed at a motel if things ran late. That's where I thought he was. He hasn't called. It's not like him. Something happened to him. I just know it! He may be dead or hurt. I don't know.

MPG: Don't you think his disappearance was just a little coincidental with the enterprising research published in the East Hawkings High School paper by young Marcia Rojas? Good listeners, I believe this young woman will earn a Pulitzer prize for scooping every paper and media service in the country. So Cherylee, where do you really think he is right now?

CStJ: I don't know. Didn't I just say that? I just hope he's safe. If he is listening, I want him to know that his wife and children love him and need him. Please come home, Peter.

MPG: And if you are listening, Peter Howell, I hope you can hear the sorrow you left behind. A good woman doesn't know what her real name is! Come home, indeed, and face the consequences like a man, wherever you are. And friends, in a moment we'll come back and talk about whether pornography belongs in our schools. That's right! We'll be talking about *obscenity* that goes by the name of *poetry* in *your* children's classrooms, and we'll have a teacher here who believes that deviants like Allan Ginsberg and D. H. Lawrence have something to offer your children. I'm sure they do! *We want to know!* Back after this.

A rush of anger swept over him. In the sedate warmth of the library, he felt like he was exploding. He pulled his sweater off, pulled it off as if it was on fire, yanking his tee-shirt up to his chest and exposing his belly and back as patrons warily observed him. He dropped the sweater in a rumpled ball on the floor and straightened his tee-shirt, leaving his hair tussled. He reread the transcript and debated whether to drive straight home or go to the police station here and surrender. No, not that. He had to see them first. He would call Cherylee. At least she would know he was alive. Then perhaps he could make it home and see them again before he surrendered. Yes, if surrendering was the price of seeing them, that's what he would do. This was all wrong, to be here, to leave them alone. Nothing else mattered, just getting home, seeing them again.

He pulled his shirt up off his belly to wipe his brow and now felt a powerful urge to use the bathroom. The greasy food and refilled Cokes were coming back on him. He rushed from the computer, leaving his clothes on the floor, unaware of Kristen's gaze as he passed her desk. In the stall, he sweated and strained impatiently, regretting the money he wasted on that meal, money he would need to get home. He washed at the sink, tossing cold water on his face, running his hands through his hair. His last shower was in a campground stall weeks ago. He was ragged with hair, his cheeks sallow, his eyes dark pits in the puffy gray skin surrounding them. Then he remembered his coat. His keys were in it, and his change from the meal!

He pulled the door open with more force than he realized, slamming it into the wall, and then stepped into the hallway, surprised to find it full of people, all leaving the building. The lights inside had been dimmed, and the librarian, Kristen, stood beside the inner door as they passed.

He wedged through the crowd and asked her, "Is it closed?"

"Yes," she said, "we're closing early, because of the storm."

Panic rose in his voice. "But I left my things inside!"

Before she could respond, a woman took her elbow from behind and asked, "Will you need any help closing up?" Bundled in her coat and scarf and gloves, the woman appeared more ready to leave than to help close. Kristen just said, "No, I'll be fine." The woman smiled and stepped into the hallway, pausing to straighten a stack of brochures on her way to the door. Kristen followed her with her eyes before looking at Peter again, and now she squeezed her lips and tilted her head for him to pass through the door, but once inside, he found his computer blank and the carrel vacant. As he turned back, she raised a forefinger, anticipating his distress, while the last patrons passed in front of her. Then she led him to her desk and retrieved the coat and sweater from behind it, offering one in each hand, and, he realized, holding them without regard for their decrepit condition.

He took the clothes and turned to leave, but she said, "Wait," and then raised her finger again as another patron emerged from the stacks, pulling on his coat as he headed for the door. "Good night," she said.

Peter now stood alone in the half-lit building with the librarian.

She asked, "Are you all right? You seemed unwell."

He wondered if she intended to give him a handout or direct him to a homeless shelter. "Yes, I'm fine," he said. "Thanks for getting my coat."

"You're…I'm sorry, but I looked at the computer you were using… you're the man on that Web page, aren't you? You're Peter Howell."

He sighed and hung his head. So this was how it would end, with a curious, almost idle question from a librarian in Wyoming, not even a question really, for she knew the answer. It was over. Even if he wanted to run, to bolt through the doors and dash for his car, with the conditions outside, he wouldn't make it out of the parking lot before a squad car pulled up and blocked the exit. But he felt no urge to run, only to sit, to rest, to sleep. When he got through with whatever they would do to him after he was booked, there'd be sleep—in a bed or cot, on sheets, with a clean blanket—and then in a few days he'd see Cherylee and the children. He was done.

He nodded and looked up, expecting her to reach for the phone, but she squinted thoughtfully, folding her arms and stroking her neck with the fingertips of one hand hidden in her hair.

"Where were you going?" she asked.

He shrugged. "Home. To turn myself in. You beat me to it." He staggered to a nearby carrel and sat, now pulling his sweater on, surprised to find himself chilled.

She smiled apologetically. "We turned the heat down."

"I wouldn't have minded earlier."

"You can't go home," she said.

"I know."

But she waved her hand. "No, I mean the storm. It's bad. No one expected a storm like this so early in the season. You won't get very far with the roads like this. Besides, you look awful. You don't seem well."

"I'm okay," he said, and looked up, understanding. "You're not going to turn me in?"

"No."

"But you should. You could get in trouble." He wondered if he didn't feel some disappointment.

She leaned back against her desk. "Perhaps. I doubt it." Then she rubbed her neck again, jangling the necklaces as she rolled her head. "You have a car?"

He nodded.

She drew a long breath through her nostrils, heaving her chest up, lifting the necklaces on her breast, and expelled it. "Wait for me outside," she said softly, "while your car warms up. I'll be just a few minutes, and then you can follow me home. I have a spare room."

He stood now, pulling on his coat. "Oh, no. I can't do that. I have to go."

She straightened herself too, approaching him. "You don't know these roads. The storm is going to get worse. You can stay with me until they're clear." Now she smiled. There was warmth in it, humor. "Besides you look like a shower and some rest would agree with you."

"I can't. It's too risky…for you…but thank you."

She put a hand on his arm. "Peter," she said, using his name with care, almost as if testing it, "people know me here. They trust me. I live outside of town. It's safe there, and quiet. You'll be safe. And nothing will happen to me. Come and stay, get yourself rested. Leave when you're ready."

He fumbled with his coat zipper, shifting the arm that she touched, and she pulled her hand back but stood close by as he latched the zipper and drew it halfway up. "Why?" he asked. "Why would you do that?"

"No reason," she shrugged. "You're in trouble. You need somewhere to go, that's all. I'm about the same age as you, maybe a few years older. I remember how times were then, how confusing. I was part of it too. You can rest and clean up. Wait outside. Warm your car. The blue pick-up in the lot is mine, but don't scrape the windows for me or brush the snow off. Just wait and then follow me. It'll be fine. You can trust me."

He nodded. Admitting who he was had come without effort, without the least desire to lie or run. It was even a relief, but he was exhausted, drained of any willingness to argue with her or do anything else. The fatigue from the turmoil of the past hour, from driving, from sleeping in the car and tent for months, from eating poorly, and from living in filth overwhelmed him and he gave in.

Outside, fluorescent lights cast a pink glow on the parking lot. Several inches of snow had fallen, and it was still coming down, falling almost sideways in a harsh and cutting wind, finding its way inside his collar and stinging his neck as he cleaned the car and watched the remaining lights darken inside the library. He got into the car and waited, warming his hands on the heating vents, looking around the lot and street, still wondering if squad cars might appear. Maybe this was just a ploy to keep him here, and to get him outside while she stayed safely within. If so, she'd been very cool about it indeed, and very smart. But soon, she emerged from the front door, little more than a silhouette in a dark, ankle-length coat and black boots, with a wool hat pulled low on her brow and her head down against the wind. She waddled along the walkway in short steps and struggled to brush snow from her door handle so she could get inside and start the truck. It had without doubt been in the lot since before the storm began. The virgin snow, pink and soft, formed an undisturbed, cottony slope from the roof, down the windshield and hood to the front bumper. In the open back of the truck a pair of empty animal cages were half-filled with snow.

He watched her struggle with the scraper and brush, but she seemed undeterred, even energetic as she chopped and scraped the ice after brushing off the snow. She never looked toward him as she cleaned her truck, and then she sat in the cab for five or more minutes, perhaps to let the defroster finish the job, and to warm up, before her back-up lights brightened and she pulled out. He waited until she crossed the lot and was ready to turn onto the street before he followed, and then he pulled out behind her. He would call home on his cell phone once he reached her house, when he didn't have to navigate the traffic in this mess and stay with her tail lights on the unfamiliar roads.

Chapter 11

He smelled cleaning solvents and dog food. The cot was under a casement window covered by a thin white linen curtain, now bright with daylight. A chorus of barking awakened him, high and low, yipping and woofing.

A door banged. Then he heard her voice in snowdrift clarity, talking to the dogs, greeting them, scolding them.

Last night seemed distant, where he was, how he came to be clean and rested. The confusing drive through a network of dark, narrow roads came back, and the small white ranch house with the lighted out-building behind it (a kennel, she said), and the wood stove inside, and Indian rugs and wall decorations and carvings, and then dirt swirling in the shower drain like chocolate syrup (him uneasy because she said to leave the bathroom door open to let the heat in), and the pantry with shelves of canned goods and cleaning solutions and assorted dog foods where he now lay, and snow rattling on the window in the gusting wind as he drifted into a coma-like sleep, barely moving a limb all night.

He was awake, needing to piss, wondering if anyone else was in the house. No one was here last night. She'd asked for his clothes, and he now found his khaki pants and his sweater, clean and folded, on a shelf by the door. She was still outside when he slipped into the bathroom, shutting the door, washing his hands and face and neck with hot water after he pissed, grateful for hot water, for soap. He returned to the pantry, but the casement window was too high to look out, and the cot wouldn't support his weight. He gathered his things and went down the hall. A breakfast bar separated the living room and kitchen. She was outside at the kennel, at the far end of a narrow shoveled path, watching several dogs romp in the snow, kneeling down to rub the head of a black lab. He was alone inside.

From the front window, beside the stove, he saw snow so deep and smooth that the only thing distinguishing the road from the rest of the landscape was the absence of trees on the lane that curved past the end of the driveway. His car was freshly covered, but even if he dug it out, there was almost no road. The house was surrounded by trees, and now he recalled driving for a mile or more on the unpaved road that brought him here.

He had charged his phone while he drove, but there was no signal. He couldn't use hers. He'd be found here...she'd be found.

The back door rattled open and she stomped her feet on the porch before she stepped into the kitchen.

"Well, hello!" she said.

"Hello."

He returned to the kitchen while she unbundled herself. She pulled her boots off and shook out her jacket. She wore jeans and a plaid flannel shirt. Without the reading glasses and shapeless dress she wore last night, she looked heartier, less the librarian. Colorful earrings dangled from her lobes. "The dogs love it," she said.

"I noticed."

As she slipped on a pair of loafers, she asked, "Are you feeling better?"

"Yes, much better. Thank you. Do you have a shovel?"

She chuckled, "Of course, I do, but there's no rush, Peter. The road might not be cleared until tomorrow. Even your Jeep won't get far. Let me make you some breakfast."

"Tomorrow?"

"I hope by then. It's a private road. There's some distance between the houses. The man who does the road operates on his own clock. The storm caught the whole region by surprise. I hate to tell you this, but there's more snow in the forecast. You might be stuck. Do you like eggs?"

Eggs, yes. And coffee and biscuits and bacon and juice, and a second biscuit, and more coffee. He was famished. While she cooked, he shoveled out his car and her truck, and the front walk. Then he sat with her over breakfast, and she told him that she owned the thirty acres surrounding the house and that two of the dogs outside were hers and four others she boarded. She had a small list of friends and neighbors who left their animals with her when they traveled. She never intended to start a business, she said. She just loved the dogs and over the years built the heated kennel and fenced in a half acre behind her house where they could run. A neighbor looked in on them while she worked part-time at the library. Her chattiness, drifting from one topic to another, seemed more an effort to absolve him from conversation and allow him to eat than a natural sociability.

As he listened, now sharpened by sleep and food, his mind teemed with what was next. Despite what she said, he thought he'd try to make it back to the highway. He had four-wheel drive. If he stayed here, he might be stuck for days. He'd have to use his credit cards to get home. He didn't have enough cash. Should he ask her for money? He almost thought she'd give it to him, but he couldn't ask her for more than she'd already done. She chatted as if she were a entertaining a guest instead of harboring a fugitive, a man wanted by the FBI. Would the neighbor stop by to look in on the dogs? Had she spoken to anyone this morning while he slept? He was restless. He ate quickly.

"Slow down," she said. "Have more coffee."

"If there's more snow coming, I should try to get through."

"You can't, Peter. Down below here, there's open range on each side of the road and the wind is fierce. The snow will drift up to your windows. You won't even know where the road is. You could be stuck somewhere for days. You could freeze. That's why there's so much food in the pantry, for me and the dogs." She tagged the last remark with a smile.

For a moment he felt a flash of anger at her, for bringing him out here and stranding him. He stroked a clump of his beard, wondering what to do next. He'd made up his mind to return, to surrender, and now he couldn't. He couldn't even call. And the echoes of Cherylee's voice in the radio transcript, her desperation, only added to urgency he felt.

Kristen took her dishes from the breakfast bar and returned for his, sensing his frustration, if not his anger. "If you bring your clothes in, Peter, I'll wash them for you."

A dog scratched at the back door, and she opened it, allowing a golden retriever to trot into the kitchen. "C'mere, Rook!" She wiped his legs with a towel and released him. "He's one of mine," she said to Peter. "Used to his privileges."

The dog approached Peter, who put a hand out. The dog sniffed it and allowed him to run his fingers through his coat and then abruptly pulled away and went into the front room and settled on a rug by the stove.

"Now you've got two friends, Peter," Kristen said.

His eyes followed the dog. "Listen," he said, "I appreciate what you've done, but I shouldn't be here."

She hovered at the table, also watching the dog. "Well, you're here now," she said, and then turned back to Peter and sat again. "After all this time, how come you're so anxious to go back now? You said it last night as if you'd just made up your mind."

The dog's front paws were stretched in front of him and his head was up, watching Peter. Then he dropped his head on his legs and settled, his eyes still open.

"I had," Peter said. "Just then."

Her lips pursed, as they did last night when she allowed him back in the library to get his coat, as if he'd inconvenienced her, and she studied him for a moment before saying, "I can't imagine how hard this is for you."

"For me? It's my family, my wife I'm worried about, what those people are doing to her."

The images on the computer screen came back to him—photos of his house, his children, his wife in the radio station with that crazed shock jock.

"But what good can you do by going back?"

His gaze fixed on the network of fine creases around her eyes and along her neck as he tried to understand the question, interpret the words. She might be older than him, though not much. She might remember. But how odd it was, how bizarre, that he was talking to her—a person he didn't know existed less than a day ago—about things he'd kept from his wife for almost twenty years, about things he hadn't spoken of to anyone in almost thirty, until Marcia Rojas walked into his office.

"I don't know," he said. "I have to see them, and then take whatever's coming so they can move on…so it will be over for them."

"It will never be over for them, Peter. And you'll just be in prison."

He frowned at her doubtfully, puzzled.

"What's the use to anyone if you do that?" she asked.

He stiffened. The question felt abrupt, and too intimate. The sense of entrapment and isolation now returned. The dog's head perked up at Peter's sudden movement. "I don't understand what you're saying. You may think you know something about me, but you don't know me, or anything about me."

She nodded. "You're right. I'm sorry. I just wanted to help."

"You shouldn't. I killed those people. I've been living in a nest of lies for decades. I haven't signed my real name on a piece of paper in so long I don't even know what my signature looks like. I've betrayed my family."

She reached across the table, gingerly, pausing, as if reaching for a stricken dog, allowing the animal to see her hand, to decipher that she meant no harm. Then she touched him, resting her hand on his arm, and said, "I only wanted to help. You seemed so distraught last night, so troubled. It seemed impossible that you'd ever want to hurt anyone. You can decide what you want to do. Stay here as long as you want. You're safe here. You can rest and leave when you're ready, or at least when the roads are clear." She patted his arm and pushed back her chair, gathering the dishes and rising.

He nodded and after a moment said, "You said you were part of it, too, the movement?"

"The way a lot of students were, I guess. I went to some rallies."

Her voice lifted, now returning to the chatty tone of earlier, and as she cleaned the kitchen, she told him that she'd been a graduate student in history at the University of Wisconsin at Madison in the late sixties. "You remember the Dow riots there, in 1967?" she asked, and when he said no, she seemed surprised and described the chaos during a protest to keep Dow Chemical recruiters off the campus.

"They made napalm," Peter said.

"Yes, that's right."

"Is that why you're doing this?"

"I don't know, Peter. But it was wrong then, and it's still wrong that they made that horrible stuff. You know, the riots on my campus, some people said the student leaders could have prevented them, that we could have had the protest without it turning violent and so many people getting hurt, but that's the risk you take. Besides, if it hadn't gotten so much attention from exploding like that, who would have noticed outside of Madison? Who else would have wondered where napalm came from, or even what it was? That's how it was everywhere. That's the risk you took, wasn't it?"

"I suppose."

She paused at the sink and turned to him, smiling, "Hey, you want to hear something weird? I just remembered, I had a sort of brush with fame back then. You remember the defense secretary during the Gulf War, Richard Cheney?"

Peter nodded.

She continued, "I think he's running some oil company now or something, but he was a graduate student while I was there. So was his wife...I can't remember her name...but she was in the English Department, and she…this is funny…I haven't thought about this in years…she wrote these trashy porno-romance novels about lesbians or something, something like that. Our library board probably wouldn't even allow that stuff on our shelves. Anyway, that was my brush with fame. Isn't that funny? He got a deferment to stay out of the army and then he ended up running it. Well, anyway, I met them once or twice there…you know, at wine and cheese or whatever…and then years later, there he is on TV."

Peter's outburst of laughter startled her. He laughed harder than the story was funny, and she laughed mildly with him, thinking that with all he'd been through, he probably hadn't even smiled in many months.

During the afternoon, he brought his clothes in to be washed and dug a path to the wood pile and stacked wood outside the back door. The sky turned gray, and as she'd predicted, more snow fell.

She showed him the artwork and photos that decorated her front room. Her brother was a jeweler and artist and made some of the carvings, as well as much of her jewelry. She said she was half Blackfeet Indian and showed him a photo of her parents in full Indian dress at an outdoor festival. Her father sat in a wheelchair. "My mother was white," she said, "but they got married in a traditional Indian ceremony. That photo was from over ten years ago, at the homecoming festival."

"I like their clothes," Peter said.

"Mom did too. She really took to it."

"I've never seen a headdress like that."

"It's a standup headdress. Dad was very traditional. The warrior headdresses you see in old westerns—they were the Sioux-style bonnets. The railroad companies, and even Glacier National Park, when it first opened, required Indians to wear shoulder-hang bonnets instead of standup bonnets if they wanted jobs. Dad was proud of that headdress. He was very defiant about the traditions."

"Do they live there?"

"They did, after Dad retired. He was a civil engineer. They lived all over the world, but they've both passed away. Dad bought this land many years ago, while I was still in college. My brother has a parcel not far from here, and the rest was subdivided and sold. It was a smart investment. Neither of us has to work now, but I enjoy the library, and the dogs, and he sells his work in a couple of shops in town."

Her candor about finances surprised him, as did the news that her brother lived nearby. She picked up on his concern before he could ask. "He's away right now," she said, "up at the rez." She held up a framed photo of man in his fifties, with a pony tail and a pronounced gut, standing beside an intricate wood carving of an eagle in flight. "That's him. He would have liked meeting you." The resemblance was clear, especially in the dark eyes recessed beneath thick eyebrows, and his hairline, which came to a point on his brow, as hers did. Peter noticed, too, that she gave no hint of whether she'd been married or had children, or even a relationship, and he didn't ask.

While he was outside earlier, he'd heard trucks in the distance, but they never came any closer, and by evening the road was still unplowed, and now the snow was deeper, up to his thighs, but it had stopped falling. He went to the kennel with her and helped clean the cages and feed the dogs, and he learned some of their names. She was on the phone several times during the day but never mentioned that she had a guest.

After dinner, she turned on the TV and they watched an old movie on AMC, *The Day the Earth Stood Still.* But the movie agitated him, though he remained still, even stiff, in an easy chair while she sat on the sofa, her legs curled up, with the dog at her feet. The persistent irony of the space man's secret identity and the great power he controlled, and the drama of revealing himself to the mathematician by solving an immense problem on the blackboard in his study, only inflamed Peter's inner turmoil and underscored the sordid reality of hiding his own identity from the world for so long. He should be doing something other than watching old movies in a stranger's cozy house in Wyoming while the world he'd left behind in Kansas was burning.

Before the movie ended, before the earth stood still, he said, "I'm tired. I think I'll get some sleep."

She muted the TV and said, "Wait." She arose, leaving the dog looking curiously after her as she led Peter down the hall and opened a room that had been shut until now. "You can sleep in here," she said. "I had too much stuff in here to clear away last night, when you arrived. I made up the bed. You'll be more comfortable."

A bird's-eye maple four-poster bed, with a matching dresser and nightstand, looked as neatly prepared as if he was checking into a bed and breakfast. Fresh towels were stacked on a chair in the corner. A row of paperbacks lined the cove under the nightstand.

"I was fine in the other room," Peter said.

"Don't be ridiculous, Peter. It stinks in there. That cot was still out from when I had guests weeks ago. But you'll need to open the door to get the heat," she added.

"I'm leaving tomorrow," he said. "There's no point in messing up the bed here."

Her shoulders slumped. "You are obstinate. Look, it's easier for me if you sleep in here. That way I can go in the pantry if I need to."

He nodded and brought his few things from the pantry into the guest room and shut the door while he undressed. He turned on his phone again, as he had a half dozen times during the day, but it was the same—no signal. He wasn't really tired, just didn't want to sit in front of the television, so he browsed in one of the paperbacks until the movie ended and he heard her pacing the house, letting the dog out and back in, turning things off, washing in the bathroom, and finally settling into bed. She left her door open too. He turned off his own light then and eased the door open a few inches before getting under the covers. A crease of light still glowed in the hallway. Perhaps she was reading. He could hear the rustle of her covers as she shifted, and then the click of her light, and the hall went dark.

Unlike last night, when he fell into the cot, exhausted and drained, enervated by the hot shower, and then slept deeply, now he was awake, churning with worry, at once anxious and fearful about leaving. He'd become less certain he should try to call before he went back. If the phones were tapped, it would give the FBI a warning to look for him and possibly aggravate whatever they were doing to harass his family. He had no idea how Cherylee would react to hearing him on the phone. He wanted to see her and the children again without being whisked off, and without making things worse than they already were. And he even wondered if he could do so without surrendering—just find a way to see them again and maybe hold out longer, maybe even…no, it was out of the question. This was it. He had to go in. But even so, he still had to get there. His credit cards would alert them—they'd quickly see the pattern: he was returning, driving straight east on I-80. They'd pick him up before he ever got close. Kristen had money. He was certain she'd loan him some, probably give it to him. What chance was there he'd ever repay her?

He must have dozed, a light sleep, filled with the sounds of the house, the dog shifting and padding in the hallway, settling in her room; the erratic popping of the fire in the wood stove; her breathing from across the hall, and then the abrupt rustling of her bedcovers and her clothing, maybe putting on a robe; her footsteps on the way to the bathroom, next door. But she stopped in the hallway, and now stood at his door, motionless, and then eased it back. He thought at first she was just pushing it open for the heat. He heard her breathe, and a soft footstep inside his room, and then felt the movement of his quilt. She lifted it and slid in beside him, bringing herself close, laying a hand on his shoulder. As she drew near, he realized she was naked. She sensed he was awake, already awake. "There's no need for us to be alone, is there, Peter?" she whispered. "We're both so alone. You must be lonely too."

He was too surprised to speak, more stunned than aroused, uncertain what to do, surprised into near immobility. But she remained still, allowing her closeness and the touch of her body to envelope him like warm air. He soon understood, from her words, from how she clung to him, that sexual desire had not brought her to him as much as the need to escape, if just for a few moments, the vacuum of loneliness that surrounded her life and that she knew surrounded his—which had, in fact, surrounded him for much longer than the months since Marcia Rojas showed up, and which had become a buzzing white noise of fear that had pervaded his life for as long as he could remember. She allowed her presence, her musty scent, and the confidence of her age, to create a low-burning desire long before she stroked his back and his legs with her fingertips. She nuzzled beneath his chin and then turned away, spooning her back into his belly and guiding his hand toward her breasts, inviting him to find in the creases and folds of her warmth respite from the chaos of fear and isolation in which they both lived, appealing through her hands for him to help her find the same. When he finally came, the moment had more relief than pleasure in it, as if it was merely the resolution, the final scene of a cathartic play whose substance lay in all that came before it, for the outcome was predictable, known. She gasped, a throaty breath, a quick sniff, a loosening of her limbs, and he lay beside her, his shoulder against hers, in the pleasure of a peaceful and drowsy doze, such as he had not felt in many years.

She was gone in the morning, gone from the room, from the house. Again he awoke to her voice outside, now hearing how she spoke to the dogs as if she knew their language, as if she understood their syntax and grammar, understood nuances well beyond the needs for food or attention or the expressions of fear that most people hear in their barking and growling.

The road was still not clear. After checking at the front window, he got into the shower, agitated, fearful now that he'd recklessly added yet one more complication to his troubles, yet one more betrayal to all of the others. He decided that the road would be plowed when he emerged from the shower, and he should be ready to go. He hoped it would be clear so he could leave while she was still out back, so he could be gone without adding another wrinkle to this bizarre situation, so he wouldn't learn one more dog's name or find out more about her heritage or sit through another movie. He had to go.

But the snow drifts on the road were white and rippled from the wind, and undisturbed, just as they were before he went into the bathroom, and now she greeted him from the door, "Good morning," a softer, more familiar greeting than yesterday, her voice offering the delight of finding someone inside the house, just as there were creatures outside, to fill her world. "There's coffee," she added, inviting him to the kitchen, but seeing him dressed and sensing his reluctance, his agitation, she came to him and said, "It's all right, Peter. I know you have to leave soon. It's fine." She rubbed his arm and smiled, and then went into the kitchen and shared her contentment through the sounds of water running and plates clanking and eggs breaking.

‡

The billboard over the parking lot said, "Thermopolis 'Home of the World's Largest Mineral Hot Spring.'" Photos of a gleeful boy on a water slide and a smiling cowboy on a horse dwarfed the Jeep, now parked beside one of the sign's stanchions at a gas station on I-25. From up close, the colossal size of the figures distorted their faces and bodies into grotesque shapes. The boy's open mouth seemed large enough to swallow Peter and the car.

He fingered the change from the gas as he crossed the lot on his way back from the men's room. He'd paid with two of the five twenties that Kristen finally shoved into his pocket after arguing with him. She had filled a cooler with food and then hugged him, reminding him yet again that he could stay longer if he wanted—and he could return if he changed his mind. Her eyes were moist, but he was agitated, eager to leave, to be already on his way, perhaps now agitated even more by his guilt after spending several weeks with her and now leaving her like this, and from delaying his trip home all this while.

He hadn't wanted to stay, had every day felt the urge to leave. A simple toothache had done it—a bothersome soreness that he'd felt for some time but that turned into an aching throb before the snowplow came through, and then erupted into unbearable pain on the very afternoon the plow appeared, after more snow had fallen, on his third day at her house. She'd made him sit at the kitchen table while she peered inside his mouth with a flashlight. She pulled his lips back with the same firmness she'd have used on one of the dogs and put her fingers in back of his mouth, and it felt as if she was ripping one of his teeth out when she broke off a chunk of plaque as large as the topaz stone in her ring and held up the glistening ivory-like piece for him to see. "God! When was the last time you saw a dentist?"

He groaned and muttered, "A long time."

She tapped his chin to look inside again and he reluctantly parted his lips, which she widened, pushing down on his lower teeth.

"Peter, I've looked in enough dogs' mouths to know an abscess when I see it. If you don't get this treated, you'll be so blind with pain that you won't be able to see the road. I'm going to mix up some rinse with baking soda and water."

"Just give me some aspirin. I have to leave."

"You should see yourself right now. You look worse than the day I found you. You couldn't drive into town much less all the way to Kansas. I'll take you to the dentist after we're plowed out."

"Dentist?! You're joking!"

"I'm not joking at all. Whatever is wrong with you is serious."

"No, I've got to..." but a jolt of pain stifled him.

"Oh, Peter, listen. Even if you're going to turn yourself in, you have to get this treated. You can't wait, and I'm sure you don't want some prison dentist taking care of it, whatever it is." She touched his forehead with the back of her hand. "You're warm too. Go inside and get out of your clothes."

He was defeated, drained. The pain was so distracting that all he could do was what she told him. He rinsed with the bitter solution and took aspirin.

She called her dentist that afternoon, who said to bring Peter in as soon as they could get through.

He needed a root canal, but the dentist wouldn't touch it until Peter had his teeth cleaned. The hygienist seemed to relish the challenge. She numbed his mouth into immobility for a session of scraping and poking and buffing that lasted nearly two hours. Then he was told to come back the next day for his treatment. Meanwhile, he could live with the pain or take the pills that Kristen paid for at the drug store, which left him listless and groggy. He couldn't stay awake to drive, but the pain was unbearable without them. He succumbed to Kristen's pleas to stay until he was treated, but he was depressed and withdrawn, and ate almost nothing. It was too painful to chew; he nibbled at bananas and toast.

He needed more than a root canal, too. There were cavities, and one tooth was so badly deteriorated that he needed a crown. He argued with Kristen about leaving after each treatment, but she wore him down, relentlessly insisting that he'd never get another chance like this and painting gruesome images of prison dentistry—which made treatment there seem worse than letting his teeth rot. She also paid for everything and refused to discuss the cost with him.

But beneath her arguments he sensed a larger desire to keep him there as long as she could, which manifested itself in making her home as pleasing as it could be for him. She prepared food such as he'd never tasted—elk sausages, blueberry fritters, corn chowder, Blackfeet fry bread. She allowed him to repay her hospitality by carrying in wood and helping with the dogs, instinctively sensing the quiet satisfactions such chores brought with them. To fill some of his time, he reread *A Stranger in a Strange Land*, which he found in the bedroom and hadn't read since college, and he started *Middlemarch*, which was also in the nightstand cove. Her home and land were quiet, serene; sometimes hours went by without a vehicle passing in front of the house. And a dozen or more times in those weeks, she came into his bed after he put out his light, always following the same pattern, always coming in the dark and leaving while he slept, or while she thought he was sleeping, as if she only wanted to be seen or touched in darkness, as if exposing her aging body to him in daylight would drain his desire, even his willingness. He felt as if he'd been suspended in limbo or taken a drug, but when the dentist asked him about getting some cosmetic work done, he knew it was time to go.

Even the hundred dollars she gave him wouldn't be enough to stave off using a credit card for long, but at least he'd get a few tanks of gas closer to home once he got on the interstate at Casper.

He opened the cooler in the back of the Jeep for the first time since he left. It was packed to the brim with sandwiches, drinks, fruits, and canned food. The unfinished copy of *Middlemarch* lay on top with the bookmark where he'd left it. He picked up the book as he grabbed one of the sandwiches, and it felt thick. An envelope was inside, at the bookmarked page. In it, he found money and a brief note. *I'll be here, if you ever come back. K.* She'd written her phone number beneath her initial. He counted out ten one-hundred dollar bills and then looked around to see if he'd been watched. Then he realized that the phone number would lead the cops back to her if he was picked up. Back in the driver's seat, he ate the sandwich and considered a different route, now that he could pay in cash.

Chapter 12

October 1999

She missed grocery shopping with the children.

Oh, there were sometimes arguments, and fussing, and maybe a broken jar or crushed cookie package, and there was the time Todd needed changing—it was so long ago now—and she opened the changing table in the ladies room to find…well, at least she wouldn't have to do that again.

But she missed it—the outing, the adventure—as if they were all on this…mission—traveling in the car, exploring the store, unpacking the groceries. They were her friends, her partners, on shopping days. The quiet pleasure of it was as satisfying as anything she ever felt as a mother.

Now, Emma would rather walk barefoot on broken glass than go with her, though Todd still went occasionally. Cherylee would give him tasks in the store—go find these items, help put the case of soda under the cart. He seemed energized by helping her, by having a job. Plus he tested all the samples offered by cheerful retirees in colorful aprons at stations around the store—sizzling cocktail sausages, new flavors of ice cream, hot mini-pizzas. Still, she missed having them both with her, Todd in the cart and Emma at her hip. She nurtured her children on such outings. Grocery shopping was so much more than getting food. It wasn't a chore, and Cherylee savored it.

Such thoughts preoccupied her as she pushed her cart listlessly through the same Tasty Pantry grocery store in East Hawkings where she brought her children when they were small. She knew the store so well that in the babel of juice flavors and cereal brands, she could probably find what she needed blindfolded. Several clerks and the butcher knew her by name. The butcher now folded a bundle of ground beef in paper and ran his finger along the tape to seal it and said he hoped she was doing well as he handed it to her. She smiled and nodded and thanked him, and placed the package in the empty child seat, aware that he was still watching her as she turned into the canned vegetables aisle. He knew. People knew. Strangers who stared at her in the aisles—they all knew.

She had begun to see herself as little more than the husk of a human being. If it were not for the children, she thought she would already have dried up and blown away. They kept her going, the instinct to protect them, not only from the policemen and reporters and crazies who seemed to come out of nowhere after Peter disappeared, but worse, from the sadness and emptiness that was eating away at all of them.

In the coffee aisle, she dropped a five-pound can into the basket for the office. She only had one cup herself, but Luanne always kept a big thermal mug next to her computer, and people came and went all day for refills. It was a small enough thing to keep everyone happy, and Cherylee liked the traffic, the busyness. She didn't know what she was doing there. Mostly she just tried to keep what Peter had set in motion from falling apart. All she knew how to be was a mother. If only she could just mother the business too. What did she know about running a company? She hadn't intended to take over, but others had come to her with questions, expecting her to know the answers. "We've always restocked the inventory this way," they'd ask. "Can we go ahead with it?" Or, "It's time to paste up the holiday catalogue. Would you like to see what we did last year?" And so it went, no decisions turned into small decisions, which then became bigger decisions, and soon she was working full time to keep things going.

Oh, she'd gotten rid of that tart assistant of Peter's. How had he put up with her for so long? Anyone could see that you couldn't trust her. Cherylee felt more delight the day she asked Luanne to step into that woman's place than she thought Luanne did, and they worked so well together. It was comforting to have people around that you knew, that you trusted.

There were legal matters pending. The district attorney wanted to freeze the company's assets, had been trying for months. Peter had foreseen this, she now realized, and even the business was in her name. She had signed a lot of papers over the years, never understanding what he was doing, or why she had to use her maiden name, but she understood now. A red flag that large had flapped in front of her nose and she never saw it! How stupid could she be? Along with all the turmoil and pain that consumed her, she was also mortified at her own naivete. He'd always said that putting everything in her name would simplify taxes and estate planning. It never occurred to her that he wasn't filing taxes for himself—and never had. Her lawyer said the D.A. would have trouble proving she was a conspirator, but these tax issues could be sticky. Whatever...all she could do was try to keep going while everything else took its own course.

She no longer doubted that Peter was a fugitive and had once been somehow involved with those terrorists, though she still didn't believe all the things people said of him. The man she knew and loved wasn't capable of murder, of anarchy...of terrorism. Still, she knew that Peter Howell was his real name, and that he was indeed the man wanted by the police. She had known it in her heart the day she stood at Rita's desk and saw the bank withdrawals on the computer screen, though even then she didn't want to admit it to anyone, or even to herself, but that was the moment. She later discovered that he'd taken much more clothing than he needed for an overnight stay in Topeka, that he'd taken camping gear and food, and some papers, too, though she didn't know what they were, only that some file drawers were empty. And she had seen so much more since then, recognized so much, or had it forced on her during endless interviews with the FBI. Friday and Gannon—that's what she and Jean now called the two agents who first sat at her kitchen table six months ago, after the characters on *Dragnet*. And she saw plenty of them—to go over financial records, phone bills, photos, to answer more questions. How did they get all that stuff?

She saw how Peter had fitted things together over the years to protect himself—to protect all of them, really—insisting that she pay cash, putting accounts in her name, building his own business rather than working for a company. How difficult it must have been for him to harbor this secret for so long! What a burden! But she vacillated in her sympathies. At times, she was simply enraged, slamming cabinet doors and stomping around the house. At others, she understood the fix he was in. He couldn't tell her without dragging her into it. And if he had, she would have wanted to know more; she would have demanded it. She might be in jail herself right now if he'd said a word to her. Or she might have given it all away—not intentionally (she didn't think she would intentionally)—but it would have consumed her. Could she have slept in the same house with him if she knew, or allowed the children to do so? He must have thought of that too. But in all those years she never had a clue.

Creating a false trail, or no trail, with money and bank accounts was child's play compared to doing the same thing in a marriage, and as more and more came out, as she accepted that this was the way things were, she realized that she was getting to know a part of his life that had never existed for her. He had filled in the past with falsehoods that she now recognized as variations on the truth—that he'd attended a small Catholic college, that he'd grown up in New York, that he'd been a laborer, even that his parents were dead. None of it a lie. There was never a reason to doubt what he said. He had no immediate family. He said he'd lost track of the few college friends he had; he never went to a reunion and received no mail from the alumni office. He'd been a loner and traveled and worked while he was young until he settled down with Cherylee, and then the children came. Kansas became his home, and he supported them by working hard. It wasn't a complicated story. She always liked thinking it was an American story.

But within that story, she now recognized, his past was a great void. She'd never met anyone—relative or friend—who knew him before she met him. And until that photograph appeared in the high school newspaper, Cherylee had never seen a picture of him as a young man. By the time she met him, his face was sun-worn and bearded, and his hair was already receding. He was thick but not overweight; rather, thick as men become, enlarging almost from within, and he was darkened and lined from long exposure to the sun as a construction worker. He was also tall, and he told her later that his misshapen nose was from playing basketball; he'd tried to stop someone's elbow with it, he said, and she laughed.

The first time she saw him, he held a door for her at a convenience store in Clearwater, Florida. He wore a dirty tee-shirt and jeans and work boots. He had a tape measure on his belt and carried what was probably his breakfast, a Coca-Cola and a sweet roll, both in one hand, as he stood aside for her.

She and Jean were there on vacation, or what passed for a vacation. They were visiting their parents, who had retired to a tiny cottage just outside of Clearwater. Cherylee was twenty-eight and Jean past thirty, and their vacation was gathering in this little house for a couple of weeks in late winter. Cherylee had suggested they all go on a cruise, but June Horstman had laughed in the irritable and familiar scoffing ripple that came out when she suspected she was about to be overcharged or cheated. "This *is* a vacation place!" she declared. "Why would we go anywhere else?" Cherylee would have skipped this trip altogether if wasn't also her mother's birthday. She slept in the spare bedroom between her mother's sewing table and her father's desk, and Jean got the foldout in the Florida room. Last trip, it had been the opposite. There was one bathroom, and Cherylee hated showering after anyone else, when the tile walls and curtain were still dank. But, at least there was the beach and the town, and Cherylee would wander off for hours, sometimes with her sister, sometimes alone, to drink in the Gulf breezes and sunshine and lie on the beach. The house was such a depressing place, even on nice days.

She knew from the outset that Peter was an itinerant laborer. He said he came south in the fall to work construction until late spring, and that he had done so for years, but he hadn't told her how adept he became at working in a subculture of semi-skilled labor that disdained social security numbers and insurance benefits and taxes—and that paid in cash. Over almost ten years of roofing and siding, and building decks and fences, Peter had acquired a truckful of tools and enough skill to work steadily. And he adapted well to this nomadic and anonymous life. He liked working among immigrants, legal or not. Most were Latinos, but some were Indonesian and Filipino and Middle Eastern. He learned smatterings of Malaysian and Tagalog, and gained proficiency in Spanish. He even picked up a few Farsi words. Occasionally people thought he was an INS agent or a relation of the boss, but he either won them over or left them alone. Either way suited him.

He had a network of regular employers and stayed in cheap motels, or he rented mobile homes in nearby trailer parks, always paying in cash. He worked on shopping malls and mansions and even small ranch houses, like the one occupied by Cherylee's parents. He was just another laborer—faceless and nameless to people who made fortunes in software and footwear enterprises, people who had yachts and slips and estates in Sanibel and Palm Beach and San Padre Island, people whose homes and businesses he built. He was just an anonymous white guy on the crew. He avoided hassles with bosses and coworkers, and when they were unavoidable, he packed his tools and left—more than once foregoing a day or more of wages. So the pattern went for most of ten years, through the seventies and eighties, through Jimmy Carter and Ronald Reagan, from soaring inflation to a soaring stock market, as greed became good and Woodstock became a myth and Vietnam became the war we couldn't make up our minds to win.

She wore a sundress that morning, and Jean was miffed about it too. Jean had put on shorts and walking shoes, thinking they were going out to power walk while shop owners hosed off the sidewalks and delivery trucks parked in the center of the streets and the sun was still low enough to cast shadows from the buildings. But when she saw Cherylee dressed as if they were headed to a lawn party, she sniffed, "Are you going like that?" And Cherylee said, "I don't want to get all sweaty." They drove to town in silence, and then Jean hustled off, elbows flying and shoulders pumping, while Cherylee enjoyed the bustle of the streets and screech of the gulls and peered in the windows of dark shops.

It was a whim to dress like that. She'd packed the dress and didn't know when she'd wear it. The afternoons were hot, and they never went out to dinner. She wanted to enjoy the morning breeze over an iced coffee at an outdoor café, but when she couldn't find a place, she unceremoniously stopped at a convenience store for a cold drink when she grew hot and thirsty.

He smiled as he held the door and she passed in front of him, and then he flicked his head at her when she turned back. His smile filled his eyes and radiated from his cheeks. The door eased shut behind him, and she watched through the front window as he climbed into the driver's seat of a pickup truck with two Latinos beside him.

To Jean's thinking, Cherylee invited men to flirt, but in reality she was much less sociable than she'd been as a girl. She had long ago grown bored with happy hours and sports bars, and her school friends had moved away or been drawn into their own families and children and new homes. She shared an apartment with another woman, who, like her, preferred romance novels and movies to drinking in smoky bars. They worked together as sales clerks at Sears. (Cherylee had made the mistake of dating a guy from appliances, who continued to make a nuisance of himself, and she refused to date anyone from work again.) Her life was uninteresting, and although she was slender and attractive, with dark blonde hair feathered below her ears and hazel eyes set close together that betrayed a sense of curiosity, she'd become shy and had lost confidence in her ability to make new friends as she approached thirty. But on this day in a Clearwater convenience store, feeling pretty in her sundress, feeling like she might easily be one of the residents who lived nearby in an expensive home, feeling not at all like one of "the good people," she savored the lingering smile of the burly man with the tattoo, and she relished, too, the satisfaction of having this unspoken encounter while Jean was off somewhere huffing and puffing.

Later that day, she saw his truck a few blocks from her parents' house and spotted him throwing old shingles into a dumpster. He was not what she imagined she would find if she ever found someone. He was the very opposite—a worker in a tee-shirt and boots with a faded tattoo. She never dreamed of herself with a man who had a tattoo, and this one seemed odd, indecipherable—a cat grinned mischievously from within a circle of barbed wire, while beneath it, the fuse burned on a stick of dynamite. He told her that he'd gotten it on a dare when he was young and said it didn't mean anything, that he'd just picked a pattern he thought was funny. He usually wore shirts that covered it. (She now knew what the logo meant.) Perhaps it wasn't so much that he was the opposite of what she imagined as that she hadn't really imagined someone at all. She had envisioned a life—but not a person—a life with children, in a large home filled with closets and cut flowers and toys. She never considered whether her husband would be a lawyer or a plumber, only that her life would be filled by the absence of frugality, which was all she heard about from her parents—what the price of this or that was; how much they saved by going to one store instead of another; what a triumph one of them had by pointing out a flaw and then getting something for half off.

But her attraction to Peter was out of kilter with her dreams.

She wandered past the dumpster. He watched her and asked if he hadn't seen her before. She could see that he remembered her, but she still replied, with a smile seeping from her lips, yes, she thought so, and that evening she was waiting for him under the front porch awning, and she climbed into the truck beside him as Jean and her mother looked on from behind the curtains. She had never before taken such risks with a strange man, or felt such passion. But this was different. It wasn't something that would last; it was just a diversion from the stingy and close life in the linoleum kitchen, where they seemed to spend all of their time, with a couple of electric fans moving the thick humid air.

He was not her first sexual partner, but the last one had been many years ago, so sex with Peter was almost a new experience for her, and in the Gulf heat, and with the salt air blowing up from the water through the flapping curtains of his motel room—and with some wine to loosen her limbs and her senses—she made love to him without inhibition, and also without contraceptives.

Jean was quick to conclude—and never fully let go of the idea—that Cherylee's pregnancy with Emma was all that brought them together, and whatever the truth of it, Cherylee convinced herself that Jean was eating sour grapes, though she avoided saying so, despite Jean's mean-spirited conclusion.

Before she left Florida, and several weeks before she knew she was pregnant, Cherylee gave Peter her address and phone number in Hawkings and implored him to come see her. For his part, Peter had not spent more than a night or two with one woman in all the years since he fled New Paltz, and those occasions had been rare. She made no demands of him and seemed uncomplicated, and he also found plenty of work in the growing suburbs around Kansas City. He did not grasp the real cause of her distress at finding herself pregnant—that her dream of a comfortable life would be swallowed up by what amounted to little more than a belated teenage pregnancy—but he would not leave her with a child, and she was staunchly enough a Midwesterner that she refused to live with him and raise the child out of wedlock. He convinced himself that his documents would hold up through a marriage certificate, which they did, and that he could be absorbed into this new place, where he was known to no one, on the simple strength of their shared story about a chance meeting in Florida.

He was nothing like what she thought of construction workers. He was smart and articulate, though reticent about himself. She gained the impression, not that there were secrets, but rather that there were painful memories for a man with no family, so she didn't press him when he changed the subject or answered in clipped sentences. She noticed that he preferred the editorials in the newspapers to the sports pages; that he read books in the evening rather than watch TV, mostly paperbacks that he picked up at library sales with his pocket change; that he seldom drank; that he was careful with his money, though not cheap; and that he seemed devoted to nothing more than giving her and their child a good life. Emma was barely walking when he came up with an idea for a business, an idea gleaned over many years of seeing fortunes made by all the mansion owners whose places he helped build, an idea that he thought would free him from the risks of working for a corporate employer and yet make enough money to create a life for them.

Cherylee was nervous when he left his job and took their small savings to invest in this new business, but the unconcealed skepticism of her parents and sister helped motivate her enthusiasm as Peter started a catalogue and mail-order company which he ran from the garage of their rented duplex until complaints from the neighbors about the continual traffic of UPS and Fedex trucks led to a series of visits from the landlord. It soon became clear that the business would support the cost of leasing a warehouse and hiring a couple of employees. Cherylee's humiliation from the neighbors' complaints gave way to gleeful satisfaction as she recognized that these problems resulted from Peter's rapid success, and although the business required long hours, and weeks and months without a day off, by the time

Emma started school, they were able to put a substantial down payment on their first house, which Peter insisted on putting in Cherylee's name. He paid cash for their furniture, and her cash allowance for groceries and expenses now grew. Soon after Todd was born, they moved to a second home, the expansive place in East Hawkings.

She didn't know what to make for dinner.

She dropped things into the cart out of habit, not from any plan. Emma was away at college. It was just her and Todd, and maybe Jean. There was little that appealed to her. Maybe macaroni and cheese. Comfort food. Todd liked mac and cheese. That's what she wanted. And applesauce. That was something her mother made well, she had to give her that. You couldn't find applesauce like hers in any of the jars on the grocery shelves.

The store was busy with people on their way home from work. Cherylee recalled how pleasant it was to shop in the morning, when it wasn't crowded and the aisles were bright with sunlight pouring through the front windows. Clerks would stock the shelves as she strolled the aisles with her children. Now she had to weave through the rush hour crowd. Maybe she'd make brownies, too. The kitchen was so cheerful when brownies were in the oven. She would have tea while they baked, and she would put on some music tonight instead of television, which always left her agitated. She needed to revive herself. Comfort food wasn't just about eating. It was about preparation, ambience, aromas. That's what she needed, what they all needed. She missed Peter so much, and she wondered continually where he was, what he was doing at that very moment. She was always waiting for his voice to be in the phone or to find him standing at the door. Always. Passion had once brought them together, and then a child kept them together, but she loved him now—and she thought he loved her too. No, she knew he did. She couldn't be wrong about that. She knew he did. But all of this was so puzzling—that he would simply leave them without calling, without a note. What did it mean? She refused to believe that there was no other explanation than what everyone else wanted her to believe, and she also refused to let her children believe that.

She pushed on with more purpose now, even backtracking to gather items she needed for dinner. As she considered making a second tray of brownies for the office, she turned into the frozen foods aisle and saw the rumpled figure of Melvin P. Gash leaning over the pizza case.

Too late! He looked up and spotted her before she could turn away.

"Mrs. St. John!"

She drew a short quick breath and exclaimed, "Oh!" and started to push her cart around him, but she had to wait for an older woman who chose that very moment to stop in front of the frozen peas.

She looked at Gash and demanded, "Let me pass!"

The woman turned sharply, thinking Cherylee meant her. "What!? Oh!"

Cherylee's cart banged into the freezer door and then bumped the woman's cart as she fumbled past, now followed down the aisle by Gash.

"Mrs. St John!"

He pursued her out of frozen foods, and as they swerved on each side of a Halloween display in the aisle, he said, "Mrs. St. John, please wait. I'm so glad we ran into each other. I tried to call you. I was hoping we could talk…"

"We have nothing to talk about. Just stay away from me and my family!"

"No, no, no," he continued. "Look, we're not on the air. I just happened to stop here. We were on assignment nearby."

"What?! What is it that you want? Isn't there some law or other that says I can go grocery shopping without finding you behind every shelf?"

"I don't think there is, Mrs. St. John. Besides, I just want the same as you, for the truth to come out."

"Truth! You wouldn't know the truth if it smacked you in the head. All you do is twist things around with your ranting about all these horrible things you've been saying about my husband. Haven't you done enough damage already? You've ruined my family. And don't you dare presume to know what I want!" Her chin began to quiver, and her throat went dry. Her voice cracked and trembled as she added, "Whatever you may say about Peter and me, you leave my children out of this! They have no part in it!"

"Part in what, Mrs. St. John?"

He paused and frowned, and she drew back from him, gripping the shopping cart handle, reeling from this assault when she'd only moments ago been quietly trying to remember the ingredients for homemade macaroni and cheese.

He sputtered once more, "Part in what?" He thrust his lower lip out and waited for an answer, looking over the thick rims of his glasses, and then he added, "Perhaps you haven't been forthright with the public, or even with the police. What else *do* you know that you haven't shared yet?" And he paused again, lowering his voice, and asked, "Have you heard from him?"

"Oh!" Her rage and frustration stymied her, and she tried to push her cart around him.

By now they had attracted some attention, and the store manager, a young man with a white button-down shirt and clip-on tie, approached them as they blocked one of the checkout lanes.

"Is everything all right, folks?" he asked, as if venturing into an argument between a husband and wife at the risk of having both turn on him.

Cherylee slumped and said, "I just want to check out."

The manager gestured toward a closed aisle, pulled a register key from his pocket, and said, "Right here, ma'am."

Shaking with anger and humiliation and confusion, she bumped the cart into the counter and began putting items on the conveyor belt. She gazed into the basket, aware of Gash's presence until he finally turned and headed back to frozen foods. Tears came as she pushed one item after another on to the counter. She stared into the basket, wishing it was bottomless. As long as she could continue emptying it, she would avoid facing the clerk and the dumbfounded shoppers who had watched the spectacle.

The manager came around the counter to pack her groceries and then he escorted her to the car. She could not even remember paying. She was numb as he asked whether she was all right to drive. But she nodded that she was okay and offered him a five-dollar tip, which he refused.

He knew too.

At home she found cookie wrappers and crumbs on the kitchen table and heard a gun battle raging on the TV downstairs in the family room.

After a halting exchange over the din of the battle, Todd trudged almost to the top step, hopeful that he'd be released to return to his program.

"Did Aunt Jean call?" Cherylee asked, damping a sponge.

"No," he said.

But that wasn't the real question—though Todd gave her the real answer.

No one had called.

Peter hadn't called.

Cherylee wiped away the cookie crumbs and told him to help her with the groceries, which he did languidly. Homemade mac and cheese now seemed like a lot of work. She was tired. The encounter with Gash had drained her. The house was so empty, and they were so alone.

Chapter 13

So let us not talk falsely now, the hour is getting late.
–Bob Dylan, "All Along the Watchtower"

March 1970

Magnus

See, here's the thing, you take just a little bit of this purple shit, just the eensiest, teensiest, weensiest bit of it, no bigger than a clump of toenail dirt, and you put it on your fingertip and swallow it with a gulp of o-j, and what you get is the truth—the total, one-fucking-hundred-percent truth—the world turned inside out for all to see—in living color—like the fucking peacock—in bright, bright living color—oh, yes, colors!—and traces!—and truth!—and grok this—the dicks at CIA had it all along! Is that fucking real or what? Didn't even know what they had—didn't get it—no imagination!—they hear the fucking truth and what do they think it is?—manic depression, incoherent raving, insanity!—and you know why?—*because they never did it!*—just sat there and watched—lazy fucks!—locked people in little white rooms for hours and watched them draw pictures and put together puzzles and sing songs—who wouldn't go crazy? Here's some truth—right now I'm sitting on the top step of this looonnng old wooden stairway around back of the house that goes all the way down to the driveway from this rickety, lopsided porch—the wind's gusting and dead leaves from these huge motherfucker oaks out back blow every which way—everywhere, leaves blow—I love days like this, cloudy and gusty—the wind reaches up under your shirt and tickles your nipples—people call this *bad weather*—but there's no *good* weather or *bad* weather—there's just weather—it is what it is—today, it's busy, full of turmoil, action, stuff happening—it's like your soul, like all the shit that's going on inside you all the time when you're just walking around doing your thing—all these thoughts and ideas and feelings, all the shit that you don't even have words for, just piling on top of itself, one thing on another—and there it is right in front of you, like you can see what the planet is feeling, what's going on inside of *it*—it's trying to talk to you—that's it!— your soul is the planet!—this is how it talks to you!—in the swirling leaves—and I'm sitting here watching them blow—watching it talk to me—listening!—dried brown leaves, dead leaves—swirling and swirling—gusting everywhere, every fucking which way—and suddenly, I see one, like I'm looking through a rifle scope—just one!—one leaf—a solitary leaf in a swarm of thousands—and I follow it—I watch it—I focus on it—a dead leaf, a dried brown dead leaf—and it's free, like me—death freed it!—free because it's dead—you have no fear when you're dead—there's nothing left to fear—that's the thing, you're alive and you're afraid, but you're dead and you have no fear—that's how you live without fear—when know you're already dead—you imagine it, and see it, and feel it—fear sucks the life out of you—dries you up, like the leaf—it kills you but doesn't kill you—you become the living dead—apathetic—afraid—it's easier to believe what they tell you—go back to your fucking television and watch your living color—gather the kids, honey, it's time for *Bonanza*!—there—isn't that better?—no pain now—no fear—and no life—who's really dead? But…wait—boots clomp on the steps and vibrate through me—who's that, coming up the stairs?—seen the guy around—that big black motherfucker Fu Manchu—they look weird—something weird about them—she clings to him—cling! cling! cling!—on the stairs—both in peacoats—that's it, what's weird!—the same clothes—peacoats and jeans and work boots—*the same clothes!*—they're wearing *the same fucking clothes!*—they have *style!* Holy shit!! I'm gonna lose it!—don't look!—at them—at…now Robin looks at me!—I smile…but—don't look—don't look back—I'll lose it!—I will lose it!—the peacoat twins step on by—I lean forward, look down the stairs, find the leaf—and don't look back—they don't say anything—don't even say anything!—she…clings—I'll bet she's good pussy, though—so many fucking people coming and going today—all these people here—it's cool, though—cool—take a clump of purple toenail dirt—find out who's for real—that's all we want to know—who's real—now Robin sees the leaf too—*Dja see that one?* I ask—she stares into the swarm—she saw it—Peter saw it too. The door opens, the peacoat twins go in—go on in and have a purple toenail—we'll find out soon enough—what's that smell?—from inside?—like burnt toast, like breakfast and funny papers and soggy cereal and cartoons in the bright warm kitchen on Saturday morning. Peter smiles—at the twins—he knows—he saw the leaf too.

Corinne

Baking a pie is so simple, and so pleasant—so easy—easy as pie!—its delights are endless—*how much butter?*—yes, even the delightful recipe card—propped on the coffee canister—that canister—all that's left from Mother's set—with faded pink orchids, folding over and under each other, like snakes—such a lovely color for snakes!—I could love a snake of such a color, so benign and graceful—and the card—the little index card—worn and faded, used and useful—a thing of beauty, of character, with folded edges and splotches and stains, in her loopy, rounded handwriting. How many pies has it spawned? How much joy from the aroma, the taste of sweet, juicy, thick apple pies, all from this one little card? Now, that is something to ponder—*how much butter again?*—two tablespoons—now mix it in—mix mix mix—with the spoon, with my fingers—it feels so good, like squeezing a cock to life—squishy—then...ooooh!—now, flour on the board and roll the dough—roll it out—roll it and dust it with flour and roll it some more, and line the pie plate—and slice the apples and measure the sugar—but not too close—a little extra this, a little extra that. No one's pie ever tastes like mine, or like hers—and no pie ever tastes the same—they're like—like what?—yes, yes! I know! snowflakes!—that's it!—each pie is a snowflake—no two alike, but each one perfect—I have to tell them, Terry and Simon—they're watching, watching me bake a pie—I have to tell them—*Imagine,* I say, *imagine, a snowstorm of apple pies! Just imagine it!* That's it! I've told them—it's like...poetry—it fills their minds, like a newsreel—and now Simon looks out the window—and... sees them!—pies gliding gently down from the sky, landing all around us—apple pies invading from the sky!—and Terry asks, *Should we use a shovel or a fork?!*—Simon turns—his eyes brighten. The right question. The perfect question! Yes! Eyes brighten—we look at each other and wait... wait...wait—and then it comes—like an avalanche—the laughter—it pours out, rolls over us, buries us—omigod! I can't stop, I can't stop!—it rolls over us—we laugh like, like...like a big truck winding through the gears, gaining, pausing, gaining, pausing, and more, and more—Simon's out of his chair now, on the floor—*We have to write this down!* he says. *We should write things down!—But,* I say, *but but but I have to bake!*—lifting my head, smiling, breathing now, picking up the card, staring at it, suddenly noticing the pleasant little Fahrenheit circle, a tidy, tiny circle that Mother drew, and I wonder, *Who came up with that?*—a long time ago someone put a little circle next to a number to show how hot a pie should be baked. Imagine! And now the pie's ready and I put it in the oven—and the rush of heat feels so good, so warm—my old thermal shirt's dusty with flour, and hot, and splotchy with sweet syrup—I wipe a dab with my finger, wipe it off my boob and lick it—and there's Terry, watching, fixed—staring...at my boobs—he's so sweet—*Brother What-A-Waste*, I call him—he's never... he can't go without...the pie's in the oven—he has to know, has to know—you can't go on a diet if you never tasted food—he has to know—*Today's the day!* I declare—out loud—a business decision—Simon squints, curious—then he knows, and he smiles, nods and smiles—shares the mischief—a prank on Terry—he has to know—he's still sideways in the chair, where he landed from laughing—his wiry red hair jiggles when he laughs—and now he looks up—he knows too—I know he knows—I told him he couldn't go to the brothers without getting fucked—I told him—told him he couldn't go—and I love tripping and fucking!—it's like, like vibrating with color, swimming in music, running as fast as you can on a cloud—and Simon, well...not today—we fucked last night—he's thinking about the others now, who all they are, in the front room, and on the porch—and today—well, today's the day!—I wipe another splotch with my finger...and put it on Terry's lips—oh, such a look, like a kid at the carnival gates—so much to behold, to ponder—but it's too much for him, and I laugh, *Holy shit, Simon! He's scared to death!* Simon pats him on the shoulder. *It's okay, man. Today's the day!* And I set the timer and take his hand. *Ooooh, your hand is cold! C'mon, we don't have forever!* And I point to the timer and take him down the hallway, people are everywhere—we step around them on the stairs—and the pie's sweet aroma fills the house.

Simon

You can't live like you own stuff—that's a fraud, a fraud on yourself—you're just lying to yourself—like you own a piece of dirt, or another person—that's where all the trouble starts, from the beginning of time, or the beginning of man, anyway—that and God—where all the trouble starts!—look at Palestine, for chrissake—for Christ's sake, indeed—when the world blows up, that's where the fuse gets lit—it's all about Vietnam now—I'm all about Vietnam—but the fucking crusades never ended—for a piece of dirt, for Allah, for Christ, for oil. You think a piece of paper lets you own someone?—a person?—another person? That's fucked up! I hope

Corinne fucks his brains out, fucks him so hard that he has to pick up the pieces of himself all over the room. She's offering him a gift—what greater gift is there?—a gift of life—to send her life pulsing through him—she wants him to see and feel and touch the very source of life—is there a greater gift? Hmm, this is mellow shit. Keub said there was Dexy laced in, but I don't feel it—might be wired later, when the glow fades. I should go inside—kibbitz, whatever—it's just mellow sitting here—I can smell the pie now—people all over the house—music out front—just far enough so I can still smell the pie—sometimes the noise gets in the way—it fills you up too much—like static on the radio—keeps you from hearing your own voice, seeing your memories, smelling a pie—looks peaceful out on the porch—but if I go out there too...it'll change—everything'll change—whenever you do something, it changes everything else—they'll talk—what would they not say, or think, or see, because I'm there? or what will we all lose if I'm not?—holy shit!—the stuff's more intense than I thought—Peter's out there—I'm glad he's back—*he's* changed, *he's* different, since the ROTC thing—they beat the shit out of him, out of all of us—barely saw him while we were inside—we passed in the hallway once, when they were dragging him from one place to another—*Keep the faith!* I yelled, and then the pig's fist landed in my gut—pricks!—tried to turn me, tried hooking me to a bank bombing and an oil well blowout in sunny Ca-li-for-ny-ay—tried everything—said I was dealing drugs, selling porn—we don't even sell the paper!—we give it away—that's when I knew they had shit—that was the shoes, too, not even the pigs—suddenly two of them showed up between sessions with the pigs—I'll bet the pigs were more pissed about that than they were at us—once the feds show up, the pigs are done, sitting in the back seat like scolded children—the pigs didn't even know how to beat us, and the shoes were pissed about it too—(not like the pigs in Chicago last year—they could beat you without leaving a mark)—then we went in front of the judge with swollen eyes, our faces a patchwork of red and blue—we wore short-sleeve shirts so the bruises on our arms would show—Peter had a sling because his shoulder was dislocated—and Robin limped in with a crutch and sat while everyone else stood—beating up a woman put him over the top—ha!—what a joke!—she'd rather go to jail than think that being a woman had anything to do with getting off. Peter took months to recover—we poured out of the courthouse doors hooting and screaming—but Peter was quiet, somber, withdrawn—chastened is what he was—I thought that was the last of him—he went into hibernation at home in Long Island—we didn't even know he was back until weeks later—suspended from school, like the others—and so bruised you wouldn't recognize him—but then he sent some copy to the paper, good stuff, too—none of that SDS-Weather gibberish he was writing before—now it was real, authentic—he had a voice—writing about the student uprisings in Czechoslovakia, and the massacre in Mexico City—and he savaged "Revolution"—*Lennon's a rich fuck*, he wrote, *making money by playing with our ideals!*—trashing Lennon!—good stuff!—pull down all the idols!—that's how you start a revolution!—and then Régis Debray!—holy shit!—I was dumbfounded—where'd he find that!—but Robin grinned—she sent him *Revolution in the Revolution?* —and Peter wrote that the student movement had it backward, trying to form itself into one big organization—classic Debray!—instead, we should form small, independent revolutionary bands if we want to change the system—*It worked for Fidel!* he said—Fidel!—Peter said that! I went over to his place and we talked for hours—about the stuff he was writing, about what we'd do next—talking helped him thrive, like rainwater and sunlight for a sick and shriveled plant—when Susan was there, she'd send off a vibe—she has a reserve of them—the disappointed surprise, the unwelcome welcome, the strained smile—but Peter wanted me there—he wanted to be part of something—he passed through the fire and now he wants to see where the journey takes him. I should go out front—see who's here—sounds like fun, all the laughing—intense but mellow—a good glow—you can just sit and look at things—like the door handle on the refrigerator—just seems to crawl down the door like a soothing lizard—that's good!—*soothing lizard*—I have to remember that one!—*soothing lizard*—I'll write it down—write it down—find something to write on—there, that card—the recipe card—room at the bottom—but where's a pen?—counter?—drawers?—utensils in the drawers…look…*intense!—will my hand come back out if I reach in there?*—just…close…the…drawer—what did I want to write?—oh, oh, *lizards!—something lizards*—in the front room—that's good—the front room, where the music is—that's where I'll find a pen—the music and a pen, remember that.

Robin

See what?
Ice cream in a trunk downstairs, and people just come and go.
Simon's having too much fun.
Pranks, graffiti, street theater, protests.

What good has it done?

The louder you shout, the more of you there are, the less they listen.

Sixty thousand in Bryant Park last October. Speeches and songs, and a lot of people. But nothing changed. More troops went over. More bombs, more napalm, more free-fire zones.

Then Washington. A quarter-million people. *A quarter-fucking-million people!* But all that organization. Marshals with armbands, like the MOBE was all of a sudden the fucking thought police! Is that a revolution? Yippies shout at the pigs, and the marshals start a counter-chant: *"What do we want?" "Peace!" "When do we want it?" "Now!"* And the pigs!—smiling at the stupid college kids, who smile back and offer them food. Food! Pigs everywhere in helmets and riot gear, just waiting for us to step out of line so they can unleash the tear gas and start swinging their clubs! With that many people, we could have had some real Days of Rage. Chicago was a set-up, an ambush. Daley baited Weather right into his trap. At least Weather tried to turn Washington into something besides a picnic on the mall. That was cool! While the kiddies went back to their busses like sheep and slept on the ride home to their cozy dorm rooms, we marched on the *In*-Justice Department. Busted out windows, splattered paint bombs, tossed bottles and rocks, set garbage cans on fire. What a rush! You could feel the momentum building, people getting pumped up. The pigs threw canister after canister of tear gas. But that didn't stop us. Took two tries, but we raised the National Liberation Front flag at the *In*-justice Department, and then on we went, down Connecticut Avenue, with NLF banners flying, smashing out windows at every bank and business we passed, while the pigs just kept the tear gas coming. Clouds of it wafting through the streets. The pigs herded us this way and that. You'd get to the end of a block and find a line of them waiting. Then you'd hear the clanky thump of canisters hitting the street and the hissing of spray ballooning into waves of noxious burning smoke.

It was big—and real!

It was the start of something.

Chilly out here.
My knee.
Throbs.
In the cold.
Where that fucker hit me.

But it helps me remember…

What do we have here?

Costume revolutionaries!

Just a couple of years away from the house and garden and PTA.

Magnus knows. Look at that grin. I love that grin.

And Peter.

He even got the tattoo.

Barbed-wire and Yippie the kitty laughing as the whole kit-and-kaboodle gets blown to smithereens. Simon came up with that. The artist. His cat too. (Where is the cat? He should trip.) Kitty Yippie immortalized on our shoulders.

I figured Peter was gone when he got out of jail. He just disappeared. I drove down to his house and tried to see him, but his mother wouldn't let me in, so I left some books for him. He's screwed up about that girl, too. Still is. Probably loves her. But this thing has lit him up. I saw it last month, at the draft office rally on Market Street. He burned his draft card along with the others. They passed the flame, and we sang and danced like Druids at the solstice while a pair of soldiers with buzzed heads and unvarnished contempt watched in the doorway, and the pigs looked on, and the shoes took pictures. Might have sputtered out if Simon hadn't pulled a flag out of his coat and set it on fire and started waving it like a toreador while it burned, taunting the buzz-cuts behind the glass doors. When they saw the flag crumbling into charred wisps, they burst through the doors and rushed the crowd, and people milled this way and that and the pigs were wondering what to do. The shoes snapped photos so fast they probably ran out of film. I got in the middle of it, kicking the soldiers, grabbing the flag. Got my ear boxed too, and then I jumped one and straddled his back and clapped his ears and rode him like a pony! The pigs finally plunged in, batons swinging and bullhorns blaring, until the crowd scattered.

Amazing! None of us got busted.

The shoes probably didn't even share their snapshots with the pigs.

Whatever they're saving them for will come down soon.

I don't want to get rounded up before we get something done.

How much longer can we wait?

What's that smell? Something burning…

Peter

Maybe someone burning leaves.
Did I say that or just think it?
What're they grinning at?

—something about that couple.
Don't know.
Smell's gone.
Don't know.
Door bangs.
Duck and cover.
We file in two lines down the stairs and line the walls,
kneeling in the dust,
clamping our fingers behind our necks,
while Sister Anne and Sister Benedict walk the rows,
and push our heads down,
leading the rosary.
The explosion will blow the school away while we kneel here,
then we'll come up from the rubble
—the only survivors.
I'll marry Patty McCormick,
for the sake of humanity.
My father said we should strike first.
Said Kruschev is a lunatic.
Said we have more missles than the Ruskies.
Said Kennedy was just a kid and should listen to his superiors
—the generals.
Said Nixon would never let a commie walk all over him.
Not many Catholics voted for Nixon,
but my father did.
But he's not a true Catholic.
The one true faith!
Converted from Episcopalian when he married Mom.
She voted for Kennedy, and I wore a Kennedy button to school.
"Prosperity for All," it said.
The night I scored fifty points,
I cried because he wasn't there.
He died of a heart attack two years earlier.
Kennedy died two years before that.
Mom sobbed on the edge of the sofa
as the cortege passed on the fuzzy screen
and John-John saluted.
She didn't even cry like that when Dad died.
I didn't know Robin came to the house until days later,

when I found the box she left,
full of books and magazines.
I don't want them here, those people! Mom said,
tearfully, bitterly.
You should stay away from them.
I had already decided to come back, but I didn't leave for weeks.
I couldn't.
I had doctor appointments.
Susan came too.
I awoke one afternoon to the sound of her voice in the kitchen.
When I saw her, though, it felt different,
as if she and Mom had agreed
—had decided for me—
that I was sorry,
that I made a mistake and got mixed up with the wrong people,
that none of this had anything to do with war
or American foreign policy
or corporate greed.
And I was angry.
Do you see what they did to me?! Do you see?
My anger blossomed.
Hearing them nourished it.
Susan thought
—maybe she convinced herself—
that I'd start over again.
I was claustro there.
Aunts and uncles always around.
And the rosary guild.
Mrs. O'Reilly and Mrs. Hannity.
I heard them in the kitchen from my room.
The spics'll take over soon. More and more of 'em all the time.
Don't you worry yourself, Alice. He'll turn out right, like his father.
I worry. It wasn't like him. It was those hooligans, it was.
They didn't disagree with me.
They just didn't believe me!
They didn't hear me!
Good grades, a varsity letter, a scholarship,
but I couldn't think,
couldn't speak for myself.

I was allowed no ideas but the ones they expected me to have.
But I'd seen how the world worked.
I now knew why Jimmy Carmichael,
three years ahead of me at St. Boniface,
died in Vietnam.
Why having a war made more sense than not having one to people with power.
I was breathing clean air for the first time in my life.
The house was musty and close,
like a funeral parlor.
I imagined myself laid out while the rosary guild said a novena.

Robin huddles in her fatigue jacket,
watching the leaves blow.
Thin cheeks and pale skin,
and a hard look.
When she works her jaw muscles,
you can almost hear the dark busy chatter in her head.

She told me about a Filipino village
where she worked in the Peace Corps
—how the village women spent days and weeks making beautiful scarves
that they sold to tourists for a fraction of their value.
And the tourists would try to barter them down!
The Americans were the worst, she said.
The free market keeps these people in poverty! she said.
She made me drive her to the cemetery one day.
We need ID's, she said. *Just drive.*
The cemetery is across the highway from a new shopping mall.
A hundred yards from the wrought iron gates to eternity,
people hurry into the mall for new toasters and shoes.
Cemeteries are such a waste! she said.
This should be a farm or a commune. You should see the farms in Cuba, Peter.
It's such a beautiful country.
They haven't fucked it up,
like here.
And the workers—
they still have weapons.
The revolution goes on.

Just look at this place,
all these monuments and tombs.
You can't beat death.
How arrogant can you be?
Just throw some gas on my body when I'm done with it
and light a match.
The traffic noise receded behind rows of pine trees,
and when we crested a hill with a sweeping view of the Hudson
and a single mausoleum on top,
she exclaimed,
See!
This is what I'm talking about!
Some rich fuck buys the primo land and plunks himself here
for a thousand years,
until a new civilization comes along
and digs him up,
like we dug up the Egyptians.
Why should one person with money control all this?
She tromped ahead.
Over there looks good.
They don't look new.
We wandered among the headstones
and looked for birth dates close to ours.
Children, if we could find them.
Are the others getting IDs? I asked.
I told them to, she said.
I can't do everything for everyone.
Look! Here's one for you. It even has your first name.
St. John.
Peter St. John.
It's got a ring.
You can still be a nice Catholic boy.
I copied the name and dates,
and the family members,
into a ten-cent notebook
and found a few more over the next hour.
We were cold.
We laughed at the names,
at remaking ourselves with new names and new personalities,

and we huddled together while the heater warmed the car.
Soon our hands were inside each other's clothes.
It was too cold to take everything off,
and we fondled each other,
and she grabbed my dick in a tight fist,
squeezing it,
shaking it,
and her lips tightened and her arm vibrated until I was raw and sore,
but I didn't want her stop.
Don't stop!
And a car glided past as I came.
Over her shoulder, passing slowly,
a few feet away,
from the back window,
a tiny woman in a Jackie Kennedy pillbox watched me gasp
as come damped my belly and shudders of pleasure swept through me.
The woman's lips parted as she realized we weren't bereaved,
and her rouged and pancaked face turned,
and her eyes fixed on mine,
as the car passed,
and Robin looked back and burst into hot laughter,
pressing my hand inside her pants as she laughed.
We joined the Y and got library cards
and stood on line at the DMV and Social Security offices
with our new names.
We fucked for real in her bedroom on Brook Street,
with the door wide open,
but it was like when I had breakfast with her.
Her breasts are large and loose
—way big for her thin frame—
and her skin is dark,
and when she fucks, she's aggressive and intense.
I played against people who play like she fucks
—not even competition,
but fighting.
To fuck is to fight.

And the last time at my apartment—
Susan showed up.

Hendrix pounded through the speakers.
Shock.
Tears.
I stumbled down the narrow staircase as she rushed to her car.
She drove away while I stood on the front steps in bare feet.
You still don't know where you are, Peter! Robin said.
Here or there. What's it to you if she shows up?
Why doesn't she join us?
I'm the one who should be in a huff.
We fuck our brains out
and then you rush out the door after another woman.
Ha!
You lose either way.
She gathered her clothes.
Don't you get it, Peter?
This movement
—the real movement—
is about changing everything!
The war has opened the door so that we can see all that's wrong
—all the fundamental things—
like capitalism and ownership,
and monogamy.
You don't know what you want
—but you can't have it both ways.
Now, gimme your car keys.
—My keys?
—Just gimme your keys.
The car will be at my house.
—But how will I get there?
—You're smart. *You'll figure it out.*
She patted the bulge in my left hip pocket,
stuck her hand in,
pulled the keys out,
before I realized what she was doing.
Thought you were gonna get fucked again, didn't you?
She laughed and jangled the keys as she swept out the door.
She stirs.
Her grin shifts from Magnus to me.
She rises from the lawn chair.

I'm cold. Goin' inside.

The guy with the pea-coat leans out the back door:
Something's burning.

Chapter 14

Saturday, January 1, 2000

Maroon gowns swish and hiss in the undercurrent of chatter. Names resonate from loudspeakers. Cheers swell up and cameras flash as graduates cross the stage.

Then she sees him.

Right there! Behind Mom and Todd and Aunt Jean!

There, in the bleachers!

Just turn around! He's right there! *You can't miss him!*

In that filthy red Kansas City Chiefs cap, sweat-stained from years of mowing the lawn.

She watches him.

Don't stare! Nobody's seen him yet.

But she can't stop looking.

He sees her.

He smiles.

She tries running to him but can't budge from her seat. Her legs flutter, but she can't move!

Then…

…the terminator between light and shadow crossed her brow and harsh white, white sunlight pressed on her eyelids.

She shuddered, still trying to run.

Bright, too bright.

The same loop had recycled a dozen times. Now it dissolved in the light.

The glare, seeping through a slit in her curtains, had chased her to the edge of the bed, a glare that only came on bright days in winter, when the sun crossed the southern sky, when it was late. She knew by the light that it was late, maybe past noon.

Emma tried rolling over to escape the light and return to the gymnasium, to her father, but he was gone. Now there was the brightness of the room, and the urge to hurl.

She gave in, pulled the covers back, slogged across the hall to the bathroom, only to find that once again her brother had not flushed, on purpose, she was sure.

Number two!

"Fuck!"

She dropped the lid with a clank and hit the flusher.

She might lose it any moment.

She decided to shower. She locked the door and stood motionless in the shower, steadying herself, allowing the water to warm her. She would heave soon. She always did. If she had to, she'd force herself and get it over with. But it came before she was dry. She found Tylenol in her mother's bathroom. Now that she'd puked, recovery would begin. She'd had practice.

She ignored Aunt Jean calling from down in the kitchen as she pattered back to her room. Not ready for Aunt Jean yet.

No messages on her cell phone. What time did Sharon drop her off? Four? Five? She'd call her later. Maybe do something.

She tried going back to bed, but the curtains wouldn't block out the light. The room glowed, too bright, too hot, too stuffy. The heat was up in the house.

Cabinet doors banged and dishes clanked.

Sleep was hopeless.

Dr. Pepper.

She suddenly craved one. If she had one she'd feel better.

The nacho taste was still in her mouth, in the vomit.

She brushed her teeth and went downstairs. The Aunt Jean gauntlet might be worth it for a Dr. Pepper.

"Oh, Emma! There you are—finally! Happy New Years!"

Emma succumbed to the hug and returned the greeting. She wanted to correct her—Aunt Jean always said New Year*s*—but it was too much effort.

"What can I make for you? How about an egg?!"

Egg was a gaggy word. "Nothing."

"Oh, you have to have *something*. I just made soup for lunch. But you have to catch up first, don't you."

She was subtle like that. There'd better be a Dr. Pepper. The fridge was within reach now.

"You go ahead. Where's Mom?"

Jean folded a napkin beside her bowl before she sat down at the table. The newspaper was propped on a vase. "At the warehouse. Todd went with her."

The aroma of soup in the kitchen enveloped and warmed Emma, though she didn't know what felt good.

Two Dr. Peppers glinted behind the dish with the leftover ham. *Yes!*

"On New Year's day?"

Jean shrugged, looking over her reading glasses. "Oh, I don't know what she's doing there. She has this idea…this notion…it's consumed her…to put this…what do you call it now, comfort food?...into the catalogue. Used to be just food! That's what we ate. And she's adding other things, too. Old-fashioned nightgowns, bath soaps, frilly curtains, homemade jams, fancy soups, canned fruit." Jean shook her head. Skepticism flooded her face. "Who would buy things like that?"

Emma slugged a long gulp, jittering her shoulders for *I don't have a clue*, more avoidance than response.

Jean interrupted herself, "Wouldn't you rather have some juice and toast?"

"Not really," Emma said.

The cold sweet fluid in her throat, the sugar finding its way into her arteries, the aroma of the soup, the quiet buzz of the Tylenol—recovery had begun.

Jean blew on a spoonful of soup, tasted it, sipped it. "Still too hot," she said, and took off her glasses, ready to pick up with her unanswered question. "You can buy three boxes of macaroni and cheese for a dollar at the grocery store. Who would pay twelve dollars *plus shipping* to have it delivered frozen? And those long nightgowns…my mother didn't even wear them…they're awful to sleep in…they get bunched up every time you roll over."

Emma had no response, though Jean seemed to expect one, as if they were conspirators now, which instinctively felt wrong to Emma, though at that moment she couldn't have said why if she was asked—or, given the chance (and out of earshot from Jean), she might have said that agreeing with Aunt Jean about anything sent convulsive warning signals through her whole being. This idea that Cherylee had about changing the catalogue was coming back to Emma. Cherylee told her about it on the phone one night weeks ago. Sales had fallen off, she said. The sales manager said they'd gone down for several quarters, not just recently—since Peter left. (He didn't say that outright, Cherylee added, but that's what he meant. She heard him dance around it.) She had to face reality, she told Emma, almost as if confessing to her. Sales had tumbled since her father disappeared but Cherylee was terrified of changing anything. What did she know about business? She just signed things, let people do what they'd always done and hoped it didn't fly apart before Peter returned. (Emma recalled thinking that even then her mother still clung to a dim—and unrealistic—hope that their lives could somehow be restored after her father was found or came back.) Cherylee described to Emma how, at a meeting with the sales manager and Luanne and a couple of others, she told them—she was frank with them! she said—that she didn't know what she was doing. She was a mother, not a business woman, and…then it came out…this notion…just a natural segue as she explained herself, as she apologized to them for not being anything other than what she was—a mother! a housewife!—she did what mothers did…made mac and cheese, and brownies, kept her home a happy and warm place for her family…and the idea lit them up. Yes, that's what they'd do! People wanted these things. *They* wanted these things! They would sell brownie and pancake mixes, aromatic candles, knitted afghans, wooly slippers. It wasn't because of Peter's disappearance that sales fell (nobody said that, but that's what they meant); it was because the extravagant gifts and promotional trinkets, which sold by the gross—the mugs and squeeze balls and mousepads—were getting whittled out of budgets this year. The stock market had fallen. Everyone had lost money. People were staying home, watching movies, curling up on the sofa, drinking cocoa. Couch potatoes were a new market—that's who they'd pursue!

"I swear, she'd throw herself in front of a train for you kids," Jean concluded.

Emma didn't hear what came before that.

She nodded, acknowledging her guilt—for living, for accepting the bounty of her life, for wanting Dr. Pepper instead of orange juice.

Guilt. Aunt Jean's special blend—Emma's now to bear, as if she didn't have enough of her own, as if she didn't wonder what they had all done to deserve this. There must be a god, she often thought, and he must be really pissed at them!

When she tossed her can in the waste bin, soda splattered on her hands and she rinsed at the sink. "Hey! The water works! I didn't even think about it when I showered."

"Why wouldn't it? Oh, that nonsense about the computers? How ridiculous!"

"C'mon, Aunt Jean. I'll bet Todd checked the water and turned on the computer when the ball dropped."

"Well, I don't know. I was already home in bed. I guess I've rung in enough New Yearses. And I'm happy to say I don't have a computer."

"What if they'd been right?"

"Nonsense!"

"People were going whacko about it."

"Oh, I know! It says in the paper that a congregation in Independence barricaded themselves in church because they thought there'd be rioting in the streets."

Emma poked in the pantry. She wanted some Oreos but she didn't know if it was worth the battle if she pulled out the package.

Jean said, "I can fix you something. How about some hot cereal? You'd probably rather have breakfast, wouldn't you?"

"I'm okay. Not that hungry after all."

"So how was your party?"

"Okay."

"Anyone from school there?"

"A couple of people."

Emma felt her fishing. She thought about telling her how many beers she had just for a goof, but it didn't seem funny.

Jean gathered herself and said, "Now, sit down, dear, and tell me about school."

Emma sat sideways in the chair, not quite committed. "Not much to tell. It's okay." She knew what Jean really wanted. She'd soon get around to talking about her father, asking *How are you doing?*—prying the whole thing open. Emma just didn't want to talk about it right now. She felt so exposed, here alone with Jean.

"How's your roommate? Any better?"

That was touchy.

"Miss Perfect? Joining a sorority," Emma sing-songed. "Probably won't see much of her in the spring. Once they have you, you're theirs! It's like the mafia."

"It's hard if you've never shared a room. You've always had your own.

You're such a bright girl! Do you like your classes?"

She hated being told she was bright—especially that word, *bright*. Not smart or intelligent. *Bright* meant you *could* get good grades if you tried. She heard it all the way through high school.

"Mostly boring," she said. "Religion is okay. Just took it cause I heard it was easy," she shrugged, "but it's interesting. We talk about other religions, like Buddhists and Hindus. Imagine being reborn as a frog or pelican!"

"Nonsense," Jean shivered.

"Half-a-billion people don't think so. I don't know what makes us right and them wrong. We don't have any more proof about what we believe than they do about what they believe."

"Of course, we do. There's the Bible."

"All religions have holy books. And they all feel the same way about theirs."

"That doesn't sound very religious to me."

"Well, they're not trying to preach, Aunt Jean. It's a course about different religions. Christianity is just one."

Emma saw the incredulity in her aunt's face. If this conversation had been a year ago, she knew what Aunt Jean would say next: *You're every bit your father's daughter!* Instead, Jean drew a breath and said, "Well, I think they should at least put more emphasis on Christianity if they're going to talk about all these other…religions."

"Oh, don't worry, Aunt Jean, plenty of Christianity to go around, even in Lawrence." She slid out of the chair and said, yawning, "I'm going upstairs."

"Must have been a happy New Years!" Jean said.

"It's New *Year*, Aunt Jean."

"That's what I said."

"Whatever."

"Sure you don't want something?"

"Not right now. Gotta pee."

"Emma!"

"Well, that's what I gotta do."

Upstairs she checked her phone again. No calls.

She hung the damp towel over the window and then slept through most of the afternoon. When her phone woke her, it was near dark. The whirring ring tone startled her out of sleep. She couldn't identify the sound at first. "Hello," she grunted.

"Hey!" It was Sharon.

"What's up?" Emma mumbled.
"Nothin'. You still fucked up?"
"Not so much, just tired. What time is it?"
"After four. What're you doin' later?"
"Don't know. Nothin', I guess."
"Wanna hang out?"
"Where?"
"Not here. My mom's pissed about the mess."
"Not here either. I gotta get outta here."
"What's goin' on?"
"Usual. My aunt was here. Probably still here."
"Aauunt Jeeeaaan!"
"Aauuntiee Jeeaannie!" Emma moaned in a hoarse whisper.

They both snickered weakly. The joke had worn out long ago, a mimic of how Jean sounded on the phone to Emma. She'd been friends with Sharon throughout high school, but Sharon didn't go to college. She worked at Target.

"Hey," Sharon said, "let's bounce through some movies at the plex."

"I don't know. Maybe. I'll call you back. Not awake yet."

Emma heard her mother downstairs talking with Jean. She didn't want to see anyone, but she had to go to the bathroom. The doors and toilet would announce that she was awake. She padded across the hall barefoot and eased the door shut.

While she was in there, her mother climbed the stairs and her footsteps stopped at Emma's door. Now she tapped on the bathroom door. "Emma?"

"I'm in here." She squirmed on the seat, wondering if the door would open.

"Why is it dark in there?"

"It's not dark. I can see. How do you know it's dark?"

"I can see under the door that the light's not on. Are you all right?"

"I'm fine, Mom. I'm just trying to use the freakin' bathroom!"

"Okay. We're going out for dinner."

"I'm not hungry."

"Honey, you should come. We'll all go together. We can wait a few minutes."

"I really don't want to go."

"Are you okay?" Her voice got lower, closer to the door. "Did you get sick?"

"I'm fine. Just not hungry. I'm trying to use the bathroom."

"Okay, honey. Can we bring you something?"

"No, but I might go out."

"Call me if you do."

She stayed in the bathroom until the garage door went down.

Cherylee had turned on the lights in her room. It was dark outside. The whole day was gone. The lights revealed a mess—clothes everywhere, the bed rumpled from twelve hours of sleep, CDs, food trash, makeup smeared into the carpet. But she felt better. She was hungry and could eat what she wanted now that she was alone.

A remnant of the dream came back to her. It felt eerie, as if he was a ghost. But he wasn't dead. Well, they didn't know. They didn't know anything. And she didn't know what she should feel. Sometimes she thought it would be easier if he had died. At least she'd know what to feel. Then she felt guilty for thinking so. More guilt.

She got mad at him, too. She wouldn't have been mad if he told her what he'd done. She had so many questions. He could have told her. He could have trusted her. She would have kept his secret. She would have embraced it. She would help him, if she could. He should have trusted her.

She'd been in trouble herself in recent years—for drinking, for vandalism; the BIG one was for smoking weed, and she realized now how much jeopardy she'd placed him in. The night her parents claimed her at the Hawkings police department, after she and Sharon were stopped and the cop found a joint in the car, seemed like the end of the world to her mother, but her father calmly dealt with the officers as if they were teachers and all she'd done was cut class. When he scowled at her on the way to the car, she caught a glimmer of his smile, and she felt safe now that he was there—safe from the cops, even from her mother, who motored through waves of lecturing and yelling and industrial-strength silence. He took her to juvie court, listened alongside her to the judge's lecture, agreed to keep her out of trouble, and paid the fine in cash. He made himself her partner, but now he'd abandoned her. She hoped she'd be the one to answer the phone, if he ever called.

The yearbook was all she had now. She kept it under her pillow. It meant as much to her as her favorite photo of the two of them, dressed as Dorothy and the Scarecrow for the father-daughter Halloween dance when she was a girl scout. He trailed hay all over the school. She'd read every page of the yearbook and found some of the other people in that group, the Circle. She studied their faces—the girl with dark, stringy hair; the guy with a thick mustache and wire-rimmed glasses—both of them dead, killed in that explosion. She also found the man who escaped, the Vietnam veteran, and she wondered if her father was with him now, if he might be the key to finding her father. Well, the FBI had surely thought of that. But her father—he was the same age in those photos as she was right now. Right now! The same age. If only she could look inside them and see what he was thinking at that very moment. If only.

Her mother said he was trying to protect them, to keep them out of it, to avoid leaving clues—but she didn't know. It was all just speculation. No one knew *anything*. Nada. Nil. There was just this void, this big black hole, and he'd disappeared into it, and the rest of them were spinning at the edges, just inches from getting sucked in themselves.

Emma had not unpacked since she arrived home for winter break weeks ago. She pulled clothes from her bags when she needed something, and the laundry had piled up. Amazingly, her mother hadn't said a word. She never would have put up with it in the past. She even ignored the towel hanging over the window. Emma could hear it: "Do you think we live in a trailer?" That's what she would have said then, but now, nothing.

Emma pulled the towel down. It was dry, so she folded it. Then she made her bed and propped Winky, her stuffed bear, on the pillow where her mother put it while she was away at school. When she stacked her CDs, she found an old Smashing Pumpkins' album, *The Aeroplane Flies High*, and slid it into the CD player, and the dry nasal voices and urgent drums seemed to echo from inside the black hole. She folded her clothes and gathered her trash. She even tried to scrub the make-up out of the carpet.

Then she cranked up the music and went downstairs. The house was lit as if guests were coming. Cherylee must have turned on every light before she left. Smashing Pumpkins pounded through the stairwell and into the kitchen, filling the house, shutting out the emptiness. Emma found it easier to be alone with the noise and light than surrounded by people who reminded her of the black hole at the center of their lives.

She made a peanut butter and potato chip sandwich and grabbed the package of Oreos. The last Dr. Pepper was still there. She took the food down to the family room and thumbed the TV remote, finally settling for *Leave It to Beaver* on Nickelodeon because she was more eager to eat than to find something to watch. The music from upstairs reverberated through the walls. Wally was in trouble for staying out too late after a dance. He called his father "Sir." His father wore a suit and tie while he read the newspaper at home.

The album ended, Wally was forgiven, and she washed down her fourth Oreo with the last gulp of soda.

She noticed the computer in the corner, which she hadn't touched since she came home. When she hit the ON button, Darth Vader filled the screen. Todd had taken over. She surfed the Web pages of musicians and movie actors while *Bewitched* started. Samantha sent Darren off to work with a kiss on the cheek, looked slyly around the kitchen, twitched her nose, and all the breakfast dishes magically washed and dried themselves while she folded her arms and grinned.

Emma wondered where he was. Did he have friends helping him? Was he going back to being a terrorist? (Maybe it was true that he was still involved with them.) Was he still in the country? What was he doing *right now*? She'd rather be with him, whatever he was doing, than *here*, dealing with all the people who came and went—lawyers, cops, reporters, insurance people, *whoever!* Total strangers knew all of their business and were always in their faces. Whatever he was doing—wherever he was—had to be better than this!

She went to the one website that she knew followed him relentlessly. She had avoided it for weeks. Seeing the things that appeared there left her feeling as she imagined she would if she was raped. She couldn't imagine feeling worse. It was sickening—the wild accusations, the smug tone, the cartoons. It was all a game, entertainment. Her whole life, her whole family, had been destroyed, but it was just a game. And there was Marcia—a photo of her in headphones when she was interviewed by that cockroach. Marcia. Emma hadn't spoken to her since the day she confronted her in the newspaper office, but she'd seen her on campus at KU. They both ended up there. They couldn't escape each other—for their entire lives, they couldn't escape each other—but now, seeing how small she looked in those oversized headphones, and with that fat cockroach crowding her at the microphone, Emma thought for the first time that maybe she'd been bowled over too; maybe she'd unleashed something that was much bigger than she ever imagined.

Samantha scowled as Endora made a snide remark about Darren. Canned laughter swelled up.

Emma shut off the TV and computer, gathered her dishes, and hurried up the stairs so she'd be gone before everyone else returned.

✣

Brenda Rojas wasn't expecting more guests. Alan's assistant called during the afternoon to say that her husband had the flu so they couldn't come, and Brenda thought everyone else had shown up. Most of the newsroom staff was here, except for the Havermales, but Jonas had asked Alan once too many times about interviewing Marcy. Alan had had it with him.

But maybe for this one day they could put all of that aside. Maybe with the new year, all of the commotion and attention were finally behind them. Brenda always liked that January first was Alan's birthday. Having a party on the evening of New Year's Day was different; it was mellow. People were coming down from the holidays, and usually from last night too. She felt...not radiant, but cheery. There was chatter, the smell of meatballs, of sauces, of coffee brewing. Her home was filled with football, jokes, stories, and laughter this evening.

She almost missed hearing the doorbell in the happy chaos.

She smiled as she went to the front door, expecting to find another guest clutching a casserole dish or brownie pan, but the smile froze on her lips as if she'd been hit by an arctic blast when she found Emma St. John standing in the glow of her porch lights. Brenda's smile began to melt, but she saved it before it dripped into a puddle at her feet.

"Emma?...hello. What a...surprise! Happy New Year!"

Brenda had not seen the girl since last spring, when the whole mess blew up, and she couldn't have named the last time she'd had a conversation with her. It had been years. She knew it was Emma instantly, of course, but she still needed a moment for recognition to take hold, not just because of her surprise, but because, like Marcy, she had changed. She'd grown up. She was taller. She'd always been tall, but now the long legs rising from her black boots to her short black skirt were those of a woman. Her rounded jaw line had lost its girlish pudginess and had the defining contour of an adult face. Brenda saw more of her father in her than she'd ever noticed before. She had the poise of an adult. She looked at Brenda without the skittish side glances of a child. Her black eye-liner and black beret were a little too much of a statement for Brenda's taste, but Emma always seemed to find a way to make a statement. She did look cold.

"Come inside," Brenda added.

"I'm sorry. You have guests. I wanted to talk to Marcy. I can come back."

"No, no, that's all right. You must be freezing. Come in."

"I had to park down the block. I didn't realize all these cars were for your house."

"It's Alan's birthday."

Emma scrunched her shoulders up from the cold as she stood in the hallway. "I didn't mean to intrude."

"You're not intruding at all. Are you hungry?" Even as Brenda offered her hospitality, she wondered what disaster awaited if Emma joined a party of news people.

"No, I just wanted to see Marcy for a minute."

"Well, she still doesn't like the adult parties even though she's a college girl, just like you. I'll get her. Come in and join us."

"No, I'll just wait here."

"It's okay, Mom," Marcia said from the stairs. "C'mon up, Emma."

Brenda stood aside for Emma, and now, left alone in the hallway, she recovered her smile, took a breath, and returned to her guests as the girls disappeared around the corner of the stairway.

Marcia led the way to her room. Over her shoulder she said, "Wish I'd seen my mother's face when she saw you."

"She did pretty good, considering."

They both noticed—though neither said it—not only how the joke spirited them over a vast chasm, the distance of all the years and all that had happened since they were children, but that it was a joke that could only have passed between them because they'd known each other for so long.

Marcia glanced down the hall before she shut her bedroom door behind Emma. Music played so low that Emma didn't hear it over the din of the party until the door was closed. Marcia turned the stereo off.

"Not much room to sit," she said. "Here, sit on my bed. You wanna take off your coat? You'll roast up here."

Emma perched at the corner of the bed, and Marcia spun around her desk chair.

"I'll wait," Emma said. "I'm still cold." She looked around. She hadn't been in Marcia's room since she was a child. It looked more like an office than a bedroom now, with papers and folders everywhere. Photos crowded the bookcase and desk—Marcia with the high school newspaper staff, with her parents at graduation, showing off her medals, holding a soccer ball.

Emma still couldn't believe she'd come here. Even as she trudged past the cars outside, she debated whether this was the right thing to do, and when she stood before Marcia's mother downstairs, she felt as if she was inside a glass snow dome. Just shake and watch the snow swirl around her.

She'd been terrible to Marcy and said awful things about her, but Marcy never tried to dispute any of it. She just seemed to take it. Emma heard from others at school that Marcy even said she felt sorry for her. Maybe that was true. Emma didn't know. Her resentment had metastasized.

A couple of bags spilled over with clothes. Marcy hadn't unpacked from school either, just lived out of her suitcases until everything went through the wash, just like Emma. By then it would be time to go back to school.

The computer was on, with written text halfway down the screen. Marcia said, "It's just a story for the *Kansan*."

Emma smirked, "Picking right up with the college paper."

"Nothing very exciting. Updating the bus schedule for spring semester. The upper class journalism students get all of the good stories. I can't even apply until next year. Anyway, I don't mind." She paused and asked, in almost a whisper, "How's your mother?"

"It's been hard, but she's been working at my dad's business. I think that helps."

"I'm so sorry, Emma. I tried to tell you. I'm so sorry."

Emma hesitated. She saw that Marcy was tired with the same fatigue she felt from this ordeal. Its endless presence had left them both weary, exhausted. The sniping and name-calling her friends inflicted on Marcy last year seemed petty and childish now.

"I suppose it was gonna come out anyway, sooner or later," Emma said, and then she added, "I guess it wasn't all your fault."

"That's not how it feels to me. Have you...have you heard anything more?"

"No, nothing."

"Oh..."

"Why I came over is...well, you were the last person to see him."

Marcia slumped and shook her head. She was near tears. "I know," she said.

"I never got to ask you...what did he say?"

"Oh, Emma, I had no idea what I was in! And I got so caught up in the story. You know, it was like a mystery. Things just kept coming up, and I couldn't make sense out of them. But he was way ahead of me. Your father is a smart man. I truly think he's a good man, too. It just seemed like he'd already made up his mind that it would all come out before I ever went to see him. He told me about some of the stuff he did, the stuff I wrote about, like he wanted to set the record straight. He must have said a dozen times that they never wanted to hurt anyone, that the whole thing was all about sending a message. He was so sad, so full of sorrow. He said how much this would hurt you and your family. That was the worst of it, he said, what it would do to you. But it just seemed like…I don't know…it was already a done deal that he was going to come out. I wasn't even sure my story would be the one that broke it open, but…"—now she did let out a sob—"…but I just got caught up in the whole thing, this image I had of myself being a journalist, breaking a big story. I just never thought about what it would mean to you, and I never imagined he'd…he'd leave like that."

Emma was warm now and slid out of her coat. She found herself in the unfamiliar position of feeling sorry for Marcy, as if she'd survived a horrible accident in which others had died.

A voice disengaged from the muffled din of the party downstairs, now in the stairway, and footsteps passed Marcia's room, followed by the bathroom door opening and closing. Marcia watched her door. It was obvious that she'd barricaded herself in here, that she also feared the hordes of invading forces, that she heard them gathering at her walls.

"Have you looked into this any more since then?"

Emma's voice startled her. "No…really, Emma!…I haven't."

Emma waved a hand. "I didn't mean like that. I just wondered if you found out anything else."

"I followed some if it, what's already out there, but I've done enough damage. Besides, now I'm part of the story, too. My father tried to keep those people away from me." She wagged a hand at the door, at the hordes. "I'm not a reporter to them. I'm just a freak. Kids my age aren't supposed to scoop them."

"I can't even stand to watch the news," Emma said. "Every time the phone rings, everyone in the house goes silent. It's like we're living under this big avalanche and if you even breathe the thing will come thundering down and bury us. We're always expecting to hear a key in the door or footsteps in the middle of the night or a tapping at the window. I listen for stuff like that. We all do. Every time I walk into the house I wonder if he'll be there…or someone…with news about him…or maybe a call came while I was gone…something."

"I can't imagine it."

The bathroom door shut and the footsteps passed the other way. Emma smirked, "Maybe you can, a little." She got up from the bed and fluffed her sweater. "You're right, it is warm up here."

"You want something to drink? I can go down…"

"No, I'm okay. It's not worth it. We'd both be better off dying of thirst."

Marcy opened the front window. "That'll help."

Emma studied a photo of their girl scout troop in a collage on the bulletin board. She stood at the end of the second row, taller than the others, grinning widely. Marcy sat on the ground, her legs folded, her lips tight, and her mother stood behind the group. Emma knew—her own mother always said—that it was really Brenda who sold all those cookies, not Marcy. No doctor or nurse or attendant at the hospital escaped Brenda and her cookie sign-up sheet. Probably everyone downstairs had eaten cookies delivered—no doubt reluctantly, even apologetically—by Alan Rojas.

Emma said, "It's weird. I don't even know what other relatives we might have."

"His mother and father both died."

"Yeah…and he didn't have any brothers or sisters. Probably nobody'd want to claim they were related," she sniffed. "I just keep trying to imagine where he'd go."

"It still amazes me that he…oh!"

Emma turned. "That he what?"

"I'm sorry, Emma. It's still so hard to talk about this with you."

"What?"

"Just that he managed to stay concealed for so long, right out in the open too. And then to run for the school board…"

"What was he thinking," Emma said, less a question than a sigh.

"He told me that back then, when all this happened, you could just feel all of the stuff going on…you know, the war and the protests and all of it…like it was part of your life, like everything they did, the government, it affected you. The draft, the war. He said the government had spies everywhere and they were doing horrible things. Like they'd decide that certain professors were too outspoken so they'd send out anonymous letters accusing them of being perverts or communist spies or using drugs. People lost their jobs and got kicked out of school. The government wasn't just spying on people but they were trying to stir up trouble, like they'd turn peaceful protests into riots. He said how different things felt now, with people just going along like none of this could happen again, how weird it was to be a businessman, part of all he was revolting against. It reached the point for his group, like, that the only logical thing for them to do was try to change the whole system. They figured there was already anarchy in the government, so if there was anarchy in the streets too and the government couldn't function, then the people would take control again."

"That's crazy."

"I know. He even thought so too, when he told me, but he was trying to explain how it felt then, you know, how one thing led to another, and not all of them felt the same way, or even thought they were doing something for the same reasons. But it is hard to imagine—I've thought about this—like, what if soldiers came on our campus and starting shooting at us, and people got killed?!"

"That's impossible."

"But that's what happened, Emma! Just before his group went underground, that's what happened. They were occupying a building on their campus when the Kent State thing went down. It was the second time he was arrested—and you saw what they did to him the first time."

"I know, but it's just so hard to believe that that was him, that he's the same person, that was my *father*. He's not like that!"

"Emma, he was so sorry about those people…the people who got killed. He said it wasn't supposed to happen and he'd been wrong…they'd all been wrong…to try to solve their problems with bombs."

Emma slumped onto the bed now, and Marcia sat beside her, taking her hand. Emma sniffed as tears came, and she said, "Oh, God, he's a murderer. I never thought about that way, until now. He's a murderer."

"He didn't mean it, Emma. It was an accident. They meant for it to go off when no one was there."

"But it did! People got killed!"

"Listen to me, it makes a difference. It's not the same as throwing a bomb into a crowd."

"The result was the same."

Marcia lifted Emma's hand in both of hers. She was crying now too. "Listen, Emma. His friends died also, three of them did. You already know this. I know you do. He's lived with it every day of his life, without telling anyone. All I got to see was a little glimpse of how sorry he was. He told me that life just keeps moving you forward and you don't even get to decide most of what happens…and then, what can you do? He had a family, he said."

Emma sniveled, "He didn't have to have a family."

"Even that, he said. It just happens."

Emma looked up now, looked at Marcia as if she'd just appeared in the room. "What do you mean?"

"Oh, no!"

"What?"

"I thought you knew."

"Knew what?...knew what?"

Marcia covered her face in her hands and began sobbing.

"What?" Emma said, shaking her by the shoulders.

"I…I…it's like I'm doomed. Everything I do just makes it worse."

"What are you talking about? Tell me!" Emma said sharply.

"Your mother…I don't know…probably your aunt, too, they were trying to protect you. Your mother and father…they were expecting you before they got married. That's why…he wanted to take care of you, of your mother. I thought you already knew."

"What else did he say?"

Marcia got up, looking for a tissue, and when she couldn't find one, she picked up a tee-shirt from the pile on the floor and wiped her nose and eyes. Then she dropped into her desk chair. "I just keep making it worse."

"You have to tell me everything."

"There's nothing more, Emma. That's all. He said he never imagined he'd find himself in this situation, even when he got married. It wasn't something where he could look so far ahead that he could see things coming apart like this. Your mother was pregnant. No one knew him here. He just thought it would work out. That's all. Your mother's trying to protect you too."

"Yeah, everyone's taking such good care of everyone else that our lives are totally fucked up forever."

Emma got up now, wiping her eyes with her sleeves, and began to put on her coat.

"Wait, Emma, please don't go yet." Marcia went to her. "I can't stand any more of this. Please don't be mad at me any more. Please!"

As Emma looked at Marcia, with her face streaked and hair matted and her eyes filled with her plea, she felt only pity. Her will to be angry was gone. What was anger but a way to defend yourself? And she had nothing left to defend. She was exposed, stripped naked. What else could anyone do to her? And what good would come from leaving Marcia with more pain than she felt right now? "It's all right, Marcy. I'm not mad at you."

She pulled her coat on, and Marcia suddenly hugged her.

"I'm sorry," Marcia said.

"I know."

"I'll come down and run interference so you don't have to talk to them."

In the car, shivering, Emma remembered that she was supposed to call Sharon, but she didn't want to talk to her now, or go to a movie, or do anything but go home.

Chapter 15

New York

Cars came and went in the Keubler Real Estate Agency parking lot. People milled in the front office. Peter recognized him flitting past in the window, even after all these years. That's what he'd wear now, how he'd look—a two-toned shirt and bright silk tie, with his hair buzzed around his ears, erect, easy with himself, slender and fit, like a mature model in a *GQ* ad. Now he burst into laughter and patted a man in short sleeves on the shoulder. Then he retreated from sight, reappeared, looked over papers, talked with others.

The agency occupied one end of a rundown strip mall that had been there since Peter was a student. The stores had changed and a couple were vacant, but Keubler's end of the strip was busy. Near the highway, a sign announced, "Zoned commercial. Pads available. Contact Keubler Real Estate." At the bottom of the sign was the same phone number that Peter had scrawled on a Starbucks napkin, now folded in the cup holder.

Peter watched the office from behind an overgrown juniper beside the Jeep. Empty bottles, crumpled papers, and dog shit littered the sparse mulch around the shrub. Traffic rushed past on the six-lane highway in front of the shopping center, and across the road, cars poured into the entrance of the Groenkill Parke Mall. A dairy farm had once been there. Its pastures rolled all over the brown hills that surrounded the mall. Cell-phone towers now sprouted from the summit of the tallest hill.

A day earlier Peter had driven through the area for the first time in three decades, slowing as he passed the college, tempted even to drive through the campus. Some of the buildings were as he remembered—the chapel and Driscoll Hall, mostly concealed now behind rows of pines and budding maples along the highway. A new building stood beside Kieran Union, with a high, angular roof, perhaps a theater or performance center. Other buildings had gone up too. The river could no longer be seen from the road. Around the city he recognized landmarks, but many were gone. An off-ramp swept over the site of his old apartment building, and the house on Brook Street—in fact, all of Brook Street—was now a Home Depot and Sam's Club. The diner in the warehouse district had morphed into a Starbucks, where Peter bought coffee and asked for a phone book to look up Keubler. People all around him, mostly white, chattered on cell phones.

He couldn't go into the office and ask for him; that would surely be a problem, for both of them. He'd be easy to remember in his filthy, smelly clothes, and no one in his condition would be there to buy a house. He would wait until Keubler came out to his car, without doubt the white Lexus with the tag *LK*. He'd catch him then.

A tapping on the window next to his head startled him. He couldn't recall where he was. He must have dozed off. For how long?

Keubler peered in the window. "Peter…is that you? What're you doing here?" His voice was muffled and he grinned widely. A mouthful of even, white teeth glistened inches from Peter's eyes.

Peter rolled down the window, and Keubler said, "I wondered if it might be you. My girl in there said some guy had been parked here for hours and maybe we should call the cops. What's the deal, man? What're you doing?" The grin was still there, but his tone had an edgy directness.

"I…I wanted to talk to you. I need help."

The grin lingered, but tightly sealed lips now hid the white teeth. He hesitated. "Man, we don't have long. There's a klatch of girls watching back in that office window. I said I could probably take care of this rather than bother the cops for a vagrant. I own this strip."

"I'm sorry, Keub…I shouldn't have come here. I'll get going."

"Listen, man, you're putting me in a spot. The heat was here a few months back, asking if I heard from you."

"They were here?"

Keubler arched his eyebrows and nodded. "That's right. They came to the office…only once, thank God…but they called back a couple of times. I don't know if they're watching now or tapping the phones."

"If they were watching, they'd have picked me up by now."

"Peter, you got money?"

"No."

Keubler pulled a thick money clip from his pocket, shielding his movements from the office window, and handed Peter a couple of fifties. "Here, take this. We can't be seen around here. You remember up in New Paltz, there's a diner near the Thruway entrance?" When Peter nodded, he continued, "I'll see you there tonight, say eight or so. Right now, I'm gonna step back from the car and wave my arms around and shout, and we'll put on a good show for the girls while you drive outta here, okay?"

Peter put the bills in the cup holder and played his part. He didn't know what he expected from Keubler. Aside from a handout, it didn't appear that he could do anything else. Peter could only be a problem.

Keubler stood in the parking lot and watched him turn onto the highway. Then he turned back to the office and smiled at his assistants in the window, throwing his arms out wide and brushing off his hands in big, exaggerated strokes.

At a quarter to eight, Peter sat in a booth with a cup of coffee, considering whether to stay. It was plain that Keubler wasn't happy about seeing him today, and Peter knew he had a right to be mad about getting jammed up. But the damage was done. A pair of state troopers had just come into the diner and taken a booth near the door, and Peter didn't want to walk past them, or stand nearby to pay at the register while they got a good look at him. By eight-thirty, while he nursed a refill and watched the troopers pay their checks, he thought maybe Keubler had blown him off.

Then he appeared. One of the troopers, with his gray, smoky-bear hat pushed low on his brow, stood aside and held the door for him before the pair left. Keubler wore a black North Face parka with the collar up and a baseball hat and tinted glasses. A gold chain jangled down his wrist when he grabbed the table and slid into the booth. He looked back at the door, making sure the cops weren't returning, and said, "Holy shit, man! I saw the squad car outside when I first came by so I took a drive. Saw your car too. It was still here when I came back, so I figured I'd just sit at the counter until they left, and then I bump into them head-on as I'm walkin' in the door. What's the deal?"

Peter shrugged. "They stopped off the Thruway for dinner. Good call on the rendezvous." He offered the last remark as a joke, but it came out flat, like dropping a pebble into a puddle of oil, almost no splash. The whole situation was simply too grim.

"Yeah, well, I guess I'm outta practice. Not like you," Keubler said, without a hint of a smile.

This encounter looked even less promising than the one in the parking lot.

The waitress arrived and Peter ordered meatloaf. Keubler asked for a diet Sprite and dismissed her with a flick of his hand. He kept his cap on and his back to the door. The cap bore a Titleist logo. Now, with Keubler sitting across the booth from him, Peter noticed how lined and toughened his face was, like worn and cracked leather. He hadn't merely aged, he had survived. Even dressed down in the cap and parka, he appeared outwardly fashionable, even genteel, but his thick hands and timeworn face suggested that he was accustomed to getting quickly to the point—whatever the point may be. He seemed impatient, irritated.

Peter knew it was a mistake to come here, to step back into Keubler's life at all. But more than money or help, he now realized that he wanted something else from him. He wanted some connection to the past, some reassurance that whatever they had done, whatever had happened, at some point they had been friends, had shared something. He recognized, acknowledged now, the instinct that had brought him here and compelled him over miles and miles and days and days until he drove past the college yesterday and then some of the places that had shaped his life. He'd seen no one who knew him by his real name since the day he drove away from the safe house, and now here was someone—maybe irritated, maybe even resentful (and not without reason, Peter conceded)—but here he was, and Peter did want something from him before they parted. It came to him in the moment that Keubler slid into the seat, as Peter looked into the only face he'd ever seen from so long ago in his life, that this was what he needed so he could end this nightmare in which he—and without a doubt, his family—were living. He needed to return for just a short while, to pick up the broken threads and tie them off, so he could leave them behind for good. He would go to the cemetery where he stole his name, and while he was there, he would visit the graves of his victims; he would drive down the tree-lined lane that led to the front entrance of Merval Corporation, which he'd left behind while smoke poured from the sixth floor and crowds milled in front of the building and emergency vehicles rushed past him; he would go back to Long Island and see if he had any living relatives. He would find…no, not that…he couldn't do that…he had to leave Susan alone. Wherever she was, he had to leave her alone. Look what happened just for showing up in Keubler's parking lot. He couldn't do that to her. But he had left himself here, buried himself without a word over the grave, and he would have those words now, silently and privately, before he ended this odyssey, before he surrendered and gave his family what he owed them, too. Keubler might own the high ground here—and he literally did seem to own it—but he'd used the Circle once. They bought dope from him; they were some of his best customers. He was indeed a survivor, and he'd survive this too. Peter would be gone soon.

"No dinner?" Peter asked.

"Nah, had a salad at home. I'm good. You go ahead, Peter. It's on me. You don't look like you get a lot of regular food. How you doing?"

Peter shook his head. "Some bad days and some really bad days."

"Where you been? What's goin' on?"

Peter noticed how thick his clipped New York was accent now, much more pronounced than Peter remembered, when Keubler wanted to become an actor and played Shakespeare. He was a businessman now—and an ex-con. His voice was edgier than Peter recalled, even allowing for these strained circumstances.

"Oh…a lot of places, no place. It was a bad idea coming here. Even if you give me some money, it'll just be gone in a week or a month, and I'll still be in the same spot."

"You came a long way to figure that out."

"Yeah, I guess." He paused, and Keubler waited. "You're the first person I've talked to in decades who knew me."

Keubler grinned for the first time since he arrived and peered out from under his cap, a hint of recognition, of acknowledgement that Peter was perhaps more than someone from the long-ago past showing up now just to hit on him. "I heard about you being outed last year. I don't know how you lasted so long. I always wondered what happened to you, and then all of a sudden there you are on CNN. 'Holy shit!' I thought. 'There's Peter!' Then a week or two later, the shoes appear at my office. Fuckers! I thought I was done with them for good. So where you been all this time? By the way, you look like shit." He snickered now. "You gotta get cleaned up. You even stick out in a place like this."

"I can't go much longer. Seems like every time I was about to turn myself in, something stopped me, and I just couldn't do it. It's not even like I'm running somewhere. I've been driving for months, sleeping in rest areas, hanging around truck stops. I'm like a highway zombie. I've been all over the country. I just go from one place to another but never really go anywhere and never stop anywhere. It's like my legs keep waiting for my brain to send a signal to quit."

The waitress slid Peter's dinner in front of him and left the check on the table.

Keubler watched her down the aisle and asked, "How'd you get out, Peter?"

"Out of where?"

"The building, after the bomb."

"Just walked away. Nobody noticed me in the chaos. People were running this way and that, covered with debris, looking up at the smoke, talking about what happened. I just walked out and kept going. Never stopped. Still haven't stopped." He ate a forkful and asked, "What about you? Where were you? I saw the car."

"The car got blocked in, and I took off into the woods. Tried to get to New Paltz. No car, couldn't hitch, so I started walking. Over forty miles! I went through woods and backyards for two days. Mighta got there too, but some housewife got spooked when I cut through her backyard and called the pigs, and they picked me up on a side road up in Highland. I kept my nose clean inside, though. Wasn't easy, but I did it...did nine years. Nine fucking years."

"I'm sorry. I shouldn't be here."

The grin faded. "It's a problem, man. I'm takin' a huge chance just talkin' to you. Those fuckers are gonna call again, and I'm gonna have to lie now that you showed up. Why don't you just turn yourself in? You have a family, don't you? What about them?"

Peter laid his fork down and stared at his plate. "That's the worst part. My wife, my kids...what I've done to them. At first, I just couldn't face the time, going to prison, but more and more it became that I couldn't face *them*. And then...I began to think...maybe I should just let them be, let them get through this and go on, and the longer I was away, the farther I went, the harder it got to turn around. It's like interest compounding on a debt, you know. It gets bigger and bigger, worse and worse. And some days, I think, this is my punishment, my dues, to have no place to go, nothing to live for, no name. Nothing but guilt. I got too comfortable. Sometime...I don't know...maybe eight, ten years after I got married, I thought I'd made it, that the walls around me were thick and high enough, that we'd be safe. I'd raise my children and send them to college. I couldn't take all that away from them. I couldn't tell them, or anyone. It was too late. I thought I was who I'd become. But it's like...this, what you see right now in front of you...that's who I really am, just a shell, nothing left of who I was before, and what I turned into was never real. The person I was is gone now. There's nothing left."

Keubler blew a breath and shook his head. "God, Peter, you are fucked up. I haven't seen you in so long I can't tell if running like this made you crazy or if you were crazy all along, but I can tell you that living in your car for seven or eight months isn't the same as living in a penitentiary for nine years."

"You're right. I know that. For a while I thought about trying to keep going, getting in touch with my wife and kids to let them know I was alive, to tell them I loved them, and then trying to disappear again…one way or another…just disappear." His voice trailed off as all possibilities of what disappearing meant spun before him, and Keubler waited, wondering if there was more, about to say, *So...what now?* when Peter continued, "It's gonna end soon. I'm almost done. And I have to see them again." The last came out as if he was affirming it, remembering that whatever else he did, he had to do that. Then he looked at Keubler intently and leaned toward him, assertive now, as if to let him know that on this one thing Keubler's ground was no higher than his own, that he was here and would do what he had to do before he left. "I just needed to come back here first, to shut the doors behind me."

Keubler glanced around toward the front window and watched a car pull into the lot. Then turning back, he said, "So, now you're here, Peter. Go ahead and eat something."

Peter looked down at the plate without picking up his fork and then at Keubler again. "What happened to Simon?"

"Dead. Been dead for years. He got out too, just you and him. He made it out of the country, went to Mexico and then got arrested on a drug charge. He was stabbed in a prison fight. That was over twenty years ago."

"I've never known anyone like him. I sometimes wonder what he'd be now, if all this was really behind him, like you…how you became a businessman. That's what I did too."

"Yeah, I heard. You did pretty good, didn't you?"

"I did what I had to do, but Simon…I don't think he would have done anything he didn't have a passion for. I've wondered about him, if he'd still be painting, what his paintings would look like, and what the others would have become, if they hadn't…"

He let the sentence hang.

Keubler shifted in his seat, twisting his straw wrapper around his finger. "I don't know. I never really believed all that shit about revolution, even then, but it just seemed to sweep over us like a hurricane, and you could barely figure out which way was up. Planting that bomb…to me, it was just an oversized prank. I never imagined getting caught any more than I imagined anyone getting hurt. That's what's fucked up about being young…you never look past today, never think about the downside. You want to hear something weird? I'm a Republican now. I was in prison when Reagan was elected, but I would have voted for him. Communism was bullshit. I did my time and then came back here and built this business from nothing but borrowed money and an empty junk lot that I bought and sold. The land under that strip mall where you found me today is worth millions. I'm gonna bulldoze the strip and build something there…I don't know what, a shopping center, an office building, something. I'm gonna put my name on it, too. Right there in big letters for the people of Groenkill to see. When they get a bill from their doctor or lawyer, it'll say, 'Keubler Building, Suite One.' Or some kids'll be trying to figure where to hang out on Friday night and one of 'em will say, 'Let's go down to Keubler Mall.' Won't that be a kick in the ass?! I've made a small fortune here, Peter. This was my home before you and Simon and the rest came along, and I'm still here. People know me. Some remember what happened, but it didn't stop me from getting rich. Hell,"—he lowered his voice—"this isn't all that different from selling nickel bags to undergraduates, except you pay taxes and now the pigs are the good guys because you might need them to help move some low-life off a property for missing their rent."

Peter scraped the plate, cutting his meat. "I shouldn't have bothered you. I'll be gone in ten minutes and you won't even know where I went."

"Ah, Peter, it's not for me to decide whether you still have dues to pay. You have to figure that out. But you look like shit. Listen, you can crash for a couple of nights in one of my apartments. We're doing some painting, but the lights and hot water are on."

"You shouldn't do this."

He waved Peter off and asked, "You remember Brother Luke?"

"Yeah, I do remember him."

"I called him this afternoon after you left. I see him once or twice a year at homecoming or a regatta." Keubler smiled. "You'll get a kick outta this…I'm a big booster at the college. I even took night courses and finished a business degree after I got out. Took some courses in the pen, too. Anyway, Luke lives at the Selly retirement home now. He's the youngster up there…takes care of the old guys."

"Where?"

"It's up north of Saugerties, almost to Albany. They have an unbelievable piece of property on the river. You ever go there on retreat in college?"

"I didn't stick around long enough."

"Beautiful place…very wooded, very dense, with a big meadow that runs straight down to the river. No railroad tracks or roads in between. Used to be a religious training school. They called it a novitiate then. Anyway, he's expecting you in a couple of days. There's a retreat going on up there right now. That's why you can't go yet. Here. Here's five bills." He slipped the tightly folded bills under a napkin and pushed it across the table, where Peter covered it with his hand. "The key and directions to the apartment and Brother Luke's are in with the money."

Peter shook his head. "I can't go there."

"Ah, it's just a handful of old men and half of them have Alzheimer's. You probably won't even have to have much to do with them. Just tell them a story about recovering from alcoholism and getting religion, or whatever. I went on retreat myself a few years ago. Might be good for you."

"It wouldn't be fair."

"No, maybe not. That's up to you." He paused and added, "Peter, I don't mean to sound harsh, but you gotta move on. I'm just helping out, like the underground railroad. If you decide to turn yourself in, find somewhere else to do it. Don't drag me into it, or Luke either."

"I won't," Peter said. "Thanks."

Keubler shook Peter's hand, laid a twenty on top of the check, and mumbled "Being seein' ya." He never looked back as he went down the aisle and through the door.

‡

The apartment building resembled a stack of shipping containers piled alongside the highway near the power lines that cut through the middle of Groenkill. Across the parking lot were a liquor store and a Hardee's. Fried grease hung in the air like a dank, invisible mist.

Peter took his first shower in weeks and spent a long time at it, washing his thin hair, scrubbing his crotch and his ass, and then standing in the hot water to breathe the steam. Still damp from the shower, he slept on the floor, awakening a few hours later while it was still dark.

The front window had no blinds or curtains, and the highway felt like a presence in the hollow living room, though few cars passed now. The hum of the high-tension wires and the clatter of building noises reminded him in a strange way of the forest noises in Colorado many months ago. He made coffee in his camping pot and watched the highway, grateful to observe the world from the sheltered side of a window.

He felt as renewed from knowing what he'd do next as from the shower and rest. He was more contented than he'd been since the day before Marcia Rojas first appeared at his office. He would spend a day or two here, then go to the Island for another day or so—drive past his old house, look up names in the phone book, maybe cruise by their houses, and then he'd return home. He would call Cherylee soon, talk to her, let her know he was all right—and that it was nearly over.

The visit with Keubler stayed with him, and he realized that he'd underestimated him. It wasn't hard to imagine Keubler taking advantage of you if he could, and that made it difficult for Peter to assume that he would help him, especially like this. He could have told Peter to go to hell, or worse yet, he could have brought the police. Robin had doubted him, whether he could be trusted, as things had moved along in the later stages, as vandalism and even occupying buildings began to seem tame. But he never turned on them; he'd been one of them too. Just because his motives were self-serving now didn't mean that he wasn't also helping Peter. Keubler had more risk, and more to lose, than Peter, whose life had already disintegrated.

Peter decided not to go to Brother Luke. It seemed like a needless risk for him, and also for Keubler. He had no need to go there now, but hearing his name made Peter regret not asking Keubler about Terry Finnegan. He might still be alive too. Peter had also wanted to ask about Susan, and he'd thought of it while they sat in the diner, but it seemed transparent, as if he might even try to see her, and he knew, too, that by not asking about her, he was concealing more than just curiosity. Perhaps being here and submersing himself in the past fed the long-buried regret and desire that was also part of the awful sense of loss that he carried for so long, and now, rather than purging himself, he seemed to be nurturing these feelings. Still, he hadn't so lost himself in the past that he would do anything more foolish than he'd already done by coming here. Seeing his effect on Keubler was lesson enough. Besides, none of it could be changed. And trying to touch too many things would just tarnish them and lead him off course. He knew what he had to do next. Keubler had given Peter what he was comfortable giving him. It was more than Peter had a right to expect, and it was enough.

As he watched the nighttime pass in the window, a car pulled into the Hardee's lot, and a man went in the back door and lights brightened the windows, though the highway sign remained dark. Another car slowed on the highway and came to a stop in front of the apartment building before it turned into the lot. An old car, maybe an Oldsmobile, late 80s, rusted, sitting low, lumbering and rumbling deeply with muffled music and a faulty exhaust system. Its lights dimmed and the music went off as it cruised the front of the building, and with the car still moving, a kid in oversized jeans and a baseball hat emerged from the passenger door and hustled alongside, peering into the parked cars. Peter's was still loaded with most of his gear, and when the kid approached it, he signaled to the driver that he'd found the mother lode. He smashed the driver's window before Peter even realized he was carrying a hammer. As Peter fumbled with the window latch, the driver got out and smashed the rear window, and the pair began throwing all they could grab into the trunk of their car. Peter finally got the window open and shouted, surprising himself as his voice echoed across the lot. They each grabbed another armload, piled back into their car, and squealed out of the parking lot, rounding the curve on the highway with their lights still off. All that remained of them by the time Peter got outside was the distant roar of their engine.

The Jeep was trashed, with broken glass and cookware and clothing strewn about the car and pavement. And he now realized that with the racket, the police might already be on the way. He ran back upstairs and gathered his things, and with his sleeping bag slung awkwardly over his shoulder, he stumbled back down and out to his car. Jagged glass lined the driver's side window. Fragments and shards covered the seat and floor. He cut the heel of his left hand hastily sweeping off the seat, a painful, sharp slice just above his wrist. Wincing and groaning, he shook out a filthy rag and wrapped the hand, and then climbed into the driver's seat. Glass crunched under his feet as he backed out, and the wind blew through the broken windows. He wore only a sweat shirt and he shivered as he drove with his hand still wrapped in the rag. He thought some glass might be embedded in it.

He headed the opposite way as the thieves, driving through the empty streets of Groenkill in the gray pre-dawn quiet, hearing his engine's rumble echo from the dark storefronts, and wondering if a local cop would suddenly appear from a side street. Then he drove north on Route 9, taking the by-pass around Poughkeepsie and crossing the Mid-Hudson Bridge in a thick, dense fog. He saw nothing of the river. The ponderous silver-gray struts alongside the road were a blur in his headlight beams. A few cars passed him east-bound—headlights emerging from the fog and whishing past almost to within arm's length—perhaps on their way to an early shift somewhere in Poughkeepsie. He was across the bridge in minutes and rushed around the bend enclosed by hills on the west side of the river, and as the bridge receded behind him, he recalled the night he took Susan out on the walkway.

They had gone to a party at nearby Marist College, where Susan had a friend, and later, much later, when the party had run down and they'd gotten bored, they left, still brimming with energy. The bars were closed, and it was too early for breakfast. They just wanted something to do, and as they started south on Route 9, Peter saw the bridge and exclaimed, "Hey, let's go out there!" He thought for sure she'd say he was crazy, but she surprised him; she brightened. She didn't even ask if it was allowed or if it was dangerous. Instead, her smile expanded with the delight of discovery and adventure. They parked on lower Main Street and tromped through the grass alongside the ramp up to the bridge. It was a cool autumn night, and the wind swept down the river from the north, stiff and cold. They locked elbows, fearful and excited, leaning into the blustery wind as it rushed and swirled around them. They were the only pedestrians, and they were isolated from the few cars that passed on the other side of the massive struts criss-crossing the length of the bridge. They passed through an ominous stone tunnel and when they emerged, the expanse of the bridge and walkway lay before them, with only the railing between them and the dark, empty void on the other side.

At the center of the bridge, they leaned on the railing, tentatively at first, testing its strength, and then they looked down into the blackness. They couldn't tell if they were seeing the river or just the vast emptiness between them and the water. There was no moon, no light on the water from anywhere. Leaning into the void thrilled them. They huddled and peered into the darkness and laughed and kissed. "This is what I like about you," she said. "What?" he asked. "That you would think of this, that you like adventures. I would never have come out here without you." "Somebody else might have suggested it." "Nobody else would." She kissed him again, and he thought he'd never been happier and could never want more than to be here, hundreds of feet above the cold, dark water, inches away from oblivion, wrapped inside her warmth and their shared desire. He hadn't thought of that night in many years, until now, as he sped away from the bridge, with his hand throbbing and his chest and shoulders shivering and tears streaming along his cheeks.

Soon, it was fully daylight, and he crawled painfully through Kingston in rush hour traffic. On the north side of the city, he found the traffic circle where he remembered it, near a Thruway entrance ramp, the same place where the group ate after they graffitied the overpass, where, indeed, they took the idea from the traffic loop and became The Circle as they joined their hands at a corner table and vowed to stay together until they could end the war and bring change to the country.

He pulled off the road and parked beside a semi-trailer that idled while the driver slept or ate breakfast. The truck shielded him from the traffic. His hand was pulsating with pain; broken glass was all over the inside of the car; and he was uncertain of what attentions he might have drawn back at Keubler's apartment building. The cut was long and deep enough to require stitches, but he found no glass in it. He tore a strip from a tee-shirt and wrapped his hand tightly. Going to a hospital never occurred to him. It would heal, he decided. There didn't seem to be more to it than the pain. Cleaning the glass out of the car and sorting what was left took the next hour, most of it spent picking jagged shards out of the windows. The thieves had gotten his cooler, his tent, a couple of bags of dirty clothing, and some cooking utensils. They'd also gotten the bag with Susan's CDs, and Peter smiled wryly at the image of them playing one. They were probably long done cursing their foul luck and tossing away what they'd gotten from him.

The car was still a mess when he'd done as much as he could without a brush or dustpan, and he was angry and disgusted, wondering why this had to happen now, right now, just as he was almost ready to turn back. Maybe it was best to be rid of the junk. And the clothes. Like molting. He'd find a Salvation Army store. At least the money Keubler gave him was still in his hip pocket. Right now he was hungry. He looked over the cars in front of the diner. No cop cars, marked or unmarked. After some breakfast, he'd decide whether to go see Brother Luke. He couldn't drive around with the windows broken out, and after rushing off with all that chaos behind him...well, he didn't know what any of the residents might have seen, or what they might have told the cops.

Chapter 16

Gelatinous fat coated Luke's fingers. He sniffed at a plate of sliced ham. Easily two pounds left. Such a waste to throw it away, but what else could he do? Someone had come down for a snack and left the meat out. Maybe Brother Clement. The plate was room temperature—might have been here for hours. He'd put the mustard away and left the meat out. Streaks of grease and mustard zig-zagged across the stainless steel counter. Luke tore off a piece and sniffed it. Maybe all right. He ate it. Tasted okay. He covered the meat with the crinkled greasy plastic wrap that had been on it until Brother Clement's snack and put the plate back in the refrigerator.

Before he could wipe the counter or wash his hands, Brother Francis's hoarse voice echoed in the stairwell at the back of the kitchen. "Luke! Brother Luke! You down there?"

"Yes, Francis."

"Luke! You down there?!"

Luke called over the running water. "Yes! Yes, I'm here!" Francis was hard of hearing. Even face-to-face conversations required a lot of repetition. Luke soaked a wash rag and wiped the counter.

"Luke! You there? Come up here quick!"

"Be right there," he said.

Brother Francis called again, his voice now drifting away, looking for Luke elsewhere.

Up on the loading dock, Luke saw him shuffling down the driveway, shoulders scrunched, his hair thick and white. Luke called, and Francis heard him now and then pointed to the vegetable garden, where Brother Artaud was flailing his arms and arguing with a man standing in front of a car. Luke started in a trot toward the garden.

"*Va t'en! Va t'en!*" Brother Artaud shouted. "*On n'a plus rien à vous donner! Va t'en! Allez*!"*

He had backed the man up to the driver's door, and the man seemed to be trying to reason with him, which Luke knew was useless. Brother Artaud had almost completely given up speaking English. Still sometimes, over dinner, when Luke addressed him in the French he had learned from him over forty years ago in a classroom just down the hall from the dining room, the old man would smile and quietly correct him in his thick English, "Use the imperfect subjunctive...*que nous finissions.*" Brother Luke was still his student.

Luke stepped breathlessly in front of Brother Artaud without greeting Peter and said, "It's all right, Brother. It's all right." The frail old man hacked a phlegmy cough and allowed himself to be walked along a grassy path toward a statue of the Virgin Mother decorated with small tricolor flags.

Peter heard none of what they said, only the calming voice of Luke and the assenting mumbles of Brother Artaud, punctuated once by an outburst, and followed by another cough and then the appearance of an overused handkerchief.

When he returned and Brother Artaud was kneeling in the dirt and pulling weeds, Luke said, "I'm so sorry. He's slipping all the way back to before the war. Hard to believe, isn't it? He thought you were his father's landlord before the Germans came. If his parents hadn't sent him to the brothers, he would have been shot along with them. His father never even tried to conceal his hatred for Germans. He was re-enacting an incident between his father and the landlord." Luke gazed at Brother Artaud as he narrated the story and then interrupted himself. "I'm sorry. Can I be of service?" He noticed the bloody cloth on Peter's left hand now. "Oh, you're hurt! And your car! Oh my! Was there an accident? Let me take you inside and look at that."

"It'll be all right," Peter said. "I'm sorry if I surprised you. You probably weren't expecting me today."

Luke looked puzzled for a moment and then said "Ah! So you're the visitor from Larry Keubler. Yes, that's no problem. Things are very informal here. Now, we have to take a look at that hand. What happened? Oh," he hesitated, "I'm getting ahead of myself. We don't get many visitors. I'm

* "Get out! Get out! We have no more to give you! Get out! Go!"

Brother Luke, and that was Brother Artaud, and this is Brother..." He looked around and now saw Brother Francis back at the loading dock, watching them. "Oh, over there. That's Brother Francis. And what's your name?"

"Larry didn't tell you who I am?"

"No, he just said it was an old friend and that you needed a place to stay and..."—Luke squinted at Peter, studying him, and continued—"... he didn't say much more than that. He said that...well, he thought an environment like ours might be helpful to you right now. It's very quiet here, and we're very spiritual. These men have done God's work all their lives. I always remind myself that this is their last stop before they journey on to be with Our Lord, so I do what I can to make things comfortable for them. But we welcome visitors from our friends, and we're very fortunate to consider Larry among them. He and Shirley have been very generous, very helpful. Now, here I am going on and on, and you do look like you could use some rest and maybe something to eat. I talk too much sometimes. You'll find that about me, but then, conversation here can be a little... routine." He studied Peter and looked over the car as he spoke, and now he paused and said, almost a question, but not quite, "Now, tell me your name."

"Peter."

"Peter?"

"I'm Peter Howell, Brother Luke. Do you remember me?"

"Peter...Peter Howell!" Luke's eye widened. "You?"

Peter nodded.

Luke peered into the worn face before him, trying to find in it the face of his student from so many years ago. Deep creases were furrowed into Peter's cheeks, and puffy shadows swelled beneath his eyes. His hair and beard were ragged. If it were possible to wear your soul on your face, Luke thought, this is how despair would look. "Peter!" he gasped.

Peter's head fell as he shook it and sighed. "I thought you knew, Brother Luke. I thought he told you. I should leave. I wasn't going to come here at all, but then..." He waved his good hand at the car.

"What happened?"

"Some punks...a smash and grab."

"And your hand..."

"The broken glass...look, you could get in a lot of trouble."

"Nonsense! How can I get in trouble for helping someone who's hurt? Our Lord never asked the sick and needy what they might have done before he helped them. Oh, I have thought about you many times, and… then there was news about you, about your being found after so many years! We only get the Albany TV stations, and the brothers don't want the news. They like the Mets and *Jeopardy*. Father Daniel is very good at *Jeopardy*! But, oh…I'm such a talker. I never knew what happened to you. I prayed for you, but to have you standing here now after all these years! Yes, well, we have to get you settled inside. It'll be lunchtime soon. We're not very formal, just a little sandwich buffet. Everyone helps themselves. I'll get you set up in a room and you can clean up, and…"

"Brother Luke, what about the others? Is there anyone here who'll remember me?"

Luke pressed a finger on his nose while he took a mental inventory of the residents. "You know, Father Alfonse passed away about…it's six years ago now. He's buried here in our cemetery. And there's Father Daniel… well, no, he was in the Philadelphia province, and Brother Clement…no, he taught at St. Helen's and then at the college, but that was after your time…and Brother… well…"

"What? Who is it?"

"I'm not sure. It's so long ago. Was Brother Joseph in your time?"

"Brother Joseph Stedman?"

"Yes."

"I should leave right now."

"Now wait, Peter, wait! Things aren't like that. He's very, very old, and there's senility. You know, he has the Alzheimer's. It's very sad really. He was so sharp, so lively, and now…well, he can't even recall what he had for breakfast some days. He's quite different. He's even smaller than he was. It's such a sad thing about old age, how the bones just seem to shrink. I can't imagine he'd even recognize you, Peter. You know, he taught so many students. And…well, all those things happened so long ago…it wouldn't mean anything to him anymore. Trust me, it'll be all right. He's the only one. The others are from other schools and missions. You really should stay with us for a while. Please, Peter, let's go inside, and you can get settled and get that hand cleaned up. You'll be safe here."

Peter gave in, thinking at most it would be for a night or two. Getting the glass replaced would be expensive, but he thought he could buy some heavy plastic and duct tape, and at least vacuum out the car.

The residence was but one section of a large brick building that circumscribed a courtyard of stone walkways and flower beds with sprouts now pushing through the moist black dirt. Brother Luke told him that all of the gardens were Brother's Artaud's province. Peter recognized the familiar design of the maroon brick walls and mortar casing around the portals from the original buildings at the college.

Luke led Peter past a chapel and rows of empty classrooms at the center of the complex and around to the dormitory, a three-story building where the brothers occupied the main floor.

"The dining room and kitchen are on the other side, across the courtyard," Luke said, and he added, "Most of this is all closed up now. So much space. It costs a fortune to heat. Well, we have the retreats from time to time, but I don't know what will happen to all this. It's so beautiful. They're such marvelous old buildings, and the property is hundreds of acres, most of it still wooded."

As Peter looked around, admiring everything for Luke's benefit, he now wondered if Keubler's generosity toward these old clerics had more to do with real estate than philanthropy.

Luke led Peter to a room in a vacant wing just beyond the hall occupied by the residents.

"Brother Francis's room is on the other side of the door that separates the wings," Luke said. "He likes to be near the bathroom. Oh, yes, you'll have to use that bathroom because the water's turned off in this hallway. The pipes freeze with no heat down here. Sorry Peter, it's either no heat or lots of company. I'll bring you some extra blankets, and I have a box of clothes for the needy. You can take whatever you want. It's all been laundered. The days are getting warmer, but the nights are still cold. I remember getting snow storms in April when I was young, but we haven't had weather like that in many years. Here, see this doorstop. Make sure you leave the door ajar when you go between the wings. Brother Francis likes the draft on the hallway. He says it's too stuffy when the steam heat goes on. You never came to the novitiate, did you Peter?"

"No, I never did."

"Brother Francis was my math teacher here. He's still very sharp with numbers. He's got Parkinson's now and has trouble with his hands. His hearing seems to be going, but not all the time." Luke chuckled and continued, "He's a good man, a very holy man. You could always get extra points on your homework if you put J-M-J on the corner of the paper."

"J-M-J?"

"Jesus, Mary, and Joseph."

Peter fidgeted with the wrap on his hand and looked around the room as though he'd find something he needed.

"Oh!" Luke exclaimed. "Here I am carrying on, and you're standing in front of me bleeding. Let's take care of that now. I'll be back in a moment."

While he was gone Peter located the hallway exits and looked out the windows in his room and the one across the hall to get the layout. Luke returned with a metal tool box that turned out to be the first-aid kit. He took Peter into the bathroom and unwrapped the wound. "Oh my! This needs stitches, Peter."

"Not possible. Not unless you want to do it."

Luke studied his hand and said, "Mmm, I see. Well, we'll do what we can then." He washed the wound and used thins strips of tape to pull it shut and then dressed it, chattering all the while about the residents, their eating habits, a bobcat they'd seen recently, and then sometimes clicking through his teeth, "Tstch, tstch, tstch!"—which seemed an all-purpose expression of dismay about everything from the severity of Peter's wound to the terrible circumstances of his arrival to the demise of life as Luke and the other residents had once known it. "That's as well as I can do, Peter. I'll give you a bottle of aspirin. I'm sure it's painful."

"Not so much now."

Back in Peter's room, Luke said, "Are you…how should…? Oh, I don't know how to ask…the others…what can I tell them about you?"

"I'm sorry, Brother Luke. This isn't fair to you. I'll be gone soon. You can just tell them I've had…alcoholism…family troubles…"

"Well, good. Now, we won't say that you attended the college—or any of our schools. They'd be on that in a heartbeat, asking about your teachers and…I know! You could tell them you went to school in New Paltz, or better yet, that you moved away to…wherever…Kansas? Is that where you've been?"

"It's okay, Luke. Lying doesn't suit you very well. I've had a lot of practice."

Luke smiled and nodded. "Well, then, Peter, tell me how you are. You look awful. I'm sorry, but it's true. I do talk too much sometimes. And the car, you were robbed?"

"They didn't get anything valuable." He paused, trying to avoid talking about himself, and asked, "So it's just you and the old brothers here?"

"Nobody else, Peter. We don't get many visitors. An occasional retreat, like the group from the college that just left, and that was only a few. Some family members come, but there aren't many still alive. No one here ever got married or had children, so there's no one else. Now, you look exhausted. Maybe you'd like a shower and some rest. Can I bring you a sandwich?"

"No, but..."

"What, Peter?"

"What happened to Terry?"

Luke sighed and sat beside him on the bed. "He served his term in prison. He got nine years, the same as Larry, but the parole board released him a year early. Still, it was hard on him. He was not suited to that sort of life, you know, to be among some of the people there. I went to see him as often as I could...a federal prison in Pennsylvania. I took his mother too, but the distance...it wasn't easy. His father never forgave him for the bond money they lost. It nearly cost them the house...but his father...it was his pride even more than the money. But Terry studied and he counseled other prisoners. He taught reading and writing...so many of them, you know, they can't even...oh, well, he prayed and studied for the seminary. He also mastered Latin and Spanish. It's truly amazing! He translated several books of *The Aeneid* and some of *Don Quixote.* Wonderful translations! I hope he'll finish them someday."

"Where is he?"

"He joined the Maryknolls when he got out, and now he does missionary work in San Salvador. He's been there for the past three years. He's been all over Central America. I get a letter from him once or twice a year."

"It's what he always wanted, isn't it?"

"Peter, I think much of the good he's done came out of his personal suffering. His sorrow is with him every minute of every day. God's miracles come in strange forms, don't they?"

"I suppose they do."

"Maybe you'd like some rest. Don't worry about anything right now. Just get some rest." He patted Peter on the shoulder and left him alone.

Peter dropped his shoes on the floor and threw himself back on the bed, intending to close his eyes for a few minutes, but it was nearly dark when he was awakened by a sonorous chanting that seemed to resonate from the walls. A familiar sound. The same vespers music the Celixine brothers had sung in the college chapel when he was a freshman and the music echoed across the campus in the evening. He hadn't heard that melody in all the years since then. The Latin verses surrounded him:

Tantum ergo Sacramentum
Veneremur cernui,
Et antiquum documentum
Novo cedat ritui;
Praestet fides supplementum
Sensuum defectui.†

He listened for a few moments, surprised that these geriatric men could sing with such strength. Then he realized that he could use the shower alone while the residents were in the chapel.

The service was still underway when he had dressed, putting on one of the clean sweatshirts that Luke gave him, and he found his way to the courtyard outside. In the chilly, damp April air, he wandered outside the compound along the wooded road that led to the highway. Brother Artaud's flower beds smelled of moist, freshly turned soil. The grinding engine of a barge or ship on the Hudson vibrated through the dense, budding maples and oaks.

When the music ended, he walked back through the courtyard and found the dormitory locked. His knock on the heavy wooden door had all the resonance of tapping on a seat cushion. He tried again and listened, but no one came.

It was dark outside the courtyard, and within, only two dim bulbs were lit, one at the gateway and the other at the main door, near the chapel. A stained glass panel over the door glowed with an image of Saint Celixine teaching Indians in a meadow filled with flowers and grazing deer. That door was locked too. Peter tried knocking, but again no one heard him. He started around to the dock entrance, where he'd gone in this morning with Luke, but just then the side door opened and Luke called his name.

"Over here!" Peter called, and he stumbled through the shrubs toward Luke's voice.

"I looked all over inside for you," Luke laughed. "Shouting into the darkness was my last resort."

---

†*Down in adoration falling,*
Lo! the sacred Host we hail,
Lo! oe'r ancient forms departing
Newer rites of grace prevail;
Faith for all defects supplying,
Where the feeble senses fail.

"I was just getting some air. I didn't realize I was locked out."

"Well, it's not like there's any crime here, but with so many doors and windows, it's hard to keep track of what's open, so we just keep it all closed. This door is unlocked all day, and the one at the dock too. We're just sitting down to dinner. Come inside. By the way," Luke whispered, as they went into the dining room, "what's your name?"

"Peter St. Clare."

"Ah, that should be a hit."

Luke guided Peter to a place that had already been set for him and then announced to the table, "Brothers, this is an old family friend of mine, Peter St. Clare. He'll be joining us for a short visit."

There were seven men already seated and passing platters around, and they all looked up and nodded. Several smiled and offered "Hello Peters." Peter shook hands on each side of him, with Brother Clement and Father Daniel, whose hand was little more than a leaf on a corn stalk. He nodded and went back to arranging his napkin.

From behind Peter, a raspy, high-pitched voice announced, "St. Clare! Patron saint of TV. Imagine that! Hi, I'm Brother Brendan." He grasped Peter by the shoulder as if they had known each other for years and shook his hand. He was a squat man, with a large belly, a ruddy face, and a full head of white hair that was parted on one side and combed in a wave over his brow. As he took his place across the table, he asked, "Did you ever dream there'd be a patron saint of TV?!"

"No, I always thought she was the patron saint of music." As soon as he said it, he wished he'd kept quiet. He should have known her patronage, or just shut up.

Brother Brendan blew past this oddity as if Peter was a schoolboy who'd given the wrong answer. "That's a reach for her. Now, the telegraph, good weather, and laundry workers, those are in her domain, though I don't know how she got that last one. She got TV because she was too sick to go to mass at the end of her life so she had an image of the service hung on her wall. That was in the thirteenth century, so I guess the picture on the wall passed for TV. Hard to believe she's now overseeing *Seinfeld* and *Who Wants to Be a Millionaire?* Oh well, TV needs all the oversight it can get. Cecilia, she's music. Clare, she's also got gold workers and television writers, also eye disease. Well, brothers," he said to the table, "with all the cataracts and macular degeneration among us maybe we should have a mass for St. Clare. Anyone know what her day is?"

The group mostly ignored him. Only Brother Francis offered in a nasal tone, "August, I think. It was changed after Vatican II. Sometime in August."

While Francis and Brendan debated the saint's feast day, Peter was startled to find Brother Joseph Stedman staring at him from the farthest corner of the table. His face bore the remnants of his fixed look of incredulity, with his eyebrows arched high on his brow, but Luke was right. He was smaller and thinner, and he was bent over his place as if he might suddenly tilt into his food. Luke brought the bowl of mashed potatoes down to him, distracting him from Peter.

Food and plates passed busily around the table, but nothing had been consumed yet. When Luke finally settled at his place, the chatter stopped as if by a silent signal, like birds changing course in flight, and at once the group plunged into grace: *Bless us, O Lord, and these thy gifts, which we are about to receive from thy bounty, through Christ our Lord. Amen.* They prayed rapidly, but still enunciated each word. Their voices all found the same baritone pitch, and they intoned the words almost as if they were in Latin and the grace was being sung on a single note. Peter recalled the prayer, though he hadn't heard it in years. He didn't catch up until *bounty.* Then he quietly added *Amen* along with the others.

"And how long will you be with us, Peter?" Father Daniel asked.

"A day or so."

The priest nodded and began a rapid slicing and quartering of his meat.

"Luke, did you say Peter was from Kansas?" Brother Brendan asked.

Surprised, and wondering what else Luke might have said, Peter responded, "Yes, that's right."

"Never been there," Brother Brendan said.

He took a mouthful of food, perhaps expecting Peter to tell him about Kansas, but Brother Francis now said, "Brother Luke, don't forget we have to get the weather stripping tomorrow."

Peter now saw Brother Joseph watching him again.

Luke said, "I haven't forgotten." He turned to Peter, "We have to insulate some of those old windows in the hallway. The cold was just too much this year. Now, will anyone else's room need treatment?"

Only Father Daniel replied, "Mine. I might as well be sleeping outside."

The others continued eating. Brother Francis struggled with the encrusted cap of a mustard jar. "Let me get that," said Peter, and he added, "Maybe I can help. I used to do construction work."

"Oh, we'll be fine," said Luke, giving Peter a puzzled glance. "You should get some rest."

"I'll rest better after a day's work."

"Work's good for your soul, Luke," added Brendan. He seemed eager not to let the opportunity pass. "We'd be very grateful for your help, Peter."

Luke glanced once more at Peter and hesitated before saying, "We should check everyone's room in the morning before we buy the materials."

Brother Artaud now spoke up. "*L'étranger...est-ce que tu vas le laisser entrer dans nos chambres?*"[‡]

"*Il est venu pour nous aider,*" Luke said. "*Il est des nôtres.*"[§]

"*Pour aider,*"[¶] Brother Artaud corrected, grinning, offering an idiom.

"*Que Dieu nous aide!*"[**] Brother Joseph mumbled.

‡

The outing included Father Daniel and Brother Artaud, who had doctor appointments, and Brother Brendan, who simply enjoyed outings. After the breakfast dishes were cleared and the bathroom revisited, all five of them piled into the old Crown Vic and set off for the doctor's office and then Home Depot, where Peter also wanted to get the materials to repair his car.

They spent over an hour in the waiting room, and Brother Artaud was on a long bathroom visit when he was called, so they had to wait through another patient until he was finally taken. Peter browsed some magazines, but the place felt close and warm, and Brother Brendan's attempts to converse with him carried all over the room. He was jovial and eager for fresh conversation, but Peter was thinking about his family, especially Emma. The task had fallen to him about a year ago to take her to the doctor for a feminine issue, an appointment that Cherylee would have done but she was volunteering in Todd's classroom that day. So Peter sat in the waiting room with Emma, who was mortified by his presence, by him knowing why they were there, by being alive at that moment. They

‡ "The stranger...are you going to let him into our rooms?"

§ "He's come to help us...He's one of us."

¶ "To help out..."

** "God help us!"

were silent until Peter took up a celebrity magazine and asked, "What's a Bennifer?" Emma shook her head, scowling, ignoring him, but her scowl cracked into a grin when he asked, "Two legs or four?" The memory pressed on him now, and he told Luke he was going outside for some air. The group was hungry when they finally emerged, and they all went to McDonald's and sat in immobile vinyl chairs, staring in different directions at the TV monitors. Ronald McDonald smiled at Peter over Brother Artaud's shoulder.

In the Home Depot, Brother Luke tried to keep the little band together like a mother goose crossing a busy road with her young. They wandered the aisles in fits and starts, blocking shoppers, becoming distracted at bins of sale items, handling tools, kitchenware, metal flanges, anything within grasp. Brother Artaud had never been inside such a place, and he muttered in French as he took in the rows of lawnmowers and stacks of gardening chemicals. He picked up a leaf blower and turned to a small boy perched at the front end of his mother's cart like Leonardo DiCaprio on the bow of the *Titanic*. "*Est-ce que c'est pour chasser? Tu pourrais tuer un ours avec ça!*"†† He erupted in laughter at his own joke, which even Luke did not get, and his laughing morphed into a phlegmy cough that frightened both the child and the woman, who wheeled a u-turn and disappeared into the toilet aisle while he wiped spittle from his lips with a dirty handkerchief. Luke gathered him back to the gaggle, but now Father Daniel had stopped at a bin of night lights and said to Peter, "A few of these would be a good idea…for the bathroom and hallway."

Before Peter could respond, Luke said, "Father, we're blocking the aisle here." He herded them all to one side to let a flotilla of shoppers drift past as if a stiff wind had just caught their sails.

Brendan finally announced, "We'll be in here all day at this rate. Peter, you take the list. You were in construction, so you know what you're doing better than any of us. We'll wait up front."

Luke looked helplessly at Peter and said, "Do you mind? I'll meet you at the register."

Peter shrugged indifferently, took the list, and pushed the cart off into the vast store, which felt even closer than the waiting room. It was a near replica of the same one at home in which he'd logged countless hours and spent thousands of dollars. He knew his way through all the departments and knew what he'd find on each aisle. And what he found now were the materials and tools for all of the painting, repairing, yard work, and

†† "Is this for hunting? You could kill a bear with it!"

carpentry he'd done on his house over the years. In the plumbing aisle, he recalled laughing at Emma's horror when the toilet backed up and spilled over; in the lumber section he saw Todd, with his jaw clenched and eyes focused behind protective glasses, as he swallowed his fear the first time he braced a piece of wood and pushed it through the power saw; and in paint supplies, he heard oldies songs playing on a warm afternoon as he and Cherylee painted the living room and then rushed up the stairs on a lustful whim, pulling off their clothes and pouncing on the bed before the kids came home from school, while rollers and brushes soaked in the paint trays. He guided his cart past other carts pushed by people who had homes and names, who belonged somewhere, who belonged here, and he felt like a ghost walking among them. He threw a dozen boxes of weather stripping into the cart, selected the other items he'd need for the repairs, and then found the plastic sheeting and duct tape for his car, now angry at himself for offering to help these old men, for coming here at all to see Brother Luke, for squandering a day sitting in a doctor's office and eating at McDonald's while he'd left his family to who-knows-what kind of hell. He had to fix the car and leave. He couldn't delay any longer. He had to go home. He was sullen and withdrawn on the ride back to the residence. Brother Luke chattered with the others about their doctor visits while he drove and left Peter alone with his thoughts.

At dinner all the conversation was about the outing today and the impending repairs tomorrow. Peter began to see that Brother Luke, good-hearted and well-meaning as he was, did not have the skill even for a job this simple. Brother Brendan's eagerness for Peter to help now became clear, and even more so the next day. Luke was willing and energetic, but he didn't know a ratchet wrench from a putty knife. Little wonder that this chore had been put off so long. Peter soon found that more than weather stripping was needed. Some of the window casings had water damage and had to be replaced, which in turn meant that painting and staining would need to be done, all of which meant removing the blinds and drapes, which were broken and filthy. The brothers had stuffed towels into rotting sections of window casement; they had tacked sections of drapery to the walls to block the drafts; they had neglected leaks from aging gaskets in ancient steam heaters, which led to mold and rot in the floors. Brother Clement had even repositioned his bed to avoid rain splattering on his pillow through a broken window pane.

Still, Brother Luke insisted that Peter shouldn't worry about the brothers. He should just fix his car and go. But Peter had already pried rotten molding from the windows and pulled up sections of the floor, and he couldn't see how any of it would get fixed if he didn't stay. And so one day led to another, and then one week led to a second, with more trips to the Home Depot, and with several brothers displaced from their rooms while he repaired the windows.

For all his chattiness, Brother Luke said nothing to Peter about what his plans might be. Luke even wondered if Peter weren't perhaps offering a penance to the clerics by his labor, but nothing in Peter's demeanor suggested that was so. He was quiet and withdrawn, and as skilled at turning the conversation away from himself when anyone—mostly Brother Brendan—became inquisitive as he was at carpentry. Gradually the questions stopped and the talk turned to the day's work or the Mets' prospects or the correct answers on *Jeopardy*. But one afternoon, while Peter and Luke worked alone in one of the rooms, Luke asked, "What will you do next?"

Peter was squatting at the window, fitting a length of molding into place, and he paused, without looking up, as if he'd seen something unexpected outside. "I'm going back. As soon as this is done."

"What will happen?"

"I'll turn myself in, go to prison. What should have happened long ago."

"Have you...I don't mean to pry, Peter...you've been so generous... but I think about your...well, all that's going on with you...I think about it constantly. I can't seem to stop myself. I worry and pray, and I wonder about your family too. Have you been in touch with them?"

Peter pulled the molding away from the window, brushing sawdust from the edges and studying the grain of the wood, running his fingers on it. "No. I can't."

"Why not?"

"Even if I drive fifty miles to use a phone, they'll figure out...the FBI will...that I'm here in this area. They'll harass Keubler. They might even show up here. Besides, I don't want to call. I just want to go home and find a way to see them first."

"What about a letter?"

"The postmark will tell the same story. I've written dozens in my head. I ramble on about a thousand things, but I never put any of it down. Funny, too, considering all the writing I did back then. I thought I was so glib. But I don't even know what I'd say now, after all this time. I never should have run. Some days, I can't tell if I'm dead or alive. They're better off without me. It even seems selfish to want to go home, like I'd be doing it more for me than for them. Sometimes I think about going back to the bridge and just throwing myself in."

Luke took his arm in a firm grip, much firmer than his affable manner would have hinted. "Peter, you mustn't ever think that! You're one of God's children. Please promise me right now that you won't do that."

"I can't promise anything to anyone, Luke. I'm not even sure where I am each morning when I open my eyes, and I have no idea where I'll be when the day ends."

"Peter, it's so important for you to communicate with them. I know you miss them, and I have no doubt they're terribly worried. Do this for me…just write the letter and let me worry about mailing it."

"Maybe," Peter mumbled, and he put the molding in place and told Luke to brace it while he set the nails.

✣

Vespers was dead time to him. No hammering and sawing. He showered and walked the grounds while the old men sang. Luke said he'd be welcome in the chapel, but he never pressed Peter to come. The chanting permeated the building and courtyard, resonating from the stone walls and carrying easily through the trees, which had begun to leaf. At first, he found it oppressive, almost maddening, but as the tunes grew familiar, he found a liveliness, even vigor, in them. The notes seemed sharper and more defined than the melancholy sound he awoke to on his first day. One of the songs had a kind of dance rhythm, like a waltz, that he tapped out on his thigh until he realized what he was doing.

It should have been obvious to him that this was where Susan had found her inspiration, that the performance he sat through with Cherylee and the music he'd heard on her CDs began with these voices. She'd heard them, too, much more than he had. And she had absorbed them, rechanneled them, made them her own. But it wasn't until a combination of notes struck him one evening that he recognized the connection—just three notes as he came downstairs from his room while the music saturated the hallway, startling him as forcefully as if he'd seen her waiting at the foot of the stairs. He had to steady himself on the bannister. She might as well have been standing in front of him. There she was, in the music.

He'd seen some record albums in the reading lounge near the chapel, and now he went there. The stereo was probably twenty years old. It stood on a wire rack with a shelf of albums below it. Peter knelt down and fingered through them, and quickly found two of hers. Of course she'd be here—such an achievement by one of their own. He held her face in his hands now, with longer hair and a serious but doubtful look, as if the camera had surprised her, older than when he knew her, but still young, still fresh. The photo was as old as the stereo. He sat on the floor to read the liner notes and didn't notice that the vespers music had ended.

Luke was in the doorway before Peter realized footsteps were clattering through the hall. He recognized the album cover instantly. "Ah, Susan! I haven't listened to that in years. Such wonderful music! Would you like to put it on?"

"No...but what happened to her?" he asked before he could stop himself.

Luke squinted as if trying to recall, but then said, "You were...you and her..."

"It was just for a short time," Peter responded, and then, as if trying to shrug off his question, he added, "I never knew what became of her."

Luke folded his arms over his belly and stroked his jaw, frowning, reassembling images of Susan and Peter as students. He eased into one of the lounge chairs, leaning forward, and said, "I haven't seen her since she graduated. The alumni office has tried to get her to come back. Everyone is so proud of her...and to have such a famous graduate. But she never has. I don't understand it. I've heard nothing of her for years, but the last I knew, she was teaching music at a small college in Maine. I couldn't even tell you which one, and that was years ago, like I said. But you..."

"I never knew, that's all. It was nothing, Luke. Just for a few months. She had a better path to follow than I did."

Luke paused, shaking his head, and said, "No one but the Lord knows where our paths lead. But..."—he slapped his hands on his knees—"...I have to get dinner for the brothers. Please stay and enjoy the music. There's time before dinner."

Peter nodded and continued reading the album liners in silence until the dinner bell rang, and then he put them back on the shelf.

Chapter 17

"We will not be defeated."
—President Richard M. Nixon,
announcing the American
incursion into Cambodia.

Thursday, April 30, 1970

As Susan climbs out of her VW Bug, she might as well be stepping into the polluted Hudson, so fetid is the air that hangs over the desolate alleys, run-down buildings, and gritty bars of the warehouse district. Long ago, just a few blocks from the newspaper office, the wharfs bustled with steamboats and barges loading bricks and grain and livestock from the brimming warehouses. Trucks, horse-drawn wagons, and people hurried this way and that on the streets. Now…an occasional tug lays over while its crew ties one on at a bar near the wharf, and the buildings that aren't abandoned have been converted to low-rent apartments and offices or let out for storage.

The day is sunny and warm, but the noisy highway overpass drapes a shadow over the street. Inside, Susan's footsteps echo on the dirty tile floor and creaky wooden stairs. She steps over a greasy splotch of something rotting on the first landing.

Two more flights.

The pungent scent of marijuana thickens as she climbs.

It occurs to her more than once to retreat down the stairs—to get back into her car and drive away. Her world is so much the opposite—the very opposite—of this place. She likes brightness, fresh smells, wholesome food—and clean stairways with *lots* of light. She pulls her hand back from the banister, imagining the hands that have touched it. This was a bad idea.

Chatter and laughter echo through the frosted glass of an office door. File drawers slam shut.

She's seen Peter on campus, but never out of his car. He's still suspended. She knows he was looking for her—knows it because he always managed to find her, and then she would turn away, ignore him, head in the opposite direction, pretend to be having a gay conversation with whoever was nearby. The semester is nearly over. She graduates in a couple of weeks. But her senior recital is tomorrow night and she wants to invite him—an offering, a gesture of friendship. She wants to part well. She even entertained a daydream of him celebrating with her and her parents over dinner, though now, this dark and filthy place reminds her it was just a daydream.

A loud, barking laugh breaks her reverie. Voices emerge from an office upstairs. Robin's voice. What to do? Well, she's come this far. At least Robin won't be in the office when she gets there. But they'll pass in the hall. Oh, they'll see each other anyway. She'd look even more stupid scampering back out of the building. She stiffens and marches upward. At the top of the stairs, Robin glances at her and smirks, but says nothing. Susan doesn't recognize the other woman. She's certain that the eruption of laughter as they descend is about her.

Che Guevara guards the office door with an automatic weapon. Above him, a handwritten sign on the transom proclaims, "*The Word* is the Truth and the Truth Starts HERE!" The office is laid out like a railroad car, rooms strung along a narrow hallway. A haze of tobacco smoke hangs like fog, but she now realizes that the marijuana smell didn't come from here. It had receded as she approached the door.

The place is lively and busy—and loud. Paul McCartney prayerfully sings "Let It Be" through bursts of radio static. A couple of students huddle over a typewriter and ignore Susan, while somewhere down the hall another typewriter rattles like a machine gun. She hesitates and then wanders through, looking in offices along the way. A burly, long-haired man pounds the machine-gun typewriter. Next door, several people crowd around a table covered with posters and newspapers. They look up expectantly when she appears. "Peter Howell?" she asks. A girl she knows from school smiles and points down the hall.

In a small office at the end of the hall, she finds him with Simon, who sees her first. "Susan, what a surprise!" His tone is warm, but bemused. She didn't know what to expect—sarcasm, silence. She'd risked more than she realized coming here.

Peter now turns, rising, a hesitant smile glimmering. He musters

"Hi" with an upward lilt as she steps inside, surprised at how pleasant the office is, with warm, fresh air from three stories above the street drifting in through an open window.

Simon lopes around from behind the desk. "I gotta run down the hall," he says, heavily, humorously, and then, over his shoulder, "Good to see you again, Susan." And she says, "You too," to the empty doorway, which feels like a strange thing to say to him, but things seem different today. Maybe it's even good to see him again. Maybe she can leave on good terms with everyone. Well, almost everyone.

She plunges ahead. "You look better," she says. "The bruises have healed."

In fact, he looks *a lot* better. His skin has color, his hair is brushed, his clothes are clean. He shaved his beard, though he kept the mustache and sideburns, and he looks bright, confident.

"How are you?" he asks.

"Okay, I guess. Almost done."

"Yeah," he says faintly. School seems distant. "I don't think I'm going back. I don't know what's gonna happen yet."

"What about the draft?"

"Oh, the deferment's gone," he chuckles, "out the window with the suspension. Doesn't matter, though. They already sent mail. To my house. You should have heard my mother on the phone."

"When?"

"I don't know…a month ago. Doesn't matter. I'm not going."

"What will you do?"

"Maybe Canada. Don't know yet."

Susan's daydream of Peter sitting at a table with her father, the proud World War II veteran and active member of the American Legion and the Knights of Columbus, evaporates, but that was never really part of her plan. "I was thinking…"

"What?"

She tries again. "I was wondering…"

His smile interrupts her, rising slightly at the corner of his mouth, his lips sealed and his eyes discovering the forgiveness she's here to offer even before she's offered it. "Hey, wait a sec…I'm about done here for now. You wanna get some lunch?"

She's not hungry but she says yes, grateful to leave, grateful for his smile.

In the hall, John Fogarty wails *doo, doo, doo* through the static and watches all the happy creatures dance across his lawn.

A couple of doors down, Simon reads typewritten pages while the machine-gunner leans back in his chair, his arms draped on the armrests. A boxer between rounds.

Peter says, "Hey, man! See you later."

The machine-gunner stares at the typewriter and breathes through his mouth.

Simon nods, and from behind, as they head out the door, Susan hears him over the music, "Good to see you too, Susan!"

The neighborhood now seems less intimidating as she navigates the streets with Peter. Busier than it appeared. Traffic flows through. People come and go, mostly blacks. Was that it—what really bothered her before? Peter greets people along the way.

He takes her to the same café Robin brought him the day he met her, guiding them past the counter, wedging his way between the chrome backrests of the swivel stools and the tables lining the wall, to a table in the back, across from the coffee urns. Most of the counter stools are occupied. The din of conversation and cooking hovers over the place. It's crowded. Now settled, she looks around after a young black woman takes their order.

"Feels different, doesn't it?" he says.

"What?" Her feint is weak.

He smirks. "You know...I can see it."

She feels the warmth flooding her cheeks.

He smiles. "I'm glad to see you again."

"Me too...I mean, you too...oh, you know."

"I'm really sorry. I've wanted to tell you. I even went over to campus. You did so much for me, and then...well, I'm just sorry."

Yes, he is sorry. Her cheeks are still warm, but different warm now. This is too fast—too much and too fast. "You look better," she says. Didn't she already say that?

"I feel better, too. There's so much to do, and it feels like, I don't know, like we're getting ready for something, like something's gonna happen."

She recovers now. Conversation. Something to talk about. "You were right about Nixon. I've read your articles. You were right."

"Well, I wasn't, not at first. I had a lot to learn. It was like you said...I was just parroting things I'd heard. You were right about that."

"But you seem...different now. What happened?"

"A lot. It was...you know what? It was the look in their faces when they beat us up, especially this one pig. He was like a junkyard dog, just full of piss and hate, swinging so hard he was drooling. It was running across his cheek while he looked for new places to hit me."

"Oh God, Peter."

"No, I learned something then. I realized…I saw how scared they are."

"Scared?"

"It's true. They are. That's why they did that. Justice isn't their job. Our message is our civil disobedience, and they're just supposed to arrest us and take us to jail. But they're like mafia enforcers, you know, sending a message that this is what we'll get if we mess with the system. It's like we're all just actors in a play and most of us don't even know it, but when you lift the trap doors like we did, these Rottweilers are down there to keep the play going."

About four minutes—that's how long she figures it will take for Peter and her father to combust.

The waitress brings their food, and Peter looks at the sandwich and then at Susan. "I'm sorry," he says. "About everything. And now I'm preaching. You didn't come down here for a speech."

"No, it's interesting. *You're* interesting. Things have to change." She hears herself babbling. Before she touches her food, she says, "Why I came…I'm playing my recital tomorrow night. It's the last thing before I graduate. I wondered if you'd like to come. I just thought I'd ask." More babbling, not at all as she planned.

Perhaps not, but the effect is palpable. His gaze lingers as he absorbs the invitation, its import, that he truly is forgiven. "I'd like that…to hear you play. I will. I'll be there. I'd like that a lot."

"I'd like it too."

Yes, she would, to have him there when she plays. For now, that will be enough. Everything else is so confusing, so chaotic, especially him—now better, healthier, happier, yet doing she-knows-not-what. Wasn't he just talking about Canada? If only he—all of them—didn't have to be so extreme, so fixated. She just can't bring herself to think that breaking the law is the only way, but for now she just wants to set all of that aside, not think about it. It has nothing to do with right now. What matters is that she's here with him, that she'll play tomorrow night, and that if he's there, her playing, the music—it will all be complete, fulfilled. Beyond that, she can't think right now.

"So that's all you have left, then graduation?"

"That's it. Just the recital. I'm going to practice for a couple of hours this afternoon, and then…"

"Then what?"

"Oh, my mother and father will be here tomorrow."

"So, what's wrong with that?"

"Nothing…I don't think you'll like my father much."

"How do you know? Maybe I will. Maybe he just won't like me. Are you worried about that?"

Once again, blood pulses into her face. It's always bothered her that she's so fair-skinned—that she can't hide anything.

Peter laughs. "Don't worry. I'll be nice. I still remember how to consort with the silent majority."

"Oh, he's not silent."

"I'll bet your mother is, though. Let me guess. She's the long-suffering Irish mother, and your father's got all the opinions, but when it comes to the real decisions, the money decisions, nothing happens till your mother says so."

Susan laughs. "Well, she's not so silent either, but she does keep the checkbook."

"So what are you playing?"

"Something special. A surprise."

"Hmm." He folds his hands, touching his forefingers to his lips, and asks, "Do your parents know?"

She gives a tight shake of her head. "No, but it will mean a lot to them, especially my father. He was so supportive of me studying music. You know, I had a friend when I was little whose father wanted her to become a stewardess. He said it was the perfect job for a girl because you'd learn how to do your make-up and hair and take care of your looks. And you'd meet lots of businessmen flying everywhere. He even got her a little Pan-Am flight bag and a make-up kit. It was sick. But my father encouraged me to keep playing the cello. He always said if I loved what I was doing, everything else would work out."

"So not even a hint?"

"No, but it's something special. You'll see."

Her eyes have welled up, and he reaches across the table and puts a hand on hers, lightly, tentatively, yet his touch vibrates through her with the resonance of her cello's low C. She leaves her hand under his until he picks up his sandwich, and she dabs at her eyes with her napkin. "Oh, this is silly. I feel like such a fool. It's everything…the recital, graduating…

everything. I've practiced so hard for it."

"You'll do fine. I can't wait to hear it."

At her car, he asks, "Where will you be later?"

"I don't know. I have to practice some more, but I'm afraid of over-practicing."

"You need to take your mind off it. Let's get some dinner."

She barely allows an eighth rest. "Okay."

As she drives away, she feels as if she's tying together all the pieces of her life here, and this is the final loose thread.

That night, after a lingering dinner at an Italian restaurant in Peter's neighborhood, she lets him make love to her back at his apartment. Well, she wants to think she let him—but she knows that in the playful talk, the touches, and later the kisses, she encouraged him. She hadn't planned to, hadn't even considered the possibility that they'd land in bed that night when she went to the newspaper office or even when she agreed to dinner—and she knows, too, that this is the wrong time of month for her—but she is so completely happy tonight, with her music culminating in her final recital and with Peter seemingly reborn, that she surrenders not so much to him as to her own joy. Everything that matters to her fuses in a single moment, a tremor, a perfect chord.

And while they tangle joyfully in Peter's narrow bed to the rich harmonies of a Brahms symphony, President Richard Nixon goes on national television and announces to the world that United States troops have invaded Cambodia in pursuit of the Viet Cong. During the broadcast, he loses his place, clutching a sheaf of papers, and a dumbfounded nation learns that the United States has been illegally bombing Cambodia for over a year.

‡

Friday, May 1, 1970

It's after eleven the next morning when she returns to her dorm room and finds a note on the door. Her father's assertive script declares, "Mother & I arrived but can't check in at the Holiday Inn yet or it'll cost another day. Might as well get some lunch. Love, Dad."

They weren't supposed to arrive until late that afternoon. The tone sounds almost miffed at finding her gone. Or maybe she just feels guilty. She didn't expect to see them until the recital, and there's no reason they should think she wasn't here all night. Oh, what to do now? She needs a nap before she performs. She only dozed in fits in that little bed; the mattress is like a pile of cardboard. She pushes aside the clothing and books on her bed and curls under an afghan.

She's no sooner nuzzled her head into the pillow than the phone rings. An insistent ring. Her father's ring. As she reaches for it, she sees the clock...*four-thirty-six!*

Omigod! Is that right? Four thirty-six...P-M?!

A familiar gravelly voice: "Susan?"

"Hi, Dad." She squints at the clock. No mistake.

"We stopped by. I left a note."

"I got it, Dad. God, I fell asleep!"

"Hold on. Mother wants to say something." He talks off the phone while Susan frets. Then he's back. "Have you eaten something, she wants to know? Do you want us to come get you?"

"No, not now. Tell her I'm fine, Dad. I have to dress and get over to the music building. We'll go out later."

"Okay, honey. We'll see you there. Good luck!"

"Thanks, Dad. Bye."

Senior recitals have been going on all week in the orchestra room, with several students playing every night and maybe a dozen or two people to hear them, but her slot is special—the final performance of the week, and the longest. A piano student will perform a short program before she plays. Professor Ritchdorf regards her as the finest musician the school has ever graduated, and she's not alone in thinking so. The room will be full for her performance.

Susan finds her parents in the vacant orchestra room over an hour before the recital. She hasn't seen them in months, but she's too anxious for them right now—still unsettled from sleeping late when she wanted to practice, from rushing her shower and hair, from eating vending machine food instead sitting quietly over a bowl of soup. She needs to be alone. This isn't at all how she imagined it.

They both appear puzzled at finding the place empty.

After she hugs them, her father asks, "So where is everyone?"

"You're early, Dad. I'm sorry."

Why sorry?

And what difference does it make? Here they are, all three of them—right where they're supposed to be. All together. Everything's fine.

But she's so...frazzled, unnerved.

Her mother clutches her purse in both hands and wanders the room, admiring the tympanum and double basses, reading posters about music history, finding something to appreciate everywhere in the cluttered room, where music stands, a couple of dusty rolling blackboards with staves, and a second piano have been crowded against the walls to make room for extra seating. She's slightly taller than her husband, and she stands erect too, never hiding her height. Susan considers telling her about the new recital hall Professor Ritchdorf has been campaigning for, but there's no time now.

Her father wears his raincoat, though it's a beautiful evening, and carries a hounds-tooth fedora in one hand. Susan now recognizes how he's aged, slowed down. His greased wave survived the transition to gray hair, and the nearly perpetual smile on his face still endures, a fixture even when he's irritated or angry. But his world has shrunk since he retired. The people he knew from the insurance company, his clients, his friends, have also retired, moved to Florida, passed away. He still goes to the Legion and Knights meetings, but they've lost the familiarity that once gave him a foothold in the world.

"Did you check in?" Susan asks.

"Oh, we did!" her mother erupts, strutting back with a purpose, a story to tell. "But the room was in such condition. The bathroom…it was…"

"Now, Mother, we don't have to go into all of that right now."

Susan can't recall when he started calling her *Mother*, but he rarely calls her Kathleen in front of her.

"Yes," he says, "it's all fine. But what's going on outside? A lot of people out there."

"Nothing," Susan responds. "I guess I didn't notice. I was in a rush and came in the back way. Exams ended today. Everyone's probably celebrating."

"Raising hell, looked like to me, but that's no matter to us. You go and get ready and we'll make ourselves comfortable. Looks like we can have any seat in the house."

"Not the front row, Dad."

"Okay, not the front row. Mother, let's sit up near the window. We'll have some fresh air and we won't distract Susan."

She watches him climb the steps, though her mother hasn't budged. The decision about where to sit absorbs him. He starts down one row and then another, and then he looks back at them with a grin. "Mother, are you coming?"

At that moment, Professor Ritchdorf leans in from the faculty door. "Oh, Susan! There you are!"

"Anne, these are my parents."

Her father scoops his coat up from the chair he finally selected and retraces his steps down to the front of the room.

The professor wears a familiar white blouse, buttoned to her neck, with her eighth note pin and a small cross on a chain glittering on her breast. She appears agitated, distracted, as if she'd just come from an unpleasant department meeting, but she musters her smile and graciously meets Russell and Kathleen Mallory.

Now Susan worries that Peter will show up early, too. He's so unpredictable! He could walk through the door at any moment or not appear until the intermission. She told him she wasn't playing until later. She doesn't need these distractions right now.

The professor appears ready to run interference. Susan's father has engaged her in discussing some new method of music instruction he's heard about that was developed by the Japanese. The professor has opinions on this subject too. New soul mates bond.

Susan slips away as others drift into the room and find seats.

Finally!

She shuts herself inside a sound-proof practice room, toward which every nerve ending in her body has been urging her since she awoke.

She breathes. She rosins her bow. She tunes her instrument. She opens her music.

And she plays the familiar opening notes of the D-minor suite, a simple and mournful tune. She's been playing and studying Bach's Cello Suites for most of her life, and soon she will play the entire work publicly for the first time. She has dreamed of this day and worked toward it for years. Practice now absorbs her and carries her into the *allemande* and *courante*. A long time ago, her father—a non-musician himself, yet a man who loved music as much as any musician she has ever known—took her by the hands, after he'd dropped the needle on a recording of these suites, and led her through a playful ballroom dance as the music filled the room, and she heard something she wouldn't have heard if she listened to the recording a hundred times while sitting in a chair. Her head was barely higher than his waist, and she only had the skill to play a few passages, but the memory of that dance, of learning how this music could fill the spirit and liven the body, stayed with her throughout her life as she studied this work and returned to it. Now, soon, she'll play the Cello Suites for her parents, a tribute to them, her way of thanking them. And her way, too, of inviting Peter into her soul. She couldn't expose herself more if she stood naked before the audience that now assembled in the orchestra room.

She runs through other passages, plays some scales, and driven by temptation, wanders down the hall, which echoes with piano music. She peeks inside to see where her parents have landed and whether Peter has appeared. He's still not there.

During the break, while people mill in the hallway, she sips tea in Professor Ritchdorf's office and reads titles on the bookshelves. With only minutes until her performance, she's settled, ready—recovered from the earlier chaos. But now an unexpected sound rumbles over the hallway buzz. The window is open a few inches, and from outside she hears voices, many of them, talking, now shouting with rhythmic consistency, the sound of…chanting, just outside, on the quad. "No more war! No more war! No more war!"

Susan pulls the drapes back and watches in horror as hundreds of people crowd the lawn, with more pouring in from the football field parking lot and the main entrance to the campus.

Just then, Professor Ritchdorf opens the door and says, "Oh, good! You're here. Almost ready, Susan." But when Susan doesn't turn away from the window, she asks, "What is it? What's going on?"

The chanting is louder. The crowd moils on the quad.

"I don't know. Some sort of protest march."

"Oh, no." The professor's voice dissolves with recognition, even despair.

"What?"

Anne rushes to the window and pushes it up, leaning out, allowing the noise to invade the office. They raise their voices just to hear each other.

"What's happening?" Susan asks. "Did you know about this?"

"There was a rumor on campus today…and flyers, but no one knew if it would come to anything."

"Rumor?"

"About this…this protest. Oh dear, this is so much more than we imagined. There are hundreds out there. Oh…"

"But why? What's this about?"

"Didn't you hear…on TV last night…the president? We invaded Cambodia! It's all so much worse than we thought. Oh my! I better go inside." As she starts away, she says, "Susan, just stay here for a few minutes. Just wait. It'll be fine. But let's shut that." She returns to the window and pulls it down, and now, seeing the drained look on Susan's face, she adds, "It'll be fine, dear. We'll just wait a few minutes until things settle down." But even with the window shut, the noise continues to vibrate inside, rattling the panes.

Left alone, Susan watches the throng gather in front of Celixine Hall. Crowds surge over the quad, flowing like hot lava, smothering it in a searing rush. Signs are pumped and waved. On the narrow road along the far edge of the quad, campus security cars pull up with lights whirling as crowds swarm past them. The security guards remain in their cars and watch.

Too agitated to wait any longer, Susan hurries to the recital room, where most of the audience has gathered at the open windows overlooking the quad. With the crowd now just below the windows, the noise overwhelms the chatter inside. A couple of students in the recital hall lean out and call to their friends. The music department chairman comes and goes, as do several faculty members. When the chairman returns and tries to address the group over the din, no one hears him. Anne taps a baton on a music stand and says, "Everyone listen, please! Everyone!!" But her voice is drowned out by the screeching of a bullhorn.

Susan is numb as she realizes that after a lifetime of preparation, after years of learning this one piece, after all the work, her moment is vanishing in this chaos. Her mother puts an arm around her as they watch the spectacle, and her father attempts a stilted conversation with a nearby faculty member.

Now a familiar voice croons through the bullhorn. In the glow of the walkway lights, Simon stands on a balustrade above the crowd. Before him, from the steps of Celixine Hall to the darkness at the far edge of the quad beyond Driscoll Hall, the crowd swarms and gathers, many at the rear still chanting. But gradually, as he begins to speak, the shouts subside. The trees outside the music room partly block Susan's view, but it's not Simon she's trying to see. Peter never showed up, but she now recognizes a pale blue Jimi Hendrix tee-shirt that she had worn herself in his apartment. There he is, along with the rest of the group behind Simon. She didn't want to believe he'd be out there, but now she sees him through the rustling leaves.

Her father steps up beside her and declares, "Anarchy, pure and simple. Communists!"

But she says nothing.

And Simon's voice booms through the bullhorn. "Last night, we were insulted! Our intelligence was insulted! We watched bad theater by the acting company in Washington. Nixon couldn't even remember his lines as he recited that pile of bullshit about why we invaded a peaceful country! This government has lied to us, and its leaders should be turned out *now*!"

The crowd applauds and shouts, and he waits until they quiet themselves. "We have been told that this war is winding down. We have been told that the South Vietnamese will fight their own war. We even have a new word in the English language thanks to the lexicon experts in Washington...do you know what the word is? Can anyone say it?"

He pauses. Someone shouts, "Fuck Nixon!"

Susan feels her mother's arm stiffen on her shoulders.

Then Simon answers his own question. "*Vietnamization*!" The word rolls out slowly. "*Viet-nam-i-za-tion*!" he repeats, as if teaching them to pronounce it. "*Vietnamization!*" He lets the echo fade and continues, "That's right! The military establishment that runs this country has tried to confuse us with their garbled language, with their cartoon maps, and with fear...fear that Communists are about to overrun the world starting with an insignificant little place called Vietnam. Well, you know what? Vietnam would be better off with the Communists! Better off than having Agent Orange spread over its rice fields and villages and forests! Better off than having whole villages slaughtered by bloodthirsty troops! Who are the good guys? It ain't us!" And he shouts now, "*It ain't us*!" Which sends the crowd into a frenzy of applause and chanting.

He pauses again and restarts in a lower tone. "When you think about it, there's much more wrong here than this crappy lying administration. What are they, after all, but products of a system that for two centuries has consumed itself with conquest and manipulation and greed, all in the name of righteousness? We've heard all our lives how we're the good guys, how we stand for democracy, for fairness, for justice, but what is all that except propaganda? Let's look at the record. Slavery is gone in name only! A black man takes his life in his hands to order a cup of coffee in a diner in Mississippi or Alabama. The red men have been murdered in an organized system of genocide, while history books and Hollywood treat them like an infestation of vermin. The land has been raped and the water polluted so badly that there are probably ten kinds of disease you can get from skinny dipping in the Hudson. And our schools and universities are nothing but cogs in the military-industrial machine that runs this country, with no other purpose than turning out clones to run the bureaucracy and make the bombs and weapons and computers that the government needs to destroy the lives of peaceful Cambodians and Vietnamese!"

The crowd erupts in cheers, and he makes several false starts before continuing. "This school is no different! We all know where the money comes from. It's our good friends at Merval Corporation. And *their* biggest customer is...*who*? We all know that too, don't we? It's the Pentagon! Yes, it is! The largest, most aggressive military force on the planet depends on this place to produce workers and research for its operations. Well, it ends today...with the illegal bombing of a peaceful nation, with the revelation that tens of thousands of innocent civilians have died by this illegal act. We are occupying this building in the name of peace, and we will stay here until the president of this college and all its trustees either resign or agree to sever their ties with Merval!"

As he flourishes the key to Celixine Hall and pushes open its wooden doors, the crowd resumes its chanting and the lava flow bubbles once again to life, now pouring through the doors behind him, shouting, chanting, piling in, rushing the building.

The crowd on the lawn is so large and dense that police officers and security guards can't get through, so they remain at the edge, watching as the crowd surges forward, congested, packed together, flowing up the steps of Celixine and through the doors, all the way up to the fourth floor. Lights go on, windows fly open, banners and signs appear. From the shadows of the rooftop, a flag unfurls, a single gold star on a red and blue banner, the flag of the National Front for the Liberation of Vietnam.

The gathering in the music room is uncertain, frightened, wondering if this building will be invaded too. The chairman now announces that security guards will take them through the hallways and escort them out the building.

Susan packs her cello and music, tearfully, shaking with anger. She walks briskly ahead of her parents, around corners and down stairwells so familiar that she doesn't even think about which way to turn in the dizzying haze that envelopes her.

Outside, she waits for them to descend the steps into the alley. From the quadrangle on the other side of the music building, the noise swells up like ugly raving in a stadium after a bad call or a cheap shot.

Her father mutters about communists and agitators, while her mother watches others from the recital drift away into the darkness. Behind them, the security guards disappear as the door closes.

She is stunned, unable to choose which emotion to hang onto now—rage, despair, loss—yes, an overwhelming sense of loss. Her parents have been turned into frightened refugees in this chaos, when they should be listening to the music she has spent a lifetime learning. Instead they stand in this filthy, dim alley beside a dumpster, wondering if they might be murdered. Her moment is gone, stolen, not even stolen, just flicked away like a crumpled gum wrapper.

Chapter 18

December 2000

In an unfinished storage room downstairs, Peter built a workbench with a peg-board for his tools. It was often a busy and noisy place on weekends. The table saw's piercing, violent shrieks would startle Cherylee up in the kitchen, and a stained clock radio stuck on *2:09* would crackle with oldies songs, straining for a signal in this remote corner of the house. But now, in the gray glow of fluorescent lighting, an assortment of parts from projects finished and unfinished littered the workbench and shelves—toilet valves, gutter drainpipes, flooring tile, unopened wallpaper rolls—just as Peter left them.

Todd's model-building table was the only uncluttered section of the room. Peter built it years ago so Todd could work on models while he stained a chair or cut wood for a cabinet. Todd covered his ears at the high-pitched racket from the saw, but he liked the smell of saw dust—and he liked sitting at his own worktable while his father built something. He giggled when his father swore at the slip of a screwdriver that drew blood or the whirring of a drill that led to a stripped screw head. Usually it was "Shit!"—a low, hissing, involuntary gasp, almost a sneeze—but sometimes it was the F word. Peter would glance at the boy, and then his eyes would brighten and a tiny grin would appear. They shared the mischief.

The model table had been through several incarnations, beginning as a child-sized picnic table that appeared many Christmas trees ago for this very purpose, so that Todd and Peter could work together in the storage room. When Todd outgrew the colorful plastic table, Peter built a worktable with a light and shelves and a pegboard, just like his, and Todd helped him.

Todd's skill at building models had grown in the years since he sat at the plastic picnic table snapping together toy cars and boats. Model kits were always on his birthday or Christmas list. Whatever else he received, there was sure to be a model box, which consumed him before the sun had set on the day it appeared. He was so good at model-building that a hobby store in Hawkings displayed some of his handiwork, and the store owner occasionally gave him a model to assemble for display in the front window.

Peter chose the gift models for Todd, usually old muscle cars—Belairs, Firebirds, Camaros, Super Sports, Chevelles—cars with rear-ends jacked high off the road, chrome exhaust pipes running along the rocker panels, intake valves peering from the hoods like periscopes, thick tires and gleaming upholstery and stick shifts. Todd painted them in clever designs and finished them with the doors opened and the hoods up—displays that delighted Peter. Cherylee was happy because they were happy.

But Todd preferred military models. When he spent his own money or had a gift certificate, he bought a tank or destroyer or an F-16. In the year and a half since his father left, he had thrown himself into model building, and his collection of military models had outgrown the cars. The hobby-store owner encouraged him to enter contests and submit photos of his work to model magazines. He said Todd could even review new models for the magazines. Cherylee reminded him that Todd was just twelve. Todd only cared about getting another freebee.

As he worked on an Abrams tank on a cold Saturday afternoon in December, unaware that the plows had cleared the streets after last night's snowstorm and the other kids in the neighborhood were zooming down a nearby hill on their coasters, he studied the arrangement of tools on the pegboard over his father's workbench and listened to the rapid, almost breathless, sputter of a radio announcer.

Who else, to get back to my point, who else, is going to say it if I don't?! Not the liberals, that's for sure! I know, friends, that you have figured out the difference between the First Amendment and the perversions that liberals and the ACLU try to hide in the skirts of the Constitution. But we don't have freedom of speech so we can publish pornography and filth! We don't have freedom of speech so Americans can burn the flag! We don't have freedom of speech so criminals can hide behind their "rights"! No, we have it so we can speak the truth! And that's what you get from Melvin P. Gash. The truth! I like to think that what I'm really doing here each day is offering you a reflection of what you're already thinking, what you already know. I think of myself as a sort of Ben Franklin of the airwaves, just sharing the wisdom and insights that you already have in your hearts and minds. Think of me as your vocal chords. Together we'll continue our unrelenting search for truth, wherever it may take us, because, my friends—say it with me!—We Want To Know!

Todd listened and gazed at the tools on the his father's pegboard. He hadn't touched any of them since Peter left, though if he found a pliers or screwdriver on the workbench after his mother used them, he restored them to their places on the pegboard. He liked the pegboard's lack of symmetry, the randomness and functionality of the way the tools hung. Few belonged to any one set. None of the screwdriver handles matched, and the hammers, chisels, and wrenches, everything for that matter, were old and worn. These tools had built things—many things, things he would never see in places he would never go. Or maybe—he would go there and see them, but not even realize he was looking at something his father built. These tools had knowledge of his father; they had been in his hands; they had gone to faraway places with him; they kept secrets about him. His mother, the police, all those reporters—they were all looking for his father in the wrong places. The entire story was in the tools, if only someone could decipher it.

Todd stared at the peg board over the workbench and daydreamed while he waited for the glue to dry on his model. He studied the gadgets and half-finished projects, figuring out what his father was doing, what had broken that needed fixing, what improvement he was making to the house. There was the refill valve from the toilet (that was a mess, the day that backed up!), and the molding from after the new carpeting was installed, and the leftover hardware from the new cabinets in the laundry room. Also strewn about the storage room were assorted racks and bins and mailing trays from the business. All with a story to tell, but Todd couldn't fill in the gaps. It was like reading a mystery book with missing chapters.

The announcer ranted on in familiar strains:

Well, now, back to business! As you know (unless you've been visiting another planet), one of our main items for over a year has been to follow—no, it's not too much to say that we have assisted in—the investigation and pursuit of a fugitive from justice, one Peter Howell, a-k-a Peter St. John, who has been living under a false identity right here in the suburbs of Kansas City, in a self-respecting town in the heartland of America—in Hawkings, Kansas—a place built on Midwestern values, family values, where people go to church on Sunday, where children learn the importance of growing up in homes with a mother and a father and not some perverted two-mother or two-father homosexual arrangement…

Todd avoided asking questions about all that happened. Well, he just didn't like to ask questions in general—he didn't trust people to give him honest answers, and besides, you could learn so much more by keeping quiet and listening. Why ask? Kids in school were always asking questions that were answered in the book. Why would you ask a question and show the teacher that you hadn't done the reading? But then, even more amazing, the teacher would say, "Good question!" Like not doing the reading and then asking a dumb question made you a good student. Todd thought that if you eliminated all the dumb things people said, you could cut out half of all talking, maybe more.

He tried keeping to himself at school, but it wasn't easy. At first the taunting was so unbearable that he dreaded walking the hallway, going to his locker, and worst of all, gym. He ate lunch by himself, but one group or another would show up and the abuse would begin. There was one kid, at least, who wouldn't bother him again. Todd pounded the shit out of him in the lavatory when he called Todd's mother a whore and said he and his sister were just little bastards. The kid was bigger than Todd, but Todd attacked with such ferocity that he might have killed him if a couple of teachers hadn't lunged into the bathroom at the racket. In-school suspension was okay. You just sat all day in a little room. He wouldn't mind getting suspended again, and kids bothered him less after that. They lost interest as the luster of his father's story faded.

A couple of boxes in the shadows of the storage room overflowed with camping gear. Todd had known right away that stuff was missing from there. His mother never would have noticed if he hadn't said so. His hot cocoa mug was still there, in one box. He remembered spilling the fresh hot chocolate as he tried to balance his breakfast while seated awkwardly on a log. His father got irritated because he had to boil more water, and he said the smell would attract animals. He'd been cranky all weekend—mostly, it seemed, because of things Todd didn't do right. He failed to brace the tent when they were setting up and the whole thing came crumpling down; he snagged his fishing line and his father had to climb into a thicket of shrubs to untangle it. The strangest thing of all was that the trip later became this great memory—a memory that others didn't even share, like his mother and his aunt, who said what great outdoorsmen Todd and Peter were. His father didn't like camping, but he went anyway, went because of Todd. It was Todd's fault that they had a crappy time.

The TV went on in the family room. Emma. She came home almost every weekend this fall. Now she was home again, even though she'd just been home for Thanksgiving break a week ago.

Todd worked on the turret section of the Abrams tank, setting the Ma Deuce, the fifty caliber machine gun, at a different angle than the tank's main gun. The tank commander would be firing the Ma Deuce. The tank was taking fire on all sides. When it was done, Todd would mount the tank on a hill or bluff with scenery from his railroad train set.

...but like the snake in the garden, Peter Howell, a terrorist with a long list of felonies—pardon me, alleged felonies, for he never was brought to trial—has slithered among us, entering into a marriage, fathering children, starting a business, and even—oh! this is the final insult—running for office! That's right!—a seat on the school board, a position in which he might do untold harm, spread lies, perhaps even run his underground terrorist network!

The store room door flew open and Emma stood there. "What're you doing?!"

"Nothing. A model."

"No, I mean that garbage!" She found the OFF button and snapped it.

"Hey, I was listening!"

"You don't need to listen to that trash."

He turned back to the model, and she moved a box from the stool at the workbench and pulled it over near him.

"They were talking about Dad," he said.

"That's all they do is talk. They don't know anything."

She looked around. "It's so gloomy in here! How can you stay in here all day?"

"If I do this anywhere else, someone will mess with it."

"Who's gonna mess with it?"

"Like if Mom's cleaning."

"So what's that?"

"What?"

"The model."

He stared at the model and shrugged. "A tank."

"C'mon, I can see that. What kind?"

"An Abrams."

"God, Todd! We have to drag everything out of you."

He shrugged again, and Emma watched him. Music from MTV drifted into the storage room. Then she said, "It's just the same shit over and over again." And after a pause, she added, "But he's still ahead of them. He's out there somewhere."

Todd's grin encouraged her.

"There's no one else like us," she said. "Other people with problems get their own self-help group. Doesn't matter what...AIDS, booze, cutting, irritable bowels, whatever! There's always people out there with the same problem. But not us. We're like freaks or something...always waiting for something to happen that never does. And we don't even know what we're waiting for...Dad to appear, a cop to show up and tell us he's been arrested, or..."—she hesitated, skidding past the obvious example until she found another—"...or some suit to be standing at the door with a pile of papers, telling us we have to move. I don't know what, but something. Every time I get this outta my head for two minutes, someone comes up and says, 'Hey, you're that...chick, aren't you?' or 'Any word yet? Any news?' like I'm even supposed to know what they're talking about, like I owe them some fucking explanation. Jesus, I'm so tired of it! Sometimes I think about booking, you know, just taking a hike, but then I think I'll just end up the same way, going off and having to change my name." She looked at Todd. "Isn't that weird? It's like we're doomed to be fugitives, too, with fake names and nowhere to go, and then we'd go off and have families and their names won't be real either. We'll, like, spawn this whole race of fugitives with fake names. We'll probably need a special hand signal to recognize each other. Hey, maybe there's already a secret society out there! Maybe we're not the only babies from hippie-terrorists in the sixties. We should be looking for the others. We could start some sort of group or get a country of our own on an island where people would leave us alone."

She spun herself out, and he looked at her expectantly. "Are you gonna leave too?"

She shook her head. "No. Don't worry. I wouldn't leave you here alone with Mom and Aunt Jean. There's no self-help group for being alone with them."

He smiled, but said nothing. His thoughts went back to the Abrams tank. Maybe it would go on display at the model store. The store owner could help him set it up in an action setting. If his father ever came back,

Todd would take him to see it.

"Turn that TV down, please!" Cherylee called from the top of the stairs.

Emma grinned at Todd and left him at the storage room door while she found the remote. Her cell phone rang, and now she chattered over the music.

Todd picked up the turret section and studied it in the palm of his hand. He'd added many small details with a tweezers and the sparest amounts of glue—night-vision equipment, antennae, door hatches, handles, railing, a second machine gun. The turret alone had been hours of work. It wasn't ready to be glued in place yet, but he gingerly put it on the tank and held up the model, admiring it, studying it. How fragile it was. How easily he could crush a mighty Abrams tank in his hand. Its beauty, he realized, came from its small size, its fragility, its intricacy. He placed it back on the table, shut the door, turned the radio on, and settled on his stool, listening to the broadcast while the glue dried.

✣

The mail arrived later than usual because of the snowstorm. Cherylee would have left it in the mailbox, but the man down the street had come over with his snow blower, and when she went outside to thank him, the mailman came crunching through the snow-crusted street in his truck and pulled up to her driveway with her mail.

Now the thick, cold bundle, bound with a rubber band, sat on the kitchen table, and the music pounding downstairs just added to her anxiety as she began to unravel it. She went to the top of the stairs and called down to Emma to lower the TV.

The mail always made her anxious. For one thing, there was usually a lot of it, and not just seasonal catalogues and sale notices. Ever since Peter left and their story became public, she got solicitations for everything from private detective services to financial management; there were offers from real estate agents to sell their home, and from others to buy it; she received ads for moving companies, retirement communities, legal services, and psychological counseling. As many times as she'd gone through this daily ritual, she was still cautious leafing through the envelopes. She feared getting a notice that the bank was foreclosing on the house, or even finding something moving in an envelope. The letters from strangers bothered her most. Sometimes signed, sometimes not. Oddly enough, people asked her advice on their own bizarre circumstances, their divorces from incarcerated spouses, their runaway children. Being famous and having problems seemed to endow wisdom and authority. Sometimes there were vile and frightening letters, accusing her of being involved in Peter's crimes. She gave these to Friday and Gannon whenever they came around. She had also been notified recently that the family of one of Peter's victims of thirty years ago was filing a lawsuit. These things hung over her each day as she tried to keep the business going and protect her children from the chaos that surrounded them.

The envelope had no return address, and she didn't recognize the handwriting, a swirling, elongated script. It was thick, with a postmark from the Bronx. She slit it with the letter opener. Inside was a note, and an envelope addressed to her and the children…*in Peter's handwriting!* A shiver rushed through her. The whiteness of the bright, fresh snow outside the windows seemed almost blinding. The handwriting was unmistakably his. The note said,

> Dear Mrs. St. John,
>
> Peter was worried about the postmark, so I waited until I was home to visit Mother and sent it from the box down at the corner.
>
> I think the time he spent with us helped him in this awful journey. He was not in very good shape when he arrived. But the injury to his hand healed, and he got back some of his color with food and rest. He was very troubled, but we were glad to have him among us. I know how much he worried about you and your children.
>
> You are always in our prayers.
>
> Yours in Christ,
>
> Brother Luke Finnegan

Just then, Emma passed through the kitchen talking on her cell phone, and Cherylee felt as conspicuous as if she was reading pornography. She slid the letter under an L. L. Bean catalogue and flipped through some envelopes. Emma took a can of soda from the refrigerator and went back downstairs. Cherylee was vibrating inside; she decided to take the letter up to her room. She had no idea how she might react to whatever it said.

She locked her door and sat in the club chair. The letter was several pages in Peter's rounded handwriting.

Dear Cherylee and Emma and Todd,

I have begun this letter many times over the past year, sometimes on paper and sometimes in my head. It is so difficult even to find a place to start.

I love all of you, and I want to beg your forgiveness. I have no right to expect it. As deep as my sorrow is, it is nothing compared to the pain I have brought on you.

I don't know why I ran in the first place or what has kept me going for so long. I had no plan and no place to go. I just ran. I was afraid of being caught, and then I was afraid of facing you—all of you. What I have done to you is unforgivable. A prison term may be the price of my crimes, but it's impossible to measure what this has done to you, and now, nothing can change it. I'm sorry.

Where I've been doesn't matter. I've survived, if this can be called survival. Most of the time, I feel more dead than alive. I think about you constantly, knowing that even if I return, there will be nothing I can do to help you.

None of this is anyone's fault except mine. Marcia Rojas is not to blame. She wrote accurately about my past. I told her about some of it.

It's difficult to explain some of the things I did so long ago because so much has changed. When I started college I didn't know much about politics, and now I can see that thinking I'd later become an expert really meant that I knew even less. But we lived in a time of fear and anger—and immense frustration. It seemed like the world had gone insane. No amount of reasoning mattered to the people in power. They seemed incapable of compassion and decency. People were beaten and killed because of their skin color or because they disagreed with the government. The government lied to us every day. War was good for business, which meant that war would continue as long as business had anything to say about it. Tens of thousands of soldiers were dying in a remote place under horrible conditions for no good reason, and no one knows how many foreigners also died while American corporations enriched themselves by producing the weapons that killed them. It's hard to describe how these issues consumed me with rage. The people I was with felt the same way. We fed on each other's fear and anger. We reasoned that if our government and our capitalist economy were that poisonous, then they needed to be destroyed and a new system put in its place. Up until the tragic and senseless act that put this whole play in motion thirty years ago, we had tried everything to make our voices heard, but nothing worked. The government was indifferent and unyielding. The FBI and CIA were spying on U.S. citizens. They incited riots and sabotaged the careers of college professors and others who opposed the war. I helped to organize rallies and protest marches. By now, you probably know that I wrote articles for a newspaper. Nothing worked, and the web that we spun around ourselves got thicker and thicker. Three of my friends died on the day that bomb went off. I saw one of them killed, and I saw a man horribly mutilated. I have relived those moments every day since then.

All of this happened long before you came into my life, and none of it justifies what I have done to you. Now it's all come tumbling back on me, and the things I did so long ago have infected all of us. At the time it seemed that nothing would ever change unless we forced it to change.

But of course, everything did—for the world and for us. That horrible war and the vile thing our government turned into seem unimaginably distant now, like a nightmare that sometimes flashes back at you but that's finally over and can't hurt you. We're safe from it now. The country has healed. We learned the lessons of that time and moved on. Yet I still carried this cancer inside, and now it's spread.

Cherylee, I don't know what I could have done differently once we fell in love and began a family. Every day I carried the secret of my past with me and wondered if that would be the day when agents would show up at the door and tell me to come with them. But life went on, day after day, year after year. It seemed like the more time passed, the worse it would be if I shared anything or decided to turn myself in. And every day, I continued to love you and the children and to want what any husband and father wants for his wife and children, which is a happy and safe and prosperous future, something that a long time ago I thought might be a vanishing hope for the entire world.

Emma and Todd, I have loved you each from the moment you came into my life. My sorrow for betraying you is impossible to describe. I don't know how to make it better. I don't think I can. I know that your mother's strength will help you to go forward.

As I write this letter, I have had a little borrowed time in a remote place. I have eaten what I needed and had a warm place to sleep, when I've been able to sleep. But I won't be here much longer.

I don't know when I'll see you again. Coming in means that I'll probably spend the rest of my life in prison. The little time I have right now is borrowed from that, and it will surely run out soon.

I don't know when you'll get this letter or where I'll be when you receive it. I'm afraid that just by writing to you I may have dragged you further into this horrible mess. I'm sorry. I love you all.

Your loving husband and father,
Peter

Cherylee's cheeks and brow were warm, her eyes moist, and her chin quivering, but she was surprised at how calm she felt, and how relieved. He was alive. He had burrowed his way under the sights of all the people looking for him. She'd been warned many times by Friday and Gannon to report any contact from him, in any form, but there was no chance she would give them this letter. She still didn't understand all of it. It wasn't even dated. When did he write it? Where was he now? But still, she felt as if everything had suddenly changed. She had something to hold on to—he was alive, he loved them. What more was there now? She had long since arrived in a similar place to where he was, namely, that even if he returned, if he ever did, they would never go back to what they were and what they had. Life had changed forever for her and the children. Like him, she felt that she was on borrowed time too. She could lose the house and the business at any moment; she would have to start over again with the children, probably somewhere else. She would have to file papers to change their names. (She had already decided that they would use her maiden name.)

But these things he wrote about—the war and the protests—she had thought about them too, what they meant to her, how they had influenced her life. She was younger than Peter, and her recollection of that time was in hazy television images of race riots and war protests, of policemen on horses in the streets of Chicago, of oceans of people in front of the Lincoln Memorial. Sometimes she couldn't separate what she remembered from what she'd seen when these images occasionally reappeared on television and in movies. Back then, when she was a girl, none of it affected her. Her father had grumbled about Communists inciting the riots. A few boys from her high school got drafted, but she didn't really know them. Her life just went on. And now, she might not have cared a wink for any of it, might have thought, as many in this conservative suburb did, that it was just an age of anarchy, a time of loose morals and social chaos, except that as she heard the terrible things people like that radio person said about her husband, she knew—not knew, but her instincts were screaming at her—that something was amiss in what they said, how they portrayed it, as if history wasn't as simple as this one thing that was so easy to believe, as if there was more to it. This was, after all, a loving and devoted man they were tearing down, sincere and thoughtful, humorous and clever. The man she knew was incapable of cruelty, of murder. Shouldn't he get the benefit of the doubt? At least from her, if from no one else. Maybe there was a reason for what happened. Even now, in the midst of this nightmare, here he was writing to her about it, trying to tell her that things just weren't that simple. And she wondered, too, if he—if all those people like him back then—hadn't done some of the things they did—maybe not…no, not all of them, but some of them—would anything have changed? It was true, she reasoned, that changing things meant rupturing what existed. That's what was happening to her—right now. They had all been living on this thin, shiny veneer, living comfortable lives, fretting over trifles, burying themselves in the vicarious lives of celebrities, entertaining themselves with the false realities of reality television, but the veneer had cracked, and when they crashed through, nothing was underneath it, and they were still falling. And now she looked back up as she plunged downward and saw that all around her, that's how others were living, though they didn't know it yet, and anything could change their lives, just as hers changed. That was how she lived when she was young, too—while a war exploded, while the country nearly came apart. But she knew so little of what was beyond her small world. She'd been oblivious to everything else. Boyfriends, dances, dresses, music—that's what that time meant to her, while all of this turmoil bubbled beneath it, and she wondered now, if everyone had just gone along like that, oblivious, indifferent, would the war have ever ended, would blacks still drink from separate water fountains, would the FBI spy on you? She'd seen something of them up close lately, and they made her more nervous than protesters ever did, and she had come to resent it, too.

But she was frightened for him—even more for him than for the kids right now. He'd been injured, the brother said. He might be in danger. He surely had little or no money.

She considered whether to share the letter with the children and decided to wait. She didn't know how they might react, and also, she didn't want to burden them with keeping it secret. Peter's dilemma had now fallen on her. So be it. She welcomed it if the price was knowing he was alive. Talking to Jean was out of the question. Cherylee looked out the front window and saw that the driveway was done. Her neighbor had even brushed off the Expedition.

She found the roads passable all the way to the warehouse, but the parking lot was still not cleared. She parked on the road and trudged through the snow, clutching the bag with all the papers and files she'd collected since the turmoil began.

The place was dark and cold inside, while outside, the afternoon sunshine had faded to a luminous amber glow in the west, casting streaks of gold and orange across the ribbed underbelly of the clouds. The temperature was falling. It would probably go below zero tonight.

Normally on a Saturday, she and a few others would have worked through the morning. Luanne was always willing to come in if Cherylee needed her. But with the storm last night, no one had been here today. Cherylee was alone in the vast, dark warehouse. She left the thermostat at its overnight setting and kept her coat on as she booted up the computer.

She'd gotten better with it. She didn't want to depend on others for information. She wanted to see things for herself, especially when it came to the bank accounts. Now, she went to Melvin Gash's website. She usually avoided anything to do with him, but she knew that if something was known about Peter, it would be here. The website was a study in self-promotion. In his photos, Gash looked thinner, smarter, and friendlier than the aggressive and nasty man she knew. Photos showed him in his radio broadcast booth wearing a headset with a huge globular microphone in front of him; signing copies of his book at a mall in Overland Park; shaking hands with a U.S. senator. Still others showed Marcia Rojas being interviewed about her article on Peter; and Gash near his truck in front of the warehouse, and with his back to the camera as Cherylee's SUV sped out of the parking lot. Cherylee found profiles of Simon, Magnus, Robin, and the others, along with mug shots and surveillance photos. There were old news articles about the bombing, about the apprehension of several members of Peter's group, about the death of Simon Phelan in a Mexican jail fight. There were even items implying that Peter's group had been involved with the Irish Republican Army and some airline hijackings in the 1970s; and more innuendo about recent environmental sabotage, and even the World Trade Center bombing in 1993, with the question at the top of the column, "Did Peter Howell's days of anarchy end in 1970, or was that just the beginning? *We want to know*?"

Finally, she found what she was looking for—a link to the college Peter attended. Once there, she entered Luke Finnegan's name in the search box and discovered an address and phone number for the Saint Celixine Retirement Community.

"Brothers residence," the voice said. It was assertive, lively, not what she expected.

"Hello, is this the Celixine retirement home?"

"Yes, it is!" the voice boomed, as if delighted that the call was indeed for the residence and not a wrong number. "This is Brother Brendan. Who would you like to speak with?"

"Brother Luke, is he there?"

"Ah, Brother Luke…let me see…he might be down in the kitchen… hold on, please."

Hollow footsteps receded and then a door slammed. After several minutes, another voice greeted her on a different line. "Hello, this is Brother Luke." There were voices in the background.

"Yes, this is Cherylee St. John."

A pause. "Oh…Mrs. St. John…yes, I'm so pleased you called. How are you, and your family too? I'm sorry, you caught me off guard. I was cleaning up from dinner. Are you…in Kansas?"

"Yes, yes I am. I received your note and…"—she hesitated, just shy of saying Peter's name, and then continued—"…when did you see him? How was he?"

"Oh, of course! My hands are wet. Can you hold on for just a moment?"

"Yes."

The phone clunked and then the first voice boomed through the earpiece. "Hello? Luke? Have you got it?" Cherylee pulled the handset back from her ear.

"Thank you," she said. "He's there."

"Luke?...I don't hear him."

"He's there...he just..."

"Mrs. St. John?" It was Luke again.

"You got it now, Brother Luke?" Brother Brendan asked.

"Yes, thank you, Brother."

The first line clunked dead, and the connection improved.

"Mrs. St. John. I'm so glad to hear from you. Yes, Pe...he...was here for several weeks. He left rather...suddenly, but he must have known something because we had a visit from...from some men only a couple of days later. Have you heard more since then?"

"No, just your letter."

"Oh, I hope he's all right. Tell me, how is your family? How are you?"

"We're doing the best we can. It's been difficult, especially for the children. But we're getting along."

"I'm sure it's been hard, especially not knowing. Well, let me see... what else can I share with you? Yes...he was here for several weeks. As I said, he was not well when he arrived."

"You said he'd been injured?"

"A nasty cut on his hand. His car window had been broken and he cut his hand on the glass. He wouldn't go to the emergency room, so I cleaned it up the best I could."

"How did it happen?"

"He was robbed..." As he said it, she let out a sob, and he paused. "Oh, Mrs. St. John, I'm so sorry. This is all so awful. Are you all right?"

"Yes, just please tell me everything, all you can."

"Well...he was robbed. Thieves broke into his car. They were gone by the time he discovered it. He came here and we took care of him for a few weeks. I should say, he took care of us, too, repairing some things around here. He's very good with his hands. There's only a few of us here, and most of the brothers can't do things for themselves. Well, I'm sorry, I can go on sometimes. When he arrived I don't think he could have gone another mile. I'm sure he hadn't eaten or slept well in a long time. He was tired and very run down, very thin. It took some time for him to recover, and the brothers...well, several of them knew him from school, although they didn't let on while he was here. Those...people were here and told me we could be in trouble, but I don't know what they'd want with a bunch of sickly old men. And even if they took me off to jail, I'd do it all over again. Our Lord preached mercy and forgiveness, not punishment..."

"Did you go to school with him? Were you part of that...group?"

"No, I was one of his teachers. But I was young then, too, and he was only a little younger than me. He was lively and bright. He just couldn't seem to find his way in college. Like most young people, he went a little crazy his first year, but then he got mixed up with those people. He had a girlfriend, too...oh, maybe I shouldn't..."

"It's all right. Who was she? Maybe she'd know something about him."

"Oh, I doubt that. She graduated with honors at about the same time as all the trouble started. She was a musician. She became well known, too. Maybe you've heard of her, Susan Mallory?"

Cherylee hesitated. "I don't think so. It rings a bell, but I don't think so. He never spoke about the past. Do you know where he was going?"

"No. But he's a smart man, very shrewd, too. He fooled the police for all these years, and..."

"Yes, he did."

"Oh, I'm sorry. I do talk too much. I didn't mean..."

"It's all right, Brother Luke. I just wanted to talk to someone who had seen him."

"Mrs. St. John, I haven't stopped thinking about him since he left, or about you either, you and your family. I can't...well, none of us can imagine how hard this must be for you. You have been in our prayers. The brothers pray for him, and for you and your children. Please call me if I can do anything more."

"I will. Thank you, Brother Luke."

Susan Mallory? Cherylee couldn't place it. The name probably meant nothing to Peter or anyone else now, but she thought she should look it up when she had time. Right now, she wanted to call her lawyer. He'd probably double bill her for calling him at home on a Saturday evening, but she didn't care. Time was getting short for Peter, wherever he was.

Chapter 19

"You see these bums, you know, blowing up the campuses."
—President Richard M. Nixon

Friday, May 1, 1970

The drive over felt rushed and weary. They'd slept too late, slipping off again after waking in the gray hour before sunrise, drowsy and aroused, making love once more, and then collapsing in an awkward tangle as a light breeze drifted through the window on the noisy tide of rush hour traffic outside Peter's apartment. But before she got out of the car at her dormitory, she slid across the seat, pushing her hips against his, and took his cheek lightly in her hand as she kissed him. Her lips lingered beyond the kiss he expected, warmer and moister, and her fingers stiffened now, holding him to her. Then she released him as if recovering, as if remembering all that awaited her.

"I'll see you tonight," he said.

She nodded, a small nod, slight, smiling through pursed lips, yet betraying her happiness in tiny movements, in her hesitation, even in her fatigue. Her eyelids drooped as she smiled, as she stopped time for just a moment before she rushed back to her music, her practice, her parents, to everything happening at once—for just a moment before she got out of the car.

He watched her on the walkway, until she waved at the door and disappeared inside. He leaned across the seat and rolled her window down, and then he dropped into first and snapped on the radio…

…turn on your legs while you walk, and the prettier the legs the groovier the walk. When you want the walk the girl watchers watch, ask for Scholes Exercise Sandals, the original, walk-pretty sandal, with the exclusive, patented toe-

grip. ♪Se-ven-ty-se-ven double-you aay–bee–seeee!♪ Bonnng! This is Ron Lundy takin' you through the morning. (♪gritty guitar erupts♪) Aaah-ha! Play that thing! Don't you love it? Here's Crosby, Stills and Nash, and those other guys...

...and Stephen Stills sings crustily of meeting one of God's children on the road to Yasgar's farm. Music and radio banter mingle with the warm spring air rushing into the car and pleasantly ruffling Peter's tee-shirt as he drives off campus, tempted to return to his apartment for a couple of hours' sleep, tired, and also uneasy. But not from being on campus. If anything he feels aloof from it. It seems merely a curiosity to him now, a fishbowl, full of weird, exotic creatures (though she is unique among them—delicate and floral, and more suited to a rich and colorful warm-water reef than this toxic bowl). His mother and aunts want him to return, but it's over. His scholarship is gone; the draft board wants him; and more than anything, he just doesn't belong here, though tonight should be interesting. He wonders who else will be there, what anyone will say to him. She probably hadn't even thought about that, but he won't make a spectacle of himself. Wouldn't be fair. It's her night. She said she plays later. He'll arrive then and quietly take a seat in back. Let the professor give him a curious look. What can she do? What can any of them do?

But none of that bothers him. No, it's her. Her...and B. J. Thomas and Freda Payne and The Carpenters, and Simon and Garfunkel, and Stevie Wonder and Edwin Starr and Norman Greenbaum, all stirred in with Ron Lundy's happy chatter, and with ads for tanning lotion and shaving cream and perfume, bleeding all over the songs. Raindrops falling on his head, bands of gold, troubled waters, war, signed, sealed and delivered to the spirit in the sky who's only just begun. Begun what? He's not part of that world any longer. Yet, here he is enjoying it. Yes, enjoying it as he drives—the songs, the wind rushing into the car, the sunshine, even the ad jingles, as if she's pulled him back, brought him back. As if he could just hurdle the wall between them, her world and his, straddle it at will. But for how much longer?

When she found him with Simon yesterday, they were discussing an article he was writing—which he has to go finish right now. The paper has to get out. A special edition to distribute at the Jefferson Airplane concert in New Paltz next week. Bring the fight out in the open—*that's* what he's writing about. Defy even the organized antiwar movement. What's the point of *legal* protests? That's not civil disobedience. It's not disobedience at all. Nothing changes without destroying something else. The group has been choosing targets. Maybe the recruiting offices in Poughkeepsie and Kingston and Peekskill. Late at night, when no one's there. Turn them to rubble. And that will change everything. A declaration of war. They'll have to go underground, disappear. Soon. All of this laced his conversation with Simon when she appeared and stood in front of him and then later asked him to come hear her play. And it will still be there when he smiles and shakes hands with her father tonight, when he applauds her wondrous performance. He knows it will be wondrous, knows there will be tears and joy, hope and sorrow. And he knows things no one else there will know.

⸸

Something has happened. It's obvious before he's out of the car. People have gathered on the sidewalk and steps in front of the office building, spilling out from the vestibule. He recognizes a few faces from antiwar groups and SDS chapters on other campuses. The scent of cannabis hangs over the street.

He takes the stairs two-at-a-time and finds the office crowded, busy, loud. Robin is squeezed into the narrow hall with her back to him, talking to a couple of people. A grin fills her eyes when she turns and sees him—irony, curiosity, something. He's puzzled at first and then recalls Simon's cheery send-off when he left with Susan yesterday. Oh yeah, now they all know. So what's it to them? Fuck that.

"What's going on?" he asks, with more irritation spilling out than he meant. She hadn't even said anything yet. Maybe he read too much into a little grin. He's tired. He wants to finish the article and go crash before Susan's recital.

But now she leans on the wall and allows the jostling of the crowd to push them closer together. "So you're finally here. I tried calling."

"Yeah, what happened?"

She smiles broadly, chuckling through a snort. "You don't know?"

"I wouldn't ask if I knew."

"They're bombing Cambodia, Peter!"

"What?"

"Just what I said..."—she mimes a plane flying with one hand and little bombs bursting with her other hand—"...pchoow! pchoow!"

Her irony or jealousy or whatever is tiresome. He looks around. "So what's all this?" he asks.

"Organizing. We're gonna march. So you back now?"

"Back? I'm here. Simon down in the office?"

She nods, and he turns away before she can grin again, or snort or ripple her jaw muscles, and he works his way along the hall.

A dozen people have crowded into the small office. Terry leans on the window sill and greets Peter with a flick of his head and a smile. Simon is at the center of the group, arguing with the SDS president from St. Selly.

Peter stays at the edge of the group and makes his way around to Terry, perching himself on the window sill beside him. No irony here. Just a smile, a soul shake, a bemused nod at the entertainment.

"What's this about?" Peter asks.

"Turf…who's in charge, what the flyers say, who gets to speak, more turf. Right now it's about showing the NLF flag. SDS doesn't want it."

"And we do."

Terry nods, with an acquiescent grin.

Peter gets the whole story while they sit there—the TV broadcast, the maps, Nixon shuffling his papers, the outrage, the impending response on campuses all over the country—at first, taking it in, sharing the outrage, becoming excited, swelling with eagerness, and then realizing what's about to happen. They plan to march on St. Celixine in a few hours.

When the SDS people leave, Simon sneers, "No balls is what! They just don't get it, the big picture. They don't see it. We're in a war! Who knows, maybe this is the first day of *our* revolution!" He laughs, turning to Peter and Terry, and says, "Wouldn't that be a kick, May first?! May Day!" Then he throws an arm around Peter, as if welcoming back a prodigal. "You're here, man! Just in time. So much to do!" But even before he's let go of Peter, more people fill the room. The place is manic. Simon is manic. Fueled on high-octane, ignited by the energy all around him. They're going to rally everyone, not just the students. Nixon's gone too far this time! Everyone will see it, everyone will know! They'll send a message all the way from Groenkill to Washington. This is it! This is the big one!

Whatever doubts anyone may have gleaned in Peter's reluctant smile when Simon shook him are soon swamped in the roar of this engine. Its power ignites him too. Nixon *has* gone too far this time. The only way to respond is loudly, raucously. Yes, the people have to be rallied. Yet even as he gets his marching orders—to pick up bundles of leaflets from the printer and deliver them all over the region—he wonders what he ought to do, what it's even possible to do. He can't stop this, and he wouldn't if he could. It's too important, too large. He's a soldier in a war, too. He has to fight today. But—years later he would wonder if this was the moment that changed everything—here, in this hot, crowded office, tired as he was and still absorbing the events around him. He could never say for sure that it was one moment—when it was that he actually chose one thing over another, because it felt less like a decision than an impulse, a surrender, as if he was swallowed back up after floating briefly in limbo, in a place where nothing existed but the songs and radio banter and her fingers on his cheek, holding his lips to hers for a moment longer than he expected when she leaned up to kiss him.

And from here, events just seemed to carry him forward on their current. With his trunk full of flyers, he drove all over Groenkill County and then up to Dutchess County and across the river to Ulster County, hitting the university and college campuses, dropping bundles at bookstores and handing them over to students to distribute in unions, in cafeterias, on the streets, and still hoping that even though he would miss the recital, it might go on as planned, that nothing would change for Susan and her music, trying to convince himself that a massive protest rally on the quadrangle in front of the music building would have no impact on her recital. He even considered, momentarily—just momentarily—skipping out on the rally to go hear her play. (How naïve could he have been, he would later think!) But the wall he'd been straddling just hours ago did not seem taller and more imposing now, but rather, weaker, and crumbling, and everything and everyone on one side was about to pour over onto the other. He tried calling her several times, but something always conspired against him—a store owner wouldn't let him make a toll call, a phone booth was out of order, another swallowed his dime and dropped the call, and finally, at a booth alongside a busy highway, his engine began idling erratically, and after he dropped the handset to go rev it, he returned to find the line dead, and now all his coins were gone. He would call when he got back to the office, but time was running out. And sure enough, he never even got inside the building when he returned before eight people squeezed into his Plymouth and they joined the caravan of cars and vans headed for the campus.

So now, in the twilight of a warm spring day, his voice goes up with hundreds of others, as they chant and shout in pulsating, angry rhythms. Hundreds turn to thousands as traffic outside the campus jams the roads and people swarm through the entrance on foot. The members of the Circle link their arms at the head of the crowd and march across the quad, gaining speed and gathering momentum as the crowd swells, until they reach the wide mortar stairway at the front doors of Celixine Hall.

The lights outside the building provide a theatrical glow as speakers shout through the bullhorn, their voices screeching and crackling over the crowd.

Terry leads one chant after another through the bullhorn.

End the war now!
End the war now!
End the war now!

Ho, Ho, Ho Chi Minh!
Ho, Ho, Ho Chi Minh!
Ho, Ho, Ho Chi Minh!

Finally, Simon climbs onto the concrete balustrade above the walkway, and as he begins to speak in a somber and deliberate voice, the mood of the event shifts as if a priest had stepped into the pulpit to address his Sunday flock.

Peter takes a place on the steps, a few feet from Simon, alongside others from his group and from SDS, mesmerized by the immense spectacle, as people continue pouring onto the quad, seeping through tree stands, arriving in waves. In the fading daylight, the whirling red and amber lights of police and security cars now accumulating at the edge of the crowd have a bizarre, almost decorative effect on the gathering. Signs bob up and down everywhere.

As Peter crossed the quad and mounted the stairs, he'd seen the glow of lights in the recital room windows, and now he peers through the budding leaves as silhouettes collect there to watch the chaos outside. The windows are open. Students down in the shrubs shout to others up in the music room. The recital has undeniably been interrupted.

Simon rallies the crowd, which sprawls all the way from the steps of Celixine Hall to the stadium parking lot. People sit on tree limbs and crowd the front steps of other buildings for a better view. They shout and chant as he waves a key over his head and unlocks the door. (The same SDS student who let them into the union had stolen this key from the security office.) Peter glances back once more at the faceless shadows in the music room as he's swept into the torrent rushing through the massive oak doors and into Celixine.

They march up the wide, carpeted stairway lined with portraits of trustees living and dead, of past college presidents in their dark brown robes, clasping beads and prayer books, and finally beneath the huge crucifix over the landing in the stairwell. Students rush into the building like children at the gates of an amusement park. They spread out, rampaging, overturning desks and furniture, emptying waste baskets, pulling books from the shelves and pictures off the walls. The windows are thrown open and they rally the bulging crowd in front of Celixine, heaving files and books and papers into the night sky. A group at the top of the stairway breaks through the door to the roof and from the front of the building they unfurl the NLF flag, red and blue, with a single gold star representing the Viet Cong, which now flaps in the white glow of floodlights that illuminate the building.

‡

Saturday, May 2, 1970

Father Alfonse LeClerq is a slight, amiable man in his mid sixties, with thick, flowing white hair and a soft manner that has served him well to calm the periodic turmoil at faculty and trustee meetings. His resilience has led to a long tenure as the college president, over twenty years. Every so often, a new faculty member or trustee mistakes his inoffensive nature for weakness, an error in judgment that is soon corrected, for his quiet manner conceals both immense reserves of strength and a formidable intelligence.

Even now, as he surveys the aftermath of last night's chaos, he doesn't betray his fatigue and stiffness after dozing for barely an hour in the back of a police cruiser. He'd refused to leave the scene and return to his residence even for a few hours. He washed this morning in the athletic center locker room, borrowing a razor from the basketball coach, shook out his black coat, straightened his stiff white collar and black dickey, and accepted a cup of coffee and doughnut from a sheriff's deputy. He also accepted the use of his binoculars to study the windows and rooftop of Celixine Hall. There's little to be seen through the windows in daylight, just shadows and sometimes a student appearing and shouting inaudibly to the crowd camped on the quad. On the rooftop, he recognizes figures as they come and go—the campus SDS leaders, the students who were suspended last fall, others. Oddly, they worry him less than the growing contingents of sheriff's deputies and city police officers, and soon a company of national guardsmen being sent by the governor, all on his beloved campus. He had argued futilely against having men with weapons here. The sheriff scoffed at him, and Father Alfonse recognized in the sheriff's eagerness and the easy offense he took to the protesters, and especially to that flag on top of the building, that this situation had become far more combustible even than the initial rampage last night.

He hands the binoculars back to the deputy and wanders through the rows of police cruisers to the edge of the quad, which is now surrounded by uniforms of one sort or another, all of them sweating in their helmets and hats and straps and buckles and guns. Wooden barricades separate the protesters on the lawn from the uniforms and from clusters of ROTC students, jocks, and hecklers who taunt and jeer at the protesters. Those on the quad who want to leave are allowed to pass, but no one can enter. Yet few have left, and music plays and frisbees fly as the uniforms look on and sweat. Bright sunshine bathes the quad and the brick facing of Celixine, and most of the uniforms stand in direct sunlight behind the barricades, as the morning warms, with temperatures possibly headed for ninety by afternoon. Whatever the Lord's plan for this day may be, Father Alfonse thinks, this heat will certainly be part of it. Yet he won't remove his own jacket as long as these men have to stand here like this, and he's aware that his black suit and white collar also make it easy for the students to recognize him. He'd like to go out and talk with some of them, but with the barricades and line of policemen and the hecklers, he's afraid of sparking trouble where there's now a détente of sorts. At least, he was able to get a couple of water stations set up. The sheriff's first choice last night was to unleash his deputies on the quad in riot gear and clear it, but the sheriff learned, as others have, how determined Father Alfonse could be when he opposed something—and he absolutely opposed responding to this situation with violence. The second choice, which even Brother Stedman favored, was to starve out the protesters, but Father Alfonse was convinced by last night's proceedings that many of them would willingly suffer hunger and thirst in this heat. Water and a few dozen cases of Twinkies weren't just merciful; they were politic. Saint Celixine is the only martyr Father Alfonse wants associated with this campus.

He waves to a group of students on the lawn, pleased that one girl smiles and waves back, as if she's sitting on a blanket at the beach.

"She missed her final yesterday," a voice behind him says.

Father Alfonse turns to find Brother Stedman at his elbow.

"She must have thought this was more important, Joe."

Brother Stedman scowls. "Well, she'll have a chance to rethink that when her grades arrive."

"Yes, that's something the faculty may have to review in light of these events."

"I don't know what there is to review, but you'll have no doubt where I stand."

"No, I won't," Father Alfonse says, smiling, "no doubt at all."

"How can you smile at any of this, Father? Look what's happened. The quadrangle has been trampled, the administration building raided, who knows what's going on in there—and all those records inside! Oh, this is just a disaster!"

"A disaster, maybe. But not a tragedy, not yet. In all my years here I never imagined men with guns entering these grounds."

"It's the people in that building who frighten me. Frankly, I don't understand why they started this. We should have invaded Cambodia long ago. At least the president went on television and explained it all. I for one don't know why he'd even use maps. Isn't that just telling the enemy what we're up to? Let the army go in there and clean out those infestations, I say. And then what do we have here—outside agitators, townspeople, students from other schools, the Lord only knows who else. Well, this can't go on forever."

"No, but we have to give it some time. Nothing has been destroyed that can't be fixed or replaced. This will pass. I just want all of us to get safely through it. These policemen, and now soldiers coming…I don't know why we need all this."

"You're not that naïve by half," Brother Stedman responds, now grinning himself. "All that traffic backed up on city roads, a trustee who went to law school with the governor…I'm hearing that this is the biggest protest in the entire region. Even those nut-jobs up at New Paltz don't have a mess this big. Now we've got television crews and reporters showing up."

"I'm not going to allow this to turn into another Columbia, Joe. It's just too easy to look at these students and write them off as agitators or troublemakers. But I listened to those speakers last night. I listened closely…especially that one—he was a student here…"

"Phelan. He's one of the leaders. I had him in class a couple of years ago."

"Yes, well, he…all of them…there's great conviction driving this. You can't just muscle that down. This country has gotten itself into a terrible fix with this war. We can't separate that from what's happening here right now. And some of these…oh, Lord forgive me…"—he lowered his voice—"…

these thugs all around us...they're just too eager to go in there and...well, who knows what will happen once that starts. We can't let it. We can't! You know, I have to confide something to you. It's something I've thought about for a long time and not just since last night. But those protesters may be right. Perhaps we are too knotted up with Merval and other donors who expect us to do their research for them. Maybe that's something else for the faculty to review—and the trustees too, for that matter."

Brother Stedman's caterpillar eyebrows now droop into a frown, and he says deliberately, "It's a sorry day, Father Alfonse, when we let rabble rousers dictate our policies to us."

Father Alfonse is grateful for the interruption when Brother Luke emerges from the cluster of parked cars, headed toward them, his face flushed and sweat beading on his brow. He's out of his robes, dressed in jeans and a white tee-shirt, already damp around his armpits and neck.

"Working in the garden today, Brother?" Brother Stedman asks.

Brother Luke smiles, letting the sarcasm roll off him. "No, just seemed like the right outfit for the job."

"What job is that?" Father Alfonse asks.

"I should go in there and talk to them, Father. I wanted to ask you first and see what message I can bring."

"Absolutely not!" Brother Stedman exclaims.

"We have to talk to them, Brother Joseph," Luke responds. "I understand they refuse to talk on the phone."

"That's true," Father Alfonse says, and adds, almost amusedly, "The bullhorn has been their preferred means of communication, though it's been a little one-sided. That's your nephew among them, isn't it, that novice, Brother Terrence?"

"My cousin. He's a few years younger. Yes, that's him. I want to go inside and see him and the others."

"They've barred the doors," Father Alfonse says.

"They'll let me in."

"But you may not get back out," Brother Joseph says, "and even if you do, dressed like that, you could find yourself in the middle of something when these policemen move in."

"It hasn't come to that yet," Father Alfonse responds stiffly.

Brother Luke shuts his eyes and folds his hands at his lips before turning to Father Alfonse. "We're not talking about terrorists but about some of our own students. I hardly think they'll prevent me from leaving if I wish to. We have to find out what's going on in there. Maybe I can start a dialogue. Unless you order me not to, Father, I'm going inside, and I'd like to know what message I can bring."

Father Alfonse smiles and nods approval. "Ask them to think of the safety of all of these students before this goes any farther and tell them that I'd be pleased to talk with them too…and also, tell them they're in my prayers."

"I will, Father."

Brother Stedman abruptly adds, "And tell them a company of soldiers is on the way."

Father Alfonse glances impatiently at Brother Stedman and then says, "Brother Luke, use your best judgment, and call the athletic office number if you or any of them wish to speak with me."

Brother Luke nods to Brother Stedman as he passes, and Father Alfonse watches him navigate the perimeter of police officers, now stopping to tap one on the shoulder. The cop looks around for his commander, who in turn looks back at Father Alfonse before giving an okay. Brother Luke exchanges a joke with the officer and then ducks under the barricade. He greets students all the way across the lawn, sometimes stopping to talk, even to throw a frisbee on the way. It's nearly a half hour before he reaches the front steps of the building, and then, after a few words with someone at a window, the door opens and he disappears inside.

✣

By late afternoon, in the torpid heat and dead air inside Celixine Hall, a contagious fatigue has spread. The protesters have sung songs, chanted, talked themselves out, and listened to more speeches. They've smoked dope and drunk wine. One couple even fucked in a place that no one ever imagined fucking. Now, many are exhausted and sleep where they've landed, on the floors in hallways and offices.

The water fountains and rest room sinks still work, but the toilets are filthy and several jammed, and the vending machines are empty. A few boxes of sandwiches were smuggled in, and some of the protesters on the quad threw their rations of Twinkies in the windows, too, which led the sheriff to cut off the food. He told Father Alfonse that he couldn't keep his men here indefinitely for a picnic, and besides, he said, the human body could not only survive without food for quite a long time, but it would be to everyone's advantage if the protesters were in a weakened state. He also added that they were free to leave, the ones on the lawn, anyway. In the end, Father Alfonse gave in to that reasoning, as long as water was still available. Protesters and police alike are certain the stalemate will soon be broken by a sweep of the quad and a raid on the building, yet at the moment nothing seems imminent.

Peter steps over splayed legs and curled up bodies in the hallway, handing out jars of Vaseline, worried about the flagging energy all around him. Down the hall, Robin smokes a cigarette, sitting cross-legged with a cluster of students. A speech in front of the building echoes through the windows.

"What's this for?" a kid asks.

"Slather it on your arms and legs before they come in. And your neck, too…they like grabbing the neck. Pass it around."

He moves on, chatting and joking with those not sleeping, speculating when the raid will come. From the windows, they all saw the national guard troops arrive and disburse at the far end of the quad, to the cheers of rotsees and jocks. As he passes it, Peter looks in the mailroom. The coffee pot is dry, and even the sugar packets are gone. The room has been trashed and mail litters the floor, with a mess of blue booklets scattered about. He picks one up: the program for Susan's recital, its cover smudged by a boot print. A stack of them must have been delivered to the administration building.

He opens it, almost hoping to find a mistake—that her recital was scheduled for another night—but there it is. It would have been in the past now. Today. Last night her parents would have slept in their motel room, and she would have wrapped herself around him in his bed. This was everything to her. Across from her name is the music she was to play. She hadn't told him what it was, but he knew. He'd guessed it when they had lunch together. He'd heard sections of it so many times that it couldn't be anything else. And he knew its special meaning for her, and now recognized also what it meant that she wanted him there when she played it. There would be no other moment like this one. The possibility that she would play Bach's Cello Suites again and he'd be there when she did now seemed as remote as a distant galaxy. Besides, that would be another night, not last night. That's when she would have played it for him. And last night would always be what it was.

He folds the soiled program and slides it into his back pocket.

‡

The raid would have come early Sunday morning, before dawn, when most of the spectators and hecklers were gone and the protesters drowsy. The sheriff and national guard commander said the lawn could be cleared without much trouble and the hundred or so inside would probably offer little more resistance than going limp when they were arrested. A covey of trustees and administrators also argued that TV cameras would not get good images, that there'd be no live audience at that hour, that most newspaper deadlines were over sixteen hours away. Whatever happened would be long over when it hit Monday's papers.

Father Alfonse knows something of managing publicity. The college phone lines have been swamped with calls from parents. Yes, all this makes sense.

But now he also knows that situations like this one have occurred on campuses all over the country, and he believes that everyone here is underestimating the potential reaction. Indeed, the students themselves anticipated such a raid. On the lawn a bonfire and hundreds of candles burned through the night, while inside, the lights were bright and music blared out the windows from the stereo that had once been upstairs in Father Alfonse's office. Also, people came and went freely in the building as the occupants opened the doors for bathroom use. It's impossible now to estimate how many are in there, and Father Alfonse doesn't see how the building can be taken without people getting hurt.

Brother Luke has been busy in Celixine Hall, debating and arguing with the leaders, visiting among the students, and calling the athletic office regularly. Somewhat to Father Alfonse's ire, he refused to say anything about the situation inside that might help police officers plan their strategy. "If I betray their trust," he asked, "what good can I do here?" Father Alfonse reminded him that his role was to help end this thing, and Brother Luke said he was trying to do just that. His calls are loquacious, meandering, full of anecdotes about students who have friends and brothers in Vietnam, reminders that many of the students here get good grades and stay out of trouble, pleas for patience, hints that he may soon find a way to bring the students out without force. Giving in to Brother Luke jibes with Father Alfonse's instincts, but he's no more pleased with the results the young brother is getting than he is with the task of keeping the eager sheriff and young national guard commander at bay. Still, he succeeds in doing just that through another hot day, even delivering—after relentless pleas from

Brother Luke—boxes of bread and peanut butter and jelly to the quad. Father Alfonse is growing weary and impatient too, but a tenuous peace prevails through another day and night.

‡

Monday, May 4, 1970

Peter leans through a window on the second floor and looks out on the patchwork quilt of blankets, sleeping bags, and makeshift tents on the lawn and walkways. The uniforms at the perimeter appear less strident this morning, some clustering in small groups to gossip and smoke. The office he's in is small, an assistant dean for something. The students who slept here have gone up on the roof, leaving him alone. On the steps below, one of the black student leaders tries to rouse the tired crowd with an angry speech, much distorted by his harsh shouting into the bullhorn. As he finishes, Jefferson Airplane explodes from the stereo speakers in the window below Peter almost as if someone was holding the needle over the turntable and waiting for the last syllable. Gracie Slick's wavering lyrics to "White Rabbit" swallow up the fuck-you's exchanged downstairs, and Peter sniffs a chuckle at the scene.

"What's funny?" Brother Luke asks, from the doorway.

"Power struggles within the power struggles," Peter responds, and turning says, "Oh, Brother Luke! I thought you were Terry. You two sound alike."

"We've heard that before," he says, stepping forward and leaning on the sill beside Peter. "It's too relaxed here."

"I know. A lot of stuff is getting through the lines—even that music."

"There's a power struggle out there too. Father Alfonse has done everything he can to hold back the police. And now it seems the sheriff has his doubts about the national guardsmen. Look, they're the ones leaving the big gaps around the edges."

"Yeah, I noticed that."

"It will end soon, Peter."

"I know. We're ready. You shouldn't be here, Brother."

"I can't think of anywhere else I should be, or would rather be. Besides, it may be helpful if Father Alfonse knows I'm still here when they come in."

Peter laughs. "I've been through this before, and I can tell you it won't matter."

"You surprise me, Peter. I wouldn't have made you out for someone so...militant. It just doesn't seem to come naturally to you, not like some of the others."

Peter follows the flight of a frisbee above the crowd. "There's nothing natural about any of this, but what choices are left to us?"

"Not violence. What kind of choice is that?"

"No one's been hurt here. And if they do get hurt, it's the goons and weekend warriors out there who'll do it."

"Oh, don't be obtuse, Peter. You're smarter than that. Taking this building by force, rousing all these students into an illegal action...what else can it lead to? Aren't you just undermining your own message with tactics like this?"

"The problem is that so many people out there, beyond this insulated little campus, don't even know there is a message. They're oblivious to it, to what the government is doing. They don't give a damn as long as ground beef is on sale at the grocery store and Tom Seaver is on the mound for the Mets. But maybe they'll notice when something gets in the middle of all that. There are kids inside this building who've never even been to a protest rally before. I'll bet Father Alfonse has had a few phone calls from parents by now."

"That's an understatement," Luke says, with a chuckle, "but it doesn't mean they'll take your side."

"We're all on the same side, only they don't know it."

Brother Luke shakes his head. "You're a bright young man, Peter. I'd hoped you would return to school after your suspension. Now I just hope you're not ruining your future by acting rashly."

"Rashness seems like the only thing left to us. And this place...it pretends to have all these intellectual ideals, but it's here and other places just like it that war gets made, Brother. Right here. This is as much a part of the food chain of war as the Pentagon is. That's why we have to be here."

"Well, there may be some truth to that, but I also know there's much more to this place than you think. Why just the other night...well, now that I think of it, Peter, you must have heard about the recital that was disrupted. You were friends with Susan Mallory, weren't you? What a shame. She'd worked so hard, and she...everyone...well, it was so disappointing. Did you know about that?"

Peter squints, focusing his gaze on one of the yellow and white barricades in the distance, recognizing in the yellow tint the same color as the blouse she wore when she appeared at the newspaper office four days ago. He clears his throat to cover the quivering in his chest and arms. "Yeah, I heard about that."

"It was just a shame. That's where I thought I'd be on Friday evening. Many of us did. Father Alfonse planned to go. Oh, well, there's no point in going on about it now. Sometimes I do talk too much, I think. Have you eaten anything this morning, Peter? There's some P and J downstairs, or there was a little while ago."

"I'm not hungry, Brother. You go ahead."

"I think I will. You'll need your strength, Peter. Why don't you come down with me?"

"Not right now."

"I'll see you in a bit then." He squeezes Peter's shoulder and greets some students passing in the hall, and Peter hears him chattering over Jefferson Airplane as his voice recedes down the hallway.

‡

"They're coming," Robin says, grinning, looking down from the rooftop beside Simon.

Everyone up there now crowds the parapets to watch.

"Maybe," he says, "but they're not moving. All the commotion is on the lawn. It's the people on the quad."

Indeed, the crowd appears to swarm while Hendrix wails across the quad in the woozy three-four beat of "Manic Depression." But even the music is soon drowned out in the chanting below, which seems to begin at the center of the quad and spill outward: "Pigs off the campus! We don't want your war! Pigs off the campus! We don't want your war!" Soon it finds a stout rhythm of its own as bullhorns join in and the protesters in the windows and on the rooftop take it up also. "Pigs off the campus! We don't want your war! Pigs off the campus! We don't want your war!"

Puzzled, Simon turns up his palms and looks at Robin. "What is it? What started it?"

She shakes her head.

Now they watch and join the chanting as protesters gather at the barricades, taunting the soldiers and cops, shouting and spitting at them. The guardsmen form a line at the far end of the quad, and the policemen along each side brandish their batons.

‡

On the main stairway in the lobby, Peter finds Terry rushing down.

"Have you seen Luke?" Terry asks, with terror in his eyes.

"A couple of hours ago. What's happened?"

"He has to leave!"

"Why? What is it?"

Terry gasps, "On the TV, up in the president's office…they're shooting at students, Peter! National guard troops fired on protesters at a school in Ohio. Killing them! They're killing students! I have to find Luke!"

"Try downstairs. He went down to eat. I haven't seen him since then."

Terry hurries on, leaping down the steps and running through the lobby and into the hallway on the right, while students now rush and mill everywhere.

Peter looks around for others from his group and SDS but sees no one in the turmoil. He perches on the landing above the lobby and shapes his hands into a speaker cone and shouts, "Everyone here, stop now! Everyone! Stop now!"

He continues shouting until they slow and quiet themselves, looking up at him, and then he gathers them onto the stairway, crowding them into dense rows, coaxing them, calling down the hallways for more, gradually filling the stairs like crowded bleachers at a basketball game.

"Pass around the grease!" he calls.

They wipe Vaseline on, linking their arms, and he reminds them not to fight or run. "We wait here!" he yells. "We wait. Nobody moves! We wait! Who's got a song? Somebody got a song?"

He'd hoped for something livelier than "Where Have All the Flowers Gone?" but soon everyone soon joins in, and there's even laughter in this tragic song as it spreads and they try to remember what's gone missing with each new verse. And now he laughs, too, swaying with those on each side of him, losing himself in the motion and the warming sense of purpose, of commitment, now as certain of his cause as he's ever been.

As they sing, he sees Brother Luke arrive from the hallway on the left, smiling, looking up at the chorus that fills the stairway, and finally squeezing himself in among the students on the lower steps, linking his arms with theirs and joining the song.

‡

tat …
tat …
tat …
tat …
tat …
tat …
tat …
tat …

"What is that? Why are they doing that?"

No one responds.

The police officers around Father Alfonse watch the swarming crowd before them, eyes ahead, fists tightening on their batons.

The staccato rhythm continues, out of sync with the students' chantng.

tat …
tat …
tat …
tat …
tat …
tat …
tat …
tat …

"Father," Brother Stedman says, "we have to leave here now. We have to go."

"I won't go. What is that?"

"The city police, on the other side. They're banging their clubs on their shields."

"Why? They'll just provoke them. It has to stop!"

"We can't stop it now."

Father Alfonse lunges toward the line in front of him, but Brother Stedman grabs him across the chest. He's much bigger than the priest, and though he easily holds him back, they're still just a few yards behind the line, which is all that separates them from the seething, shouting protesters.

"Those shootings," Father Alfonse says, "they have nothing to do with us! They can't shoot! Tell them not to shoot!"

Just then, canisters fly into the crowd, trailing gray smoke, and protesters rush wildly through the tear gas. At every turn they run headlong into armed men in uniform. A few students grab the hot canisters and toss them back at the police, and one of these disburses a line of guardsmen without gas masks into a nearby grove of trees.

Across the quad, city policemen wearing masks march on the crowd, while the deputies wait. In their khaki uniforms and Stetson hats, they greet anyone who comes near them, male or female, whether they're fighting or trying to run, with clubs and punches. They chase down students who break through the lines and head for safety, beating them on the ground and then moving on and looking for others to pummel. The football players and ROTC students also grab anyone within reach, beating and kicking them, and sometimes finding themselves beaten by the police. Women are fondled, men pulled by their hair. Smoke blankets the quad, and people lose one another in the chaos. The city police, in their riot gear and masks, move easily through the crowds, pushing people to the ground with their shields, kicking them, beating them with clubs. The confused regiment of national guard troops withdraws still farther, to the grass on the far side of the road, where they regroup in front of the stadium, now training their rifles on the riot.

Noxious, stifling smoke has filled the eyes and nostrils of the priest and brother, burning their throats as they stumble back through the parking lot. Brother Stedman drapes his robed arm across their faces and finally guides Father Alfonse to safety inside the stadium, where they sit in a stairwell, coughing and heaving.

‡

In the hallways and offices on the first floor of Celixine Hall, students leap from the windows and run into the chaos as police in riot gear enter the building, where they find row upon row of students sitting on the stairs, singing, waiting, arms linked, glistening with grease. But the police are in no mood for passive resistance. Now pumped up from fighting their way across campus, they drag the protesters down the stairs, swinging at them, regardless of gender, regardless that no one resists.

Peter watches from a dozen steps up as they attack Brother Luke along with the others on the lower steps. Peter tightens his arms with the students on each side of him as cops maul through the crowd. The first one to reach him is faceless behind his mask and helmet and shield. Two more are right behind him. He smashes Peter square in the face with his shield, breaking his nose, and then pulling him down the stairs by his arms, with another cop taking shots at his ribs as they drag him from the building on a bruising trip down the concrete front steps. He's lost sight of Brother Luke, of any of his friends, and as he tries to climb into the police truck in front of Celixine Hall, a blow to his legs crumples him and a swarm of paws hoists him into the truck. He can't see through the blood flowing from a bruise on his forehead, and he coughs and gasps as blood and fluid clog his nose and mouth.

Chapter 20

Fall 2000

The fan whined hideously and the defroster vent on the driver's side was blocked, which Peter discovered on a hilly wet highway in northern New York as sleet caked on the windshield. He finally pulled off the road to scrape it.

The car wasn't even close to a fair trade for his Jeep. A rusty Chevy Citation, circa early eighties. Inside, it wreaked of oil…and something… piss?…animal?…human? The upholstery was shredded, maybe by dogs, and the broken door and window handles were a hassle. It had no hubcaps, and the trunk didn't close tight. Keubler had arranged the deal with a junkyard in Albany, and he wasn't too happy when he did it either. Maybe this piece of shit was his revenge. The apartment incident took many weeks to filter through the system, but it finally resulted in another visit from the FBI. His lawyer sat by while he stuck to the line that he couldn't know everyone who came and went at his buildings and it was a long stretch from a commotion involving a Jeep in the middle of the night—and no one could say for sure what color it was—to harboring a fugitive. His lawyer said they had no case, but this was closer than he ever wanted to come to this business again. He thought Peter was already gone, but weeks later, when he spoke with Brother Luke on a filthy pay phone, he found out that the "visitor" was still there, so he paid a visit to the brothers' residence himself and made sure Peter went pronto. Setting up the car deal was *it!* IT! He wanted Peter gone, and he wanted that Jeep to disappear forever.

The junkyard owner had rounded shoulders and dark eyebrows, and his jump suit stretched tightly across his belly. He looked Peter up and down, and spoke as if he'd just caught him skulking near the chain link fence that enclosed his junkyard. The place was a jungle of mechanical detritus, acres of mangled heaps of metal, a vast tapestry of knotted and tangled auto waste, bleeding over into the scruffy woods where rusted trucks and cars had been planted decades ago and never moved again. He inspected the Jeep as if he was about to pay a premium for it, while a dog barked and lunged from a chain near the trailer that was both office and home to the man. A window curtain parted and closed a couple of times, distracting Peter over the dealer's shoulder. He thought men in suits would fly out the door at any moment, but none did. The face behind the curtain was a child's.

There was no choice about the vehicle. This was the one. Soon after Keubler tussled on the phone with the man, it was brought up to the front gate to await Peter's arrival. A straight swap. No money and no papers on either car. The only other vehicles anywhere near drivable were the tow truck with *Newt's Salvage* in blue italics on the doors and a late-model Toyota Camry with a baby seat in back. Neither was remotely a prospect for this trade. But he couldn't walk away, not only for Keubler's sake but also for the brothers', and his own. They'd be looking for the Jeep around here now—and with two windows covered with plastic and duct tape, it wouldn't be hard to spot—so he moved his stuff into the Chevy while Newt watched from the porch, as if suspecting that Peter might snatch a hubcap from one of the heaps near the front gate as he left.

The gas tank was near empty, and when he filled it, Peter also had to add two quarts of oil—and he found the wiper fluid reservoir cracked. Black curdles on the side of the engine block, like an oily mud slide, meant that the head gasket was near blowing. The car would need oil whenever he tanked up. The odometer said 48,210 miles, but Peter knew that really meant *one hundred* and 48,210 miles. As he poured oil into the engine, he thought about what he needed from this car. He doubted it would get him home, but that's not where he was going. Not yet. He no longer kidded himself that he wanted anything more from the past before he surrendered than one thing…one glimpse, from a distance. That was all. He now knew that she taught at a college somewhere in Maine, and he wanted to see her once, not even to talk to her or bother her, just to see her one more time, and then he'd go back, maybe not even drive himself. He'd walk into a police station or FBI office and let them do the driving, or flying, or whatever they did. His family would be at the other end. He'd never see her again if he didn't now, and he believed this was all he needed to shut the doors on his past and never look back. He would never mention her again or tell anyone that he'd come here. That's what he wanted from this car. That, and nothing else.

This urge or desire or impulse had never formulated itself into a purpose while he stayed with the brothers of Saint Celixine over the summer. It had mingled then with the multitude of fears and longings and regrets that swelled constantly within him. The brothers, especially Brother Luke, had given him a short reprieve from what was behind and what was ahead. He rebuilt their window casings and then caulked and painted them, and then he moved on to other repairs—leaky gutters, loose porch steps, fresh paint. He thought himself cowardly at times and thought maybe they did too, but at others he recognized that they were allowing him to strengthen himself to make the choices he needed to make. They had quietly accepted him, compressing his history among them, after a fashion, into whatever tasks or accomplishments he had recently done. At meals they would talk about a room he had painted the day before as if it was part of a distant past that they now shared. They loaned him credit on history, gave him currency, so he wouldn't have to answer questions about himself. They created a shorthand from the tidbits—the full-truths, half-truths, and no-truths—of information he provided: his past acquaintance with Luke, his experience in business, his retreat from alcohol and other nebulous weaknesses.

It occurred to Peter that maybe they weren't as naïve as they appeared, that perhaps they helped create the fictions of his life because they knew more than they gave out, that they probably talked among themselves and speculated about his past. He had once been their student, and he knew they were not without wits—or resources—connections with their own families and friends, letters and telephone calls and visits. But these fictions and shared experiences were sufficient to maintain an orderly relationship among them. They saw some good in him, perhaps because they chose to see it. Perhaps they just quietly insisted that this was what he would be while he was among them, and so that's what he was. Life there was active. He could not be a passive recipient of their hospitality. He had to participate, to contribute, and physical labor helped drain off some of the overflow from within him.

But he left hastily after Keubler's visit, while the brothers were in the chapel, hurriedly throwing his things into a bag and leaving an envelope on Brother Luke's bed, without seeing any of them again as he drove out of the wooded grounds and turned north on Route 32 to go find the salvage yard. Newt the junkyard dealer was a stiff dose of reality, welcoming him back to the only world he could hope to know until he entered the one that awaited him, but he'd already made up his mind what was next before he got there, and he numbed himself to everything but the essentials of the transaction.

Sleet pelted the windshield and roof as he sat on the roadside with his motor running, wasting gas, and the heater on full and the fan whining like a cat in pain. Back drafts from the highway traffic rocked his car. He couldn't wait this out. If he stayed here, a cop might think he needed assistance. The car had current New York state tags, but who knows what would turn up if they were punched into a police computer. The car lurched and the engine knocked as he throttled onto the highway after a stream of cars passed.

He had a little over $300 with him. At a convenience store within sight of a bridge that crossed Lake Champlain into Vermont, he bought bread, peanut butter, a gallon of water, and a jar of instant coffee. Robin was from somewhere around here. He wondered if her family still lived here—and what they said of her now, thirty years later. A generation had been added who would only know her through photos and stories. He thought of Emma and Todd, now imagining them as her niece and nephew. What would they think of her if they'd been born into that family, children of a brother or sister. Terrorist?...murderer?...revolutionary?...folk heroine?...the family Che? There would be so much more than pictures in albums and family memories to assimilate. Her name—and Peter's and the others—had once filled newspaper accounts and now even appeared in some histories of that period. They'd each have to decide for themselves what she was—and how, and if, she mattered.

The sleet stopped after he paid the toll and drove onto the bridge, and now, above the flat, still water and beneath a close cover of gray churning clouds, the day was surprisingly clear, with colorful trees along the shoreline and on distant hills in crisp relief against the surrounding blank, grayness of sky and water. Everything appeared as if in a broad, well-lit tunnel, yet with no apparent source of light. Living indoors for a few months hadn't desensitized him to the weather, but once again the conditions would affect every minute of his day and night. Still, it wouldn't be for long—a week, maybe two; then it would be over.

He'd browsed in a road atlas at the convenience store and memorized the sequence of highways that would take him across Vermont and New Hampshire and into Maine. Twilight fell as he drove through the White

Mountains. It would be difficult to find somewhere to stop safely for the night once it was dark. It wasn't yet seven, but he knew better than to pass up a clean rest stop, where, in the turnover of vehicles—even police cars, if they happened by—he could remain unnoticed, undisturbed, and have the use of a bathroom and running water and soap. He parked at the far end of the lot, close to the trees and empty picnic shelters. He still had the unfinished copy of *Middlemarch* from Kristen; he hadn't touched it in months. He thumbed the pages, but the light was too dim to read. He put the dome light on long enough to look at her note once more. He would never go back there, and that phone number could only get her in trouble. He crumpled it and dropped it in a waste barrel near the car. Then he resettled himself and listened to the traffic pass, all of it going somewhere, having a purpose, a destination. Well, now he did too.

‡

He wanted to find a public library and use the internet, which again reminded him of Kristen, and now he wondered if he should have thrown away her number—but then he was glad he did, for himself. There would be no other options now. This was a one-way road. And there'd be no more Kristens or Keublers or Brother Lukes.

As he drove across New Hampshire and Maine, he passed through towns that seemed to be from another time—old mill towns, along a river that paralleled the highway, with steel arch bridges, abandoned factories and warehouses, stores and offices with faded awnings and lettering painted on plate glass windows. Such places only existed in Frank Capra movies now, he thought, but there, at least, they had life, vibrancy. These weren't idyllic postcard towns. He saw ample evidence of poverty. The only library he passed was no bigger than a single-bay garage. Even if they had the internet, in such a small place he'd be conspicuous just walking in the door.

He had noticed, too, the absence of fast-food chains along the way, but at a busy intersection outside of one town in Maine, he found everything clumped together, all around the Wal-Mart—tire and liquor stores, McDonald's, Burger King, Ken-Taco-Hut. All of it. Traffic was so heavy that he waited twice for the light to change as he inched forward in a steady rain. The heavy scent of fried food tempted him, even in the musty dampness of the car's stink. He could eat for less than five dollars. Use the bathroom hassle-free. But he found the traffic and chaos oppressive. He drove on, but now it was pointless to go far until he had some information. He didn't know what college or what town. He'd have to find a library, or somewhere, to look her up. He could have found out back at the brothers' residence, but he didn't know he would do this, or leave as suddenly as he did—and he also thought asking Luke for information about her was just too obvious.

‡

He learned that she taught at Halston College, an hour or so north of Bangor, when he browsed the literature racks in a counseling office at a junior college. He'd spent twenty minutes cleaning himself up in a highway rest stop just so he could go inside without attracting attention. He couldn't use the juco library without an ID card, but when he said he was interested in researching music colleges for his daughter—a lie that made him shudder even as it came out of his mouth—the attendant directed him along a short walkway to the counseling office. Everyone there was busy, so he leafed through the catalogues undisturbed until he found what he wanted. The cover photo depicted bronze statues of two men conversing on a park bench. Outside in his car, he read that they were each graduates, one of whom served in Teddy Roosevelt's cabinet and the other in the senate after the Civil War. He found her name—still her maiden name—and a short profile in the faculty listings, and he saw the statues in person a day later at the main entrance to the campus, but he only stood there briefly, self-conscious of his appearance, of just being there. He felt conspicuous even as a car slowed and turned onto the grounds, as if the passenger whose eyes fell on him was suspicious, wondering why he was there, what his intentions were. What if she'd been in that car? He couldn't linger. He couldn't wander around.

The college was small, much smaller than St. Celixine, with a half dozen buildings in granite and red-brick clustered around a hill at the center of the property. Thick, ancient trees studded the campus, and students hurried across the grounds. Light snow had fallen overnight.

From the map in the catalogue, Peter thought he knew which building was the music department, but so what? He couldn't just walk in there. And what was he doing here at all? The utter foolishness of being here overwhelmed him now that it was real, tangible—now that she was but a short walk from where he stood. But, as foolish and stupid, and even sinister, as his presence here might be, still here he was. He'd come this far. He'd have his look and then go—go far from here, so his surrender wouldn't be linked to her either. Maybe Boston, maybe some small town in New Hampshire or Connecticut. It didn't matter. His time was now short.

The college campus spilled over into a village, also named Halston, where he parked and walked the streets, with his collar up and his hat pulled low. He ate a sandwich in a café filled with students wearing college sweatshirts, and he studied in surreptitious glances the few women in the place who might be close to him in age. Later, at a bookstore down the street, he found a display of her CDs and sheet music. He also saw a recent photo of her on the cover of the music, her hair long and mostly gray, tinged in streaks with remnants of the reddish-orange it had once been, now pulled back behind her head, with the same broad face and glistening eyes. The upward tilt at one corner of her mouth barely hinted at a smile, which left her face unwrinkled, open, serene. She was thoughtful and mature, and beautiful. He could do nothing but hurt her, he now saw. She had a life—a rich and meaningful life. And also, what would being here do to his own family if this was where he was caught? He had to leave.

"You like her stuff?" a clerk said, from behind the rack.

Peter had felt him approaching. He was ultra-sensitive to everything around him now, as afraid of stumbling into her unawares as he was of getting nabbed here. He couldn't allow either to happen. "Yeah," he said, replacing the sheet music on the rack.

"The new one's really good," the clerk said. He was gaunt, unshaven. Too old for a student—maybe an alum. He snatched a CD from the shelf and studied it himself. The same photo was on the cover. He offered it to Peter and said, "Have you got this one?"

"No," Peter responded, turning it over, reading the song titles—"Eclipse," "Flight," "Rubato Rumble," "Angels' Samba," "Magister Ludi"—trying to imagine music from these names.

"It's good! If you like her stuff, you'll like it. She's come so far from the early stuff, you know, but one thing..." he trailed off, picking up another copy of the same CD and staring at it again.

"What's that?" Peter asked.

The clerk looked up as if he suddenly recalled he was conversing and said, "Like, other music—whatever, classical, jazz, anything—I can put it on and either sit down and listen to it or I can have it on and do something else while I listen. You know what I mean? Could be Mozart, could be Coltrane...great just to listen to, and you keep hearing it new every time, or you can enjoy it while you're doing something, like reading your e-mails or making dinner. But with her stuff, there's only one way to listen to it. You gotta sit and listen. Doesn't make any sense otherwise. It's almost annoying if you put it on and go do something, but when you do sit down, like, after dinner with some tea, and put in one of her CDs, she just takes you away. It's like reading a novel or a poem. You have to pay attention. She makes you work, too, but she pays you for the effort. One thing, though,"—he smiled now—"they're never gonna make elevator music out of her stuff. No shit. So...I know! You want to hear some of it? I got some headphones right over here. We've already got this one loaded. Here, this way..." He guided Peter to the end of the aisle and handed him a set of headphones, which Peter fitted over his ears, and then he touched a couple of buttons on the panel and nodded at Peter with a smile, leaving him inside the headphones with the music.

From the titles—and what he'd heard on the CDs he'd bought years ago—he expected somber, moody music, but here was something altogether different. Mostly, it was lively and rhythmic, even humorous at times. She played the cello with an ensemble that included a mandolin, a guitar, a flute, a bass, and a koto. From the CD photos, Peter deduced that the woman kneeling and plucking at a long, wooden instrument was playing the koto. Also pictured was a percussionist surrounded by a variety of hand drums, chimes, bells, and wooden noisemakers. The combined sound was large, rich. What amazed him most were the long, ranging solos she took. He'd never heard her play anything that wasn't written, but here she was, launching into ad libs that seemed to explore every note and sound her instrument could make, even knocking on the wood and tapping her bow on the strings. He'd never heard music like this. It was almost impossible to imagine that this had evolved from what he remembered from so long ago. He listened well beyond what was reasonable to sample the album, but the clerk never bothered him, leaving him to listen and read through the notes.

When he took off the headphones, the clerk said from the counter, "You see what I mean?"

Peter nodded, again looking over the same photos he'd been studying for the past half hour.

The clerk came around from behind the counter. It seemed like a lot of trouble to sell one CD, but Peter now recognized something other than that, as if the clerk had discovered a fellow member of the same faith, or a potential convert.

"You a musician?" the clerk asked.

"No, I just like music. I never really learned much about it. But...you must be one."

The clerk smiled, "Sort of...but I'm working here, right?" He paused, and laughed, "But I was, I am...play the viola. Not many of us around, sort of bastard children."

"You studied here?"

"Yeah. Took her ensemble and theory courses too. She's amazing. She could probably teach at any conservatory in the country, but instead she just settled here, teaches her courses, does her recordings, sometimes gives a recital. She gave concerts for years all over the world, but then she just sort of quit. Some people said the travel and practice wore her out, but that's not what I thought. I had my own theory."

"What's that?"

"You have to know her to get this...but, I don't know...the only way I can explain it is, like...you ever read any Emily Dickinson?"

"A long time ago."

"Well, Dickinson, she had trouble being around people. Not that she didn't like them, see...she loved them. But interacting, dealing with all the emotions...you know, managing all the thinking and feeling you do around people, it just overwhelmed her, so she ended up talking to people from behind a screen, or sitting in her room at the top of the stairs and calling down to her visitors. Well, I think Susan's a bit like that. In class, you never felt like she wasn't on your side...she didn't know how to insult somebody. I never heard her say something sarcastic or rude to anyone... not like some of the pricks on that faculty. But...if you played a note that so help me God wasn't the width of a dust mote off the mark on the fret board, she could hear it. She has perfect pitch, perfect everything. And... here's something...you know, it's why musicians like me work in book stores and musicians like her play Carnegie Hall. You could take a line of music that the ensemble cellist could play right through, no problem... sounded great, but then Susan would play it, the same thing, and the touch of her bow, the choice she'd make not to give a tremolo where the other player just had or to slow the tempo even though playing it fast showed off more skill...well, you could hear it, what makes her special."

The clerk's lips curled up on one side as he glanced around the store and squinted a grin that seemed to hold more back than it shared. Only one other customer browsed a rack of greeting cards.

Peter wasn't certain, but he thought the young man might be looking away to conceal moist eyes.

The clerk sniffed a chuckle and said, "Well, that's way more than you probably wanted to know."

"Not at all," Peter said. "I'll take the CD." At the counter, he asked, "So is she giving any recitals soon?"

The clerk handed Peter his bag and leaned forward on the counter. "No, she's on leave this semester. Not even here right now. I think she's in Europe teaching somewhere. Maybe a few concerts to promote the new CD, but like I said, she doesn't do much of that. She's all studio. Must drive her agent nuts."

"Oh…I see."

"Yeah, she doesn't have much to keep her here, even though she's been on the faculty for…must be twenty years or so. Just her son, and he's in the service, the Army, I think, so he's not around much."

"She's divorced?"

"Don't know if it's that, or her husband died, or what. She's really personable and warm as a teacher, but like I said, she's not much for being around people. Pretty reclusive, you know. Doesn't even live nearby. She's got a place up towards Presque Isle, I think. That direction anyway. Must be a hassle driving down here once the snow starts."

"Thanks," Peter said.

"Yeah, enjoy it."

Of course, he couldn't enjoy it. He had no way to play it, and even if he could, whatever sensations listening to it might bring, enjoyment would not be one of them. But still he bought it, not even thinking to do otherwise as the clerk talked about her. He swore the kid was in love with her, the way he talked, not just in love with *her*, but with all that she was, all that she'd achieved, with her talent and accomplishments and how she lived. Peter paced the sidewalk glumly, keeping his head down, stepping around students walking in groups, wondering how many of hers had fallen in love with her over the years. Well, someone had. She had a son, grown now, a soldier. Her life had been full with so much, including the sorrow or pain that must have come with losing a husband, however she lost him. After listening to the clerk, he found it hard to imagine that anyone would willingly leave her, yet…

The stench and dampness inside the car filled his senses, as if seeping in through his skin, as he sat there and wept, huddling himself up against the cold and the ugly filth that surrounded him. He felt as if he was gasping inside a tiny air pocket, which was now all that kept him alive in a deep, inescapable cave. There was nowhere left to go, nothing more to do. His pain seemed as much derived from seeing how she had thrived without him, how life had persisted, her life, everyone's, as from his own sense of loss, as if he was looking back from death and seeing all that happened next, after he was gone. She had moved on without him. Her life had stayed in the current of its flow—while his now seemed no more than a series of accidents. But even so, he knew it was impossible to have stayed with her. He couldn't have chosen her life any more than she could have chosen his, but now he could also see that for all the grandness of his vision at twenty years old, she was the one who saw beyond horizons that he couldn't even imagine back then, and now recognizing that his life was mostly spent, and that it had been a failure, he was filled with contempt for himself.

And her son was a soldier—wasn't that rich?

Chapter 21

Six Months Later

He pissed in spurts. A dribble now rolled back under his cock, and he wagged it off. Glistening bronze drops melted into the snow and soaked into his pants. There was more. He could either wait or he'd be out here again in five minutes, so he waited, wedging one foot on a rock to keep from slipping in the snow. And just as it began to trickle out again, and he leaned forward to guide the stream away from himself, a gust of wind, rushing up from the pond and across the open plain of the boat slip and parking lot, cold and sharp, blew the stream to one side, splattering his pant leg and foot. He couldn't stop now and tried to turn downwind, but he slipped and splattered himself. A truck rumbling past on the highway, just through the woods, swallowed up his voice as he swore and howled. The flow had stopped, and he waited for it to start again, until it built into a final satisfying spurt, but the warm dampness on his knee and socks quickly turned cold. He was only a few feet from the car, and before he zipped up, he wiped himself with a greasy rag. The pants would dry. He put on another pair of dirty socks.

Water lapped up on the concrete slip, high with snowmelt, rippling in the gusty wind. Heavy, wet snow covered the ground, ankle deep, but the concrete had mostly dried out in the afternoon sun over the past couple of days. He'd returned here several times to park at night, when the lot was empty. Last night a car full of teenagers stopped, and in the darkness, he clutched a crowbar while across the lot their woofers throbbed as they smoked up and maybe fucked, and then drove on, possibly never even seeing his car in the shrubs at the back of the lot. He knew about this place and a dozen others, just as he knew which shelters in Portland and Bangor to sleep in and which church pantries in Augusta and Waterville and other towns would feed him. That's how he stayed alive over the winter, bustling into homeless shelters with crowds of desperate men and women, pushing forward as doorways were thrown open when the temperatures dropped to below zero, minus ten, minus twenty, and staying outside was certain death. He lifted food from trash bins and sometimes shoveled snow and did other manual labor through referrals from the shelters. He occasionally worked at one shelter, washing dishes and laundering donated clothing for small handouts of cash, for a used coat that didn't carry the stench of his old one, for the promise of a bed. But surviving in these places also meant scrabbling with other men over soap bars and pillows, sleeping curled up with his belongings so they weren't stolen in the night, crowding and elbowing at the doorways for the beds inside, and being turned away when he appeared too frequently. The temperatures had risen as spring loomed, and now he stayed in his car. Often, when he slept, bundled in the back seat in two coats and a dirty blanket, he hoped the temperature would drop into negative digits and he'd just drift off and never awaken, but he did wake up after fitful sleep, stiff, sore, cold, and urgently needing to piss.

His piss was brown and rusty, and his shit thin and watery. He coughed and sniveled continually and hadn't shaven or cut his hair in months. He lived like a small animal that had suddenly been transplanted into an unfamiliar and strange habitat—like a squirrel in a field with no trees—its instincts raging in confusion. He was disoriented, dazed, withering from the effort to stay alive, and not even sure why he bothered. He hadn't made a decision not to surrender as much as he simply gave up the will to do anything, as if he'd abandoned life while continuing to live. The small air pocket in the dark cave continued to sustain him, though the air he breathed was dense and sickening. He didn't care if he was recognized, though that wasn't likely in his present state. He had a better chance of being picked up for vagrancy. Meanwhile, he went through the motions of living, finding what he needed to sustain himself just as liquid finds its way into the smallest crevices and creases that gravity takes it. He was driven only by hunger and cold and fear, and hounded by swirling voices and memories that erratically flitted through his head, often erupting in random utterances, fragments of words and phrases.

At first he was aware of his outbursts, and he would go silent, surprised at the sound of his own voice. But soon, he was talking aloud wherever he was—pissing in the bushes or putting gas in the car. "Middle-earth on the garbage dumpster! Ha!" The lady pumping gas across the island slid the minivan door shut with her kids in back. "If you're not gonna use it, what're you keepin' it here for?!" He read the headlines through the window of a newspaper box, while passers-by steered a wide path around him. When he noticed people looking at him, he didn't understand why. After a while, the sound of his voice blended seamlessly into the images and scenes that rushed through his head like a stretch of furious whitewater in springtime.

He jabbered now as he squatted on the boat slip and wet his face and hands in the icy water—"...bombs for peace peace peeee...pee pee pee...where's Robin?" He giggled. The parking lot was empty. He looked around and then crept into the bushes at the edge of the water, where he dropped his trousers and washed his crotch and ass. "...but we don't need new carpeting..." He dried himself with a rag and pulled up his pants.

The engine groaned before it caught, sending a thick black plume from the tailpipe. He had nowhere to go; he just didn't need to be here any longer. He'd become conditioned to moving on at indeterminate and regular intervals. On a frigid morning back in January, he settled in a booth at a diner and ordered coffee and a muffin, taking up the newspaper another customer had left behind. When he'd eaten, the waitress suddenly appeared and instead of refilling his coffee mug, she put a takeout container on the table. "Here's one for the road, hon. It's on the house," she said firmly. He looked up from the paper, needing a moment to process the message, and then he saw the cook watching through the service window behind the counter. He took the cup and left the restaurant. Now, he didn't need prodding; instinct alone kept him moving.

With less than half a tank of gas and about three dollars on him, he wasn't going far—just to find another place to settle for a day or two. The church food pantry in Houlton was open on Tuesdays. He thought that was two days from now. He'd go tomorrow and if that turned out to be Monday, he'd return the next day. A highway sign said Presque Isle 33 miles. What was there? He couldn't recall for a moment. At times he didn't know why he was here at all in this damp, gray, snowy place. It was just the place he was now. All tomorrow meant was whether the food pantry was open. But then he did recall about Presque Isle—and the bookstore clerk, and the music, and her. Nothing good would come from going there, yet he couldn't bring himself to leave, now that he was this close. He'd never gone back to Halston and he'd never driven into Presque Isle, fearful that she might see him. Yet he tempted fate in nearby towns, on the chance that she'd emerge from a store or drive by in a car. As he thought of her, he squinted and jerked his head back as the policeman's shield caved in his face, and then he rubbed the flat spot above the tip of his nose and touched his upper lip and looked at his fingers. No blood, no pain. That was long ago. Maybe he would go there—in two days, or three, after he'd gone to the food pantry. Just once. It was so close. He only wanted to see her once, and he'd stayed away all this time, so near yet.... He often watched people on the streets to see if she'd be among them, sometimes not even remembering who or what he was watching for.

He passed a road that looked familiar, an unpaved logging road. He thought he'd previously parked in a small turnoff down that way. The road was easy to miss. With no sign and no houses or other landmarks nearby, it blended into the gray woods that lined the highway for miles. He pulled up and made a u-turn. The slushy road was shrouded by woods on both sides, much darker here than on the highway. He drove for fifteen, twenty, maybe thirty minutes—he didn't know—driving slowly, looking for the turnoff, but he couldn't find it. The road descended and curved, which seemed unfamiliar, but he continued looking. Now it didn't matter if this was the same road or another, as long as there was someplace he could settle, but there was no turnoff on the narrow road, and no shoulder and no way to turn around. He became frustrated and worried, and he had to piss. With nothing around but woods, he stopped the car and stumbled to the edge of the slushy road, unzipping.

As he stood, muttering and waiting, he heard a deep rumble up ahead—a truck or some vehicle was coming. His piss was close to starting but the ominous noise frightened him. He zipped up and hurried back into the car, but when he turned the ignition a series of sharp clicks greeted him, and then nothing. He tried again with the same result. "Thinking it through through through," he muttered, as he tried again and again. Now even the clicks ceased. The engine rumble was no longer distant. It would round the curve ahead at any moment. "...Simon wouldn't..." He was filled with terror, and he pushed down hard on the broken driver's door handle, which snapped out of the socket as the door swung open. He grabbed his bag from the back seat, stuffing his blanket and other loose items into it and then dashed into the woods, soaking both feet as he stumbled through a stream, and then he hunkered behind some brush thirty or forty yards from the road as the grinding engine approached. It belonged to a big diesel pickup truck with four huge rear tires, and the driver was alone. He stopped in front of the Chevy, got out of the idling truck, and looked inside the car and then all around. He was in his forties or early fifties, pot-bellied, and wore a fluffy parka vest and a baseball cap. He peered into the woods and studied the ground, retracing Peter's footsteps in the snow, and then following them as far as the stream, where he stopped and stared ahead into the shadows.

"Hey! Anyone there!" His voice was sharp, angry.

Peter slunk low to the ground behind the shrubs, shivering with fear, pressing his face into the snow.

"Hey! This is private property. There's no hunting allowed! Get your heapa junk outta here!" After a few minutes of watching and listening and shouting again, he muttered, "Shit!" and returned to the road.

Afraid to move, Peter could only listen as the diesel truck backed up and the cable was unwound from the hitch in front and clanked onto the Chevy's bumper. The engine revved as the truck pulled the car forward and off the road. Then more clanking and unhitching, and the truck revved again, thwacking brush on the roadside as it angrily roared past the Chevy.

Peter was certain the truck driver would return, perhaps not alone. With his feet and pant legs wet, he cautiously approached the car, retrieving some food cans and dry clothes from the trunk, stuffing everything into a canvas tote bag he'd gotten at one of the shelters. Hurried and fearful of lingering, he looked around at the dark woods and decided the road wasn't safe, so he took off on the opposite side of the road, wanting to avoid the stream, and loped into the woods again.

He tramped on for much of the day, never finding his way back to the highway, licking snow when he was thirsty and stopping to rest when he found a dry rock. He often mistook the white noise of the forest for footsteps. Running water seemed to carry human voices within it. He would pause and listen, crouching behind thickets of shrubs and rocks, until he realized it was only the water and moved on, trudging through the woods, uncertain where he was headed and wondering how far it was to the highway.

The area was hilly and thick with pines. He tried to find openings at rises to see what was nearby, but he only saw more woods, no fences or houses, or anything human for that matter. It was hard to gauge how far he traveled. By late afternoon, he had no idea where he was or how far from the highway. There was nothing but woods in every direction. When he came upon a large rock formation that offered shelter from the wind, he settled to rest for a while. He was exhausted, and his feet were numb.

Darkness was coming and he knew he'd have to spend the night here.

He gathered deadwood and built a fire, setting his wet socks and shoes close by. Steam rose as they warmed. Almost giddy with fatigue and hunger, he scarfed the few remaining vanilla wafers from a box and then threw it on the fire. He had cans of chili and fruit from his last visit to the food pantry, but he'd left the can opener back at the car. He also had a filthy blanket, some clothing, and some crackers and cereal. Exhausted and shivering, he wrapped himself in the blanket and leaned against the rock wall, drifting in and out of sleep for hours, rousing himself during the night to add wood to the fire or piss into the darkness. Moose bugled in the distance, and nearer, the eerie nasal grunts and squeals of elk frightened him. All around, rustlings and scurryings startled him awake every few minutes.

Time had warped. The past gathered itself into one place. People from thirty years ago were no farther away than his life in Kansas. He replayed an argument with Cherylee—still frustrated by it, how it had even turned into an argument. He'd been throwing a baseball with Todd, and the boy flinched and turned away, missing the ball nearly every time Peter threw it, until finally he ran inside, frustrated and crying. Cherylee then got angry with Peter for not throwing more gently and aiming better for his glove. Which led him to think of Simon, because for some reason he'd thought of Simon at that very moment—the first time Simon showed Peter his paintings, and Peter saw not from the images on the canvases but from the willful intensity in Simon's face how dire the causes were that drove him, and that he'd allowed himself to become a filter for all of that emotion and anger and anguish, transferring it to his canvases, and Peter recognized how personal the stakes were: this came back to him—while Cherylee accused him of being too rough on Todd, though he hadn't thought he was rough at all. He was just throwing the ball, not hard, not maliciously, just playing catch. The boy, he said, was too big for underhanded, baby throws, which she took to mean that he was being hard on him. Bits of conversation—with her, with Simon, with others—erupted from his mouth, startling him awake, out of place in the quiet that surrounded him. Then he would watch the fire and listen to the forest, absent of any sound of civilization, not even a hint of distant road noise. The sky cleared during the night, but it was moonless, and the darkness nearly perfect. Through the treetops he saw the infinite thickness of stars and watched satellites whiz across the firmament at such speeds that he lost sight of them when he blinked.

Corinne had her back to him, across the lobby, admiring a picture—not just pretending, but really admiring it—with the same easy sway in her hips she would have had on a Sunday afternoon in a gallery, and then the blast came, roaring through the wall with the force of a locomotive. Then, from beneath the overturned sofa, he looked across the floor and saw her, crumpled, bleeding, unmistakably dead. Screams in the hallway. A man howling—horrible, animal-like sounds. Then, he knelt over Terry, his face shredded from glass shards, blood leaking from countless sieves. Simon shouted at Peter to get out.

The loop played and replayed, sloshing back and forth between waking and sleep, but he was never fully asleep and never fully awake.

Dawn neared and he leaned on the rock wall, huddled in his coat and blanket, with nothing left of the fire but embers and dust. The sky was the flat gray of concrete when he unwrapped himself and put on his shoes and socks, cold and still damp. The ground was wet, and there were snow packs all around where sunlight had not penetrated the woods.

He wiped his face with snow, and momentarily refreshed, he climbed atop the rocks that had sheltered him through the night. The formation extended over a long ridge, and the sun gleamed below the horizon in the distance. What he saw was more woods, more trees, and more hills, going on as far as he could see, for miles. A distant ridgeline offered the prospect of a village or town where a plume of smoke drifted upward, perhaps from a factory or power plant, maybe five or ten miles away, but there was nothing else but forest all around him. He was as isolated as he had ever been. Behind him was the old Chevy, the angry pick-up truck driver, and miles and miles from there...all that he'd left behind.

When the sun had risen fully, it shown through a blustery sky, riddled with a thousand puffs of clouds but no continuous cloud cover. He rebuilt the fire and ate handfuls of crackers and cereal, listening now for footsteps and voices, wondering if the truck driver and his friends would be looking for him. When they found him, he would accept whatever happened, expecting they'd beat him up before they marched him back to civilization. He'd been beaten up before; he knew how to take a beating. For now, the rock wall sheltered him and the fire warmed him.

During the morning, the puffy clouds gathered and crowded together, darkening, and then rain began, drops here and there, increasing, becoming steady, and then blowing in thick gusts. The wall offered no cover from the rain, and his fire was soon doused. He shrouded himself in the blanket and found a dense pine tree nearby where he could squat at the edge of a snow pack, partly sheltered.

The rain continued for hours, seeping down through the branches and gradually penetrating his blanket and coat. As he huddled there, bundled and shivering, often mumbling, images from the past flashed randomly before him—Robin's sweaty breasts shaking over him as they fucked with cases of explosives just a dozen feet from their mattress on the warehouse floor; the protesters singing in the lobby—all scrunched together, swaying and singing with all of their hearts, singing to greet the pigs—guardsmen had killed students!—no one doubted the cause now—he was one of many, just one voice in the chorus, and he'd never felt better, never more certain, more ready—he had no fear as the door burst open and daylight poured in along with men in helmets, swinging clubs—before or after that, he'd never felt more certain, never again; dogs—where was that?—dogs?—many of them—he heard their barks and yelps; and read a book—what was it?—Dorothea—he knew that name—the book—she married an old man, and he used her; "push now!…push again!"—the feet came first, gray, wet, tiny, folded together—dark, brown blood oozed out around the feet—she wasn't supposed to come that way—knees appeared—a sliver of a crease where the legs met, pressed together—he knew it was a girl before the doctor said so—maybe she had waited for him to speak, for him to be the one to announce it—but he was afraid—he'd never seen such a thing—"… and again!…"—and above the stranded legs and the moist, pulsing rim, sweating and grunting fiercely, she pushed again, and the rest came, now the shoulders, now the head, blue, mouth open, wanting to gasp but not finding what it sought, wobbling, as the nurse cleared her mouth and she drew her first breath and whimpered.

In his coat pocket, in a jumble of tissues, bottle caps, and crumpled papers, his fingers touched the photo and the blue recital program, and he took the photo out and gazed at it. They were strangers—all four of them. They might have been just an anonymous family in a photography studio display—colorfully dressed, smiling, folded together, an image of prosperity and contentment that could only leave viewers to reflect on their own failings and the unhappiness of their own families. The life that surrounded the picture came to him in hazy fragments now, like childhood memories, distant, irretrievable. For a terrifying moment, there was a black, empty gap before Cherylee's name returned to him. Of all that he'd been through until now, the frustration of that moment, the immeasurable hesitation before the synapses in his brain reconnected and delivered the name was the emptiest thing he'd ever known. What had happened to bring him here, to this place, this moment? Where had it begun? He couldn't trace his way back through the network of events, people, thoughts—all that went through his mind in a lifetime—it wasn't choices alone—things had happened, things he couldn't help—he'd emerged from his own womb, from burying himself in his navel, and found that he had to act, realized that if he didn't, if others didn't, the nightmare of war and killing and greed would roll over them, consume them—at some point, he remembered being right, knowing what he had to do, but that was so long ago, so fleeting—he was never again as sure as the day he sang with the others in the lobby, all in one voice, singing to the faceless brutes with guns and clubs and helmets; not even on the day they took the bomb into an elevator and pressed for the sixth floor.

He slid the photo into his pocket and slunk down, leaning back against the tree. Rain had puddled in a crease in his blanket and now spilled inside his collar, sending a sharp chill across his neck. He was hungry, very hungry—he'd been there for hours—but he'd get soaked if he went to retrieve food, so he waited...

...watching Magnus twist the tooth of a crimping tool into the end of a length of dynamite, beads of sweat glistening on his arms and neck, with his shirt off in the hot vacant warehouse. He is wiry and muscular. His hair hangs in his face and sticks to his temples. Wires, tools, blasting caps, and disassembled alarm clocks litter the table. Two cases, with dozens more sticks in faded orange and creamy white wrappers, lie on the floor. Across the room, Robin sits cross-legged on a mattress bent over a newspaper.

"Damn, it's hot up here!" Magnus wipes his brow with a rag. "We gotta get a window open."

"They're nailed shut," Peter says. He gets up and studies the casing of the closest window. It is tall, opaque, with wire mesh embedded in the glass. He climbs up on the sill. "You got a hammer?"

Magnus tosses one, and Peter catches it in front of the glass. "Oh shit!" he snickers.

Magnus smiles.

"We don't need to attract any attention up here," Robin says.

Peter works the nails loose, jumps down, and slides the window open. "Maybe that'll help." The river smell wafts in with the hot wind.

"Shoulda done that sooner...fucking hot!"

"Yeah, I'll get another."

"Not in front," Robin says. "Someone might wonder what's going on up here."

After he opens another, Peter rejoins Magnus. "New stuff?"

"Yeah, from a gravel site in Poughkeepsie. Me and Simon went up there a few days ago. Hey, did I tell you about the shit from the house?"

"No."

"Man, Simon's got telepathy or something. He knew that raid was coming."

"He says he didn't," Robin says. "Just that they'd probably raid us after the rally."

"Listen, Peter. I had so much shit and I had stuff assembled, too…I mean, we coulda set one off any time…so dumping it…it was such a fucking waste. Anyway, I loaded the van, and I was gonna get rid of it, but I just couldn't do it. So, I drove around and around with enough shit to blow up the bridge, trying to decide what to do. There I was, sitting at a fucking light in the middle of town, checking out the cars around me and thinking, if some honey's doing her makeup instead of looking where she's going and rear-ends me, nobody for a hundred yards in any direction will ever know what hit them. I had all this shit…you wouldn't just throw away a stamp collection you've been working on for years, would you? So finally, I couldn't do it."

"What'd you do?"

"Brought it to the office," he laughs, "and while everyone was upstairs getting all pumped up for the rally, I was down unloading the van and stashing it in the basement. There was all this furniture and rubbish down there. Looked like it hadn't been touched in years, so I just put the ice cream back there and covered it up. Then, weeks later, after we got out, I went back, and, wouldn't you know, a big rain storm had come through and water seeped into the cellar and it all got soaked. Looked like rats chewed on it, too."

"No shit?"

"Yeah, must have some rat-munchy smell. I'll bet they got fucked up good!" He bobs his head, laughing.

"So what'd you do with it?"

"Took it down to the river one night and tossed it in. Simon went too. Then we sat there and smoked a joint. Nice night, too, a little breeze off the river. Lights glittering on the water. We watched a train pass on the other side. The dynamite was in about twenty feet of water, and we just sat on the shore, smoking and enjoying the scenery. How fucking weird is that?"

"Weird," Robin snorts. "I can just see you sitting by the river and grieving for your stash…"

"…a real romantic…" The words eased through his lips with a grin, and he shuddered.

"...he's a real romantic." She smiles at Peter as she tosses the paper aside and joins them at the table. She wears a tank top, and sweat coats her shoulders. She ruffles out the back of her shirt, and her damp arm presses on his as she looks over the work.

"Check it out!" Magnus holds up the stick. "The blasting cap goes in here." He points to a hole in the end. Then he picks up a small plastic cylinder. "See the two wires coming out of the top?"

Peter nods, fascinated.

"It's actually just one wire. These two ends are insulated, but a tiny length that loops through inside is bare. That's buried in a flash charge, which ignites a primary charge, and then a base charge, and when that goes off, it sets off the stick of dynamite. What happens is really a series of explosions."

"How does the clock set it off?"

Magnus grins. "This is so cool because the alarm triggers the whole thing, so you have the alarm going off, like it's saying, 'Good morning!' and then almost instantly the explosion." He picks up an old-fashioned alarm clock with two bell ringers on top and big numbers on the face. "See, when the hammer strikes the bell, it completes the circuit in the wire that runs from the battery into the blasting cap, and when that little section of exposed wire heats up, ba-boooom!"

"What's that white stuff on the sticks?" Peter reaches for one of the cases with his finger.

"Don't touch that shit!" Magnus knocks his hand away. "It's nitroglycerine. When the stuff ages it seeps out and crystallizes."

"Nitro?!" Robin exclaims.

"Don't worry. You need a blasting cap to ignite the explosives. It's really hard to set this stuff off without a pretty good charge. Besides, it's just trace amounts, but it'll burn the shit out of your hand if you touch it. Hey, was there anything about Hendrix in the paper?"

"In the Groenkill paper?" she snorts. "Yeah, good riddance! Here, listen to this quote they dug up." She grabs the paper. "'When I die I want people to play my music, go wild and freak out and do anything they want to do.'"

"I like that! We got any Hendrix here?"

"Nah," Peter responds, "we ain't got much."

"We have to get some Hendrix and smoke a jay for him."

"You sound like we're setting up housekeeping," Robin says. "We're gonna be out of here soon. When's Simon coming over?"

What was that—coming now? Footsteps—in the rain—someone coming?

He listened, his eyes open to a bare slit, but he only heard the rain—and then a sudden rustling, maybe a squirrel—and then the rain.

A door bangs in the stairwell at the front of the building. It's Sunday, and the offices downstairs should be empty. Robin trots to the top of the stairs, while Magnus and Peter hastily clear the table.

"Helloooo!" Simon's voice echoes in the stairwell.

"Shit!" Robin exclaims.

Peter blows a breath, and Magnus picks through the mess on the table.

"Nobody here but us freaks!" Simon announces, emerging with Corinne and Terry.

"What the fuck, Simon! He can't just throw that stuff in a box and shove it in the closet. What're you doing coming in this way? And all bunched up, too! Here we are parking all over town and taking buses to get here, and you come trouncing in like it's Sunday brunch."

"It is!" Simon smiles. "We brought you goodies!"

Corinne holds up a couple of bakery bags.

Simon pats Magnus on the shoulder. "You gotta show me everything!"

"Simon..."

"I know, man. I know. Shoulda come up the back. Shoulda come in separately. Sorry about that. It's Sunday. The district's empty. Not a soul in sight."

"All the easier for them to make you," Robin adds. "Where'd you park?"

"A few blocks. We stopped at the café and got some Danish and coffees for you."

Robin shakes her head. "The three of you walking through the streets with a couple of bags of food...do you think it would occur to them to follow you?"

"Oh, c'mon, Robin! We're here. No problem. Have some Danish."

Magnus has already grabbed one of the pastries, his fingers still dusty from the explosives.

"You guys are troupers!" Simon lights a cigarette.

"Whoa! Whoa!" Magnus waves the pastry. "Not here! Get the fuck out of here!"

Simon hops away and settles on the mattress, glancing down at Robin's paper. "Hey, did you see about Jackson State? That was the same week we took over the college."

"What about it?" Robin asks.

"Here, it's in the back. They got the actual transmission from the pig who radioed headquarters. Those bastards unloaded hundreds of rounds into that dormitory. Listen to this! After they killed a couple of students, this prick calls in,

'We gawt some injured here... Theyah niggah students... They ain't hurt all that bad... Gawt two niggah gals... Still some niggah males in the niggah feeemale dormitory.' And get this...can you believe this?! That cracker's name is 'Goon' Jones?!" He smacks the paper, and adds, "Christ, you can't make up shit like that!" He cackles and blows smoke upwards.

"Did you see about Hendrix?" Terry asks.

"Yeah," Peter says, "we were just talking about that."

Simon adds, "We oughta do something for Jimbo."

Robin scowls.

"Yeah, I think so too," Magnus says, with a grin.

Simon stamps out his butt and wanders back. "So what's it look like over there? You think we can get in?"

"We checked it out, both day and night," Peter says, pulling a small notebook from his back pocket and flipping the pages. "There's a receptionist in the lobby, but people just walk past her if they know where they're going. At night there's only a couple of guards who watch TV in their office downstairs. They do a round at about midnight, and that's it. They take turns sleeping and watching TV."

"They don't go back upstairs?" Terry asks. "Nobody's gonna get hurt, right?"

"Nobody'll get hurt," Simon responds. "We'll just fuck them up good."

"We can't be sure of that," Robin says.

Corinne sits on a rug by the mattress and spreads a napkin on her lap with a pastry. "We should call in a warning before it goes off."

"Yeah!" Simon responds. "Let's do that. Terry, you could do that."

"Yeah, but who would I call?"

"The pigs, a radio station. We'll have to figure that out. What's the best way to disguise your voice?"

"Oh," Magnus shakes his head. "We gotta do more than that. Gotta write a script and time it. They'll try to pass you around and get you to answer questions, and next thing you know, the phone booth will be surrounded by pigs. So you can't say another word, you just read it to whoever answers the phone. Also, you gotta be disguised when you go to the phone booth, and you can't park near it, or someone might make the car. You know what's good?...we should make a tape recording with some background noise, traffic, sea gulls, a playground, something, and you play it while you're talking. You gotta get off the phone quick too, and wipe it down."

Simon laughs. "Where do you come up with this shit, Mag?"

Robin paces the room. "We should do one of the production buildings, where they make all that shit! We shouldn't screw around. Why not go right to the heart of it?"

"You know we can't." Simon unwraps a Danish. "The shifts go around the clock, and people will be there. At least in the corporate offices people just come and go during the day. Sales people are in and out all the time. If we knock out some computers and the accounting and executive offices, that should be a pretty good setback. Won't be so easy to keep making weapons systems if you can't keep track of what you're making. That's all up above the sixth floor, right Mag?"

"Wait a minute, Simon," Robin says. "Why are we worrying about the people who manufacture guidance systems for bombs? God knows what else they're up to in there. Aren't they just soldiers in this war too?"

"I'm not there yet, Robin," Simon responds. "I don't think most of us are. If we just start indiscriminately killing civilians, how are we different from them?"

"Besides," Peter adds, "we won't get much sympathy from the public. The way I see it, a lot of those workers are people we should be trying to convert. Maybe this is the wake-up call they need to take a hard look at what their company actually does."

Robin shrugs but says nothing.

"So, Mag, what'd you find out inside?"

"Yeah," Magnus says, bobbing his head, "I took a foray into the main building, dressed up like I was there to check on the plumbing in the men's room, and I found a utility room where I can hide the shit." He waves a stick of dynamite like a teacher waving a blackboard eraser. "If we can tamp a few of these little guys just right, we can fuck that whole floor up pretty good."

"What do you mean tamp?" Terry asks.

"It's like this." He clumps several sticks in his fist. "If you put these next to a wall and set them off, you get a big explosion and a hole. But if you can build a barricade around it, like with sandbags, it forces the explosion all in one direction, and then you get a really big motherfucker hole."

"So how do we tamp it?"

"We need to carry some sandbags in."

"Oh, yeah!" Simon laughs. "We'll just walk in the door with a wheelbarrow and head for the elevator."

"No, listen!" Robin says. "We've been talking about this. If we each carry in one or two, concealed in a coat or bag, we can deliver them to the utility room. Then Mag can put the whole thing together."

"So we all go in?" Simon asks. "I thought it was just gonna be Robin and Mag and me."

"I'm in," Terry says.

Simon wags his head, looking at Corinne, who responds, "No, no, Simon.

We're all in this. Why should I stay behind?"

"It's true," Robin adds. "We need everyone. We might need a diversion."

"What kind of diversion?" Corinne asks.

"If someone notices Magnus or gets near the utility closet, we could do a spontaneous protest, you know, burst into a song or something."

"Let's do it!" Simon exclaims.

The rain had stopped. The quiet raised him from his stupor—that and the pressure on his bladder. He looked around as he pissed. Everything was soaked. Even if his matches weren't damp, there was nothing dry to burn. He shivered, rifling through his tote bag. The only food left was in cans, so he smashed one with a rock and ate cold chili, scooping it off the ground with his fingers, and then he sat and leaned on the wall again. The skies hadn't cleared. There'd be more rain, maybe snow. He recalled the plume of smoke in the distance, thinking maybe that's where the highway was. If he could get back there—something—he would do something…

"Did you ever get to talk to her again?" Corinne asks, softly.

He shakes his head no. "I tried to call her once, but her father said she didn't want to talk to me and told me don't call again. I'm not even sure she knows I called."

"I'm sorry, Peter."

"Don't be. I mean, thanks, but it's over. She has other things to do in life. It wouldn't be right to drag her into this."

"Not if she doesn't want it."

"She doesn't." He pauses. They watch the others laugh and clap as an alarm clock jangles and a test light glows, and then he says, "It's not like I want this, or any of us does. It's what we have to do right now. I don't even feel like it's a choice, like there is a choice. They've driven us to this. Look at all we're giving up. Like you…what about you? And your house?"

"I sold it…after the raid. We're gonna need the money."

He sniffs a small laugh. "Pretty ironic."

She rubs his back and walks him over to the group, where Simon grabs him by the neck. "We're gonna get some Hendrix and smoke a couple of pipes—a little send-off for ourselves. We're going on Friday, Peter. Maybe Keub can score some clothes from the costume racks. You wanna be a Veep, man?"

He became restless and looked at the mess all around him as if he'd just stumbled across it on his way to somewhere else. He had to move on.

Nothing here could help him. It came back to him now, where he was going—to surrender. That was it. He remembered now. He just had to get to somewhere that he could surrender. And then go home, to his family—to his wife and his children; he had to see them again and beg them to forgive him, and let them see him, what he was, who he was. He couldn't change his past. He'd done the things he'd done—but to have left them—all he wanted now was their forgiveness. Nothing else mattered. He would throw the ball softly this time, if he could just throw it once more, just one more toss…

The highway—maybe he'd find it if he walked toward the smoke plume.

He shook out his coat and buttoned up and then climbed over the rock shelf, heading for the distant ridgeline.

In places, his feet sank up to his calves in the snow, and where there was none, the ground was muddy and puddled. There was little open space that allowed him to walk freely or see very far ahead. But he trudged forward, warmed by the effort and fueled by the food, and also by instinct and desire. Each step would bring him closer. He only had to keep taking steps. If he did that, he would get there.

He slogged and gushed through thickets of brush and stands of pine trees. Low hanging branches became tangled in his clothes and forced him to snake his way around and change directions. His breath and footsteps sounded remote, like someone else's, but he kept going, indifferent to the cold and wet, though he finally had to stop for short rests, leaning against trees until his breath slowed and he could lurch forward for another stretch, and gradually, the stretches became shorter and his rests longer. He would look back at his tracks and go the opposite way when he moved on.

Once, he heard a buzzing sound in the distance, like a chain saw. He stopped and listened, and then heard a second chain saw, and a third. No, they weren't chain saws at all, but snowmobiles or ATVs. The sounds were faint, echoing through the trees from all around him. He stood motionless and listened, but they were soon gone. Now he stared into the woods, looking for movement, trying to see the residues of sound, and he stumbled on to where he thought it came from.

He sobbed as he tossed himself across the snowy fields and into jumbles of shrubs and trees, with branches scraping his face, stumbling on rocks and fallen limbs in the snow. He never heard the snowmobiles again, if indeed that was what he had heard. Maybe he just imagined it.

He had been steadily climbing for some time on a low grade, his progress slower and slower, his steps less and less sure. He started across an outcropping of rocks and slipped on a loose stone, twisting his right foot sharply inward and falling hard on the rocks, banging his jaw against one. His entire body felt like a single nerve electrified with pain. He couldn't distinguish where one ache ended and another began. He slowly righted himself and stretched his leg in front of him. It was more than a sprain. The barest movement sent an agonizing shock through his spine. But once he was still, resting, with his leg settled and relieved now of the exhausting effort of walking and climbing, he felt better.

As he lay there, his shoe began to feel tight, and he loosened it, and when that gave him some relief, he pulled it off altogether and pulled the wet sock off too. The cold felt good on his sweaty foot. He pulled his arms through his sleeves and wrapped himself in his coat, and leaning back, closed his eyes, enjoying the sharp, fresh cold on his cheeks and face now. He held a clump of snow to his jaw, numbing the pain, sucking on it, and he nestled himself into the snow, now staring up into the pine branches, admiring the rich, intricate shades of dark green…

Maples and elms line the smooth, blacktopped drive and offer the first hints of autumn color. The road might have led to a country club, but the building that comes into view could not be mistaken for a club house. It is tall, ten stories tall, and eerily symmetrical. You could turn it upside down and not notice the difference. Columns surround the upper and lower floors like prison bars, and recessed windows darken the building with angular shadows that change shape with the sun's movement during the day, giving it an imposing, even sinister look.

Friday is clear and warm, and the building languid and quiet as they arrive in three vehicles, at staggered times, shortly after two p.m.—after two because Magnus can't set the alarm more than twelve hours ahead.

"This should fuck the weekend up for a few suits!" Simon laughed earlier, as they threw the last of the junk from the warehouse into a dumpster and piled into their cars. Leaving to come here felt understated, anticlimactic. "See you later," Robin said, barely swiping Peter's cheek with a kiss before she climbed into the van with Magnus.

Now Peter watches the two of them walk into the shadow of the overhang dressed in utility clothes, carrying tool boxes, looking almost clownish in their outfits, but they breeze past the receptionist, who barely glances at them. He feels the urge to talk, to say something to Corinne, who sits beside him, also watching. A dozen starts, fragments…but there's nothing to say. They'd talked themselves out, all of them, endless talk. Now here they are in front of the building. What will it look like in twelve hours? tomorrow? Behind the hundreds of shadowy windows, people are doing...whatever they do...talking also, about movies they'll see this weekend, restaurants they'll eat in, parties they'll go to; about yard work, the Yankees, the weather, money, and their children. On any other day, he'd have felt disdain thinking about all that blather, but now he's curious, as if he can hear the buzzing from within, and listening closely, distinguish the voices, hear the chatter, the laughter, the predictable jokes, the cliches, but they all have distinctive sounds, belong to individuals rather than the great buzzing mass. He said he was a soldier, but this seems an unlikely place for a battle, and the soldiers in the opposing army unaware they've even enlisted.

"There they go," Corinne says.

Terry and Simon cross the lot, walking together, both in suits and carrying briefcases, talking about a golf game they never played on a course that doesn't exist. They had giggled as they practiced the conversation last night, feeding each other golf terms. Corinne had cut their hair, but there's still an unmistakable wildness in it, and their suits fit awkwardly, and to Peter, they also look clownish, as if they wear costumes rather than disguises and are acting in a farce rather than a tragedy, playing characters disguised as other characters.

Corinne must have sensed it—his doubt or fear, or whatever it is tumbling through him right then—for she reaches over and takes his hand, squeezing it, smiling warmly at him, and holding on for a moment before she says, "Okay, let's go, Peter," in barely a whisper.

He carries a sample case and she has an oversized handbag. The lawn around the building has just been mowed, and the heavy, moist scent of fresh-cut grass lingers. Stepping into the elevator, they smile greetings at a woman whose perfume remains after she gets out on the floor below their stop.

In the utility closet, Magnus hunches behind some pipes, connecting wires, while Robin takes their sandbags and stacks them. Corinne whispers good luck as she eases out the door ahead of Peter, who carefully holds the knob until the door is shut and latched.

Sooner than they imagined, Simon, Terry, Corinne, and Peter find themselves waiting in the elevator lobby around the corner from the utility closet. All that preparation, and in just a few minutes, their jobs are nearly done. They pair off, as they had coming in, Simon and Terry now looking out the window over the parking lot, while Peter leans on the back of a sofa and Corinne admires a framed print hanging on the wall that separates them from the utility room. Peter watches her. Unlike the rest of them, she's comfortable in her business clothes, wearing a skirt and blouse that she wore to her regular job in the real world. She stepped out of that world and into this one with such confidence, disguised now in her own clothes, which weren't a disguise yesterday. He flexes the hand she squeezed only minutes earlier, still trying to grasp what this means, what life will become now, what he's traded...but he finds himself wondering about the most banal things: will he ever play another pick-up basketball game, or eat popcorn at a movie, or smell new-mown grass? There is finality in this act. They can't resurface after it's done. They will take credit for it, announce their intentions. There'll be more. Until today, they could have turned back, appeared in court to face all the other charges, possibly do some time, but this is a declaration of war, and he's trying, even now, to understand his reasons for going to war, wondering—afraid!—that his anger from the arrests and beatings, from the chaos that Vietnam has brought to his own life, though he's never been there and will never go there, is what drives him now, or whether he indeed believes that this is the solution to the political chaos that has engulfed the nation. His doubts swarm like gnats, but he can't swipe at them; he can't reveal his fear, not now—not ever—for it seems selfish, and his regrets—if these are even regrets—are for things that seem petty in the grand scale of things, and he worries more about the others sensing them than he even does about getting caught.

Typewriters patter and muted voices ripple along the corridor, but they haven't seen anyone yet. They wait through several elevator arrivals and departures, standing aside as if waiting for the elevator going the opposite way. Simon said he wanted to be the last out. He nods for Corinne to leave, and she nods back yes. A man in a white shirt and dark tie now crosses the lobby and looks around at the people there but says nothing. Just beyond the utility room, the men's room door shuts, and at that moment the stairwell door at the end of the corridor opens and bangs closed. A man whistles and clanks down the hall, as if carrying a ladder or tool box, perhaps headed for the utility room. Simon turns abruptly.

And then, the roar, as if a diesel engine had crashed through the wall and into the narrow lobby. It lifts the sofa and blows it back on top of Peter, while debris of every sort—chunks of plaster, furniture, lighting fixtures—shatter and slam into the far wall. Pipes burst, unleashing torrents of water, and when the train has plowed through, it leaves behind smoke, thick, pea-soup smoke, filled with dust, dense with an overpowering burning smell, swirling and churning everywhere. In the corridors, voices shriek—women's voices—and then call out names, looking for each other, in harsh, desperate squawks; and then worse, the howling of a man screaming in unspeakable pain.

Peter's face is pressed to the floor, with the back of the sofa covering him, but through a crease, through the debris and beneath the smoke, he sees Corinne, crumpled, mangled, her head turned away from her body at an impossible angle for her neck. Her arm stretches along the floor and her hand almost touches her feet, which are bent backward, the hand that had squeezed his. Blood covers her forehead and cheeks, and her lifeless eyes are still open, looking across at him.

The sofa seems to rise of its own power, and he looks up at Simon, leaning over him, covered in dust, bleeding at the mouth. "Peter! You okay? Where's Corinne?" His voice is muted, as if from behind thick glass. Then he sees her, lying on the floor, and stumbles away, as Peter tries to raise himself.

Through the smoke, Peter now watches him huddle over her, rolling her into his arms, cradling and hugging her, sobbing. When Peter reaches him, he gurgles, "Find Terry."

The screams spread into the lobby. A black man in work clothes lurches out of the corridor and collapses on the floor, his clothing drenched in blood, his arm dangling from his shoulder, held on by a rag-like fragment of skin.

Alarms clang in the halls and elevator shafts, while Peter staggers through the wreckage and finds Terry on the floor by the shattered windows, his face a bloody maze of cuts and slivers. He smiles at Peter and says hoarsely, "I'm okay. I can't move my right leg. Something slammed into my knee. I can't get up, but I'm okay. Just go!" Peter spots a marble stand-up ashtray lying against the wall beneath one of the broken windows.

Now Simon calls, "Is he okay?"

But before Peter can respond, Terry yells, "I'm fine." Then he says, "Go, Peter. You can't stay here."

Simon hollers, "Go on, Peter! There's nothing you can do here. Take the stairs."

"What about Corinne, and the others?"

She's gone. They're gone too. I'll stay. Just go! Get out!"

People fill the hallways now, and a sobbing woman leans over the injured man. The hallway to the stairwell beyond the utility closet is impenetrable with debris and smoke, so Peter falls in with the crowds pouring out of offices and into the stairwell at that other end of the hall.

He brushes himself off as he descends, and after two flights, he's just one of hundreds vacating the building, with more merging into the stairwell from the floors below. Voices call out to keep moving and get clear of the building, and alarms echo deafeningly in the hollow of the stairwells. Already, firemen and police officers have begun to push their way up the stairs through the dense crowd and the smoke filtering down. A pair of city policemen nudge past Peter, close enough for him to smell the fresh air lingering on their uniforms. When Peter finally emerges on the far side of the building from the parking lot, people all around gasp and stumble through the flower beds and across the lawn. Fire trucks have pulled into the circle drive in front of the main lobby, where Keubler's car is now blocked in on both sides.

Peter works his way around the edge of the milling crowds, as the employees watch the building, looking up at the sixth floor, where the lobby windows are blown out. He thinks Simon passes in front of the opening, but he's only a shadow and then he's gone. It could have been someone else.

In the parking lot, people clump into groups, leaning on cars to smoke and talk and watch. Peter struts past them, avoiding eye contact, until he reaches his car and looks around once more for Keubler, who is nowhere in sight, and then he shuts himself in, shuddering now, sucking short breaths, quivering as he starts the engine. He looks around again, before putting the car in gear and turning onto the blacktopped driveway, where he passes still more fire trucks and police cars, their lights whirling and sirens screaming, on his way out to the main road.

The pain had receded. He felt comfortable, even rested, but his nose and eyebrows were cold, sharply cold, and wet. When he lifted his hand to wipe his face, a jolt shot up through his leg and back, and he found the limits of how far he could move without igniting the pain again. In small movements, he wiped his eyes and opened them to find that a blanket of light snow now covered him. He must have slept. It was dark, and the snow drifted down through the trees…like little soldiers, he thought, an army of them, silent, dutiful, drifting downward in windless and quiet efficiency. There was near total silence but for the hissing of this delicate army as it floated through the branches, covering him and all that surrounded him. Its beauty was astounding. He had never seen anything as beautiful, for his senses were filled by the serene, light hiss of snowflakes drifting to the earth, the wondrous aromas of pines that surrounded him in untold abundance, and the clean whiteness that now covered him where he rested.

And then an image warmed him, a memory—his walk on the bridge with Susan. As he dropped into it, he felt its peace and tranquility—and its joy—and it briefly sheltered him from the quaking sorrow that rumbled beneath it, and it slipped away as he knew that he would never see Cherylee and Emma and Todd again, that he'd never won the battle against his own fears and regrets to become who he was—their husband and father—what he'd always been, no matter what he'd done or what his name was. But he would now—he would fill himself with that thought, with remembering them, with knowing that they were part of him and he would always be part of them, and perhaps they would forgive him. Indeed, he knew they would.

He suddenly felt everything with great clarity, surrounded by this unspeakable beauty. He understood how things worked together, how the earth cared for itself in its cycle of seasons, of warmth and cold, of wet and dry. He found wonder in its indifference, its persistence, how it was always correcting and rebalancing itself, reusing its own waste, absorbing it back into its womb so it might be reborn once more, continuously, endlessly. So it would absorb him. He listened and watched, enraptured by the immense beauty of it, with his senses sharper and more receptive than he'd ever felt in his life. Nothing compared with this. He had never felt such serenity or such wonder. It was the first time he had not been afraid in his entire life. Movement was difficult, but his hand found the recital program and the photo in his pocket, and he gripped them, not taking them out, but just closing his hand around them.

And then, a sound resonated in the trees and echoed through the snowy hills. Music—a simple bright melody in low tones. He heard it clearly now, closer, as if the trees themselves were playing it. A familiar melody, coming back to him from long ago, now throbbing and vibrating in the trees. It felt like the music of the earth, of life itself, and he held the program and photo in his hand as he slipped away into the music.

Chapter 22

Summer 2001

Cherylee's blouse clung to her back as if it was pasted on. The evening was sweltering and humid, and the sun hung low on the horizon, sending a terrific glare straight at them from beyond the left field fence. They were all hot—she and Emma and Jean, and the hundred or so other fans who had come out on this miserable night. Nearby, a girl of twelve or thirteen sat with her parents, her earphones buzzing and hissing with rap music. She sighed and fanned herself, sharing her misery at sitting through her brother's game.

Yet Cherylee was happy—no, contented. That was it. They were all here. She and Emma and Jean, all together a few rows behind Todd's team bench. That's what mattered. That's what Todd would remember later, she knew. It's what they would all remember, that they were together for his game. He leaned back on the chain link fence. His damp hair clung to his neck.

Snarly shouts erupted all around them when the umpire called a strike.

Jean leaned forward. "Go get one, Todd!"

"There're about five batters ahead of him, Aunt Jean," Emma said.

"I don't care. I'm cheering for him."

The boy turned and looked at them. He grinned at Emma and turned back. Emma recognized the Aunt-Jean grin. She clapped, and they all clapped.

"C'mon, Blue Jays!" Emma shouted.

The team was down by six runs and had no hope of coming back. This was their last up. Todd might not get another crack. There was already one out.

Overheated Blue Jays fans jeered the umpire, complained to one another about the coach leaving his son on the pitcher's mound to give up twelve runs, and sweltered in the heat. But Cherylee and her family were indifferent to the oppressive atmosphere. Jean believed the team would mount a comeback and Todd would get another up, and Emma cheered every batter with every pitch. Cherylee didn't care if the team won or lost. Her son was just a few feet away from her, and her daughter and sister were beside her. She had all she needed right now. Even the heat seemed to have a purgative effect, as if their sweat was cleansing them and the suffering of the past two years was oozing away in it.

This was not how she expected to feel so soon after the funeral. Sorrow and fear and guilt had been with her for so long that this spontaneous serenity took her by surprise, a forgotten emotion, rediscovered as one might find forgotten money in a coat pocket.

He'd been brought home just over a month ago, and the coroner insisted that she not look at him. He said there was no doubt about his identity because of dental records the police had sent.

Dental records?

Cherylee was astounded. Their own dentist had not even been contacted. The records came from a dentist in Wyoming. How strange all of this was.

But she did want to look. She was adamant. She left Jean in the waiting room at the funeral home, and the director took her downstairs. The coroner was already there.

The body lay covered in blue cloth on a stainless steel table, and it seemed too flat, too small for Peter. But the coroner explained that the decomposition was extensive, and the body flattened after several weeks. He drew back a corner of the cloth to reveal Peter's head, and even through the sickening patchwork of black and cream-colored flesh, she recognized his hairline, his ears, the shape of his head. Her glimpse was brief. It was enough. She would never speak of it to anyone. She never imagined that one day in her life she would have to do such a thing. It was unthinkable. But so much had changed. Her sobbing then was not from the horror of seeing him in this condition or from her own pain, but from imagining what he must have gone through, how he must have suffered. They quietly buried him the next day, without a notice in the paper. She and the children and Jean. Emma had told Marcia about the funeral, and she came with her parents too. That was all. The service in the funeral home chapel was brief. It was generic. What could the preacher say? What could any of them say? Soon they stood on a hillside within view of the corporate development that surrounded Peter's business, and a stiff, hot south wind ruffled her dress as the final words were spoken at the grave.

Another chorus of hooting bellowed from behind her. The batter went down on a called strike. Two outs. Hope faded for the crowd, but Emma clapped, "C'mon, Blue Jays!"

"Go get one, Todd!" Jean shouted, but this time the boy ignored her.

So much had happened all at once. The swarms of reporters descended again. Friday and Gannon reappeared. Her lawyer had dozens of papers for her to sign, and there would be more. That bombing victim's family continued their suit, and now her lawyer was talking about a counter-suit for the additional grief they created for Cherylee. She didn't know if she could go through with something like that. They had suffered, too. That's why they were doing this. The lawyer would work it out.

These things, she had learned, the whole machinery of the law and the news, had a life of its own, and she decided it could grind along without her at times. It would grind no matter what she did. She refused to add fuel from her family's store of emotional energy to run that machinery. Soon the reporters and the lawyers and the government agents would find some other family to persecute. To Cherylee, they were a pack of hyenas, roving from one wounded animal to another. But she refused to let them gorge themselves on her family any longer. She discovered that you fought them by starving them. Once they had engaged you in battle, they won, but when you refused to show up, they withered away. Fighting nourished them. She had learned how to deal with them, from reviewing the bills her lawyer sent each month to keeping Friday and Gannon standing on the front porch when she fetched something they required. The harder it was for them, any of them, the less they bothered her.

And what was left to bother her about?

Peter was dead. The case was closed.

Even that vile radio person couldn't talk endlessly about it when there was nothing new to say, not that he didn't try. But Cherylee found that there was less pain from him or anyone when she didn't listen to them. If she needed to know something, she'd find out. She wished she had learned that earlier in the game.

The tone changed in the crowd. There was cheering. Hope. A runner was on base.

Jean turned to Cherylee and said, "He's gonna get up. I just know it!"

"Right now, Blue Jays! Right now!" Emma shouted.

A cluster of fans did a mini-wave.

Jean took Cherylee's hand and grabbed Emma's on the other side. They sprung up when the next wave passed through.

"Go, Blue Jays!" Emma shouted.

There was clapping and shouting all around them. The crowd wanted another runner. The pitcher looked tired. He thought the game would be over by now.

The Blue Jays' batter looked over to the bench and watched his coach run through the signals. Then he stepped into the batter's box and dropped a bunt in front of the pitcher, who started after the ball in the wrong direction and then loped toward it as if somebody else should have gotten it. He grabbed it and flung it a foot over the first baseman's outstretched glove.

Now runners stood on second and third. The Blue Jays' crowd cheered as if they were about to win the game. The next batter strode to the plate, and Todd's coach nudged him to get a helmet.

"He's gonna get up!" Jean exclaimed.

Emma laughed. "God, he didn't even know it was his turn!"

"Go get one, Todd!" Jean shouted.

"Go, Blue Jays!"

Cherylee could see Peter in Todd's gait, in his rounded, liquid brown eyes, and in the slight tilt of his head. He scrunched his shoulders, too, as Peter sometimes did when he was tired. Peter had done that more in recent years. Maybe his secret had become more of a burden than she ever imagined. It must have been awful. She wished that he was still alive just so she could get to know him again—all over again—with all of this truth now in front of them. She thought she would still love him. She hadn't at first, and she didn't think he loved her either, not at first. But he'd been so devoted to making a life for them...Peter fell in love with having a family, she had decided. That's how he grew to love her. They both knew why they got married, but the result was the same. He stayed with her and made as good a home for her and their children as she could have asked. She knew when Emma was born that he would not leave her, would not leave his child. They made the best of their situation, and it was better than good. His leaving, she now believed, was for the same reason. Whether he was wrong or right about it, she believed that he thought he was doing what was right by leaving. She was past her anger at him. She forgave him, and she wished she could start over again. There was so much more than she would ever know. Maybe she would call Brother Luke again sometime, or even visit him. He'd sent a card from all the brothers after Peter was found.

"Blue-Jays-Blue-Jays-Blue-Jays!"

The crowd chanted in unison. Emma and Jean chanted, and Cherylee joined in. Todd took practice swings in the on-deck circle. There were two outs and runners still standing on second and third. The team was down to its last strike.

A foul ball. Players and coaches ducked as it clanked into the chain link screen in front of the team bench. The batter had a bead on the exhausted pitcher.

The crowd drew a collective breath and the chanting revved up again.

"Blue-Jays-Blue-Jays-Blue-Jays!"

"Right now, batter!" Emma shouted. "Right now!"

"Go get one, Todd!"

The boy was down on one knee in the on-deck circle. He'd taken all the practice swings he could in this stifling heat.

Cherylee had tried to make it easier for Peter to come home. She did all she could, and she blamed herself because it took her so long to understand what was happening. Maybe things would have come out better if she'd had a clearer head at the beginning. Jean had said, "None of this is your fault, Cherry! It's not like people get experience at this. God, I hope not!" But Cherylee did blame herself. She thought she was so close to finding him when she got his letter and then spoke to Brother Luke.

Her lawyer said he would talk to the prosecutor about a deal if Peter came in on his own. Perhaps he could get a guarantee of parole after so many years or get some charges dropped because Peter had been a law-abiding citizen and a good father and husband for so long. But the lawyer was on unfamiliar ground. This was a federal case. He didn't know the Justice Department attorneys personally, as he did the local district attorney. If the charges had been local, a deal might have been struck on the golf course.

The news wasn't good when he came back to her. Peter had charges pending, she learned, when he participated in the bombing. He was supposed to appear in court only a few weeks later, and his bail bond had been forfeited when he disappeared. The lawyer said he thought he could get a deal for Peter to serve twelve years. Cherylee hoped that if he knew he wouldn't spend the rest of his life in prison, maybe he would come in. The actual sentence might range from thirty to forty years, but even twelve seemed so long. She didn't know if he would do it. Still, she asked her lawyer to find out if they could publicize the offer, and the Justice Department agreed. Marcia's father got a TV crew to cover her appeal and the tape ended up on CNN.

She never knew if Peter saw it. There were so many things she didn't know. All he had with him was a few dollars, a crumpled family picture, and a program from a concert at his old college. The program was mostly rotted, but she recognized a name on it, the same woman Brother Luke had mentioned. Cherylee couldn't understand why he'd kept this item, but she would let it lie. Picking away at the past wouldn't help her family, wouldn't help her children get beyond this. She couldn't keep digging without doing more harm to her children. They were all that mattered now. Others out there were already preoccupied with the case—bloggers, news junkies, investigative reporters. One journalist wanted to write a book about Peter, but she told him to stay away from her and her family. She couldn't stop him from writing what he wanted, but she would have nothing to do with it. He and all the others would uncover more about Peter and his past, and if she wanted to know more she could read what they wrote. Someday. But not now. Her children had suffered in ways she still didn't understand, ways that didn't yet show. They needed all of her now.

The chants rose and fell through another foul ball and then an outside pitch. The umpire now drew jeers from the other team's fans.

Todd still waited in the on-deck circle. He got up and swung the bat. It seemed to have a life of its own, wrapping itself all way around to his back and pulling him with it. He turned around and looked toward the bleachers.

"Go get one, Todd!"

"You're next!" Emma exclaimed.

Cherylee clapped.

The crowd chanted, "Blue-Jays-Blue-Jays-Blue-Jays!"

Another wave came through. Everyone was on their feet. They waved their arms as it passed by. It swarmed over the bleachers behind the Blue Jays' bench.

The pitcher looked like he'd be willing to forfeit the game with a six-run lead if he could just go home. He lobbed a throw to the catcher and the batter took a mighty swing. The ball thumped into the catcher's mitt, and the bench and bleachers across the field exploded in cheers.

Todd stood with the bat hanging over his shoulder, and as his teammate struck out, he let the bat drop on the ground behind him. He turned and looked at his family with a grin and a shrug, as if he'd forgotten to hold on to the bat.

The Blue Jays' fans applauded their team. Parents called out to their own players. The coach barked out for help with the equipment before the kids left. Todd brought an arm-load of bats.

"Oh, that was fun!" Cherylee said.

"More fun if they won," Jean responded. "I thought for sure he'd get up!"

"They tried so hard!" Emma said.

"Jean, you haven't seen the model display yet, have you?" Cherylee asked.

"Where?"

"At the store, at Hobby Shop, down on the Trail."

"Oh…oh, I remember when that place was the shoe store. You used to…"

"Jean, that was a lifetime ago. Todd's new model is there, with a laminated copy of the picture from *Model Monthly*. Mr. Thompson did a wonderful display. It looks like a battlefield from the Desert Storm war. We should drive down there now."

"Mom," Emma said, "it's about a hundred and ten degrees. And it's all the way over on the west side."

"Oh, it won't take long. It's just a few extra minutes. Hey, I know! We can get some ice cream! Jean, you have to see it. Todd's so proud!"

For his part, Todd was ready to take his sister's side. He wanted to go home and jump in the pool. He'd already accumulated several hours of admiring his own handiwork in the store window and enjoying the accolades he received. But Cherylee insisted, and once they were in the Expedition, with the air conditioner blowing and the game traffic behind them, their resistance broke down. They were comfortable, cool. The world was out there, and they felt safe.

Todd sat in front with Cherylee, and Emma and Jean were in the back.

"You were great, honey!" Cherylee said.

"Didn't even get up again."

"I know, but it was exciting. Even with all those runs, you had the other guys worried there at the end."

Cherylee passed the turn for the house in which she and Jean grew up.

Jean asked, "Have you been by there recently, Cherry?"

She never went down that street unless there was a reason, but she never passed the corner without a flash of one memory or another. "No," she said. She thought of her father, clicking his tongue at a new Hollywood magazine she'd bought.

"It's just a rental now," Jean said. "Not even any grass. They park the cars in the front yard. It's awful."

Cherylee knew this. It had been that way for years. Her father was right about the magazine. It was frivolous, wasteful, but it gave her more than pleasure. It insulated her from the spare and harsh life that surrounded her. Although Jean and others sometimes accused her of living in a fantasy world when she was young, she did know how hard life was for her parents, how so many people lived on bare subsistence all around her as they worked dirty and dangerous jobs in the stock yards and train yards. She wanted to keep her children safe from the harshness that surrounded them. She would do whatever she had to keep them safe. A big car and a nice house seemed only the flimsiest of armor now.

"Shall we get ice cream first or go see the display?" she asked.

Chapter 23

October 2001

"It's still here?"

"What?"

"That...painting. I guess that's what you call it," Susan added, with a laugh.

The student shrugged her shoulders. "Whatever, I guess it's always been there."

She was young. Well, they were all young, weren't they? They just kept getting younger.

Susan looked up at the picture with the puffy clouds and celebrities falling from the sky. Art Linkletter was a stretch for some students when she was here, but even Sidney Poitier and Walter Cronkite were probably blanks to the kids now.

The girl was bored. She'd gotten stuck hosting Susan after dinner while the dean attended to some details in Kieran Recital Hall.

Susan wondered how long Rusty would be. He was so afraid of missing a call now, and he'd left his cell phone back at the hotel. She hoped they wouldn't call him tonight.

The girl moped, unsure of what to say to the older woman, but Susan had given up trying to make conversation. All questions led to "Whatever."

Over the girl's shoulder, Susan studied the awkward corner where the ceiling sloped to the floor and her quartet had played through the din of a cocktail party. Poor Anne! She was so flustered that evening. Susan heard that Father Alfonse got an earful at the next faculty meeting. The draperies were new, but Susan was surprised at how little things had changed. The gallery looked much the same, as did most of Kieran and Celixine. The recital hall was new, and several buildings had been enlarged. But the quad still felt quiet and serene. The trees were larger, fuller. It had been pleasant walking out there earlier.

Susan was about to take pity on the girl and release her from her duty when she heard her name called from the doorway.

"Oh! Susan!" Brother Luke exclaimed. "They said you were in here. I'm so sorry I had to miss dinner. You came back again! After all these years, here you are!"

"Here I am," she said.

He hugged her and grasped her by the shoulders. "I can't believe it. You know, I have all of your albums. Here I am with someone famous. Oh, but…I'm embarrassing you! How are you? It's so good to see you again. Have they taken care of you? I hope they took you somewhere decent and not to Lancelot's or…oh, Susan, they didn't feed you downstairs, did they?"

"It was very nice, Brother Luke." She gently stepped out of his grasp. "The Cavern is now a lovely faculty dining room. We had candles and a delightful group of student waiters who couldn't give us enough to eat."

"You look wonderful, Susan, though I was expecting long hair after seeing your photo on all those records and tapes."

"Records?"

"Yes, we have…oh, that's right! Everyone has CDs now. Well, it's pretty old fashioned at the residence."

Susan smiled. "Well, then, you're missing a couple. I'll send them to you."

Luke brightened and looked around. "You know, I don't get over here too much any more myself. And this is such a nice reason to come. Anne was such a wonderful teacher, and now for her children to endow a lecture series in her name! They couldn't have chosen someone better for the first talk."

"It probably won't be much of a talk, Brother. I was never very good at this sort of thing."

"But you're a teacher yourself now, aren't you?"

"Yes, but that's different. It's just a handful of students, almost all individual instruction and some ensemble. This is…you know, a talk. But I thought I'd play something, too. That's how I'll get through it."

"Here you've been all over the world and played for presidents and royalty and huge audiences, and it almost sounds like you have stage fright."

Susan laughed, "It's nothing. I've always had some jitters before I play."

"I'm just glad you're here. You came back after all these years. Someone told me…I think it was Brother Damien, in the music department…you met him today didn't you?…yes, it was Brother Damien…he said that this is your first visit since you graduated. Is that true?"

Susan nodded and slipped a glance at her watch. She could hear voices gathering outside in the hallway, in front of the recital hall entrance. There was still too much time. She didn't want to talk to a lot of people before the lecture. A small group had wandered into the gallery, but they looked at the pictures and seemed not to notice her. Her tour guide had disappeared. Maybe this was the handoff.

"Well, you're here now. And your son is with you too?"

"Yes, but I don't know where he is. He ought to be along. He had to go back to the hotel. He forgot his phone, and…oh…" She hesitated and took a breath. She always seemed to have trouble talking when this came up, and now she'd let it spill out and couldn't avoid finishing the sentence. Just when she hoped Luke's chattiness would bail her out, he waited with sealed lips for her to finish. "Well, he's on call. He's in the reserves now. Twelve years on active duty, and then he was done, and then…after this horrible thing happened last month, the training and meetings and calls have just consumed him. Now he thinks his unit will be activated. He's waiting to hear. He left in the middle of dinner when he realized he didn't have the phone on him. I said, 'Honey, they'll leave a message. They won't expect you to drive back tonight.' But he thought otherwise."

"It'll be all right, Susan. He's doing something good, something noble. We'll get those monsters."

"I'm sure we will. I just don't know why it has to be him. I suppose that sounds selfish, but he's all I have. He and his wife and their beautiful daughter. Who could imagine such a thing?"

"And your husband…is he…?"

Susan arched her head back. "I'm not married, Brother. I never married. Rusty was a gift from God. I named him for my father, Russell. He passed away soon after I graduated."

Luke smiled. "You're very brave, Susan. I'll pray for you."

She edged forward and started to say that she should probably go inside, but Luke looked over his shoulder and abruptly whispered, "You heard about Peter Howell?"

She nodded. She knew this would come up sooner or later. Somehow she'd gotten through dinner without a word about it. She'd been right to stay away.

"It's so tragic," Luke added. "I read that some hikers found his body after it had been there for months. If he hadn't had that dental work done, they might never have figured out it was him."

Susan knew all this and more. It was gruesome. She wanted to leave, but Luke continued, his voice even lower, "You know, I saw him last year."

She felt a rush of heat flood her face. She'd only had this exact sensation once before, and then she had fainted, delaying a concert by over a half hour. She sat down in a chair by the fireplace, and Luke sat with her.

"Yes," he continued, "he stayed with us for most of the summer. I suppose I could have gotten in a lot of trouble, but I guess the police just didn't think we were harmful enough to bother with...a bunch of old brothers living in the middle of nowhere. What would they gain from putting us in jail? There was a scandal with the administration here at the college, too, but it all passed like a puff of smoke. Most of the time I think they'd just as soon forget we exist up there."

"How was he?"

"Not good, Susan. He looked terrible. He was a troubled man. What a tragedy! I just don't think he could ever find his way out. It was like he'd fallen into a river with a fast current and could never get back to the shore. He was so bright. He could have been so many things." Brother Luke paused and then added, "You know, even back then...it turned out they were right, the protesters...that's what really stopped the war...it was them...us, I guess,"—he chuckled—"but these extremists...I don't know what they wanted...I'm not even sure they did. Look what it brought instead, so many lives ruined. I've thought a lot about all of this since I saw Peter again. He never seemed like someone who'd be part of such things, but there's so much I didn't understand about it, and still don't." Luke hesitated and looked at her. "Wasn't he found not far from your area?"

"Yes, about twenty-five miles from Presque Isle. It's right on the Canadian border."

"Hmm, perhaps that's where he was going...are you all right, Susan?"

"Yes, I'm fine. It's just all been very overwhelming coming back here. So many memories. It's good to see you, Brother. I suppose I should get across the hall."

"Let me walk with you."

"No, you go ahead. I don't mean to be rude, but I always need a moment before I'm in front of people."

"Of course." He hugged her again, and she held him a moment longer this time. As he left the room and crossed the hallway, a man passed him, looking through the group that was milling into the auditorium.

He spotted his mother in the gallery, sitting by the empty fireplace.

"Mom!" he called, and then, as he came through the doorway, he asked, "Are you okay?"

"I'll be all right."

"Are you ready to go in?"

She stood and nodded at him, noticing the familiar tilt of his head and his thick dark hair. He looked remarkably as she remembered his father, with his bright face and his clear, deep, rounded eyes. Not a day in her life had passed that she didn't see him in her son's face.

Rusty asked, "Are you going to play the new piece?"

"No, I've changed my mind. I think maybe some Bach."

As they crossed the hall, he said, "I have some news, but it'll keep until later."

The rest is silence.

about the author:

Bob Sommer's work has appeared widely in literary, scholarly, and commercial publications, including *Centennial Review, Studies in American Fiction, American Book Review, New England Quarterly, Southern Humanities Review, New Letters Review of Books, Hudson Valley Magazine,* and elsewhere. He is the author of *Teaching Writing to Adults* and co-author of *The Heath Literature for Composition*. His recent freelance work and stories have appeared in *The Kansas City Star, Buzzflash, OpEd News, Cantaraville*, and other print and on-line publications. He grew up in Hyde Park, New York, and attended Dutchess Community College (A.A.), Marist College (B.A.), SUNY New Paltz (M.A.), and Duke University (Ph.D). He and his wife Heather live in Overland Park, Kansas, where they have raised three children to adulthood.